IN THE PANTHEON PRESENTS:

IMMORTAL
FEARS

First paperback edition August 2020

ISBN (Paperback) 978-1-953256-00-3

ISBN (eBook) 978-1-953256-01-0

ISBN (Large Print) 978-1-953256-02-7

www.inthepantheon.com

FOREWORD

Like so many splendid things, it all started by chance. Three of the most genuinely creative people I've ever met stumbled across each other on social media, made a connection, and then started something amazing for writers. *In the Pantheon* (originally *All in the Pantheon*) fell into place as a project to promote, elevate, and provide authors exposure. It gave them a place to showcase their writing and stand out in a crowded arena.

Debuting in May 2019 with a small cadre of authors, it quickly grew in size. By summer's end, almost thirty authors (or scribes) wrote for various deities. Each scribe wrote two posts per month, and *In the Pantheon (ITP)* posted two posts per day. In no time, the project was producing over one-hundred thousand words of quality story-telling per month. All this time the founders (Michael "Zeus" Ryan, CJ "Hera" Landry, and Moxie "Moxie" Malone) managed a project that was growing wildly beyond any reasonable expectations they had concerning its viability. It was at this point that they offered me the honor of joining their ranks as an administrator.

Through its inception and growth, the four of us maintained one mantra about the venture. *ITP* would remain a free platform for authors to showcase their work. The message always remained that the project is about helping writers and is not an avenue to generate revenue. *ITP* would not charge authors for the right to post, authors retained all rights to their intellectual property, and we would someday publish an anthology of stories featuring many of our talented authors.

Someday took 491 days.

With our own publishing house, Rewritten Realms, we now control our publishing future. *Immortal Fears* is the culmination of this future vision shared by everyone at *ITP*. Yet as a culmination, it is not the end. Rather, it is a beginning of many more things to come. What started, and continues, as a project by writers and for writers now encompasses other creatives as our community continues to expand into areas such as audiobooks.

As we always do, we thank the readers and fans who cheered us on after they discovered our community and became a part of it. You are the sole reason we do what we do. Every time you tell a scribe how much you loved their story, I guarantee you make their day. We hold heartfelt appreciation for our fans and love interacting, whether it be in character as our deity or talking one on one as fellow writers and readers. Thank you all for your unwavering support.

Now settle into your favorite chair and get comfortable. We present to you, *Immortal Fears*.

~*Wayne "Dinlas" Davids*

THE STARS IN MY EYES

BY

ASHLEY GALLAHER - POLLARD

NYX,

PRIMORDIAL OF NIGHT

H ELLO, DEAREST MORTAL, AND WELCOME TO MY PART OF THE BOOK. The family has a great many storytellers, and I am keen on what you'll think. But for now, I invite you to immerse yourself with the dark and read on.

I am Nyx: eldest of Chaos, Primordial of the Night, Goddess of the Dark Web, the Void Queen, and the equal to Dinlas, the God of Hate and Jealousy. There is little lore concerning my life, whether truth or lies, so I will create the legends and stories. Here, you will learn how I came to have star-filled eyes.

The Void is my birthplace, my true home. It was there that my mother, Chaos, gave me life and freedom. She granted me wings and gave me the ability to create the night while personifying it. She is the reason my skin reflects the starry night skies, why meteor showers rain across my cheeks, why nebulae swirl across my thighs, and why cosmos live and die within my hands.

When I emerged from Chaos, I was naked, young, and brimming with power. I wanted to flex my wings and take to the skies. She let me. The Night was first drawn over the world in a flair of triumph. A keen victory before our dear Nike was even considered. I was proud to be the first to alight upon the place my mother built, proud to be her firstborn. My siblings came after and started the world in earnest. But first, my hands grazed the essence of everything, and it was a divine feeling. I rode that high right up until the Titanomachy, then I grew cold.

The Titanomachy, or the Ten Year War as some remember it, was the war between the Titans of Mount Othrys and the Olympians. Perhaps some of you may know of this event and its details. It began with the patricide of Uranus. His son Kronos and his wife, Gaia, killed him after imprisoning the Cyclopes and the Hecatonchires in Tartarus. Unfortunately for Kronos, his father left him with a prophecy: the children Kronos would bear with his wife, Rhea, would rise against him, as Kronos had done to Uranus.

Paranoia is a cruel mistress, and she often visited Kronos. The Titan King's mind was rampant with the fear of losing his throne, and so in true Greek fashion, instead of working it out, he swallowed his children almost immediately after Rhea gave birth to them. Heartbroken, angry, and upset, Rhea decided that Kronos would steal no more of her babies. When the last child was born, she hid him away and presented her husband with a swaddled rock.

That child's name? Zeus.

Zeus led the uprising against his father, just as Uranus said he would. With his siblings newly liberated, and the Hecatonchires and Cyclopes freed from the Underworld, he called upon his allies to bring down the Titans. The Primordials were a part of that war.

I remember all too well the war room planning, the sudden call to arms over an ambush, the nights of wondering if we would lose someone. I channeled my pride and arrogance into my fighting, as sharp as any kopis could be, and it served me well. What I didn't recognize until much, much later, was that it would not stop after the Olympians won the war. I melded my sharpened blade into my very being, and I became a terror. I grew to crave the turmoil of war, the pain and victories we claimed, and wanted more. I thrived on it, eventually I lived for it, and it bled into the mortal realm with fervor.

It started with indiscriminate killings of beggars and thieves in the streets of Greece. I kidnapped priestesses for my own pleasure, put to sleep guards and nobles, murdered mistresses and bankers. Many deserved their fate, but many more did not. As the eras flowed onward, my need became stronger.

Lord Poseidon's realm became a bit fuller the day I shot a plane full of tourists, leaving Rome for Barcelona, clean out of the skies. My reasoning was simply that they had been in my evening path while crossing the night skies.

An old woman died from a heart attack after I left a portal to Tartarus open, and she laid eyes upon the hellscape.

The senior home outing that I happened upon, where I struck down half of the elderly. Sending them to their eternal rest because I couldn't stand the sight of those mortals withering away.

A young woman whose therapist wants to commit her because she sees monsters. She turned thirty-two this year and doesn't know that it was me in the corner of her room when she was only six years old. I wanted to help her, and I never thought she would remember me. Black and menacing in the corner, I was to be a monument of protection against her abusive parents, not the cause of decline in her mental health.

However, the pinnacle was not a genocide or mass murder, as some of you may think. I was in Amsterdam, you see. I had my reasons, but I don't kiss and tell. A young couple caught my attention in a strip club one night, and I took to stalking them. I did it on a whim and because I could without being seen. I hoped they would lead me to my next high. I wasn't expecting it to be *them*.

I followed the pair through the downtown. The lights, scents and music all heady and soul-spearing. The young man's boyfriend led him into a side alley. They stumbled along laughing, and for a moment, I thought they would do the dirty right before my eyes behind a dumpster. I almost wish they had. Instead, the older man pulled out a syringe filled with liquid. I could just barely see it as he moved around, flashing it at his boyfriend. They argued over his drug usage, and he insisted that if the younger man loved him so much, he should do it, too. They were drunk, far more inebriated than they should have been. The syringe was pulled back, as if to take a stab with it.

I lost control. One moment I was a thin mist, shifting between boxes and garbage cans, the next I was arm deep into the chest of the older man, his heart in my hand. I barely processed what I had done when a shrill scream of horror pierced the air. I turned to find the remaining male on his knees, the most terrified look on his face as his eyes locked on the still-beating heart of his now dead lover. I prayed no others saw me and took off down the alley, leaving his heart behind.

I felt a rush of guilt and exhilaration at what I had done as I returned to the sky. Guilt was such a foreign feeling. I had no use for it. I brought the world to life, and I could take it away in any form I wished. No mortal built temples or cults for me, considering my presence as merely an add-on to the more *prestigious* immortals, like Zeus. If they did not deign to worship me, they meant little to me. So why did this mortal's face haunt me now?

I had not been reprimanded for my actions up until that point in my long life. Immortals and mortals alike made way for me, either ignoring or shirking what I wielded. Pure power. That night, my invincibility streak ended.

Let me tell you something about my mother, Chaos. After she gave birth to my siblings and me, she disappeared from the world. She left all realms and planes of existence. Perhaps, with her job being done, she no longer needed to be here. Maybe she discarded her physical form, ephemerality overriding her. Whatever the case may be, she lived on in her children. For myself, that was quite literal. Within my being, no matter what form I assumed, there was a jagged shard of Chaos. Obsidian black, rough-hewn like an untamed mountain, it was a reminder of what it was to be a daughter of her.

It was from within that she visited me. No warning, no words, no corporeal body. She need not be solid for me to recognize her aura.

Chaos, my mother, came to me, and as payment for the mortal life I stole, she took my sight.

Thick ichor ran down my cheeks. A sick terror filled my stomach at the emptiness of where my eyes had been moments before. And the pain. As if magma were emptied into my head. Being scared, up until that point, had been a luxury to me. But now it encapsulated me, and I had no idea what to do, where to go. I was confused and angry. Chaos was supposed to be my guardian, and she had *betrayed* me.

I fled. My wings took me to safety, for I couldn't navigate well enough to find my way home. I landed in a large cavern near Mount Olympus. The light of their fires, twinkling in the night, was lost upon me. That cave became my home for three days. I lie there, unable to cry. My emotions roiled like a boiling tsunami. I was shaken to my very core, and I couldn't stop the bleeding from my empty eye sockets, my skin slick with golden ichor. I could not die this way, but that did not mean the loss meant any less to me.

My fourth day on the mountainside saw me exhausted, so much so that neither anger nor pain could move me. It was on this day that I realized what Chaos had been trying to achieve by blinding me. I needed to look inside myself to understand that even an immortal had to pay the consequences for their actions, regardless if their quarry was a deity or a mortal. When I came to this conclusion, the bleeding stopped. I sat and meditated in that cavern until evening, my golden blood forming sharp, polished crystals around me. When the moon rose, and the cool air flowed into my space, I stood outside and waited until the atmosphere tasted correct. The star's energies were pulsing in the way I wanted them to, before I plucked several from the sky and molded them into orbs.

I polished and buffed and carved these orbs until even Hephaestus would have been pleased. When I finished, I pressed them into the empty spaces my eyes used to be. They fit perfectly, and the sudden relief I felt when my vision returned, albeit blurry and unfocused at first, overwhelmed me. I sat and cried for a long while, but I had done it.

My fury at my mother returned swiftly, only to be tamped down by a new voice within me. *Why am I angry? What would I gain for searching for an attack that would never fall?* Chaos may have maimed me, but she gave me a new lease on life. One I am uncertain I would have gained had I continued following a path of misery and death. Immortals are not usually known for their subtlety. Blinding her eldest child was not a power move. It was a revelation. I would never see the same way again.

So now, dearest mortal, when you look up at the night skies, you will find strength, inner peace, and perhaps courage to look upon this realm with a different set of eyes.

TRAGEDY IN
MOONLIGHT
BY
RENEE CHRISTIAN
SELENE,
TITANESS OF THE MOON

I CROSS THE NIGHT SKY IN MY HORSE-DRAWN CHARIOT TO MEET MY DAUGHTER. Bats, coyotes, whippoorwills, and wolves followed my course, responding to my power and energy as the Titaness of the Moon. I set down in a clearing, Dreyla's glow emanating from a nearby olive grove.

"Mother! Mother, I met someone!" Dreyla called, racing to greet me. Excitement and joy radiated from her.

Dreyla, my oldest, never played the field. Her serious nature and commitment to her duties meant that it was a big deal for her to begin a conversation with that phrase. She continued at such a rapid pace that it was hard to keep up.

"I met him about a year ago, and we spend time together as often as his work allows. He's so sweet and caring. Just the other day, he sent me a bouquet of my favorite flowers just because he was thinking of me. He's just so…" She squealed, spinning in place.

"So, can I meet him?" I asked, smiling at her with genuine parental pride.

"Yes, of course!" She beamed, barely able to contain her enthusiasm. "That's why I'm here. Will you come with me?"

Her eyes sparkled, and she vibrated with an energy I'd rarely seen in her. It was contagious.

She scrambled into the chariot and I followed her directions to the meeting place. She chattered happily as we waited. The horses snorted suspiciously as a muscular young man stepped out of the shadows to greet us. The hairs rose on the nape of my neck, the welcoming smile freezing on my face.

No, he couldn't be! Oh, Dreyla, my darling, this is why he draws you so.

I tried to shake my suspicion, but the truth was explicit in his face. My effect on him was undeniable, and it was apparent he knew I was aware of what and who he was.

"Mother, this is Acontes."

His name rang in my ears like I had been boxed upside the head. Confirmation.

He bowed in greeting, his eyes flickering marigold. "Madam." He rose, intentionally avoiding my eyes.

I turned away, closing my eyes and seeking control before looking at Dreyla.

"So, darling, where and how did you two meet?" I asked, forcing a smile back on my face.

"Mother?" Dreyla's voice was filled with concern. "Mother, are you okay? Your voice, and you've become so dark..." Her eyes widened and flicked anxiously between Acontes and me. "Mother?"

I looked pointedly at Acontes. "Are you going to tell her, or should I?"

Horrified realization broke across his face. Either way, his truth would be revealed. His mouth tightened in determined silence.

"Did you think you could keep it from her?" I pressed. "Did you think she would not eventually find out? Or," I paused, glaring at him, "are you as stupid as your father?"

He flinched, and his head ducked into his shoulders.

"So, it's on me then, is it?" I growled. "You definitely didn't get his balls."

I turned to Dreyla, who stood with a mixed expression of confusion and indignation at my side.

"Drey, darling, Acontes is a son of Lycaon, the werewolf."

Shadows shifted across Dreyla's face, and I could see her processing the situation. She shifted restlessly, and energy ebbed and flowed around her. If I'd ever wondered what she'd inherited from me, there was the evidence. I reached for her hand, but she pulled away, stiff with dawning awareness.

"When were you planning on telling me?" she said accusingly, her voice echoing between the press of trees and her eyes fixed on

Acontes. "Mother's right. Did you think I wouldn't find out?" She took an angry breath and leaned forward accusingly. "It's all beginning to make sense now. How you were only around a few days a month and gave me only barely coherent messages the rest of the time." She bit her lip, her face a bitter scowl. "I thought wolves weren't even capable of a functioning intellect, so how did you even...?" her words faded, her eyes filling with bitter tears.

Acontes stepped towards her and gently took her hand. "That's the point, my love. Typically, that would be true. I am more wolf and trapped in the wolf's mindset most of the time, but I still thought of you. I did everything in my power to reach out to you and let you know I was thinking of you. Can't you see that?"

Dreyla snatched her hand from his and drew her arm back to slap him. He winced, bracing himself, but his words must have registered, and her hand fell. She turned to me, and her face was a mask of despair.

"Mother?" She shook her head, tears pooling in her eyes, threatening to cascade down her pale cheeks. "I...I don't even know where to begin. What do I do now? How did you know when I didn't?"

"I am the Titan of the Moon, darling. I can feel them. All wolves respond to me, but werewolves are directly connected to me."

Dreyla turned away to face Acontes and took a solitary, hesitant step towards him. He lifted his hand, reaching for her, clearly still bracing himself for her retaliation. His eyes pleaded with her to listen. "Please, Drey..."

Her shoulder shifted back, a minute movement, and yet still out of reach. "I don't know what you think you can say to me that would make a difference," she said.

Acontes dropped his hand, his posture indicating defeat. "Does saying *I love you* mean nothing anymore? Does the fact that I could send you messages, even in my wolf-form, mean nothing?"

Dreyla glanced back at me.

"You don't understand, Acontes," she said, her voice strained. "I am a daughter of the moon, whose courses are so constant we order our lives, our bodies, around them."

"And I am the second son of Lycaon. The werewolf, whose every step is ordered and governed by the moon," Acontes replied, his eyes briefly meeting mine before shifting his gaze back to Dreyla. "I am human once a month. Once. And I spend it with you! And every other moment, every single moment, I spend thinking of you."

"Is that the life you would have me live, Acontes? I can't retreat into the wilds of the wolf-mind as you can. I cannot run with you, to know the scent of game or the feel of moss beneath my paws as you do. I am condemned to be unable to communicate with you. To touch you. And now I will know, every moment, every second as it passes, that you are where I cannot reach you." She took a deep breath, fighting emotions as powerful as the tides. "This lie you have given me, was it to protect yourself or me? You have made me love you for something you are not. For only part of what you are. And now you reveal that the part I know is but a thin sliver, the smallest scrap of time and love I might have from you."

Heartbroken, Dreyla stared at him, the tears finally slipping down her cheeks in silver streaks.

"You lure me to loving you, then expect me to feast on crumbs forever."

Shaking his head, Acontes took a tentative step forward before thinking better of it. "Some of that is true, yes," he agreed. "You can never feel the moss under your paws. But you can run with me, hunt with me, even. I can communicate with you. I've already found a way. You've received letters from me, haven't you? They may have been barely legible, but they were letters all the same. If you were *with* me, imagine the communication we could have. The closeness we could share. We could come to know each other truly. Dreyla, give me a chance, please!"

I stood back and watched them silently. My growing anger and fear shrouding me in darkness. Finally, crossing my arms in exasperation, I could hold back no longer.

"How can you even listen to him, Dreyla? You know this relationship is doomed. Walk away!"

She ignored me. Her attention focused wholly on Acontes. I muttered under my breath and turned away. Snapping my fingers at my horses, I waited until they drew near and climbed angrily back into my chariot. I caught up the reins and lifted into the air, rising on a rush of frustration. I pulled the pawing and snorting horses to a halt, so I could continue to observe from a distance. My fear and anxiety grew as I watched.

Dreyla stood with her gaze half-cast to the sky, aware of my continuing presence but equally aware that the choice was now hers to make alone, and I caught the tremor coursing through her. I could only imagine the conflicting emotions tumbling through my daughter's mind, and her sigh was unmistakable as she turned her attention from me, taking her first steps back to Acontes.

I had to concede there was an ethereal beauty in how the moonlight accentuated his perfect frame, highlighting every muscle and every sharp, wild contour of him. No wonder Dreyla struggled to be free of him. I strained to hear her words through the sigh of the wind in the trees.

"I cannot deny what I feel. I can only doubt the strength in me to bear it." She drew closer to him and leaned forward to drape her arms around his neck. "If all I'm to have is one night every time the moonglass turns, then show me what this love looks like. Here. Now," she said. "Then come back to me when it turns again, and I will give you my answer."

She kissed him, and his hands locked behind her head, their embrace powerful and undeniable. Knowing she had made her choice, I snapped my reins against the horses' backs, leaving the young lovers in the moonlight and not looking back.

It was months before Dreyla contacted me again. When she did, her message was urgent, and she was clearly distraught. King Lycaon became aware of their relationship, and it came as no surprise to me he was livid, his rage uncontrollable.

I drove my horses hard, struggling against panic. By the time I was circling the location Dreyla gave me, they had worked up a lather. I looked down, straining to see between the night-shadowed trees.

Acontes was in full wolf form and standing defensively before Dreyla, facing off against several of his brothers and Lycaon. They were in a stand-off, and the air rippled with violent tension. I circled lower, and every head turned towards me, focused upon my approach. Fuck! I feared this from the start.

Driving the chariot downwards, I leaped from it before the horses drew to a halt, calling to Dreyla as I closed the gap between us.

"Drey! Dreyla, please! Let's go. There's no negotiating when they're like this. It isn't safe!"

I fought to rein in my energy and control my effect over the werewolves' transformations and power. Acontes shifted his attention from his father, and his eyes met mine. His gaze was intense, burning, and I sensed more to the contact than a mere acknowledgment of my presence. He was trying to communicate with me. Fear. Gut-wrenching, heart racing, uncontrollable fear raced through me as I realized what Acontes was trying to say.

Run!!!!!

Snatching at Dreyla's hand, I dragged her forwards and turned to run. Acontes' eyes flashed, switching from marigold to red. Blood

19

red! He had finally lost control, and his bloodlust rose to envelop him.

Dreyla and I bolted. The small pack had cut us off from the chariot and our escape. They were hot on our heels as we headed into the tightly packed trees, the clearing into which I'd dropped receding behind us. Branches cracked, and the undergrowth crashed around us. My skin crawled in fear, shivers racing down my spine, and panic building in my gut. The werewolves were rapidly catching up and would soon surround us. My mind raced.

"Theia, Eos, Phoebe, Leto!"

The names resonated in my mind as I cried out to my mother and her friends. Dreyla's stamina was no match for mine, and she was already slowing down. I sincerely hoped the Titans I had called would hear and come to our aid quickly.

A pool of moonlight ahead of us revealed a small clearing, and I felt certain the werewolves would ambush us there, but there was nowhere else to run. I gripped Dreyla's hand more firmly and indicated the direction with a nod of my head, my breath hitching in my throat and sweat drizzling into my eyes.

Dust and dirt peppered Dreyla's face, streaked with tears of fear and pain. I forced my voice to hold steady and calm, masking my own building emotions. She was already struggling and did not need to see my anger and fear.

"We are immortal, and we are strong. Stronger than you can imagine," I shouted at her. "We have this!"

We hit the middle of the clearing and stopped. A single shaft of moonlight bathed us as we turned simultaneously to crouch back to back. Red eyes glittered from the shadows between the trees and shifting black shapes showed me the pack's location. They surrounded us.

Dreyla stiffened at my back, and I sensed her resolve harden. *That's my girl!* I thought. There was no way she'd go down without a fight.

A voice rang through the night, shifting and echoing on the wind to keep the wolves from tracing its source.

"You aren't alone, Selene! Let's do this!"

Mother! The Titans had arrived!

Lycaon's howl, calling the pack to action, reverberated through the air. Trees swayed, and the ground shook beneath the massive movements of the Titans and werewolves. The very earth was reacting to these large, powerful, supernatural beings. Acontes appeared, lunging at Dreyla, fangs bared, and saliva dripping to his broad, black chest. Bracing herself against me, she kicked out, catching him mid-leap and sending him backward in a violent arc. He hit the ground and, without so much as a pause, leaped again.

"Acontes. Please!" I heard her scream. "Please, Acontes, I don't want to fight you!"

He was oblivious to her voice, and she kicked him again. His teeth scored her leg, and her blood marred his black coat, causing the bloodlust to overtake his eyes. A snarl resonated in his chest as he recovered to circle us warily, head lowered and tail extended behind him, two of his brothers joining him.

I had problems of my own. I stepped forward as Lycaon and one of his sons leaped towards me. I glimpsed Leto and Phoebe racing in from our right and Theia from the left. They were too late, and in my distraction, so was I. The two giant wolf-forms pinned me beneath them. I threw my arm up in defense, and Lycaon's jaws closed on my forearm, his eyes fastened on mine. I ignored the pain and ducked to avoid the second wolf's attempt to grab my head. Tucking in one leg and pushing just as quickly upwards, I threw Lycaon backward. A hot rush of blood ran down my arm.

There was no time for thought as I grabbed the second wolf. I hurled him aside and lashed out with a foot as Lycaon came at me again. I caught him hard under the jaw, and his head snapped up, fire burning in his eyes. My respite was brief as his son was already on his feet and resuming his attack. I turned to meet him, and Lycaon launched himself at my back, his breath hot and wet on my neck. Shoving my shoulders up in an instinctual effort to protect my neck, I dropped and spun, lifting upwards and once again casting Lycaon aside. His claws raked my skin.

Immersed in my own battle, I was peripherally aware of fighting all around me. I caught sight of Leto grabbing a wolf by the muzzle, clamping his teeth shut on his tongue. She hurled him violently across the clearing, sending him crashing into a tree, the impact cutting short his yelp of rage and dismay. A second wolf flung itself at her, knocking her to the ground. A cry escaped my lips as the wolf's jaws locked onto Leto's raised forearms, blood spraying across his face. Before I could take so much as a step in her direction, Lycaon and his son returned to challenge me. I dodged them, my back burning where Lycaon's claws had ripped into me.

Theia and Phoebe worked in unison against a pair of wolves. Leaves and dust flew as they circled and spun, the wolves darting in and out, jaws snapping. Their bodies sinuous, continual blurs of motion in their efforts to tear my family apart. Catching Phoebe's hand, Theia pivoted, swinging Phoebe outwards, sending both legs in a sweeping arc. She caught the first wolf in the ribs and sent him flying into the second. They tumbled end over end but rebounded, scrambling back to their paws and flying in for another attack.

I barely managed to sidestep Lycaon's launch for my throat before I was ducking under a leap from his son.

That was it! I was done with this bullshit!

Gathering my power, I darkened like a full lunar eclipse. I no longer needed to see with my eyes, my mind stretched outwards allowing me to sense everything around me. Time slowed, everything slowed, as if I walked between individual heartbeats. I saw the three Titans, Lycaon and five of his sons, and my daughter. Dreyla was lost beneath the full weight of Acontes, struggling for her life.

Rage surged through me. Leaping past Lycaon and his son, the pair seemingly suspended in front of me. I fell upon Acontes, grabbing him by the scruff of his neck and hurling him upwards and away. He somersaulted through the air to land high in a tree, his body thudding and crashing against the branches as he plunged back to the ground.

I barely glanced at Acontes' still form, dropping to my heels at Dreyla's side. She was in bad shape. Focused on avoiding harming Acontes, she hadn't fought back. Her wounds were entirely defensive, and she lay limp and still.

"Why didn't you fight?" I breathed with anguish in my voice, gathering her into my arms. She made no reply, her soft face smeared with tears and blood.

Damn it! I couldn't heal her while in eclipse, and the fighting continued around us. None of us were safe. Laying Dreyla under the shelter of an arched tree at the edge of the clearing, I straightened, swearing under my breath. *"Where was Eos when I needed her? We could have sent Dreyla away, somewhere safe. Eos was never where I needed her when I needed her!"*

Turning away from Dreyla, I sought Acontes, but he was no longer under the tree. Scanning the area, I discovered Acontes and Lycaon, shoulder to shoulder, stalking our way.

Keeping my gaze fixed on them, forcing them to focus exclusively on me, I edged around the clearing. I drew them away from where I had placed Dreyla and they followed. I could see two wolves down, though it was impossible to know if they were merely stunned or just incapacitated by their injuries. I couldn't discount them from the fight. I couldn't place the remaining wolves, though the sounds of continued fighting echoed around me, and I had two wolves determinedly stalking me. The fight was far from over.

I rolled my shoulders, ignoring the searing pain in my back and the hot wash of fresh blood seeping through my tunic's remnants. I focused on drawing Lycaon and Acontes with me. I dropped into a crouch and watched Acontes. His fur rippled, shifting, the effects of my presence gradually wearing off under my eclipse. Lycaon, stronger, his transformation far more stable, continued to glare at me with ruby-red eyes, still deep within his rage and bloodlust.

A spark of marigold appeared in Acontes' eyes, and I knew it was Lycaon who was now my greatest threat. I tensed and waited.

The yellow returned to Acontes' eyes, and he paused, his body losing aggression. I launched into an attack, channeling energy directly from the earth. I was a blur of motion, powered by Earth and Moon and maternal rage. Lycaon leaped at me, and we collided. But he was unprepared. The impact of our bodies sent shock waves through the clearing. He arced through the air with a howl of pain and fury, spinning end over end to disappear into the enveloping shadows of the forest.

There was no time for celebration. I had no guarantee that Lycaon was permanently out of the fight, and we were not yet the victors. I spun on my heel, seeking Acontes. I wasn't surprised to find him at Dreyla's side, whimpering and howling in grief and remorse. No doubt, the memories remained fresh in his mind, and the taste of her blood lingered on his tongue. I had no time for him either, but I could have faith he'd now protect Dreyla with his life. Theia, Phoebe, and Leto wearily faced the remaining three wolves, one on one, three on three. Assessing their positions, I circled them and silently approached the snarling wolf trio from the rear. Their bodies were taut with the desire to fight, their ears flattened to their skulls, lips raised over their fangs, and hackles raised across broad shoulders. They sat back onto their haunches, ready to leap, and backed directly into where I waited.

"Did you lose count?" I asked quietly.

I gave them no time to respond. Taking the tail of one of the wolves in both hands, I spun, launching him far from sight with a crescendo of fading howls. Seeing a window of opportunity while the remaining two wolves were distracted, Leto and Theia raced forwards and quickly dispatched them with cutting blows to their heads. The wolves fell limp between us.

Phoebe bent with her hands on her knees, out of breath and smeared in blood, managing a grateful nod. "It was a good fight," she said. "Thanks for the call."

Leto placed a hand on my shoulder. "Selene," she murmured softly, "it's over. You can let go now. We no longer need an eclipse."

Looking around me, I realized she was right.

Taking a deep breath, I took a step back. I was drawn tight as a drum, my powers centered and contained, my body and heart aching. Closing my eyes, I began releasing and balancing my energy. Gradually, my normal gentle glow returned, and with it excruciating pain. Theia caught me as I stumbled and fell forward, a wave of weariness washing over me. Theia, Phoebe, Leto, and I made our way to where Acontes remained at Dreyla's side. He flattened at our approach before rolling over in a gesture of submission.

"Selene," Theia said, ignoring Acontes, "you need to heal yourself before you try to heal Dreyla. You're too weak in this state."

Much as I hated to admit it, she was right.

I knelt at Dreyla's side and fought the intense need to touch her. Instead, I closed my eyes and focused my healing energies on myself. I sought my injuries one by one, feeling the soft rush of power as they drew closed. I rocked back and drew a deep breath, gathering my composure for the work still ahead. Dreyla. It was time to reach out to my broken daughter. I opened my eyes.

Leto and Theia had escorted Acontes aside, and he sat curled against the bole of a giant oak, whimpering, his marigold gaze focused on Dreyla. In a way, I pitied him. How broken must he be, knowing all the pain he had caused the very one he claimed to love with his entire being? But his burden was his alone to bear. It meant nothing to me. I laid my hands on Dreyla.

Blue tendrils of energy passed from me, through me, winding like smoke down into Dreyla. It was slow. Healing another is not the same as healing oneself. Each injury has to be found, isolated, focused upon individually. It is painstaking and exhausting. My head spun, and my body ached. Gradually, painfully slowly, Dreyla's injuries began to knit and close.

Dawn was filtering through the forest canopy in a soft mist of gold by the time her eyes fluttered with the first signs of awareness. The forest held its breath, and a deathly silence surrounded us.

"Dreyla, rest," I whispered at her. She relaxed, and I felt her drift into a healing sleep.

I turned to my mother and the friends who had willingly sacrificed their strength to come to our aid.

"How are you all holding up?" I asked. "Phoebe? Leto? I sense your need of me. Let me help you."

Phoebe waved a hand at Leto. She sat near Acontes and watched him warily, keeping a careful watch over him. I suspected he had no intention of doing any harm or going anywhere. His eyes were pools of remorse, his head laid on his outstretched paws, and his tail curled about his haunches. He was done.

I turned my attention to Leto, moving to her side and drawing one of her hands into mine. I closed my eyes and focused once again on healing. My power isn't infinite. Even when I draw from both the earth and the moon, healing is no simple task. I had expended a great deal of energy in the fight, in the eclipse, and in healing myself and then Dreyla. I was tired, and it was becoming increasingly difficult to focus. I would have to ration my energy or risk collapse myself.

I left a connection in place with Leto, permitting a tendril of energy to continue flowing through to her. I gathered myself and dropped alongside Theia. My mother had been brave, as was to be expected of her. While not as serious as Leto's and Dreyla's wounds, her injuries were still extensive.

"Thank you," I said as I placed my hands on her. "For coming."

"What else would I do?" Theia said. She nodded towards where Dreyla was stirring.

"Did you not do the same?" She coughed, a thread of blood appearing at her lips. "Besides, I haven't had this much fun in years."

"Fun?" I scoffed. "Look at you."

The words barely left my mouth when a sudden drain of energy left me gasping for breath. My vision darkened, and my head spun. I turned to check on Leto, thinking I must have made an unforgivable mistake, only to discover it was not Leto.

Before me played out one of the most astounding scenes of self-sacrifice I have ever witnessed. Acontes lay stretched between Phoebe and Leto, creating a physical conduit of my energy with his own body. I made a mistake, but it was Phoebe's injuries I'd missed. Acontes saw what I had not and took it upon himself to come to the aid of someone he had seen as an enemy. And he was dying.

As seen by Acontes' uncontrollable need for blood upon my arrival, my energy works counter-effectively on werewolves. Instead of healing him, my power flowing through him was exacerbating his injuries.

"Acontes," I breathed, darkness threatening to take me as my power ebbed.

He turned profoundly sad eyes my way without moving the position of his head. A slowly expanding pool of blood spread around him, his life ebbing away, yet he refused to move. His muzzle lay in Phoebe's lap, where she sat, eyes closed and pale, and his tail lay across one of Leto's legs.

"Acontes!" It was Dreyla, struggling to rise and reaching desperately for Acontes.

"Dreyla, don't!" I gasped at her. "If you touch him, you will break the connection, and they may all die!"

"Why? Why, mother? And why isn't he healing, too?"

Dreyla had crawled to Acontes side and was now sitting, rocking, sobbing, her body resonating with a desperate desire to hold her beloved wolf. Pain and confusion contorted her face as she watched Acontes bleeding out before her and unable to do anything to help any of us. "I don't understand. Mother, help him!"

"I can't," I admitted, my heart breaking for them both.

Fighting the desire to give into oblivion, I dug deeper within myself, seeking every reserve of energy I possessed. My back burned and blood welled from my wounds to seep through my tunic, drenching me in an unwelcome warmth. Reversing my healing was the only way to continue the flow of healing to the others.

Darkness claimed me.

I woke lying on my side, my head in Leto's lap while Phoebe pressed cool, wet cloths to my back. Theia sat next to Dreyla.

My dear, sweet Dreyla sat holding the lifeless form of a blood-matted wolf in her lap, her head bowed as she rocked back and forth. Her cries of anguish and despair echoed through a forest silent in sympathy. Acontes' price for his forbidden love was his life.

Another day fell to a close, and the sun set before I could garner enough strength to heal myself again.

We buried Acontes on an outcrop overlooking his favorite hunting grounds. Dreyla, Theia, Phoebe, Leto, and I, parted ways without another word spoken between us. Dreyla blamed me. She had to lay her pain somewhere. And it is always easier to blame the ones you love. We have barely spoken since, though I will always accept her in my heart. I await the day she can forgive.

The rest of us returned to our daily lives, holding the memory of those tragic events as best forgotten. Although, for me, the constant immortal fear of King Lycaon seeking revenge for the death of his second son, is one that will never die.

THE
DEEP
WILD

BY

CJ LANDRY

HERA,

QUEEN OF THE GODS

I sat curled on our bedroom couch in my nightgown. I leaned against the arm, watching my husband get ready for the day. Zeus was power in motion and didn't waste a single movement. Bringing my mug to my lips, I let the steam from the tea warm my face. It's strange being a part of the mortal world. I'm used to watching their festivals and feast days from afar, but being immersed in it makes me nostalgic for the days when my children were smaller and still had time for me.

I walked around town yesterday afternoon to get a feel for the area and smiled at all the children dressed in costumes, already anticipating the upcoming Halloween festival. I watched mothers talking to each other excitedly about holiday plans and ushering the kids into coffee shops for pumpkin-spiced drinks. I walked by antique stores with new window displays. Hoping that the fake cobwebs and spiders would help sell the items with the real cobwebs and spiders.

I went to bed last night with my heart full, a smile on my face, and woke up the same way. I stretched my legs out on the couch and went back to watching Zeus. He buttoned his shirt and combed his hair. Going to the closet, he pulled out a silk navy blue Armani tie and tied it into a neat Eldredge knot as he walked back to his dresser.

"Hera, have you seen my cufflinks? The silver lightning bolt ones?"

"They're in the top drawer there. I put them further back."

"Why would you do that? You know they're my favorite."

"Honestly, my love, you have so many I thought you might want to switch it up a bit."

"Hmpf." Zeus effortlessly attached his cufflinks and turned to me, his mouth open to say something. He took a step towards me and paused to *really* look at me. "Why aren't you dressed?"

I shrugged my shoulders delicately so as not to spill my tea. "I'm trying out this thing mortals call *playing hooky*. Apparently, they take days where they skip work and sit around and do nothing all day."

Zeus laughed. "You? Sit around and do nothing all day? If I could play hooky myself, I would, just so I could count the minutes until you fail."

I frowned at him, and he walked over to me.

"Does this playing hooky require a lack of clothing?" He slid a finger down my chest and pulled the front of my nightgown out far enough to look under it.

I swatted his hand away. "I haven't decided yet, but if it does, you won't be a part of it. You have meetings all day."

He threw his hands up in surrender and winked at me. "You could bring me lunch."

I sighed loudly, pretending frustration with him. "I'll be busy doing nothing. I won't have time to bring your lunch. Now go to work. You know how the henchfolk get when the boss is late."

He smiled and leaned down for a quick kiss. "And they think I'm a slave driver. No one holds a candle to you, my dear."

"Flatterer." I shooed him away and watched him walk out. Such a beautiful sight to behold, even after all these millennia.

I stood and stretched. I really was playing hooky today, but not to do nothing. I was going to help the nearby fire station get their haunted house in order. It reminded me of a haunted maze I put together for my children when they were younger.

I got dressed in some comfortable jeans and a sweater, and as I wrapped my hair into a bun, I smiled, remembering the fun that we had during that festival season.

I could have teleported to the firehouse, but I wanted to enjoy the crisp air, so I walked the twelve blocks. I snuggled into my bright blue cardigan and set a lazy pace so I could think back on one particular fall festival I planned for the children. I think it was when they were what you mortals call *teenagers*.

I had sent for Moxie one afternoon to join me for a stroll in the gardens. However, when she got to my chambers, she wasn't prepared for what she saw. Downy filling still floated lazily through the air, the pillows from the lounge shredded. The center table was upended, one of the legs torn off and lying across the room. Food was smeared and squished all over the floor. The drapes that used to frame the windows so elegantly were now torn and barely hanging on.

Moxie looked around in shock. "Mamá? Mamá, where are you?" She walked delicately into the room, her eyes wide with disbelief. She gently pushed a torn pillow out of the way with a nudge from one of her feet as she walked further into the room. Her breathing got faster, and she bit her lip.

"Mamá! Mamá! I need you, Mamá! Please stop hiding and come out. This isn't funny anymore."
Moxie stumbled over an apple and reached out for a pillar to steady herself. Her hand landed in something sticky. When she pulled back, she was horrified to find her palm covered in blood. Behind the pillar was a small table, empty but for an envelope with her name on it. She reached for it, her hand shaking and stained red.

Her lips trembled, and a tear fell down her cheek as she opened the envelope and read the note.

Moxie,
I hope you like the redecorating I've done. Hera is far too stuffy, so I showed her how to...loosen up.
You're probably wondering just what happened here, and why there's blood in your Mamá's rooms, no? It's only a minor injury on her part, don't worry. I'd tell you she's not in pain, but let's face it, I'd probably be lying.

You're too young to understand this fully, but Hera and I have not always seen eye to eye on children and their upbringing, or lineage. She crossed the line far too many times and I cannot allow this to continue. So, here are the rules.

If you tell Zeus, she will become one with my void, and that will be the end of that. If anyone in the Pantheon finds out, except the four I have listed below, she's gone. And please, before you say, "But immortals cannot die!"—consider who I am. There is no coming back from where I will place her if you cannot follow the rules. Not even Lord Hades could save her.

Nike, Ares, and Hephaestus are the only ones you may go to. Remember, if anyone else finds out, Hera is gone. Permanently.

You will find us in the Deep Wilds. You have until dawn.

Good luck.

Nyx

Moxie's tears flowed freely now, and she wrapped her arms across her chest to hold herself together, uncaring that blood was getting on her gown. Nyx had Hera, and it terrified her! The only thing Moxie could do was follow Nyx's orders to the letter. She had to get her brothers and sister together to save their mother.

Blinded with fear and too upset to teleport, Moxie stumbled out of the room and ran as fast as she could to the training fields.

Moxie followed the sound of Nike's laughter. She and her brother, Zelus, were racing through an obstacle course. Nike ran toward a rocky pile, leaping gracefully from one rock to the next, her wings aiding her ascent. Not one to let his little sister win, Zelus grabbed onto Nike's foot and yanked her backward. She did an awkward flip in the air and landed badly on her back.

"No fair, Zelus! That's cheating!"

He laughed as he scrambled up the pile. Pausing at the top, he looked at her with mischief in his eyes. "Everyone cheats, little one! That is life! You must learn to overcome the setbacks and claim your victory." He cackled and slid down the rocks to the other side, gaining a huge lead over Nike in their race.

Nike got up, rubbing her backside, mumbling, "I don't cheat." She flexed her wings and was about to take off to try to regain her lead when she heard someone calling her name. She turned and saw Moxie speeding towards her.

Nike wasn't immediately concerned, but then she saw that Moxie's hair was flying all over the place, she was out of breath, and there were red spots on her dress. Nike drew her eyebrows together in confusion.

"Why are you out of breath? You should have just teleported over here."

Moxie was breathing so hard she couldn't talk, so she did what she did best. She grabbed Nike's forearm and sent her a picture of Hera's sitting room.

Nike gasped. "What happened to Lady Hera?"

Moxie tried smoothing back her hair. "I don't know, but there was a note. Nyx will kill our mother! Nike, we have to help her!"

That scared Nike. No one messed with the Goddess of Night. "We should tell Zeus. He will tear the heavens apart to find Lady Hera." Nike started to walk off, but Moxie grabbed her arm to keep her from leaving.

"Nike, we don't have time! Do you know where he is? Because I don't and I certainly don't want to try to find him. What if he's with another woman? Plus, Nyx only gave us until morning. We don't have enough time to find him."

Nike growled a little out of frustration. "Fine, we'll go save Lady Hera. Let's get the boys. Ares is hanging out at the pool with the nymphs."

"Great, he's never going to help us."

"He'll help us. Even if I have to drag him away by his hair."

Nike and Moxie ran as fast as they could to the pools to get Ares. Thinking only of saving their mother, they burst through the hanging canopy and got an eye full of Ares slipping his godhood into one nymph and kissing another. The bare skin of his backside shone in the fading sunlight.

"No! No!" Nike screeched and turned around. "Gross, gross, gross." She rubbed her eyes as hard as she could. Physically trying to remove the image of Ares having sex from her brain.

Moxie just made a disgusted sound in the back of her throat. "Ares, please stop. We need you."

Ares reluctantly tore himself away from the nymph's succulent lips. Without missing a pump into the other he looked over his shoulder and winked at Moxie. "Enjoying the show, girls?"

"This is serious, Ares. Please!" Moxie huffed at him.

Still rubbing her eyes, Nike called over her shoulder, "I thought you were dating Ianthe, anyway?"

Ares released a hollow laugh. "She broke my heart, little one, and you know the saying, *The best way to get over one woman is to get inside another.* Best advice I've ever heard." Ares grunted, and the nymph under him let out a scandalous moan.

Moxie tried to reason with him, "Ares, our mother is missing. We have to find her. Please help us."

"Mother is always *missing*, which usually means she's chasing after Father while he chases another woman. Personally, I don't care. I'm busy. Now go *away* already." He leaned back into the mouth of the second nymph just as a third emerged naked from the water and started walking toward him.

Nike looked at Moxie. "I'm not going anywhere near that mess."

Moxie nodded and sent a thought to Ares, who immediately began to gag and stumbled away from the nymphs, leaving them painfully unsatisfied.

36

"Really, Mox? I didn't need *that* image of Mom and Dad in my head." He yanked his clothing off a tree branch and started getting dressed. "Why is this so urgent, anyway? I told you. She does this all the time. All she's trying to do is get the attention that Dad should be giving her. It's exhausting."

"Ares, Lady Hera is in trouble. Moxie went to see her earlier and found her rooms in disarray. There was blood." Nike finally turned to face Ares and crossed her arms.

Moxie whimpered a little. "There was also a note. She's not looking for attention." She handed the letter to Ares, who passed it to Nike once he read it.

Ares gritted his teeth. "You may be right this time, Moxie." He started pacing back and forth, running his hand roughly through his hair several times. Finally, he halted in front of them. "All right. I'll help you. I don't care what she's done. Mother doesn't deserve to be hurt like that."

Nike nodded. "We need to get Hephaestus and some weapons. We'll probably find them all in the same place."

Ares took off at a quick pace, the girls scrambling to keep up. One more stop and they could rescue their mother. Moxie only hoped it didn't take too long to convince Hephaestus to help them. He hadn't been on the best of terms with their parents lately.

The trip to the forge was long, and the teens were panting by the time they got there. As they came upon the forge, Moxie looked at the sky, nervously counting the hours they had left.

The ringing of metal on metal, resonated across the land. Each strike was a precise blow, designed to work out any imperfections in the steel. Hephaestus was standing in front of an anvil, wearing nothing but loose pants, a leather apron, and a pair of leather gloves. His lean arms strained with youthful muscles that could only be attained through physical labor. Each time he raised his hammer, his shoulders tightened. Each time he swung the hammer onto the flat metal, his back flexed. Though his movements were slightly awkward because of his youth, you could almost see the man he would grow to become.

Ares stepped forward, but as soon as he opened his mouth, Hephaestus said, "No. Whatever it is, no. Now leave me alone." He turned and dipped the hot metal into the water, watching the steam rise.

"Come on now, man. Is that any way to say hello to your favorite brother?"

"I don't have a favorite, and even if I did, it definitely wouldn't be you, *brother*." Frowning, Hephaestus limped over to a workbench and attached the long blade of metal to a vise. He grabbed a different hammer and started banging away.

Nike's wings flexed with exasperation. "Hephaestus, please. Lady Hera is in danger. She needs our help."

Hephaestus let out a roar of laughter. "Oh, that's rich. My mother has never needed me before, and she certainly wouldn't need me now. Go away, little one."

Moxie lowered her head and looked at the blood on her hand. This wasn't right. Why was it so hard to convince them to help? Hera may not have been the best mother, but she loved her children. Moxie knew this without question. She walked over to Hephaestus and put her hand lightly on his forearm.

Whispering, she said, "Please, Hephaestus. I'm begging you. She needs our help. You know I would never ask anything of you that wasn't important."

Hephaestus flinched at Moxie's light touch. "I can't, Mox. She may have birthed me, but she's never treated me as her child. She's no mother to me."

Moxie gasped. "How dare you say that, Hephaestus! You need to stop throwing a temper tantrum and get over yourself." Moxie then pushed memories into his head, memories that he had either forgotten or blocked out. She showed him visions of Hera tucking him into bed, holding him when he cried, scolding him when he did something wrong, protecting him from harm, fighting about him with Zeus.

A lone tear fell down Hephaestus' cheek, and he pulled away. "Stop it, Moxie. Those things never happened."

"That's crap, and you know it! She needs our help, Hephy, and she would fight anything that got in her way to save any one of us."

Shaking his head, Hephaestus limped over to the wall and grabbed another strip of metal.
"If you won't do it for her, Hephy, then do it for Nike or for me or for Ares, because we're going to save her from Nyx and we might get hurt. Could you really live with yourself if you could have protected us but didn't?"

Hephaestus growled, threw the metal across the forge, and ripped his leather gloves off. "Fine, Mox, I'll do it for you. But only because I know you'd probably find a way to get yourself killed if I'm not there. Hang on."

He grabbed a shirt and put it on as he limped to the far wall where the finished weapons were. Hephaestus deliberated, then grabbed two swords and a handful of knives. He handed a knife to Moxie, who tucked it into her belt. Nike received a sword. The other sword and the rest of the knives went to Ares, who distributed them in different places along his body.

"They're not perfect weapons, but they're the best I've made so far. Come on." Hephaestus limped away from the forge.

Nike called out, "What about you?"

Hephaestus patted the heads of the hammers attached to his belt. "I'm good."

Moxie called to his retreating back, "You don't know where you're going!"

Hephaestus stopped and sighed. "Fine, Mox. You lead the way."

Moxie took one last look at the darkening sky, shivered, and led the other three to the Deep Wild.

The teens crested the hill and stopped, staring across the field of flowers to the forest ahead. They were all appropriately nervous, as none had been into these woods before. The older gods called it the Deep Wild and warned of the horrors they might find if they got lost inside.

Nike flexed her wings. Moxie rubbed her palms over her arms and took a deep breath. Ares gripped his sword and furrowed his brow. Hephaestus flexed his hands and steeled his jaw. Without comment, the four of them started walking again, stopping once they reached the entrance.

The sky had nearly darkened to full night. The only light came from the moon shining through the archway created by the overhanging branches. There was nothing to see beyond, but there was definitely a chill in the air. Even though they were racing the clock, none of them were eager to move forward.

Finally, Hephaestus grunted and pushed past Ares. "Well, if we're going, let's go. I don't have all night for this foolishness. I've got weapons to make."

Nike followed behind Hephaestus, and Ares motioned for Moxie to go ahead of him as he took up the rear. Walking through the archway felt like they were pushing through a dimensional membrane. There was a force that tried to push them backward, to discourage them from entering, but they pressed forward. Once the four of them were on the other side, vines sprouted from the edges and grew to meet each other in the middle, forming a solid barrier that no one could breach.

"Damnit, Mox! Why'd you do that?" Ares pushed against the vines, trying to find some give to them.

Moxie just wrapped her arms over her chest and shook her head. "It wasn't me, I swear."

Nike put her hand on Moxie's shoulder to comfort her while Hephaestus pulled Ares away from the entrance.

"We don't have time for that, Ares. Let's just go get our mother and get out of here." Ares reluctantly stepped away from the entrance.

Nike stared at the high walls of thick trees and vines in front of her, craning her head up, not seeing any light, only seeing the canopy that had grown over the pathway. She looked to either side of them. "Which way should we go?"

"There's a corner just over here. Let me see where it leads. Hang on." Before any of them could say anything, Ares took off to the left and rounded the corner. They froze as they watched their brother disappear into the unknown. Hephaestus was the first to move to follow Ares, but just as he got to the corner, Ares came back.

"Nah, that's just a dead-end there. Let's go the other way." Ares walked past everyone and proceeded down the pathway, trying to ignore the thick hedges and trees that had grown together so tightly that it was hard not to get claustrophobic.

Eventually, the four of them loosened up. There didn't seem to be anything truly scary in the Deep Wild except for the darkness. Of course, everyone knows it's not the dark that's scary, but what is *in* the dark that terrifies.

They followed the path, with Ares leading the group and Hephaestus bringing up the rear. They paused at another turn, trying to see what lay ahead. Moxie shivered and said in a small voice, "I don't like this place, guys. It's full of some really bad energy."

Nike wrapped her arm around Moxie. "Don't worry. We won't let anything happen to you. I promise."

As the last word left Nike's mouth, the air shifted and seemed to part in front of them. There was a loud piercing shriek and the beat of wings from above. Ares cried out in surprise and barely lifted his arm in time to block the attack. Claws ripped through his shirt and skin as if it were paper. Ares switched his sword to his other hand and spun to follow his attacker as it flew past him to the others. "Down!"

Nike pushed Moxie to the ground and spread her wings over the two of them. Hephaestus rushed forward with hammers in each hand. He saw sharp talons reach for him from out of the darkness. He swung with his hammer and hit a wing, causing the thing to roll and let out another loud screech.

Moxie tried to look around Nike's wings to make sure her brothers were okay, but Nike kept pushing her down. "Let them handle it, Moxie. Please." Moxie wrapped her arms around Nike's waist and shivered in fear.

Hephaestus placed his feet to steady himself for the blow and turned to meet the creature. Ares finally got a good look at the beast as it descended towards Hephaestus. "Careful, Heph, it's a harpy!"

Ares ran forward and landed one foot on Nike's back. Using her as a springboard, he sailed through the air towards the harpy. He pulled his legs in and swung his sword as hard as he could. The harpy's head went flying, and blood sprayed over the boys and Nike's wings. Ares barely got his sword out of the way before falling to the ground into an awkward heap.

Hephaestus wiped the blood from his face with his hand. "Damn, why'd it have to be a harpy?"

Nike stood, releasing Moxie who ran to Ares. She examined the claw marks on his arm. "Ares, are you okay? Does it hurt?"

Ares tried to push her away. "It's fine. I've gotten worse sparring with Dad."

Moxie huffed under her breath, tore a piece of fabric from the bottom of her dress, and wrapped it around Ares' arm. "We can at least try to stop the bleeding."

Ares grumbled while Moxie tended to him, and Nike walked over to Hephaestus. "Are you okay, Hephy?"

"Don't call me that, Nike." He looked over at Moxie and Ares then turned away. "We should get moving. We don't know if there are more harpies nearby, and I don't want to do that again."

This time, Hephaestus took the lead, and the teenagers wandered on. They came to another turn and another decision. "Left or right?" Nike looked to the others for an answer.

Ares looked to the right at what seemed to be a partial barrier. "Let me check this corner." Before anyone could stop him, he was off again.

Nike grumbled. "He's going to get himself hurt worse if he keeps doing that."

Moxie took a couple of steps closer to Hephaestus as he frowned into the dark after his brother. "Show off."

A few moments later, Ares rejoined the others. Nike let out the breath she was holding. "Did you find anything, Ares?"

He just shook his head. "Nothing but more darkness and more forest." He looked down the path to the left. "Honestly, either way could be the right one." Everyone turned and looked at Moxie.

"What?"

Nike looked around and shuddered. "Well, you have that feeling thing, Moxie. Do you know which way to go?"

Moxie snorted. "I'm not an oracle, Nike."

"Well, I mean, I know you're not, but can't you feel the energy or something? Which way feels better to you?"

Moxie sighed and closed her eyes. She was still strengthening her powers and wasn't really sure this would work, but she tried. She sent her feelings out in front of her, following the path that Ares took, but only felt the darkness. She reached down the path behind her and felt nothing. Wait. She reached a little further, and there was a faint whisper.

Opening her eyes, Moxie said, "I don't really know, but I felt something alive back that way."

Hephaestus groaned. "That's not helpful, Moxie. Alive can mean more harpies, snakes, or a chimera."

Moxie put her hands on her hips and stared Hephaestus down. "I know that, Hephy, but it could also mean our mother. Besides, it's the only clue we've got."

Hephaestus looked away and grumbled under his breath, "Don't call me that."

Ares adjusted his belt. "Okay, then that's the way we're going. After you, ladies." He held out his hand for the girls, and Nike took the lead this time.

Eventually, they turned another corner, and soon came upon an opening on their right. "Should we go through it?" Moxie tried to see past the opening, but it was too dark.

Ares looked further down the path and, with a shrug, took off at a quick trot. "Be right back!"

"Ares!" they all yelled his name, but he just winked over his shoulder and waved before the night enveloped him.

Hephaestus growled, "That's it. I'm gonna kill him."

Nike patted Hephaestus on the shoulder. "It's okay, Hephaestus. Ares will be fine...I hope." She looked worriedly after her brother, but heard a faint rustling sound on the other side of the opening. "I hear something."

Moxie and Hephaestus followed behind Nike as she walked through the opening, running into the back of her when she stopped suddenly.

"Nope. No, no, no. A whole lot of nope right here." Nike attempted to back up and ended up pushing the others into each other. Moxie grabbed hold of Hephaestus to keep from tripping. Hephaestus managed to lean against a nearby hedge to hold himself up.

Hephaestus gently moved Moxie aside. "What's up, Nike?"

Nike crossed her arms. "Spiders. A lot of spiders. Like a whole nest of really big, gigantic, flesh-eating spiders." Hephaestus looked at her in disbelief. "Well, okay, maybe they're not flesh-eating spiders, but there's a lot there."

Hephaestus moved Nike behind him and looked around the hedge. His muscles tensed, and he eased back to stand next to the girls. Ares still hadn't returned. "Look, I don't know when Ares will come back, but in my experience, if something is blocking the path, that's probably the way you have to go." He frowned in thought. "There's really too many of them to attack with my hammer or a sword." Hephaestus ran a hand through his hair. "Hey, Mox? Can you do something to tell these spiders to leave us alone?"

"I should be able to. Let me try."

Hephaestus walked through the opening in front of Moxie, and Nike followed close behind. Moxie saw the nest of large tarantula spiders and focused on a few in the front. She sent them images of bugs in the webs behind them, and after a moment, they scurried off in the opposite direction of the children.

"Keep going, Moxie. You can do it." Hephaestus laid an encouraging hand on her shoulder and offered a lopsided smile. She smiled back and focused again on the spiders. Slowly but surely, the nest of arachnids wandered off, following the first group. Not used to focusing this hard, Moxie started to shake a little.

When all the little spiders had gone, and all that was left was the queen, Moxie took a deep breath and concentrated harder. All of a sudden, they heard a noise behind them, and Moxie spun around.

"Hey, why'd you guys leave? Whatever, there's just another dead end that way, so you're going the right way." Ares sounded quite pleased with himself.

With Moxie's attention diverted, the queen realized that there were large bodies of prey in front of her, and she scurried towards them.

"No, no, no, no! Damnit, Ares, why did you ruin it?" Nike started backing up the way they came.

Hephaestus pulled his hammers out, and Ares drew his sword. Hephaestus looked behind him. "Moxie, can you fix this?"

She shook her head and followed Nike. "I don't think so. I'm too shaken up to concentrate enough for her."

"Hmph. Fine." Hephaestus banged his hammers together over his head. "Come here, ya big, ugly thing!" He maneuvered so he was through the opening and away from the girls. Ares followed.

The spider scuttled towards the noise. Its mouth opened wide enough that they could see the fangs covered in drool. It reached Hephaestus' knee, and he managed to spin out of the way on his good leg. He slammed one of his hammers on the spider's head, and it let out a pained shriek. Moxie covered her ears and huddled into herself.

Ares waited until the last moment and then slid himself under the spider, swinging his sword out and cutting off its legs. The creature shrieked again.

Ares stood, covered in blood, a smile on his face. He bowed elegantly at Hephaestus. "Go ahead, brother. This one is yours."

Hephaestus took two steps to the bleeding, shrieking queen, raised one of his hammers, and swung it down onto her head with all of his strength. There was a sickening crunching sound as the tool forced its way through her exoskeleton. Blood and bile flew everywhere.

Moxie was kneeling on the ground, her hands pressed tightly against her ears. Nike stood over her and rubbed her back. "It's okay, Moxie. It's done."

Ares wiped his bloody hands on his pants and went to help Moxie up. "C'mon, let's get out of here before her babies decide to eat us for killing her."

They rounded the next corner, hurrying down the path for a bit, hoping to put the spiders as far behind them as possible. They came to another opening on their left, and turned to look, seeing that this one was different. At the end of the path was a wall made of rocks instead of trees, and about midway up, a burning torch cast shadows. The light allowed them to see that not only was this a dead-end, but there was a very large pile of snakes writhing over and around each other.

Ares slowly backed away and whispered, "We don't need to go this way. Let's just move quickly and quietly past it. Hopefully, none of them will decide to come and play with us."

Nike shivered and mumbled, "Thank Zeus."

Nearly running down the path and eager to put the snakes far behind them, they found their way partially blocked by a hedge. Having learned their lesson about things that hide in the Deep Wild, the group moved carefully around it, to find another choice. They could go through the opening on the left or keep going straight.

Before Ares could run off around another corner, Hephaestus grabbed him by the back of his neck. "I know it will be difficult for you, but think for a minute, Ares."

Ares grunted and pulled away from Hephaestus' grip. "It's quick for me to check, so we don't go the wrong way."

"And what happens when you disappear around a corner and don't come back, huh? What are we supposed to do?" Hephaestus crossed his arms. "You would endanger all of us by having to go after you. Now stop being a flaming idiot and *think!*"

Ares grumbled. "Fine."

Nike cleared her throat. "Guys, that was the first time we saw a wall of anything but trees. What if that's the center where Lady Hera is?"

Hephaestus rubbed his chin. "It makes sense. If we follow that logic, then going forward would just take us further away from the center, so we should take the new path here."

"And what if this new path is just a dead-end? Maybe the path going forward will take us around all that and into the center." Ares jutted his chin out.

"Hmph. Fine. Girls, you choose. Which way should we go?" Both the boys turned to face Nike and Moxie, who just looked at each other and shrugged.

"What Nike said makes sense. I think our mother may be behind that wall, so we should definitely try to go that way. If we follow that thought, it makes the most sense to go through the opening."

Nike nodded, and Hephaestus shifted his weight. "Fine, the girls have spoken, Ares. We're going through the opening, and since you like to discover new things, you can go first, *brother*." He offered Ares a wicked grin and bowed, his arm held to the side, allowing Ares to go first.

They walked through and came face to face with yet another hedge and a choice of left or right.

"Let's go left. It's the direction of that wall." Nike started walking that way, knowing that everyone would follow. As she turned the corner, she saw another rock wall with a torch. Much to her relief, there were no snakes this time. She turned to face the others.

"Well, at least we've got the right idea about this. We just need to find a way in."

"Fine, we'll go the other way first. Surely there's another way in." Ares turned around and led the way. One by one, they passed the opening they came through and eventually came to another left-hand turn. Ares reached behind him and grabbed Moxie's hand while Hephaestus followed.

Nike paused for a moment and looked behind her with a worried furrow between her brows. When she turned back, the others were almost completely out of sight. Not wanting to be left behind, Nike jogged after her siblings. Just before she got to them, she heard Ares shout, "Back up!"

Nike raced around the corner and dodged as a thick vine reached for her. Ares was already wrapped from head to toe in the vines, Moxie was still holding onto him, but was similarly stuck and trying to struggle free. The vines were crawling up Hephaestus' legs, and he kept trying to pull them off. He saw Nike over his shoulder. "Run, Nike!" The vines wrapped around his waist and pulled him closer to the hedge.

"No!" Nike drew her sword and, with a sharp flap of her golden wings, rose and sliced the vines attacking Hephaestus.

Hephaestus dropped to the ground and rolled past Ares and out of the way. He drew his hammers, but couldn't see a way to help his siblings. He had to just stand there, out of the way, frustrated that he couldn't help.

Nike flew closer to Moxie, slicing vines that reached for her and dodging the ones she missed. The situation was about to get desperate as she saw the vines pulling Ares deeper into the hedge. His eyes were wild with fear, but she met them with as much confidence as she could muster.

"Don't worry, Ares." She swung at another reaching vine. "Moxie, can you help?"

Moxie struggled against her bindings. "I'm trying, but it's hard to concentrate right now, Nike!"

"Fine, lean forward when I say." Nike maneuvered her body toward the left, rolling out of the way as another vine reached for her. She ascended as high as she could and then looked down at Moxie. "Ready? Now!"

At Nike's signal, Moxie strained forward from the hedge and tightened her grip on Ares, trying to pull him with her. Nike dove the short distance and sliced her sword behind Moxie. The vines fell lifeless onto the ground. Nike rolled, and as she sailed onto the other side of Ares, she pushed Moxie out of the way and into Hephaestus' arms.

"Keep her safe! I'll get Ares!"

Moxie struggled to go to Ares, but Hephaestus' grip was firm. Nike flipped around and hovered in front of Ares. She swung her sword around him, cutting the vines from his arms. Once his hands were free, Ares pulled them away from his face. A quick slice from Nike and the vines fell to the ground.

A vine reached out from behind her and wrapped around her ankle. Nike tucked into a forward roll and sliced it from underneath. As she straightened out, she sliced through the vines that were tightening around Ares' ankles.

Ares was free everywhere, but his neck, and the vines were choking him. He gasped, "Nike!"

"I've got you, brother! Lean your head forward!"

Ares struggled for breath and did what he was told. Nike soared as high as the canopy would let her, then dove towards Ares with vengeance in her eyes. In one breath, she slid her sword between Ares and the hedge, slicing him free. She wrapped her other arm around him, lifting him with her as she flew away from the vines toward the others.

"Follow me!" Nike flew to the end of the path and around the corner, not stopping until she got to yet another rock wall illuminated by a torch. She gently lowered Ares to the ground, and Moxie rushed to him, fussing over him. Hephaestus gave Nike a grateful smile.

"Thanks for the assist, Nike."

"We were bound to be victorious. There was no other option." Nike settled her feet onto the ground and looked protectively over the others as they caught their breath.

The four of them huddled together under the torchlight, trying to soak up the heat and the light into bodies that had gone cold with fear. No one said anything while they sat. They just kept touching each other with their hands, a brush of an arm, or the press of a leg. Movements designed to reassure themselves that they were still alive. The further away they got from that last experience, the more they were able to rationalize it as not as bad as it was. No one forgot Nike's bravery, though.

Perhaps an hour passed with them breathing in the torchlight, perhaps less. One by one they stood, ready to move on.

"C'mon, guys. We're running out of time. Let's go this way. The other way's a dead end." Ares started walking, reluctant to leave the safety of the torchlight. They quickly came to an opening to their right. Through the opening they found themselves in an open chamber, surrounded by hedges. The area lit by torches positioned on poles in each of the corners.

"Damn it all to Hades! It's a dead end." Hephaestus spit disgustedly off to the side. "We'll need to go the other way."

Moxie wandered further into the chamber, exploring a small stone dais. A narrow pillar about waist high stood at the center with a card sitting on top. Moxie followed her feet up the steps. When she saw what was written on the card, she gasped loudly and stumbled back into Ares, who had shadowed her.

"What's wrong, Moxie? Something scare you?" Ares steadied her and turned her to face him, but she kept looking over her shoulder. "Moxie, answer me."

"What? It's just that card. It-it has my name on it." Moxie turned to look at Ares with confusion in her eyes.

"Oh, yeah? Well, let's see what it says then." Ares marched up the steps to the pillar and plucked the card off of it. He frowned as he turned it over and over. "It's just a stupid card with your name on it, Moxie."

"Put it back, Ares." Nike walked over and joined Hephaestus next to Moxie, silently supporting her.

Ares threw his hands up in surrender. "Fine! Man, you three are the biggest scaredy-gods I've ever met." He roughly tossed the card back towards the pillar. They all startled when it stopped in mid-air and gently floated back down, settling so that everyone could see Moxie's name.

"Well, that's not freaky at all." Ares joined his siblings and stared at the pillar and the mysterious card. Minutes later, when nothing happened, they all relaxed. Hephaestus and Ares walked a few steps away from the girls, and Nike wandered around the chamber, looking for another way out.

"We can't go back the way we came, Ares. Those vines almost took you."

"I know, Hephaestus, I know, but there's no other way out of here. Look around. This chamber has one entrance, and we just walked right through it." Ares stretched his sore arms above his head. "We're prepared for it now, so we'll be careful. Besides, Nike can fly us over it, and we can go the other way."

Hephaestus frowned and nodded while he turned to watch Nike walk around the edges of the chamber. She ran her hands over the leaves and randomly pressed against them with her weight. She even flew up to the top to see if there was a way to get out of the chamber that way.

Meanwhile, Moxie stood and stared at the card. Suddenly, she felt a pull on her heart. It was as if the card was enticing her, teasing her. She found that she couldn't resist it, and her feet drew her forward. As she got closer, the card sparkled and shone as if covered in Nike's victory glitter. There was a soft humming as Moxie approached the dais. She was so entranced by the card that she didn't notice anything else.

Hephaestus saw Moxie walking toward the pillar and didn't really think anything about it, but wanted her opinion on what to do next. "Moxie, what do you think? Should we just get Nike to fly us over those vine things and look for another way around?"

Moxie said nothing and kept moving forward.

"Moxie? What are you doing?" Hephaestus took a hesitant step towards her and grabbed Ares to get his attention. Moxie had almost reached the pillar, and something felt off. He saw her hand rise to grab the card and suddenly knew he had to stop her. He lunged after her, knowing he'd never reach her in time.

"Nike! Grab her!"

Nike spun around in confusion and saw the boys racing towards Moxie as she reached for the card. No one was fast enough, though. Her hand lifted the card from the pillar, the torches flared, and the light in her eyes died.

"Moxie!" They all rushed to her, scared that she had somehow died. Ares waved a hand in front of her face, and Nike shook Moxie's shoulder. Hephaestus positioned himself so he could see the front of her. Moxie just stood there with dead eyes, arm outstretched, hand gripping the card.

"Oh, this is bad. This is so very, very bad, you guys!" Nike started pacing back and forth.

Ares gripped his hair and pulled. "What do we do, Heph? We have to bring her back to life! Who can do that?"

Hephaestus was quiet for a long moment, ignoring Ares' begging prayers to the gods that Moxie was not dead.

"Guys, look." Hephaestus nodded his head toward Moxie.

"We've already seen her! She's gone!" Ares felt like he was on the edge of losing control. He loved his sister and couldn't imagine a world in which she didn't exist. Who else would he tease?

"No, Ares. *Look* at her!" Hephaestus demanded.

Nike stopped pacing and looked at Moxie, but all she saw was an empty shell. "She's not there."

"Exactly, Nike. *Moxie* isn't there."

"What the Hades does that mean, Hephaestus, and why are you getting all cryptic on us?" Ares stood in front of Hephaestus, angry and scared and wanting to lash out at anyone.

"You're an idiot, Ares. You know that this isn't really Moxie, right?"

Ares opened his mouth to yell some more, but his jaw slammed shut as soon as Hephaestus' words registered. "Huh?"

Nike was still confused. "What do you mean?"

Hephaestus turned to look at Nike and gave her a small smile. "Moxie isn't this body. She *inhabits* this body. Well, she did. She's not in there anymore. This is just a shell."

Nike peered into Moxie's empty eyes. "Well, where did she go?"

"I don't know, little one. But I bet it has to do with that card she's holding onto."

The three just stared, unsure of how to save their sister or even what to do next.

She was sucked into a whirlwind of lights and sounds, unable to determine which way was up or if she was moving forward. If she'd had eyes in this form, she would have been blinded. If she'd had ears, she would have been deafened. As it was, as soon as she realized she no longer inhabited her previous body, she could make sense of what was going on around her and simply observe. She grounded herself by focusing on just one sound. The soft hum of a bee.

Unable to determine the exact passage of time in her bodiless form, Moxie floated in this liminal space for what could have been hours or simply minutes. Eventually, she felt her form tumble forward and finally stop, inches above the grass on a hill that overlooked a small village. She gathered herself and followed the road, trying to determine where she was and what happened to her previous body.

As she got closer to the village, she heard faint crying. Moxie followed the sound to a barn on the edge of the town. She slipped her essence between the boards and around a large stack of hay. A young girl, perhaps nine, was being assaulted by a grown man. He held the girl against the wall with his thick, farmer's hands and pressed sloppy, unwanted kisses all over her face while she tried to move out of his way.

The man pressed his pelvis roughly against the girl, rubbing one of his thighs against her, trying to lift the hem of her shift. The girl cried out softly, begging him to leave her alone.

Moxie gave it only a breath of thought before she found herself inhabiting the young girl. Her new body froze in place as she merged her essence with it. The man, thinking the girl had finally given up, missed the look in her eyes go from helpless to fierce. Moxie gave him a moment longer as she feigned interest, feeling the girl's presence squirm at his touch. Moxie gave her a quick, comforting thought and reached for the knife on the man's belt.

He was so enraptured with what he was doing that he didn't feel the knife slide into his gut or hear his blood drip heavily on the barn floor. It wasn't until he started to feel weak that he pulled back and looked at her face. Moxie met his eyes and let a wicked smile slowly form across her new face. He looked down and saw the blood. He was still confused as he backed away, tripping over a bucket and landing on his back.

Moxie straddled his waist and smeared the blood from the knife onto his cheek. She bared her teeth at him and growled.

"No means no."

She took her knife and deftly sliced it across his neck, leaving a gaping hole. Tilting her head, she watched the life seep from his body before wiping the bloody knife clean with some hay and walking out of the barn.

As she headed towards the girl's home, Moxie looked inward to check on her, but she was met with complete silence. It wasn't an empty silence, though. There was a weight to it, a patient hunter hiding in the darkness. It felt like a predator watching from the shadows as a new animal ventured into its domain. It was waiting to see what Moxie did.

Moxie quietly hummed as she walked. "I wonder what your name is."

Lydia

Moxie froze. She'd never had a consciousness talk back to her. She turned inward to check on the girl, Lydia, and found her silent, waiting to see what would happen next.

"I'm sorry I didn't get to you sooner, Lydia."

It's okay. I've dealt with him before. His wife would have come in soon and chased me off with the broom.

"You? Why?"

Moxie felt a mental shrug from Lydia. *She says I encourage him.*

"That is completely ridiculous, Lydia. None of that was your fault. He should have never touched you."

Well, now I won't have to worry about him anymore.

"Yes. I'm sorry you had to see what I did. I didn't expect you to be aware. None of my other hosts have been."

You've done this before?

"Yes. It's how I take form." Moxie started walking again, slowly approaching Lydia's home.

What are you?

"Well, I suppose you would know me best as a goddess."

...are you going to sacrifice me?

56

Moxie stumbled on a rock. "What? No! Absolutely not. That's not what I do."

Oh. What are you going to do with me?

Moxie finally reached Lydia's home and opened the door. As she stepped through the threshold, a variety of earthy smells hit her. There were bunches of herbs hanging from exposed rafters, and a stew simmering in a small pot on the fire.

Different pieces of clothing in varying stages of wear were laid about, some looking as if they'd recently been mended. Lydia's home was small and poor, but clean and homey. Moxie took an instant liking to its simplicity.

"Well, Lydia, I'm lost, and I was hoping to borrow your body for a while so I can find a way back home." Her voice trembled with her next words. "My mamá is missing, and I have to find her."

I'm sorry about your mamá. My mam died last winter. I wish I could bring her back.

Moxie pressed her hand to her chest as she was overcome with Lydia's sadness and loneliness. "Oh, dear, I'm so sorry she died. Do you have anyone to take care of you?" Moxie felt Lydia's consciousness bristle.

I don't need anyone to take care of me. I'm old enough to take care of myself.

"How old are you?"

I've lived through almost fourteen winters.

Moxie thought back to the small frame of the girl she saw in the barn and was surprised that Lydia was that old. She wisely kept that thought to herself.

I'm hungry.

"Hmm? Oh, right. I suppose you are. You've had all types of excitement today. Let's get you some of this stew."

Lydia directed Moxie to a bowl and spoon, and just before Moxie was about to sit down and enjoy the food, Lydia made a request.

Goddess?

"Oh dear, please call me Moxie."

Goddess Moxie? There's a special herb my mam would put in my stew to help me stay strong. Would you put some in the bowl for me, please?

"Of course!"

Lydia showed Moxie to the hanging bunch and told her how much to add to the stew. They sat in the chair by the fire in companionable silence as Moxie ate. Moxie soon grew tired, and Lydia had her lay down on the bed.

Lydia lay quietly while Moxie drifted off into a deep sleep. She waited until the moon was high in the sky, and when Lydia saw that Moxie was completely unconscious, she got up out of bed and walked into the kitchen.

"Mam always said the gods listened to our prayers, but I never thought one'd actually visit me." Lydia laughed and pulled several herbs from the rafters, and two small vials of animal blood from a cabinet.

Lydia's chest vibrated with an evil hum as she mixed the ingredients. Just as she was pouring everything into a wooden cup, she felt Moxie stir.

"Now, now, sweet goddess. You belong to me." Lydia swallowed her drink quickly and then let out a laugh so wicked, the night quieted in fear.

Moxie woke the next morning feeling disoriented. For the briefest of moments, she believed herself back in the void that took her from her siblings. When she finally became reoriented, she was still confused. She was inside of a body, but she wasn't in control. This was something that never happened before. She struggled to remember the previous day.

"Ah, you're awake, Goddess Moxie. Good! I have some questions for you before we start our day."

That voice was familiar. Moxie struggled to gain control of her mind and the body, but she felt bound and helpless, a feeling she didn't like.

"You can struggle all you like, goddess. Me mam taught me the ways of binding spirits so that they can never leave. You're stuck with me forever, so just get used to it." Lydia cackled as she moved around her home, preparing for the day.

What do you want from me?

"It's simple. I want to be a goddess, and since I can't, I'll take the next best thing. You."

You'll never win, you know. I'll get out of here and leave you behind.

"Well now, it seems you're at a disadvantage. You see, while you slept, I scanned your memories to find out what type of goddess you are. Granted, I wasn't able to see much, but I did find that you're not the type to hurt a mortal. The *only* way you're going to be free is if I die, and I don't plan on doing that anytime soon."

Moxie quickly felt defeated. Lydia was right, she could never hurt an innocent mortal, and so far, all Lydia had done was bind Moxie.

"Now, let's go over the perks of having you inside of me. What can I expect?"

Moxie stayed quiet, unwilling to make this easy for Lydia.

"Hmm. It seems you need some encouragement. Fine." Lydia grabbed her shawl from the back of a chair and locked up the house. Lydia's home was on the edge of the village, and she hummed a little as she walked to a nearby house.

There was a young woman with a baby strapped onto her back in the herb garden, talking to a little boy who couldn't have been more than five years old. She looked up when she saw Lydia, smiled, and waved. Lydia returned the smile and waved at the little boy.

"You see that boy over there? His name is Conner. He brings me herbs from his mother's garden every harvest." Lydia rested her hand on the handle of the knife in her belt. "I bet his parents would be relieved to have one less mouth to feed. Don't you?"

What?! You don't...surely you wouldn't!

"Kill him? In a breath, if it will make you talk." Lydia smiled bigger at the mother and son as they turned back to their work.

Moxie couldn't believe that someone would hurt a young child like that. And to do so just to get answers? It was unconscionable.

"You're hesitating. Go ahead, look at me and tell me you don't believe I'd do it."

Moxie hesitated, not wanting to greet such evil, but she knew Lydia would do exactly what she said. Moxie saw her intentions as clear as day.

Fine. You'll heal from almost anything, even bad wounds, while I'm in your body. You'll be stronger and faster and less susceptible to illness.

"Stronger and faster, huh? That could be very useful." The corners of Lydia's mouth curled into a wicked smile, and she turned around to go home.

That night, Lydia poured herself another mug of that herbal brew and sat down to make a list. Moxie tried to figure out what was in the mixture so she could try to break out of her prison, but nothing was labeled. After Lydia had written the names of six people, she went to bed.

"Rest well, Goddess Moxie. Tomorrow we hunt."

Moxie shivered.

The next morning after breakfast, Lydia put a few apples into a basket and covered them with a napkin. She hummed the same song from yesterday as she locked up and then headed away from the village. Moxie's confusion grew as Lydia got closer to the barn she found her in initially. Lydia bypassed the big structure, went to the house behind it, and knocked on the door.

An older woman opened it and growled when she saw Lydia standing there. "What do ya want, ya trollop? I know you had something to do with me husband's death, and I'll see ya pay for it!"

Lydia sighed at the woman and pushed past her into the house.

"Get out of me home, girl! I don't want the likes of ya here!" the outraged woman yelled.

Lydia placed the basket on the table by the fire and turned to face the woman. "Oh, I'm not going anywhere, Shelia."

Shelia slammed the door closed and marched over to Lydia, only stopping when she got close enough to breathe on her. "You will get out of me home, ya trollop. You've ruined me life enough!"

Lydia smiled and reached behind her into the basket. "But don't you want to see what I brought you?"

Shelia looked momentarily confused and peered around Lydia's shoulders to try to see into the basket. Lydia turned her body into Shelia's, and before Moxie knew what she was going to do, the older woman screamed in pain and stumbled backward. Her hands grasped at the clothing covering her stomach, trying to stop the blood that was now flowing freely from her body.

Lydia followed Shelia across the room, blocking her as she attempted to reach the door. Shelia fell against the counter, and Lydia watched her crumple to the floor.

"Why are ya doing this to me? What did I ever do to ya, girl?"

"What did you do to me? You horrible slag! You let your husband assault me anytime he wanted. Then you would beat me with a broom and say it was all my fault!"

Shelia's eyes hardened. "Aye, and it were your fault! Because of ya, me Matthew wasn't happy with what he got at home. It's all your fault, and ya never once apologized for it!"

Lydia shrieked and slammed the knife into Shelia's chest over and over. "I'm a *god* now, and *gods* don't apologize!"

It was all Moxie could do to hold herself together during Lydia's outburst. She was overwhelmed with the vitriol and hatred that poured out of Lydia as she stabbed Shelia. Moxie closed her eyes and hid in a dark corner of Lydia's mind, trying to keep a hold on her own sanity.

The next day, Lydia was in a good mood. She'd finally been able to kill someone. It was an urge she'd had all her life. Her mam trained her not to do it because of the consequences that would follow her home. She would suffer as a mere mortal if she were caught for the murder of one of the villagers. However, Lydia was no longer a mere mortal, and she knew her mam would approve of her actions.

As she went about her day, Moxie huddled in the darkest part of Lydia's mind, trying to stay away from the evilness that flowed through her body. It sought Moxie out like a bug attracted to the light. She had to move constantly or suffer the poisonous effects of being enveloped by Lydia's evil side. Moxie was exhausted and didn't have the energy to find a way out of her situation. She felt despondent and was on the verge of giving up.

Lydia went about her chores, and in the early afternoon she took a loaf of bread and some herbs to another nearby home. This time, a middle-aged man answered the door.

"Hello, Corbin. I brought some herbs to help your wife." Lydia smiled and held out the basket.

"Ah, Lydia. Thank ye fer comin'. Me Bess 'as been needin' a wee nip." He motioned Lydia inside and looked chagrined. "Could ye mix it fer her please, lass? Me hands' ave been hurtin' somethin' fierce."

"Of course, Corbin." Lydia went to the counter and started mixing the herbs into a tea for his wife. When she was done, she turned around and stood watching the couple as Bess lay in the bed, and Corbin sat on his knees beside her. They were whispering with their heads together, and Moxie could see the deep love they had for each other. It gave her strength at her weakest point.

Moxie was so enthralled by the love flowing between and around the couple, she didn't realize Lydia had walked into the room and was standing behind Corbin.

"Ah, Corbin, no need to get up. I'll just give it to you from here."

Bess looked at Lydia, and her face twisted in fear as Lydia drew a knife over her head and slammed it down to the hilt between Corbin's shoulder blades. Lydia yanked the knife out and then slammed it through his lower back, deep into his kidneys. Blood splashed everywhere. Bess was screaming in her weak voice, tears running down her face, her eyes haunted with the loss of her love. Lydia leaned down, kissed Corbin on the cheek, and then ran the knife across his throat.

Nooooooooooooooooo!

"Oh, do shut up already, both of you." Lydia pushed Corbin's body off to the side and climbed onto the bed to straddle Bess's waist.

Stop this, please! I'll do anything you want, Lydia. Anything!

But Lydia was deaf to the cries from Bess and Moxie. She gripped the knife in two hands, raised it above her head, and slammed it into Bess' chest. Bess tried to cry out for help, but blood bubbled and streamed from her mouth. Within moments, Bess was gone.

Moxie was *livid*. There was no more thinking about how lost she felt, how she would get home, or if she could make Lydia see the light and stop doing such horrendous things.

Moxie just *was*.

And at that moment, Moxie exploded into her natural, deified form. Lydia's body exploded into pieces that painted the small cabin from roof to floor.

Moxie hadn't felt this much anger before, and she just wanted to rage at the injustice of these two innocent deaths until she was too weak to care. Just as she hit the peak of her anger, her sight went black. She was sucked back into the swirling void that brought her to this village.

Moxie let the anger dissipate into the darkness and huddled in on herself. In what could have been minutes or hours, she found herself back in her old body and heard her siblings around her.

"I don't know, Ares! There isn't a science to it. Moxie just jumps bodies whenever she wants. If anyone would know how to do it, Mom would, but I don't see her around, do you?" Hephaestus was standing nose to nose with Ares, practically yelling at him in frustration.

Moxie shuddered, gasped in pain, and hunched forward. Tears flowed freely from her eyes.

"Moxie's back!" Nike flew over and wrapped Moxie in her arms just as Moxie's legs gave out.

The boys ran over to them, and Ares wrapped his arms around Moxie. "Moxie, where have you been? Why did you leave us?"

Moxie just hiccupped and cried harder, unable to put into words what she'd just been through.

Never one for emotional displays, Hephaestus just stood back watching. "Moxie, can you tell us what happened?"

She rapidly shook her head and whispered, "Please don't make me."

"Shhh. No one's going to make you do anything, I promise." Nike pushed Ares away and rocked Moxie gently, rubbing her hair back from her forehead in a comforting rhythm. Moxie stayed in Nike's arms and cried out all of her pain.

The boys stood back and watched uncomfortably, eventually looking away.

"Well, we got her back, Hephaestus. Let's just get Nike to carry us over the vines and try another way."

Hephaestus frowned and looked around the chamber. "No, Ares. There had to be a reason she was taken like that. Maybe there's a secret door that we missed."

Ares opened his mouth to argue, but closed it when Nike helped Moxie stand. Moxie faced the boys. "I didn't go through all of that for nothing. There has to be a way out."

As if her words were a key, the vines on the opposite wall shifted, revealing a door.

"Well, I'll be." Hephaestus limped over to the door and gently pushed on it. All four of the gods gasped as the door slid open, revealing another path.

"Well, that's our cue to get the hell out of here." Ares ushered the girls through the door, and Hephaestus followed behind. Just around another quick corner was an opening to another chamber exactly like the one they had just left. The only difference was the name on the card.

Hephaestus.

They stood, immobile, and stared at the seemingly innocuous card with Hephaestus' name on it. Of the four of them, only Moxie truly understood the fear and pain behind it. She grabbed onto his forearm and squeezed.

"Please don't touch it, Heph. We'll find another way. Nike can fly us over everything, and we'll save our mamá that way." She looked up into his eyes and pleaded with him. "Please, please don't touch it."

Ares looked a little concerned. "Moxie might be right here, man. You're not like her. What if it takes you the same way, and you just die?" He walked over to the pillar with an inflated bravado, turned to face the others, and spread his arms wide. "Obviously, this system is broken. As the most important member of the group, I should have been first."

65

Moxie just wrapped her arms around herself and turned away from Ares' insensitivity.

"What? I'm just saying. I'm the most powerful one here. I have the most kills. I should have been first. Actually, I should have been the only one." Ares pouted as he walked back to the opening of the chamber.

Hephaestus just stood and stared at his name on the card. The weight of his decision flashed across his eyes. He knew the night had gotten longer. Time was running out to save his mother, but honestly, he was a little scared. He saw how Moxie was when she came back. How she still was. It was not something he looked forward to experiencing. He turned to look at his brother and sisters and knew that there was only one choice. If he didn't do it, their mother would die, and it would tear them apart.

Hephaestus took a deep breath and walked as quickly as he could to the pillar. He looked over his shoulder at Ares. "Watch over the girls, yeah?" Before anyone could say another word, Hephaestus grabbed the card in one hand. The moment the paper touched his skin, his essence left him.

Ares rushed over to Hephaestus and cursed. "Damnit, he's not there. Just like Moxie."

Nike poked Hephaestus in the chest and pulled his eyelids up, looking for a response. "Well, he's not Moxie, so I hope he isn't dead."

The three of them found a spot around Hephaestus to watch over him and wait.

Hephaestus spun around in a dark void, flashes of colors streaking across his eyes, and random noises blaring in his ears. He was disoriented and couldn't find a way to stop. Eventually, the void spit him out into a brightly lit hallway. His senses took some time to adjust. When they did, he looked around.

He felt weightless and formless. He moved what should have been his head, to look down at his body, and found he was just a shapeless ball of energy.

What the Hades is going on? Wait, I can't talk either? Ugh!

Hephaestus floated through the doorway in front of him, only to stop in shock. He was on Olympus, in his parents' bedroom. He could tell that this was something from the past, though.

His father looked more arrogant, and his mother looked more bitter.

An attendant stepped away from the bed, and Hephaestus saw his mother lying there, holding a newborn swaddled tightly in a blanket. His father was standing at her side, beaming down at the infant, pride oozing from every pore.

"You did good, Hera. You gave me another son!"

"Well, you did have something to do with it, dear." She smiled tiredly at his father, her hand gently caressing the side of the infant's face.

"See how quiet he is! He's not a screamer like his brother, Ares. It's as if he's waiting for something momentous to happen." His father leaned down and placed a kiss on both his mother's forehead and the baby's. "I must spread the word across Olympus. I have another perfect son!"

His father puffed up his chest and left the room. His mother leaned back on her pillows and crooned to the baby, "Oh, my sweet boy. You are going to do wondrous things. You need a strong name to help you through your life." She kissed the baby on the forehead. "I will name you Hephaestus, and all the gods will love you."

The attendant came back and held her hands out for the baby. "My lady, you need to rest. Let me care for him."

"Yes, thank you." Hera watched her take the baby away, but Hephaestus couldn't stop looking at his mother. Yes, she was exhausted, but the love she had for the baby, *for him*, was blinding.

Whatever, Mother. I know that feeling didn't last long.

The room spun, and Hephaestus found himself in the throne room, surrounded by his family. The attendant carried the baby to his father and gently passed him off before scurrying away. His father smiled big.

"Look, my brothers and sisters. Look at my son!" His father removed the blanket and held the baby under its arms and away from his body. Everyone gasped. His father grabbed the baby by one arm and yanked him up to get a better look.

"What is this!?" His father roared across the throne room. "Who switched my son with this...this mistake of nature? Hera!" The baby hung limply by his arm as his father stormed back to his mother.

His mother was just about asleep when his father pushed his way into her rooms. "What trickery is this, wife? Do you think to make a fool of me?" He held the baby out in front of him by the arm.

His mother quickly grabbed the infant and held him tightly to her chest. "What is *wrong* with you, Zeus? You were here. You know this is your son!" His mother rocked the baby, whispering little *shushing* noises, even though he never made a sound. The baby lay in his mother's arms, eyes wide, watching his father.

"This...thing is *not* my son. It is deformed. Look at its foot!"

His mother gently brought the baby's foot up so she could see the deformity. "So what, Zeus? It makes him more precious amongst us. There will never be another as unique as he is."

Lightning flashed across his father's eyes, and he yanked the baby away from his mother. "I will not tolerate this abomination in my kingdom!" His father flew across Olympus to the very edge and flung the baby with all his might. He turned away without caring to know where it landed or if it survived.

Hephaestus felt a pain where his heart should have been. He knew the story of his father disavowing him, but it was something else to see it happen. His chest constricted in pain, and he had a brief thought that it was a good thing he didn't require breath in this form because he would never have been able to catch it.

Just as Hephaestus thought it was over, he flashed into another scene. He was in a long feast hall, surrounded by men in various stages of drunkenness. He floated around and found his mother standing in a corner talking to a man who looked very familiar but who wasn't his father.

"You don't want to incur my wrath, Egemen. I will see my son whenever I want to!"

Egemen bowed his head slightly. "As you wish, my Lady Hera. My only concern was for the boy. It is difficult for him when you leave. He doesn't understand why he can't go home with you."

Her expression turned to one of anguish. "I know. I know, but I can't bring him home yet. Zeus would just harm him worse. I need more time to convince him."

"A father shouldn't need convincing to see his child."

"Watch yourself, Egemen. That is the King of the Gods you are talking about."

"My apologies, my Lady. You will find Hephaestus in his room." Egemen stood aside and watched Hera rush off.

Egemen, I'd almost forgotten you, baba. How could I have forgotten the only place that truly accepted me?

The scene changed, and Hephaestus was suddenly in the room, watching his mother play with the little god. As the baby stumbled into his mother's lap, she tickled his ribs and then leaned down to blow on his chubby belly. Mother and son laughed. A nurse came in, and Hera stopped laughing. She hugged the baby up tightly and kissed his chubby cheeks.

"Mamá has to go, little god. I will see you soon. I promise." She stood and handed the baby to the nurse before quickly walking away. Hephaestus watched his fat baby arms reach out for his mother, confusion on his face turning to tears when she didn't come back.

The scene changed.

"Zeus, please. I want my son home, where he belongs!"

"That abomination will never set foot on Olympus as long as I have a breath in my body. Stop your incessant whining, Hera!"

Hephaestus saw the rage on his mother's face. "I've only ever asked one thing of you. One thing! And you refused me. You laughed in my face as you whored around and spread your seed. You will give me back my son or so help me, Zeus! I will make you wish you resided with our brother, Hades!"

"*I already do!*"

Hera gasped and sat down hard on the bed as she watched Zeus storm out.

The scene changed.

Hephaestus was now floating in an open field. He heard children laughing and followed the sound. Eventually, he saw himself and his siblings playing what looked like a game of tag. Nike was *IT* and was chasing after Ares.

"S-stop it, N-nike! F-flying is ch-cheating!" He tried to jump over a log and stumbled, landing face-first in the dirt. Nike swooped down and smacked him on his backside.

"You're it, Ares!" Nike laughed and flew away, her small golden wings shining in the sunlight.

Ares stood up and grumbled under his breath. "Why d-didn't you h-help me, H-hephaestus? B-brothers are s-s-supposed to protect each oth-ther!"

Hephaestus turned to look behind him and saw his younger self sitting on the grass with Moxie, who was weaving flowers into his hair and making vines lazily crawl across their laps.

"I'm busy, Ares! Besides, you can't be the God of War if you let a *girl* beat you!" The younger Hephaestus winked at Moxie, who covered her mouth and giggled.

Nike flew over to Hephaestus and Moxie. "I like the crown, Moxie. Can I have one, too?"

One of Moxie's vines reached up, wrapped around a laughing Nike's ankle, and pulled her to the ground. "Of course, sister."

Young Hephaestus winked at the girls. "C'mon, Ares. You need a girly crown too!"

The scene changed.

Hephaestus now saw himself in a training ring with Ares and two other boys, who were much larger than them. Ares was at the back of the ring, flirting with a young woman.

Rehor and Vadik. How I wish I had been stronger that day. I would tear you to shreds for this.

The two boys approached Hephaestus from either side, their training swords banging against their wooden shields. Both had wicked grins on their faces.

"We heard that all we gotta do is knock ya down, and you'll go crying home to your mommy." The boys laughed and moved in quickly.

Rehor dropped his training sword and pulled a dagger from his belt. "Let's up the stakes, shall we?"

Hephaestus looked awkward standing there, training sword in one hand, shield in the other. He shuffled his feet backward, trying to get away from them and not stumble. "Hey, now. This is just a training session. You're not supposed to use real weapons!" He looked over to Ares, hoping for help. His heart dropped when he realized Ares wasn't even paying attention.

Vadik swung his training sword at Hephaestus, causing him to block reflexively with his shield. With Hephaestus's side wide open,

71

Rehor darted in and stabbed Hephaestus three times. Rehor danced out of the way as Hephaestus crumpled to the ground.

Hephaestus clutched his side, blood pouring over his fingers. The boys laughed and gave each other a high five.

"Hey, Ares! Your brother needs his nursemaid." They laughed even louder.

Ares turned when he heard his name and when he saw his brother bleeding, hurried over to him, the young woman all but forgotten.

"What happened, Heph?" Ares leaned down to help him up. Hephaestus stumbled, unsteady on his lame foot and weakening from the blood loss. He pushed Ares away.

"Nothing you would care about, *brother*. Go back to your whore." Hephaestus stumbled away as quickly as he could, the boys' laughter following him.

Ares watched his brother leave and then turned on the boys, fury on his face. "What did you do to him?"

Rehor laughed. "Nothing that he didn't deserve. He's not a real god, and someone needed to put him in his place."

Hephaestus saw Ares' young eyes flash red as he reached in and pulled on Rehor's wrist, twisting it, so the knife faced his belly. He lunged into Rehor, laughing as the blade penetrated the skin.

It took Vadik a minute to comprehend what he saw. When he did, he jumped on Ares's back, trying to pull him away from Rehor. Ares let out a loud war cry and stabbed Rehor one more time for good measure. He flung himself back onto the dirt, pressing Vadik underneath him.

Rehor looked down at his bleeding gut and paled. He stumbled backward and fell as he watched Ares flip around and straddle Vadik.

"You will NEVER hurt my brother again!" Ares yelled as he pounded the fist he had wrapped around the knife hilt into Vadik's face. Blood shot everywhere and coated Ares' chest. Vadik stilled quickly, but Ares continued to beat on him.

Then Ares rose and turned to Rehor, who immediately let loose his urine from fear. Ares stood there in full God mode, angry and bloody.

"Never. Again." Just as he uttered the last word, Ares flung the bloody knife at Rehor, watching it sink into his skull right between his eyes.

But...I don't understand. Ares, why would you do that?

The scene changed.

Hephaestus found his disembodied form flashing quickly through his life growing up. Seeing things, not from his perspective, but from others.

Zeus and Hera sitting next to each other on their bed. Zeus holding his head in his hands. Hera holding Zeus.

"I really messed it up, didn't I?"

"It's okay, my love. He will forgive you. You'll see."

Moxie crying as Hephaestus walked away. She leaned down and gathered up the broken flowers he had thrown at her feet when she tried to tell him how she felt.

Hera sitting on his bed while he thrashed around in his sleep. She pushed his hair from his forehead, singing him a soft lullaby to comfort him until he stilled.

Zeus hesitating near the forge with frustration on his face. Clearly wanting to talk to his son, but unable to find the right thing to say.

Ares beating up each and every one of Hephaestus' tormentors. Protecting his brother the only way he knew how.

Ares meeting Hephaestus at a secluded pool with two nymphs on his arm. The girls looked excited to see Hephaestus until he limped out of the water.

"You can't pay me enough to bed that, Ares."

Hephaestus grabbing his clothes and storming off. "Enjoy, brother."

The girls draping themselves over Ares, expecting an afternoon of carnal delights with him.

"You disgust me," he sneered at them. "If you are repulsed by my *brother*, then I am repulsed by you."

Ares storming off to try to catch up to Hephaestus.

Hera bringing Hephaestus dinner at the forge only to be pushed away.

"Go away, Mother. I'm busy."

"You need to eat, Hephy."

"I will when I'm ready. Don't call me that."

"You didn't mind it when you were a boy."

"That was before I realized your love was just a charade to make you look like the victim. Poor Hera has a lame son. Look how much she loves him in spite of it." He spat. "You disgust me, Mother."

Hera's chin trembled, and she pressed her hand to her chest. A tear fell from her eye, but she squared her shoulders and took a breath.

"I'm sorry you feel that way. I only hope your children never dismiss you as you have me."

"I'm never having children. Now go chase after Father. I'm busy."

Moxie bringing some plants to Hephaestus in the forge.

"I thought your place could use some sunshine, Hephy." *She smiles and holds out a potted ivy plant.*

Hephaestus taking the plant and hurling it into the fire. "Don't you get it, Moxie? My world will never have sunshine, so stop trying so gods damned hard to fix me. And don't call me that!" *He turns from*

75

her and limps out, leaving her standing alone next to the heat of the forge, her heart broken...again.

Nike playing in the field with her brother, Zelus. Each one trying to outfly the other. She saw Hephaestus sitting on a rock alone, a look of longing on his face.

"Hello, brother! Are you here to play with us?" *She smiled in anticipation.*

Hephaestus snorted loudly. "I'm no more your brother than Ares is a virgin. Go away. I don't want to play with you." *He got up and walked off, favoring his lame foot.*

Nike looked as if her world had been crushed. Zelus flew over and saw her tears.

"I'll kill him for making you cry, little one!"

"No!" *Nike grabbed hold of Zelus.* "No. He's just lashing out because he hasn't found his place yet. He'll be better. You'll see."

They both stared down the trail after Hephaestus.

Zeus standing in a room with shelves covering the walls. Each one filled with small toys, figurines, daggers, and shields. Little trinkets that Hephaestus had made over the years. Zeus grabbed an item from one of the shelves and smiled. It is one of the first things Hephaestus ever made, a small lightning bolt. Zeus rubbed his thumb over its well-worn surface.

"I hope you will forgive me one day, my son."

Hephaestus found himself back on the hill he started on. There were so many emotions seething through his body. He didn't know what to do. Did he cry? Did he throw up? Did he feel self-righteous? Just when he thought he couldn't stand the pain a second longer, he was sucked back into the dark void. It was quiet this time, leaving him with his thoughts.

He slammed back into his body, his hand out, still grasping the card. The light from the torches blinded him, and he squeezed his eyes closed. A shudder passed through his entire being, and he let out a pained cry. Quickly, he shut his mouth to keep the noise from repeating. He felt a wetness on his cheeks and wiped at them, not wanting his siblings to see his pain.

Ares spun Hephaestus around and drew him into a tight hug. "The girls were worried, brother." Ares held Hephaestus by the shoulders and looked at him. He lowered his voice. "Are you okay?" Hephaestus could do nothing but nod, but Ares didn't buy it.

Ares turned Hephaestus around again and intercepted the girls as they descended upon him. Ares wrapped his arms around their waists and walked them to the opposite corner of the chamber.

"Ares, stop it. I need to make sure my brother is okay!" Nike tried to turn around, but Ares held tighter.

"He's fine, little one. Give the man a minute to collect himself before you harpies attack him with your claws."

Moxie punched Ares in the side and slid from his arm during his moment of surprise. She rushed over to Hephaestus, who had gathered himself enough to face his siblings.

"Hephy, are you sure you're okay? I've been through it. It was...*rough*." She hesitantly reached for his arm, stopping just short of it.

Hephaestus stood up straighter and cleared his throat. "I'm fine, Mox. Now, where's that door that's supposed to open up?" He raised his face to the clouds and shouted, "I've passed your test! Let us out of here!"

A moment later, the vines retreated and exposed a stone door. It slid open as the group walked toward it..

Hephaestus led them out, followed by a worried Moxie and an impatient Nike. Ares knew his brother wasn't all right, and that he and Nike were next.

Ares shivered and followed the rest out of the chamber.

They followed the pathway around corners until they were presented with another choice. Turn left or go forward. Ares looked at the others, and they all moved through the opening on the left, an unspoken agreement that it would lead them to their mother. Warily they continued on, but stopped short when faced with the next obstacle. Nike gagged and backed up. Ares walked closer to inspect it. Moxie buried her face in Hephaestus' arm.

"Well, that's just gross. Someone didn't clean up their mess." Ares held up a bloody leg bone and shook it so that the rat attached to the hanging muscle flew back into the pile.

Nike shook her head. "Gross, Ares! Put that down. You'll catch a virus or something, and your skin will rot off."

Ares laughed and shook the fleshy bone towards Nike, splashing a bit of blood on Hephaestus.

"Put it down, Ares. It's getting late, and we need to keep moving." Hephaestus wiped away the blood with the back of his hand.

Moxie raised her head. "Nike, will you fly me over that, please? I don't want to touch it."

Nike opened her arms. "Of course, sister." Moxie stepped close to Nike. "Do you want a lift too, brothers?"

The boys just looked at Nike like she'd grown an extra head. Nike sighed, gave a great push of her wings, and rose with Moxie in her arms. She sailed over the pile of half-eaten bodies, pulling her feet up as the rats poked their heads out from between the bones. She landed on the other side, far away from the rodents.

Ares just looked at Hephaestus and shrugged. "Well, shall we dance, brother?" A large grin spread across his face as he backed up as far as he dared. He let out a loud cry, ran at the bloody mess, leaped headfirst over it, and tucked into a roll on the other side. He stood and spread his arms out for applause, but none came.

"You have bloody bones in your hair, Ares." Nike gagged, and Ares plucked the bone from his hair and tossed it back onto the pile.

Moxie looked over at Hephaestus and saw how uncomfortable he looked. "C'mon, Hephy, you can do it." She urged the vines on either side of the pile to reach for each other in the middle, forming a bridge over the mess. Hephaestus looked grateful, but said nothing as he grabbed onto the rising vines and walked across to the other side.

They traversed another dark corner and faced a new opening and a choice of left or right. They looked at Ares.

"What?"

Hephaestus sighed. "Go look around the corner to see if we should go that way. But don't go too far! I don't want to have to chase after you."

Ares nodded and hurried around the corner on the left, whistling loud enough that the others could hear him. After a few moments, he came back. "Dead end that way. Let's go the other way."

They followed along and came to another opening, and beyond it the doorway to another chamber. Everyone paused for a moment as if to gather their courage. Walking into the chamber they saw it was identical to the previous one, except for the name on the card.

Nike.

Nike took a shuddering breath and looked at Moxie. "I'll be okay, right?"

Moxie nodded at her and tried to give her a warm smile. "Of course you will. Hephy and I both did it, and we're okay. Besides, you're the Goddess of Victory."

Nike squeezed Moxie in a tight hug. Letting go, she looked to the boys and then walked over to the card. As she reached for it, she heard Ares joke, "Don't worry, little one. We'll just have a tea party while we wait for you." She closed her eyes and gripped the card.

Like the others, but unknown to her, Nike floated in a dark void filled with wild flashes of colors and random sounds. Unlike the others, she was used to flying and was able to orient herself quickly. The darkness was pushed away by the bright light of Apollo's sun.

Nike blinked and looked around as her eyes adjusted to the light. She immediately knew where she was. This was the training grounds where she and her siblings practiced. She heard voices and floated closer for a better look. Nike took a moment to appreciate the lightness of her being and had a quick flash of jealousy because she could maneuver better in a deified state than she did flying.

Getting closer to the sounds, she recognized the scene. It was from earlier today, just before Moxie came and got her. Nike and Zelus were racing to a large mound of stones, her wings helping her gain the lead over him. Not a gracious loser, Zelus grabbed her ankle and yanked her backward into an awkward roll, causing her to land hard on her backside.

"No fair, Zelus! That's cheating!"

He laughed as he scrambled up the pile. Pausing at the top, he looked at her with mischief in his eyes. "Everyone cheats, little one!

That is life! You must learn to overcome the setbacks and claim your victory." He cackled and slid down the rocks to the other side, gaining a huge lead over Nike in their race.

Nike got up, rubbing her backside, mumbling, "I don't cheat." She flexed her wings out and was about to take off to try to regain her lead when everything froze. The sky turned red and crackled with lightning, and the air roared with thunder. The ground shook so hard, Nike could feel it in her deified state.

At the far end of the course, Nike saw a giant glass box rise from a crack in the ground. There was something in the box, but she couldn't quite make it out. Curious, she floated down to it and would have screamed if she had a mouth in this form.

Frozen in the box was a very terrified, very haggard looking, very bloody, Hera. Her fists were poised by the glass as if she were caught in the momentum of banging them. Her eyes were so wide with fear, all you could see were the whites. Hera's chocolate brown hair, always so intricately done, was falling out of place, electrified tendrils stretching to the sky as if to escape. Her lipstick was smeared across her face, her lips jaggedly framing a horrified, but soundless, shriek. Her face streaked with tears.

Hera was clearly afraid and in pain, but Nike couldn't see a way to set her free. At least, not in her deified state. Nike looked closer and saw an uncountable number of little bites crisscrossing Hera's bare skin. Blood streaked her pale arms, and dripped into the hungry mouths of a tightly packed hill of snakes. Their drooling venom was all over, and they twisted around each other, writhing between Hera's legs. One cobra raised itself behind the queen and its head was poised to strike. Its demon red eyes burned a hole in the back of her neck, venom frozen in mid drip from its glistening fangs.

Nike was so terrified she didn't know what to do. She floated herself around and over the glass cage, looking for a way to get Hera out of there. In frustration, she flew at the glass to slam herself into it, but her deified state passed harmlessly through to the other side. Wanting to scream and rage, she looked around for something, anything, that would help her free her mother.

Nike paused as she saw her earlier self, standing frozen in the middle of rubbing her backside, a frown on her face.

I wonder if I can do what Moxie can do? I've got to try!

Nike rushed to her physical body. Just as she was about to jump in, it disappeared!

Whaaat!?

"I'm afraid you have to wait a moment, Madame Victory." Nike looked around to see where the voice was coming from, but saw nothing.

"Ahem, down here if you please." There was a snapping sound, and an arrow made of iridescent sparkles formed in front of her. She looked down and saw a strange little imp standing on a rock waving to her. He was wearing purple silk trousers and a bright yellow top, tied in a knot at the waist. He had numerous bracelets on his tiny wrists and a gold ring in his ear.

She floated down to get at his eye level. *What did you do to my body?*

He sighed. "What happened to common courtesies?" He put an arm behind his back and bent low at the waist. "It is a pleasure to interact with you, my Lady Victory. I am Sanflores. How do you do?"

Nike was frustrated beyond belief, but she always went out of her way to help people and make them happy. She couldn't stop now, no matter the rush.

How do you do, Sanflores? It is my honor to be here...wherever here is. Now please forgive my urgency, but I must help my mother.

Sanflores nodded wisely. "Indeed, you must, Lady Victory. It seems she is in deep peril." He looked over to the glass cage, sorrow overtaking his face. He took a deep breath and turned back to Nike. "I'm afraid there are rules, my lady."

Rules? That's ridiculous! Rules for what?

"For the race, of course."

What race?

Sanflores smiled brightly. "The race to save your mother!" He held his arm out to the side in a flourish, pointing towards the cage. A ray of pure white light pierced the red sky and illuminated the cage and everything in it. Now light usually chases shadows, but in this case, it just made them worse.

Nike let out a pained cry. *What are the rules?*

"Oh, my dear lady, the rules are simple. You just have to win."

Win?

Sanflores nodded. "Yes. You must beat your brother, Zelus, to the end of the course." He snapped his fingers and pointed, and another slim shaft of white light illuminated an ivory lever with a black pearl handle. "Beat him to the lever, and your mother will be transported safely and unharmed back to her palace. However, if you lose, she will be consumed by the fire and torn apart by monsters so wretched your imagination can't give them life."

Nike looked at the imp. *I will not lose.*

Sanflores laughed in delight and clapped his hands. "Very good, my lady. Let's begin!" He spun around on his heels three times, and Nike's body came back to its position. She was about to ask another question when she found herself in her physical form. She heard Sanflores' voice in her head.

Remember, the only rule is to win.

The sky cleared to its normal blue, and she heard Zelus laughing as he raced down the other side of the stone pile. "Great, he's already cheating," she grumbled. Nike flexed her wings and took off on foot after him. As she approached the stone pile, she leapt at the base and dove over the top, her wings giving her altitude and distance. She landed in a roll just past the stones.

She sprung to her feet and growled. Zelus still had a significant lead. She dashed after him, headfirst into a thick forest that manifested around her. "Not fair! The path was clear." Nike raised her face to the sky as she danced around the random animals that appeared to block her.

"This is not fair! Zelus had a head start and no obstacles!" She heard laughter and then Zelus' voice repeating, "Life isn't fair, little one!" She picked up her speed, letting her wings pull her faster through the forest.

Her path cleared, and she was close to catching her brother when he glanced behind him. Frowning at her nearness, he flicked his fingers over his shoulder, and the ground opened beneath Nike. She shouted as she fell, quickly stopping herself with a powerful snap of her wings. As she was just about to clear the hole, a vine wrapped around her ankle, jerking her back down.

Nike shrieked in frustration and reached for the sword on her back, only to remember she didn't have one on this body. Pulling her foot up, she grabbed her ankle in both hands, and leaned down to rip the vine apart with her teeth. As it fell to the ground, she jetted off, pumping her golden wings hard to catch up with Zelus.

Sweat was pouring down her face, but she didn't waste a movement to wipe it. She stretched her arms as far as they would go and, with just one more push of her wings, grabbed hold of the back of Zelus' tunic.

Nike slammed him backward, kicking his face with her heel as she continued past him. She heard him roar behind her, but kept her focus on the lever that was almost within grabbing distance. She spared a glance over at Hera in the cage. Thankfully, she was still frozen. Nike's relief was cut short when a glass box formed around her, encasing her in her own cage.

"What is this? What is going on!?" She spun around to see Zelus grinning evilly at her, his once golden eyes now pure black, his teeth and nails lengthening into fangs and claws, and a thick black tail forming behind him. His white wings turned darker than night as he stretched them to their full expanse.

Nike was so confused. "Zelus, brother, what is going on? Let me out of here so I can save Lady Hera!"

Zelus' rich baritone voice cackled. "Now, why would I do that, *sister?*"

"Because it is the right thing to do! Look at her. We have to save her!"

Zelus laughed louder. "I am saving her...for my dinner!"

Nike gasped and fell backward against the glass. Helplessly, she watched as Zelus strode past her to the lever. "Please, Zelus, please don't hurt Lady Hera! I'll do anything you want!" Nike's face was covered in tears. Never had she ever felt so helpless. She was Victory, so why wasn't she winning?

Nike looked over at Hera and saw the snakes slowly start to move. One by one, they slithered up Hera's legs, wrapping around her waist, weaving in and out of each other. Smaller snakes started sliding their smooth underbodies around Hera's arms, covering them to her wrists like the golden bracelets she often wore. Two snakes were working their way up her body to her neck.

Hera still hadn't moved, but Nike saw a new level of terror on her face. Nike banged her fists against the glass and screamed wildly. Zelus just stood there and laughed, his clawed hand on the black pearl handle.

Nike's anger raised to levels she had yet to experience in her young life. She was mad at herself for failing. She was mad at the imp for setting this up and tricking her. She was mad at the demon Zelus. She was even mad at Hera for letting herself be captured.

Nike's ire grew with every new burst of Zelus' laughter until her body couldn't contain it anymore. A white light grew from her center and consumed her body from the inside out. It grew bigger with every cell, every molecule, that it ate. When the light got to her wings, it turned to her signature victory gold. Color pulsed in on itself for two heartbeats and then exploded outwards, devouring everything in its path. Zelus, the forest, the training grounds, stray animals, the clouds, the snakes, and yes, even Hera.

After everything burned, there was a heavy silence in the world. Nike was numb to what she had done. All she knew was that not only didn't she win, but she killed her mother. As Nike sat in her paralysis, she found herself back in the blackness of the void. Eventually, she ended up back in her body within the chamber. Her siblings were there waiting for her, but she was so numb she couldn't move.

It was the soft sound of Nike's breath leaving her lungs in a despairing shudder that alerted Moxie to her return. Moxie wrapped her arms around her sister as Nike buried her face into Moxie's neck.

"Wh-why? Why couldn't I save her, Moxie? Not only didn't I save her, I *killed* her!" Nike lifted her face and looked at her sister with wild eyes. "I killed her. I killed our mother." Nike gasped in pain and fell to her knees.

Moxie waved the boys off and they stayed in place, standing in silent vigil to Nike's pain. She held and rocked Nike until her tears finally slowed, and she wiped her eyes. Moxie brushed Nike's hair back and helped her up. Looking at the boys, she nodded and said, "We're ready."

Hephaestus just grunted an acknowledgment and turned to the newly opened doorway. Ares was already disappearing through it, in a hurry to get away from the female tears. The group followed him past another torch-light wall and around a corner to another chamber. They all turned and looked at Ares.

"What? Do I have something on my face?"

Nike, still raw from her ordeal, started to cry again. Hephaestus took a turn comforting Nike while Moxie walked up to Ares.

"It's your turn, Ares. You're the only one left. Hopefully, all that's left to save our mamá is for you to go through your ordeal."

Ares laughed. "Piece of cake! I'm the God of War. I say, bring it on!" Ares spun on his heel and trotted into the open chamber, stopping a couple of feet from the pillar with the card that did indeed have his name on it. He turned to face the others and winked before walking backwards the last few steps.

"Feel free to miss—"

Ares's words were cut off as he gripped the card, the light in his eyes fading as his essence left his body. Hephaestus walked over to him, snapped his fingers, and waved his hand in front of Ares's face.

"That's creepy. Did I look like that?" He waved his hand one more time for good measure, shrugged, and joined the girls on their vigil of Ares' body.

Meanwhile, Ares tumbled end over end into the dark void. Colored lights flashed across his eyes, and screams assaulted his ears, disorienting him. He was spat out into another dark space, and it took a moment for him to focus his eyes. Looking around, he realized he was in a cave, the dark stone walls glistening in the moonlight.

There was a faint light ahead of him, and he followed it, seeking its source. He saw the cave opening shining with moonlight, a grove of trees just beyond. Ares started to move towards the entrance, but felt his way blocked by something.

He pushed against the invisible barrier, but it wouldn't budge. He pushed harder. Still nothing. He growled and pushed even *harder*. Just as he was starting to see red, he heard laughter. He turned to see who was laughing at his expense and frowned when he saw his mother.

Mom? What are you doing here? Whatever, you're coming with me, and we're getting out of here.

Ares reached for Hera and passed right through her. She laughed louder, her green eyes shining in the darkness. Ares reached for her again, only to miss again.

Dammit, Mom, hold still and stop that ridiculous laughing.

Hera just kept laughing, frustrating him even more. She finally took a deep breath and wiped her eyes. "You always were so headstrong, my son. So focused on what's directly in front of you that you can't see what's around you."

You're talking nonsense, Mother. Let's go.

Hera just looked at Ares sadly and shook her head. "I'm not going anywhere with you, Ares."

Don't be ridiculous, Mother. I won't tell you again. Let's go!

He reached for her and felt his hand pass through her yet *again*. She sighed. "You are so self-absorbed that you don't see what's going on."

Ares stopped at his mother's words and looked around. He saw the rocky cave wall, covered with trickles of water and spots of moss. The cave itself wasn't very high, and in fact, he should be hunched over, but wasn't. He looked down and was confused when he didn't see his legs. His confusion grew when he looked for arms that weren't there, either.

What in Hades is going on, Mother?

Hera sighed. "You never were the quickest to pick up on things, Ares. Fine, I'll tell you. You're currently a ball of golden light."

That's ridiculous, Mother. Why would I be a ball of golden light?

"Your essence went through a port-key and left your body behind."

Wait, so this is what happened to the others, too?

"Yes, my son. Though none of them had any issue with acknowledging their form."

Ares spat, *Whatever, Mother. I know you love them more.*

"Now is not the time to be spiteful, Ares. You're running out of time to save me. Or do you even care?"

Of course, I care, Mother! What do I have to do?

Hera rested her hand where Ares' cheek would have been and gave him a sad smile. "Oh, my sweet, sweet boy. You just have to use your wits."

Ares snorted. *I'm the God of War, Mother. I have plenty of wits.*

Hera just waved him forward through the cave entrance. "Of course, you do, my dear."

Ares felt his essence push through the membrane at the entrance with an audible pop, and he tumbled out into the moonlit grove. He was not as graceful as he normally was and ended up kicking himself in the back of his head.

"Ow!" He slowly stood, rubbing the sore spot. He took a few steps and stumbled, no longer familiar with the gait of his body.

"W-what?" Ares slapped a hand over his mouth, horrified. He hadn't stuttered since he was ten. Slowly, he held his hands out in front of him and turned them over, shaking in disbelief at their smaller size.

"N-no w-way!" Ares looked around the grove and then quickly headed off towards the sound of water. He broke through the trees and found a brook. Kneeling, he looked at his reflection and groaned. He was in his nine-year-old body. How the hell was he supposed to save *anyone* at this size?

He roughly ran a hand through his hair, causing it to stick up all over. He needed to maim, kill, or fuck something to release his frustration and quite frankly wasn't sure how to do any of that in this body. He leaned down and grabbed a rock, chucking it as hard as he could. Ares huffed out an angry breath as it landed with a *thunk* in the brook, mere feet from him.

Ares tipped his head back and screamed into the night, causing birds to fly away in fear. Mildly satisfied with that reaction, he turned to walk away and almost ran into a young female centaur.

"W-Woah, s-sorry, I d-didn't s-see you th-there." Ares gave his best hot boy smile, one that he'd perfected over the years and knew got the ladies to lift their skirts for him. However, on his younger face, it just looked like he was constipated. The girl burst into tears.

Ares shifted awkwardly on his feet. He'd never been good with crying females, preferring to pass them off to his sisters instead. He looked around, desperately hoping another female had magically appeared. When there was none, he sighed and walked closer, awkwardly patting her shoulder.

"P-please d-don't c-cry." The young girl just buried her face in her hands and cried louder. Ares was extremely uncomfortable and had no idea what to do. Eventually, her tears slowed enough for her to talk.

"I'm sorry. It's just that poachers took my mother, and the oracle said I would find a strong and powerful warrior alone by the brook. There's no one here but you, and now my mom's gonna die." She wiped the snot from her nose with the back of her hand.

Ares bristled at her unintended insult. "I'll h-have you know, I'm th-the G-God of War!" He puffed out his chest in pride. The girl stared at him, frozen with disbelief for several long seconds. Just as Ares was about to be uncomfortable under her stare, she burst into laughter. She laughed so hard she bent at the waist, tears again flowing down her face.

Ares was not amused and crossed his arms, waiting for her to finish. She hiccupped and wiped her eyes. Seeing the frown on his face, she said, "Oh, you were serious?" Ares just nodded. "But you're so…little, and you stutter. I mean, you're cute, I suppose. But I thought the God of War was supposed to be big and brawny, and I don't know, scary."

Ares huffed. "W-well, Th-this isn't m-my n-normal b-body, okay? And I am sc-scary!"

She broke out into tiny giggles, and Ares just threw up his hands, disgusted by his whole situation. "W-whatever. I have t-to find m-my m-mother." He turned and stalked out of the grove, not really sure where he was going. Just sure he had to get away from this girl and her nonsense.

He paid no attention to the animals scuttling out of his way as he entered the forest. He needed to find a way to help his mother and get back to his body. He was so wrapped up in his problems he didn't hear the centaur girl as she caught up with him or notice that she now walked beside him. Almost an hour passed with the two of them walking side by side, Ares grumbling under his breath about his situation, the girl silently following beside him.

Eventually, she rested a hand on his shoulder to get him to stop. Ares was so lost in his own thoughts that he shrieked loudly in surprise and jumped, tripping over a fallen log and landing flat on his back.

"Oomph!" He raised his head and saw the girl standing by the log, eyes wide. He dropped his head back to the ground and stared up at the dark sky. "Are y-you f-following m-me?"

"Yes."

Ares groaned. "W-why?"

"Because I need you."

Normally, Ares would preen about being needed by a female, however, nothing about this situation was normal. "Wh-what c-could you p-possibly n-need from m-me?"

Her lip quivered. "My mother and I were out gathering flowers, and she was taken by poachers. All the men of our village were out hunting for dinner. Our oracle told me I'd find my savior by the brook. You were there, so she must have meant you."

Ares snorted, debating on whether or not to get up from the cold forest floor. "L-Lady, I'm n-not g-gonna be anyone's s-savior like th-this."

"Of course not. You have to get up first."

Ares laughed at the absurdity of his situation. "You're r-right." He got up and dusted himself off. "L-Let's g-go s-save your m-mother. After all, m-mine is a g-goddess, sh-she c-can wait." His sarcasm was lost on the girl, and she just looked relieved.

"Thank you. I know where they took her. It's a little ways from here, so get on my back, and I'll run us there." She turned and presented her rump to Ares, who took a quick moment to appreciate the woman she would grow into. He shook his head and climbed onto her back.

"Hold on!" She took off so quickly, Ares almost fell off. He leaned forward and tightened his thighs against her flank. "Wh-what's your n-name?"

She glanced back over her shoulder. "It's Niamh. What's yours?"

"Ares."

She giggled. "You're named after the God of War. No wonder you said that."

Ares growled under his breath, "I *am* th-the G-god of War."

After running for almost half an hour, Niamh finally slowed down. Ares heard a bunch of loud laughing and lewd singing. Niamh stopped behind a large boulder and started crying again.

"What if I took too long, Ares? What if she's already dead?" Niamh started to hyperventilate.

Ares grabbed her chin and made her meet his eyes. "Listen." She opened her mouth to say something, but he shook his head. "Listen." After a moment she heard it. Men were grunting and laughing. The sound of a woman cursing and spitting at them, calling them cowards for tying her up.

Niamh let out a shaky sigh. "She's okay!" She wrapped her arms around Ares and squeezed him tightly against her body, relief flowing through her.

"C-can't breathe!" Ares choked out.

Niamh let go quickly. "I'm so sorry, Ares. I'm just so happy she's alive. We have to get her!" She walked around him, set on storming the camp, and demanding the men release her mother. Ares grabbed her, yanking her back behind the boulder. "Let me go! I have to get my mother!!"

"St-stop it, N-Niamh! As m-much as I appreciate your b-boldness, w-we c-can't just ch-charge in and d-demand th-they g-give us your m-mother. Th-the least th-they'd d-do is laugh. Th-the worst th-they'd d-do is t-tie us up with your m-mother. N-Neither result is p-productive."

Niamh let out a frustrated cry. "But she's so close!"

Ares hugged her. "I kn-know. T-trust m-me, I kn-know. N-now sit d-down and let m-me th-think." Ares had a private chuckle at himself, knowing Hephaestus would laugh at the situation. Ares was not a planner. He usually bullied his way in with his charm or rushed in with swinging swords. He never stopped to make a plan. That was something Hephaestus would do, and Ares would laugh at him for it. Plans were for people who didn't have his skill.

Ares looked down at his smaller body and grimaced. A plan it would have to be then. "N-Niamh, c-can you wait here for j-just a m-minute? I'm g-going to g-get c-closer and see where th-they have your m-mother."

Niamh nodded and chewed her lip. "Just be careful, okay? You're all I've got." Ares nodded and headed off towards the campsite. He was careful to stay in the shadows on the edge of the camp. It sounded like the men were all drunk, but that didn't mean they hadn't posted sentries. Halfway around the clearing, he saw a narrow trail and followed it. He finally saw Niamh's mother. They had tied her hands and hooves to a long pole, supported high between two trees. She looked like a hog on a spit.

Ares cringed at the blood dripping from ankles that were rubbed raw from the rough cording they used. He slowly backed away from the camp and picked his way around the perimeter, looking for guards. He counted fourteen men, but let out a relieved breath when he finished his recon and found no sentries.

Walking back to the boulder, Ares wondered how he was going to get past the men. Even though they were drunk, they still sounded like they had a lot of life left in them, and he was running short of time. His eyes caught a moonbeam shining on a patch of wild herbs that looked familiar.

"Oh, th-thank Z-Zeus." Ares smiled and pulled two handfuls of the herbs, tucked them into his pockets, and ran back to the boulder. Niamh rushed him, grabbing his thin shoulder in her hands.

"Did you see her? Is she okay?"

Ares gently peeled her fingers from his shoulder. "Sh-she's f-fine."

"Really?"

"Really, really."

Niamh sat down in relieved exhaustion. "Oh, thank the gods! So what are we going to do?"

"*We* aren't g-gonna d-do anything."

Niamh opened her mouth to object, but Ares raised a hand to stop her. "I h-have a p-plan."

"Great, what is it?"

Ares sat down next to her and explained his plan in detail. She asked a few questions, complained about her limited role, but ultimately agreed to go along with it. They waited another hour to

allow the men to get even drunker. Then the two of them made
their way back to the camp.

Niamh watched to make sure no one spotted them as Ares
worked his way to the edge of the camp and shimmied up a tree. He
climbed carefully out on a branch that hung over the main campfire.
Wrapping his thin legs tightly around the limb, he slowly lowered
himself into a hanging position. For the first time since this started,
he thanked the gods for his smaller body that didn't cast a shadow.

Ares whispered, "Auntie H-Hes, I know we d-don't sp-spend m-
much t-time t-together, but if you c-could find it in your h-heart t-
to h-help m-me s-save th-this g-girl's m-mom, th-that'd b-be g-
great." Ares pulled the herbs he'd picked and waited until no one
was watching the fire. His young muscles were quivering with
fatigue before he was able to drop the plants into the fire.

The fire bloomed, glowed a blue color, and then settled down.
Ares pulled himself up and said a quiet thank you to Hestia. When
he joined Niamh, he signaled for quiet, took her hand, and walked
them silently back to the boulder. They sat side by side, waiting for
the right time, too nervous to sleep.

A couple of hours later, Ares looked up at the night sky and saw
it brightening at the edges of the horizon. He stood up and took
Niamh's hand. "It's t-time."

They walked back to the camp and were met with silence. Ares
motioned for Niamh to stand guard and slowly crept up to a man
passed out in an awkward position, snoring loudly. Ares carefully
slid the knife from the man's belt and backed away.

"I'm g-gonna g-go g-get your m-mom n-now. Be r-ready."

Niamh just nodded, her brow furrowed in worry. "Be careful!"
she whisper-screamed after him.

Ares walked to the other side of the camp and sent up a silent
prayer to the gods that the herbs worked. He made it to where
Niamh's mother was hanging and cringed at how weak and pale she

looked. He tucked the knife into his belt and quickly climbed one of the trees. Praying it would take his weight, he carefully inched out onto the pole. The movement startled the woman and caused her to cry out until she saw Ares' small body.

"Ssshhhh. I'm g-gonna h-help you," he whispered.

Her eyes were wide with fear and exhaustion, but she nodded. He made his way closer. "I'm g-gonna c-cut th-the b-bonds at your wrists, okay?" She nodded in understanding. With a few quick movements of the knife, he removed the ropes from her wrists, and she sighed with audible relief.

Ares let out a soft owl call and smiled when it was returned. Niamh broke through the trees and gasped when she saw her mother, clamping her hands over her mouth to keep from crying out.

"G-get th-the st-stuff." Niamh reluctantly rushed away. Ares addressed her mother again. "W-What's your n-name?"

"Cliona. Please, young man, get my daughter out of here."

"H-hush. I'm g-gonna f-free your b-back legs. C-can you h-hang on?"

She looked at her bloody wrists and flexed her fingers. "I'll do whatever I need to in order to get out of here."

Ares nodded and slowly slid across the pole, careful not to touch her hooves. He turned around to face her front and looked down. Niamh had been busy layering the mats of grass they wove while they waited. Once they were spread out under her mother, she made several trips to gather leaves and moss to add to the pile. Ares waited until Niamh was almost finished before cutting the ropes from Cliona's back hooves.

"H-hang on!"

Cliona nodded and wrapped her arms around the pole, hooking her elbows onto it. Ares cut one last time and released her back legs.

Her legs crumpled onto themselves, and she let out a pained, but muffled, cry. Ares scooted to her front legs.

"Almost d-done." He focused on cutting the ropes and tried to ignore the tears streaming down both mother's and daughter's faces. Just before he was done, he paused and whistled to Niamh, who positioned herself underneath them.

"Okay, I'm g-gonna c-cut you l-lose and f-fall under you t-to c-cushion your f-fall. N-Niamh's g-gonna b-be th-there, t-too."

Her eyes got wide. "No! I will crush you! You will die! I won't let you get hurt just to save me." New tears formed in her eyes.

Ares laid a gentle hand on her arm. "It's okay. I'm a g-god."

A burst of hysterical laughter forced its way from her mouth. "You're just a child."

"I h-haven't b-been a ch-child in a long t-time, m-ma'am."

The intense look on his young face made her pause. "I just don't want to hurt you."

"You w-won't. I p-promise." He gave her a watered-down version of his trademark hot-boy smile, and it eased her enough that she could focus on the fall. Just before he cut the final rope, Ares looked at her. "D-don't tw-twist your legs under you, th-they'll b-break. L-let m-my b-body b-break your f-fall, and th-then you and N-Niamh g-get out of here."

Cliona took a deep breath and nodded. Ares sliced his knife one last time through the ropes, and just as they split, he swung his body down. She turned to her side and curled in to protect vital parts, and Ares grabbed her legs, pulling his small body directly under hers just as they hit the pile Niamh had built.

Pain shot through every part of him, forcing the air from his lungs and tears from his eyes as he was crushed under her adult centaur weight. *I really hope I didn't lie about being a god.*

Niamh hugged her mother's neck tightly, and they cried in reunion.

"G-go!" Ares pushed the word from his mouth with a last expulsion of breath.

"Oh no, Ares!" Niamh struggled to help her mother off of Ares' body. Cliona stumbled and had to lean heavily on Niamh. Ares groaned. Niamh went to help him up, but he waved her off.

Gasping, he said, "G-get your m-mother out of here."

"I'll never forget this, Ares. Thank you for saving my mother."

Cliona looked at Ares with fresh tears in her eyes. "Thank you, young man. May the gods bless you and your family." Niamh wrapped her arms around her mother, and they stumbled home. Ares lied on the damp forest floor, staring up at the lightening sky and trying to catch his breath.

Once he was breathing properly, he rolled onto his side and slowly pushed himself up. He cursed under his breath, knowing that the coming morning chased away any chance he had of saving his own mother. He felt wetness on his cheeks and roughly wiped them away. This younger version of his body was entirely too sentimental for him.

Ares grabbed the knife and headed into the camp. Fucking and fighting were the two things he was best at, the two things that gave him the most pleasure. So, he ran his knife across the necks of the sleeping men, stopping only at the leader. He took a moment to slam the knife home into the man's eye socket.

"You d-don't h-hurt women," Ares spit at the man and then stumbled into a nearby tree. He was emotionally and physically exhausted. He sat against the trunk, watching the sunrise. His heart broke into a thousand pieces, knowing he just wasn't enough to save his mother. He sat there despondently as the sun warmed his skin. He sat there as the sun crested high in the sky, and the flies swarmed. He sat there as the wolves and other wild animals emerged from the forest, their mouths dripping with saliva over the smell of fresh blood.

He sat there, tears staining his face as the sun set and the day got darker. Ares sighed, the first conscious noise he'd made in the hours since he sat down. He rubbed the grit from his eyes and wondered how Niamh and her mother fared. Finally, he got up and slowly made his way back to the cave where he started.

By the time he got there, his little legs could barely hold him. He collapsed to his knees just outside of the entrance and covered his face with his hands. "I'm s-sorry, M-mother. I t-tried t-to help, I r-really d-did." Ares sat there crying silently until he felt a gentle touch brushing the hair from his forehead.

"Shh, my son. You did very well."

Ares looked up and saw his mother looking down at him. "B-but I d-didn't s-save you."

"Oh, my heart, you weren't supposed to save me. You were supposed to save yourself." Hera kneeled and gathered him into her arms, hugging him tightly.

Ares was confused. "H-how was I s-supposed t-to s-save m-myself?"

She kissed the top of his head. "Don't you see? You put that young girl's pain before your own. Instead of rushing in like you normally would, you waited and made a plan. You used your wit and not your muscle, and because of that, you helped that girl and her mother."

Ares wrapped his arms around Hera and snuggled into her embrace. Fully taking advantage of being young again, to get the comfort from her he so desperately missed. Hera held him quietly for a time before pulling away. She took his chin in her hand and guided his eyes to hers.

"You are not alone, Ares. As long as you have your family, you are never alone." She smiled. "Now, let's get you back to them, shall we?" She stood and brought Ares to his feet and walked him to the cave opening.

"Go back to your brother and sisters and protect them as only you can. I will watch over you, my heart."

Ares squeezed Hera around the waist one last time, wiped a lone tear with the back of his hand, and stepped toward the cave. He pressed his hand at the opening and felt the resistance of the barrier. He stood there for several moments, pushing against it, trying to find a way in. He heard Hera let out a loud exasperated sigh and then felt her push him forward, his body tearing its way through the membrane with a loud rip.

He felt his essence shed his body just as he fell into the dark cave. Before he could orient himself, he was sucked back into the black void, noises assaulting his ears. Just when he was about to scream in frustration, he was slammed back into his body.

"Aaaaaaaaaaaaahhhhhhhhhh!!!!!" Ares roared as he stumbled forward a few steps.

Hephaestus grabbed Ares and maneuvered him out of the way. "Give us a minute, girls." Moxie reached for Nike's hand and nodded, pulling Nike to the corner to give the boys some privacy. Hephaestus gripped Ares' shoulders tightly to help ground him. "You okay, man?"

Ares looked around wildly for a minute while he anchored himself in his brother's grip. He took a few deep breaths and felt something wet trail down his nose. He brushed it away, angrily. "I couldn't save her, Heph. I ran out of time. I couldn't save her," he whispered hoarsely.

Hephaestus pulled his brother into a tight hug. "It's okay. It wasn't real."

"But how do you *know*?"

Hephaestus thought back to his own trial. "Because it can't be. Now pull yourself together. We're running out of time."

The four were lost in their thoughts. They startled a bit at the sound of vines and stones moving as the secret door revealed itself and opened. Each hoped and prayed to various gods that this was the last of their search. None of them wanted to relive their ordeals.

As they walked out of the final chamber, the teens were heartbroken and soul-weary. Each one prayed that the trials they'd endured would somehow save their mother. They came upon a stone door with torches on either side. The flames cast flickering shadows and created nightmares on the walls. They stood in the torchlight frozen and afraid, guiltily wondering if it was really worth their sanity to keep going forward.

They stared for a long time at the doorway. Moxie raised her head to try to determine how close to dawn it was, but couldn't see the sky through the canopy. She knew in her bones they were cutting it too close. She took a deep breath and grabbed Nike's hand. "We're almost out of time."

Ares shivered and unconsciously huddled closer to Hephaestus for reassurance. Hephaestus just tightened his grip on his brother. As the one furthest from their ordeal, Moxie was the quickest to pull herself together. Letting go of Nike's hand, she walked up to the door, looking for some way to open it. Nike followed and flew up to the top to see if there was a way to get in from there.

While the girls were looking for a way to open the door, Hephaestus kept his hold on Ares, helping him ground himself back into this moment. Ares looked around the narrow hallway. When he finally felt stable enough to stand on his own, he roughly shrugged out of Hephaestus' embrace, taking four steps to the left.

Ares turned to watch his siblings inspect the door for a secret lever, talking softly amongst themselves. He felt a sharp ache in his chest at not being a part of the group. In typical Ares fashion, he dismissed it by saying to himself that he was better off without them. But it was just a little bit harder to believe this time. He retreated to watch them from the shadows. Ares stepped back to lean against the wall and hit something that almost made him fall flat. The noise caused the others to stop what they were doing and turn. Nike floated down in front of him.

"Are you okay, Brother?"

"Yeah, I'm good. Just tripped over something in the dark."

Nike cocked her head to the side. "Why are you standing alone in the dark?"

"Staying out of the way. You all were doing a fine job of looking. You don't need me." Ares cringed inwardly at the sarcasm in his voice. Nike raised an eyebrow but didn't say anything.

Ares turned away to see what he ran into and let out a small gasp. "Damnit."

Nike walked up behind him and looked over his shoulder to see another card resting on a waist-high pillar attached to a dais. "Oh no, I thought we were done with that. Moxie! Hephaestus! Come quick!"

Not being that far away, Hephaestus grabbed a torch, and he and Moxie joined the other two. "What's going on, little one?"

"Another card."

Hephaestus grumbled under his breath, "Fuck."

Moxie walked around Ares. "What does it say?"

Ares shrugged. "Dunno. Heph, gimme some light."

Hephaestus brought the torch closer so Ares could read the card, making a point not to touch it. "It just says, *children*." Ares frowned and pushed the card with his finger, but it didn't move. He let out a relieved breath when he wasn't sucked back into the void. Using his thumb and forefinger, he carefully picked it up by its corner and turned it around.

"Huh. There's like a rhyme thingy on the back."

Nike flexed her wings with impatience. "Well, what does it say?"

Ares cleared his throat and read.

Well done, children

You've come this far.
But do you know who you are?
To save the Queen, you must test once more.
You've succeeded one by one
But this time, it's all or none.

When he was done, Moxie said, "Well, it seems pretty straight forward. We all just need to try to open the door together."

Hephaestus and Nike looked at each other and shrugged before turning back to the door. Moxie held out her hand to Ares, who tucked the card into his belt before placing his hand in hers. The four of them stood in front of the door and, as if they had choreographed it, took a deep breath, and placed their hands on the door as one. Another breath. Another breath and to their confusion, nothing happened.

"Maybe you misunderstood, Moxie?" Hephaestus said as he looked around for movement of any kind.

Moxie shook her head. "No, I'm sure this is what it meant. We have to touch it together."

Nike poked her head around Hephaestus. "Maybe we have to hold hands while we do it?"

Ares grumbled. "I'm not holding Hephy's hand."

"Don't call me that. I don't want to hold yours either, pretty boy."

Ares beamed at the insult. "I am, aren't I?"

The girls just rolled their eyes, and each grabbed the boys' hands. Nike placed her left hand on the door, holding Hephaestus in her right hand. Moxie held Hephaestus in her left hand and Ares in her right. Ares pressed his right hand onto the door. They held their collective breaths.

The moment stretched out, and nothing happened. Just as they were on the edge of giving up, the torches flared, and the stone under their hands shook so hard their bones rattled. With no warning, the doorway crumbled into thousands of tiny pebbles, revealing a silver latticework gate. Moxie stepped up and traced her fingers over the shining metal. Giving little thought to her actions, she pushed the gate at its center point. Everyone startled when the gate split in the middle and opened, allowing them to enter.

Ares pushed everyone out of the way, causing Moxie to fall into Hephaestus, who just barely caught her. "Ares! What is wrong with you?"

Ares ignored her and looked around the new area. In each corner were marble statues of a different god. They weren't normal statues, though. As Ares watched, the one closest to him shifted from an image of his father to one of his uncle Hades. Trying to process what he saw, he looked to the statue on his other side and watched it turn from his uncle Poseidon to his aunt Hestia.

Ares looked around the open space, noting the wildflowers that grew in vibrant colors at the base of each statue. In the exact center, a square platform rose a foot off the ground, and was surrounded by a thick canopy of curtains. Ares ignored it and instead walked its perimeter, seeing nothing but two more changing statues.

"Mother! Where are you?" The others joined him.

"Did you find her, Brother?"

"Not yet, little one, but there is that thing." He motioned to the curtained area. Moxie let out an excited squeak at the thought of seeing her mother again. She rushed to it, pausing only for a breath length of a moment, remembering the destroyed state of the curtains in Hera's chambers. When Moxie ripped the fabric aside, she cried out in anguish and fell to her knees, tears streaming down her face.

The others rushed over to see what had upset her. "Oh, my gods!" Nike fell to her knees next to Moxie. Ares looked green, but he and Hephaestus managed to keep themselves upright.

"Mom?" Hephaestus whispered in disbelief. In the corners of the platform were wooden poles that held the curtains and iron chains. He followed the line of the chains to the center of the platform. They were attached to the wrists and ankles of a woman so bloody and disheveled she was almost unrecognizable. The chains held her horizontally, her arms and legs stretched to their limit towards the corners. Her body hovered over the platform in midair.

With halting steps, Hephaestus walked to her suspended form and gently brushed her hair back so he could cradle her face to look at him. His heart raged with a wave of burning anger hotter than any fire in his forge. "Mom?" he whispered again. Her eyelids, crusted with blood, tears, and grime, fluttered weakly. "Ares! Come help me!"

The girls stayed by Hera's head, whispering reassurances to her and themselves. Ares and Hephaestus tried to release the manacles from their mother. Ares strained and pulled to no avail.

"Heph, this isn't working!"

Hephaestus growled. "I know!"

Moxie used her power to draw vines and foliage, forming a soft pallet under their mother, hoping to ease her pain even just a little. The boys continued their relentless attempts to break their mother's bonds. Suddenly, the torches flared with dark red flames that reached out as if to grab the children. An eerie laugh echoed through the air.

"Who's there?" Nike looked around but didn't see anyone else. The laughter got louder and deeper. The sound became thicker as it rolled in waves through the air. It gained form as a thick black ribbon and glided over Hera's body, causing her to shiver and moan in pain.

The children were terrified. They had never seen such a creature as this before. The darkness twisted around Hera's body like a thick satin ribbon, tightening around her until she gasped for breath. It wound around her neck and then slowly unwrapped and floated to a space in front of the platform. None of them could take their eyes from the abomination. Their hearts pounded in fear, unsure of how they would save themselves, let alone their mother.

The laughter coalesced around the black ribbon as it twisted and turned in a state of perpetual motion, forming itself into a vaguely humanoid shape. Two pieces of darkness formed where a mouth would be, and the laughter finally stopped.

"You're too late, children! Apollo has raced dawn across the horizon, and the queen belongs to me."

"But we didn't know how late it was!" Moxie begged.

Hephaestus walked as close as he dared to the writhing darkness. "We had no choice. We went as fast as we could."

The darkness released a wicked sound from its ribbon lips. "You knew the rules. You had until dawn. No exceptions." Ribbons formed into eyes blacker than midnight, the red flames of the torchlight reflecting in the inky depths.

"The queen belongs to me!" Each word had the ribbons expanding upward and out, encompassing more and more space. They absorbed every molecule of the residual night as well as the air that surrounded the children. They gasped, desperate for breath, but unable to find any. Lungs burning, they all stumbled towards their mother, seeking comfort in their final moments.

One by one, they realized that not only did Nyx have the queen. She would also take them. Gods they may be, but nothing could stop the vengeance of a pissed off Primordial. The air got more and more oppressive, sliding down their throats and coating their lungs, strangling them from the inside. One by one, their bodies fell to the ground, their sight dimming to complete darkness.

Another voice sliced through the thick air. "Enough!"

Nyx growled in response.

"I said *enough*, Nyx! You're hurting my children!"

Nyx sighed and released the darkness, easing the air back into the children's bodies. Slowly, carefully, hesitantly, they struggled to sit up and make sense of what was happening. Hera rushed to them and hugged each one, placing a reassuring kiss on their foreheads.

"Oh, my sweet, sweet, babies. Are you okay? I'm sorry about Nyx. She got a little too excited about her role as the bad guy." Hera continued to make soothing noises at them as they regained their strength.

Moxie was the first to speak. "Mamá, are you okay? We were so worried about you." She lurched forward and wrapped her arms tightly around Hera's waist, crying tears of relief. Nike joined Moxie, and Hera held both of the girls close.

"We tried to save you, Mother. Nyx said we were too late. Was she right? Are you a shade?" Hephaestus met Hera's eyes.

Hera snorted. "I'm so sorry, my heart. Nyx has a bit of a flair for the dramatic. I was just planning on sitting here and enjoying a light meal with her while we waited for you to come through the gate. It was her idea to have me chained up like that. Though I have to admit, she was right. The looks on your faces were amazing, as if you were actually afraid for me."

Ares stood up and sputtered, unable to form words while he processed what his mother said. "Wait. You're *okay*?"

Hera nodded. "Of course, I am."

Ares' anger rose. "You. Were. *Okay*?"

"Come now, Ares. I didn't stutter."

He stalked over to his mother, barely restraining the violent anger he would soon be known for. "What the hell, *Mother*! We were worried sick about you. Terrified we'd never make it in time! We...we fought harpies, flesh-eating spiders, and evil vines! We could have *died*!"

Hera smiled, not in the least bit worried about her son's anger, knowing he got it from her. "Oh, you all did so marvelously. The way you worked together to get past your obstacles was fantastic. I especially liked Nike's flying as she saved you all from those vines." Hera looked down to smile at Nike and found that both she and Moxie had let go. They'd backed away and were now looking at her as if they would be ill.

Hephaestus walked over and stood next to Ares, his hands flexing into fists. He gritted his teeth and forced words from his clenched jaw. "What about the other things, Mother? What about those things we went through alone?"

Hera stood, brushed off her gown, and shrugged. "I needed to test you. You each have the potential to be so much more than you know. To reach that potential, you had to face your fears."

Ares took another step towards her, but Moxie blocked his path. Looking at her mother, she asked, "What fears, Mamá?"

Hera gave Moxie a soft smile. "Oh, Mou. You are so afraid of losing control that you bury your warrior deep, and I worry you'll lose her. You had to know it was okay to use your power to destroy as well as create. One cannot exist without the other."

Moxie frowned, and Nike finally spoke up, "And me, Lady Hera?"

Hera walked to Nike and cupped the side of her face. "You had to know what it felt like to lose everything. Only then would you know true victory." She kissed Nike's other cheek and walked over to her sons.

"My boys. My heart. You are both so strong and passionate. And so alone. Hephaestus, you've created a fortress around your heart and wrapped your self-righteousness so tightly around yourself, no one can get close to you. You are always so alone, but desperately wish to belong somewhere. Even though you long to be loved, it is your biggest fear. You had to see that you are adored by so many of us. *You* are the one creating the chasm between yourself and everyone else."

Hephaestus was overcome with a myriad of emotions, most of which made him want to cry. He searched inside of himself and found a small flame of burning anger deep in his gut and latched onto that instead.

"That is the biggest lie you've ever told me, exceeded only by the lie that you love me." He spat at Hera's feet and stalked away, desperate to get as far from his mother's lies as possible.

"Fight it all you want, Hephaestus. Everything I showed you was true. Ask your siblings if you don't believe me."

Nike, Moxie, and Ares all looked at him. "What did you see, brother?" Nike asked him.

Hephaestus growled. "Lies, little one. Nothing but lies from a wretched old hag who can't stand not to be the center of attention." He stalked further away and, in typical Hephaestus fashion, turned from his family. Hera's face fell in disappointment.

"You forgot my explanation, Mother."

Hera cleared her throat and smiled at Ares. "You, my heart, needed to learn to accept that rushing in without all the information is not always the best action. You needed to face that you will sometimes have to accept help from others and that the world doesn't revolve around you and your problems. Everyone has value, even if you can't see it."

Nyx snorted from the corner. "Whatever, Hera. I just enjoyed scaring them. We should do this again."

Hera looked at her children. Nike and Moxie, still looking so confused and pained. Ares struggled with his anger. Hephaestus, already isolating himself again. "One day, you will understand."

Hephaestus spun around to face her on his good heel, vitriol consuming his face and words. "*Never*, Mother. I will never understand why you would put your children, whom you claim to love so much, through such pain."

He turned away from Hera and addressed Nyx. "Lady Nyx, I know my mother made you join her in this ridiculous plan of hers. Would you please open the way out of here so we can leave?"

Nyx raised an eyebrow in amusement. "Of course." She held her hand out in front of her face and blew. A black smoke flowed from her mouth, shaping itself into a vertical portal next to Hephaestus. "Step through, and you'll be back in the field near your forge."

Hephaestus bowed. "Thank you, Lady Nyx." He turned to his siblings. "I saw how each of you looked as you came back from your ordeal. Not a single one of you can say that this romp through the woods was *fun*. Our mother lied to us from the beginning and put us in danger. A real mother wouldn't do that to her children." Before he stepped into the smoke, he sneered at Hera and said, "She is no mother of mine."

Ares looked like he was fighting a war in his heart. He wanted so badly to understand why his mother would put them through all of this, but in the end, all he felt was heartbreak. He gave Hera and the girls a tortured look and then followed Hephaestus through the smoke.

Hera looked at Nike and Moxie. "Surely, you girls understand why I did what I did."

Nike walked over to Hera, wrapped her arms around her in a tight hug, and whispered, "I'm glad you're safe, Lady Hera." With a quick glance at Moxie, Nike followed the boys.

"Mou...you understand. Don't you?"

Moxie just stood there for a long time, staring at Hera in silence. Finally, she took a deep breath and shook her head. "No, Mamá, I don't understand. I know you love us. I feel the truth of it, but what you did here could have broken us. Mothers are supposed to protect their children, not put them in harm's way." Moxie gave Hera a quick kiss on the cheek and walked through the smoke.

Nyx waved her hand, and the smoke dissipated. "Well, that went swimmingly." Her sarcasm was not lost on Hera.

"I don't need it from you too, Nyx." Hera sat down on the edge of the platform and chewed her lower lip. "I just don't see how I was so wrong. I thought I knew my children. I thought they would appreciate the lesson and grow from it."

Nyx's laugh vibrated through the night. "There is one thing I know without a doubt, Hera. No matter how much you think you know your children, they will always surprise you. You just have to keep up with them."

Hera sighed. "I'm afraid they'll never forgive me for this, and I don't know how to make it right."

Nyx pulled Hera to her feet and grabbed her chin, forcing Hera to look into her black eyes. "They are your children. Given enough time, they will forgive you. Just give them space to sort through their feelings and come to terms with the lessons you tried to teach them. They will come back to you."

"Are you sure?" Hera asked, hopefully.

"As sure as I know every molecule that creates the night." She draped her arm around Hera's shoulders and waved her hand to create another portal. "Come, let's go have some of your sister Demeter's special brew and bitch about your husband. That always makes you feel better."

Hera laughed and followed Nyx into the night.

THE
SWORD
OF PERSEUS

BY

WAYNE DAVIDS

DINLAS,

GOD OF HATE & JEALOUSY

I PULLED MY HELMET OFF AND FLOPPED ALONGSIDE THE FIRE. The Celtic landscapes were a lesson in dichotomy. Beautiful and foreboding. Welcoming and deadly. Angelic and demonic.

The three of us camped well into the heather near a creek on Samhain's eve, and the scrubby evergreen bushes were long devoid of their spiked purple flowers. Colm and his brother Bhreac managed a small fire. The heat was meager, the flames more just to lift the spirits. We were still quite a few miles from Tlachtga, but with an early start, we would reach it before the festival began the following night.

"This is madness," Bhreac said for the hundredth time. He didn't wait for a reply, but rather pulled his cloak tighter around himself as he curled up on the cold ground.

"No, madness would be allowing this to happen without trying to stop it," I retorted from my spot on the other side of the fire.

"Both of you, stop," said Colm, "the bickering isn't going to help anything." Bhreac glared at the two of us for a moment, then rolled over to face away.

Colm sighed, then said, "I will watch first."

I nodded, "I'll go second. Wake us for anything. Now is the time for an abundance of caution."

The night passed without incident. In the morning, we set out again after sharing water and a wad of salted beef. The travel was torturous. There were no paths, much less roads, in this part of the country. We were constantly scrambling over rocks, up ravines, or staggering across the windswept moors. The wind blew incessantly. An earthy, decomposing scent of peat and heath mixed and wafted across the plain. Winter arrived, and the cold winds heralded the beginning of the dreary and miserable season.

We crested yet another low tor, and Bhreac grunted and said, "We are close, Dinlas. This is the edge of the Boyne Valley, ahead are the cairns and tombs of the Celtic Chieftains."

"Good," I replied. "We need to find the correct one."

Colm agreed, "Aye, no easy task. Many burial mounds dot this landscape. Remember when we were kids, Bhreac? We lived near here. We used to sneak into the valley to see the barrows, but we never had the spine to go inside any of them." Bhreac grunted again but didn't reply.

We walked and slid down the loose rock, descending to the floor of the valley. Everything here was still verdant compared to the withered browns of the highlands.

"They said a serpent would mark the tomb," said Colm as we walked to the closest burial mound.

"No snake here," Breac said, peering at the headstone. "T'is a ram or a sheep."

"Then we go to the next," I replied, "keep moving south. We need to reach the Hill of Tlachtga by sunset."

The brothers nodded in unison, and we headed southwest to the next barrow we could see. Cairns dotted the entire valley. Hopefully, we wouldn't have to check them all before we found that for which we were looking.

Let me back up for a moment.

I am Dinlas, a Greek God. Yes, you heard me, just like Zeus, Apollo, and all the rest. I am the illegitimate son of Aphrodite and Ares, one of many they had together. The only difference with me, my mother spurned me as an infant, for reasons that have never been clear, and cast me out of Olympus. I ended up in the Underworld with my great-uncle Hades. He allowed me to stay and raised me there. It wasn't a bad childhood, but anyone would be bitter to discover their parents didn't want them.

I came of age. In time-honored tradition, I left on a quest to earn my immortal deification as The Guardian of Lamark, a city of healers for soldiers wounded in battle. A quest, I might add, that I needed to undertake with no additional skills or protections beyond those of a mere mortal. The father of a deity usually chooses such a quest. In my case, Uncle Hades decided. You may think a father would prefer an easy task for their child, but that is not the case. A deity who overcomes a difficult challenge reflects positively on the father who raised them. Hades was no different. In an effort to shame my real father, Ares, he decided on a particularly dangerous task. One which my uncle believed would reveal himself as the better guardian.

To return to the story, there I was, toiling across the Emerald Isle in search of the tomb of Elegis Harrow, a druid king who stole the Sword of Perseus. The legendary short sword used to decapitate Medusa, disappeared into legend after Perseus's death at the hands of Megapenthes. It then mysteriously reappeared here years later in the hands of Elegis.

When Elegis died, his acolytes buried the sword with him, per his instructions. He recognized the sword's power and insisted on keeping it for eternity. My quest was two-part. I needed to secure the sword from the tomb and its horde of undead guardians, then kill the current High Druidess, Dala Rei. Dala avidly followed Ankou, a rival God of Death, and killing her would vanquish him from the mortal realm.

If there was anything Uncle Hades hated, it was competition.

We reached the next cairn, and Colm shook his head. "T'is a dog of some sort."

I nodded and pointed to the next closest mounds, almost due east of us, and we continued walking. The headstone at the following burial site held no luck either. Bhreac squinted at the carving and scoffed, "A bird. Perhaps a raven."

I paused as I peered across the valley at two more barrows in the distance. I had to kill the Priestess of Ankou in less than twelve hours, yet it could take us days just to find the sword.

"Come," I said to the two brothers as I knelt. They went to their knees, and we clasped our rough hands as I said a brief prayer. Deified abilities were out of the question here, but that didn't mean I couldn't beseech another to help. I knew just who to ask.

Artemis, All powerful Goddess of the Hunt
We have no offering for thee upon this barren and accursed valley
But please help your kinsman and his companions in their hour of need
Show us the path, that we may not squander our time searching in vain
But rather in securing our lost artifact
And destroying the foes of Olympus
We pray to you with open hearts and humble thoughts
Blessed be you Artemis

We raised our heads, unclasped hands, and stood as a shaft of sunlight broke through the dense clouds. It shined on neither of the closest tombs, but on a mound that we could barely see, several miles away and due south. The beam illuminated it for several minutes, then faded as the clouds once again rolled in and blocked it.

"That one," I said.

"Aye," replied Colm, "that one, indeed."

Bhreac furrowed his brow. "So, we are taking a brief parting of the clouds as a sign?"

"No, Bhreac," I replied, "we are taking it as *the* sign. The Goddess of the Hunt would not answer if she deemed us unworthy. She would not mislead us, to lie is not her manner."

116

Bhreac seemed unconvinced, but I didn't care. I had sought Colm when I arrived here for his skill with the blade. Bhreac, his brother, insisted on accompanying us to watch over the brash younger man.

Colm looked back at us, shifting his sword on his back. "Come then. We need hurry to get there in time."

I nodded in agreement, and the three of us began trotting to the burial mound in question. At first, we seemed to close none of the distance as we worked our way across the valley floor. However, as time passed, it became clear that the mound was getting closer, and we got a picture of just how large of an area it encompassed.

"Gods be damned," said Bhreac, gazing at the vast burial structure. He then cut his eyes at me and said, "Well, present company excluded, I mean."

I waved him off and replied, "No, I agree. Gods be damned, this place is mammoth."

We approached the entrance, and there, engraved on the keystone, was a coiled serpent. Before we entered, we paused and rested for several minutes, stooped with our hands on our knees. Jogging the length of the valley with all our gear left us breathless, and we needed several minutes to recuperate.

"Thank you, blessed Artemis," Colm said finally, breaking the silence. Bhreac and I echoed the sentiment.

"All right, let's get those torches out," I said after I caught my breath, "we have no time to waste. We must find the sword and still make it to the Hill of Tlachtga in just a few hours to kill Dala Rei."

I pulled out torches, splashed some oil from a boda bag over the tops, then lit them before entering the mound. I took the lead, moving cautiously as our eyes adjusted to the intense darkness that pressed in all around us. Against the inky onslaught, the torches did little more than hold the black at bay, keeping us just beyond its reach. Spiderwebs hung heavy at the entrance, a testament to the fact that none had entered here for many years. Burning them back, sent arachnids of all sizes scurrying away into the crevices and nooks between the stone blocks.

We moved down the rough-hewn entrance corridor, keenly aware of the scampering of small creatures ahead of us. The scent of this place was palpable, clinging in our nostrils and threatening to choke each of us. A fetid and noisome rot that originated from the age-old death that dwelled in this tomb. It had long since surrendered over the years, becoming a stagnant damp aroma that overwhelmed the senses and lent itself to the whole chilling aura. The dank air mixed with the smell of burning oil from the torches and seemed to hang everywhere.

Colm commented from the rear, "That smell. It's enough to make you run from here."

I hushed him almost immediately. We were at an intersection in the tunnel, and I paused to feel the wind. The architects of the cairn hid Elegis by sealing his tomb and disguising it. The two side passages had breezes blowing in them, but very little air moved straight ahead. We continued straight, running into a tangle of hairy roots that grew down from above. It startled me as they hit my face, and I flailed at them for a moment as Bhreac chuckled. We continued in silence, our boots crunching along the passageway. That and the occasional squeak of rodents scurrying ahead were the only sounds.

So it went. At each intersection we paused, and we always followed the one choice that had little or no breeze. I took a nub of charcoal out of my pack and marked the direction each time so we could find our way out later. Occasionally, we came across skeletal remains, a would-be thief, long since dead and long since picked clean by scavengers. At the last intersection, we turned left and followed the tunnel a short way to a dead end. I raised my torch and examined the walls carefully, then ran my hand over them. One section felt smooth and different from the rest. Upon closer inspection, I could see a plaster coating caked on the stone and flaking onto the floor.

I stepped back and looked at Bhreac. "It's fake. Smash it."

Bhreac nodded and pulled his iron battle mace. The very first blow cracked the facade, and after several minutes, the burly Bhreac knocked out the faux wall. Once the dust cleared, we peered into the chamber beyond. It was large, we could tell by the echoes of our whispers. Glowing lichens covered the walls to provide some light, but the cavern disappeared into darkness far beyond our eyesight. We scrambled through the narrow opening Bhreac created and entered the burial chamber of the infamous Elegis Harrow. The air hung thick and heavy, as if it resented being inhaled by us.

I held my hand up to stop the brothers and said, "Watch for traps. Tripwires, loose stones, magical glyphs. It really could be anything. Touch nothing, unless you must. We find Elegis, get the sword, and get out of here." They whispered their understanding, and we moved forward, holding our torches aloft to see better.

"Remember," I admonished them as we split apart, "watch for traps."

They nodded, and we began to explore the chamber. We found several torches and lamps in sconces on the walls, lighting them as we moved around what turned out to be a circular chamber. No doubt, we were in the center of the massive cairn. An arched earthen ceiling towered above us. Moving around the tomb, I watched as the torches flickered and threw crazy shadows, the curved design of the walls and ceiling exaggerating the effects.

Once we lit the room, I could see that it was over one hundred feet across. Deep cut niches lined the room's circumference, pockets created in the rock that held skeletal remains. Some, clad in rusted armor, still clung to their ancient weapons. Bleached and barren bones, covered in decayed tatters of cloth, lay in others. They filled the walls, pausing only at the narrow entrance of the passageway.

119

The remains rested upon their shelves, ten or more high and numbering well into the hundreds.

A raised square dais supporting an enormous stone sarcophagus sat at the center of the room. Presumably, inside lay the decomposed remains of Elegis Harrow and the Sword of Perseus. A throne rested at each corner of the square, facing diagonally outward. On each throne sat a skeleton bedecked in gold, jewels, and an elaborate crown. Each gripped a sword across its knees.

I pointed to the four thrones and their occupants. "The *Aes Sidhe*, the protectors of the cairn. Loot nothing from them. They are here to protect the mound and the dead within." Bhreac and Colm eyed the lifeless skeletons warily. Stepping carefully around them, we mounted the dais to the sarcophagus. We examined it but still could see no traps. Satisfied, each of us gripped the enormous stone cover and heaved. It refused to budge at first, only when we redoubled our efforts did it creak and slowly grind open. Inch by inch, it moved until we could see into the stone crypt. There lay Elegis Harrow, his hands clasped on his chest, and the sword pommel clutched between them.

I looked at my companions. "Be ready. I have no idea what happens when I grab the sword." They focused and tightened their grip on their weapons. I hesitantly reached my hand in and pulled it back several times. I finally steeled my nerve and grabbed the pommel, intending to rip it from the grip of the skeletal corpse.

Elegis Harrow, the long-dead druid priest, instantly sat up and grasped at the sword as I pulled it from him. He was, however, not our only problem. The clatter of gold and silver across the stone floor alerted us that the four Aes Sidhe were creaking to their feet and scanning for intruders.

Elegis and I fought for the sword, and in the struggle he pulled me partially into the sarcophagus with him. I twisted and flailed to get away, but never loosened my grip on the blade as I fought for leverage to get back out of the stone casket. He scratched and raked at me through my leather armor, and the stench of dead, rotten air assailed my senses. Somehow, I pulled myself free, along with the Sword of Perseus.

I stumbled back, trying to regain my composure while Bhreac and Colm kept the guardians at bay. They dispatched one of them into a scattering of bones, but we realized how outnumbered we were. Pouring out of the niches in the chamber's perimeter wall was the host of animated skeletons. The cacophony of clicking and tapping as their bony feet hit the stone floor warned us we should run.

"Bhreac! Colm!" I yelled over the din. "Never mind that! We must flee now!"

Both men broke off as best they could, all of us pushing for the passageway. I exited first, followed by Bhreac. Colm was last, but as he reached the narrow opening, one of the Aes Sidhe caught him from behind. He turned and shattered the skeleton's hand with his blade. He glanced at us and the prized sword.

"Go! Go now, put in as much distance as you can," Colm shouted as another bony hand grabbed his leather armor. Bhreac and I stood rooted to the ground for a moment, then I grabbed him and pulled him down the passage.

"No!" Bhreac screamed as his brother disappeared under the press of skeletons. They fell on Colm, rending flesh from the bone. His screams were all the more horrifying accompanied by the clicking of teeth, and the sound of wet chewing and gnawing. Several skeletons scampered around his body to chase after us. We tried to beat them back, but there were just too many to overcome. I forced Bhreac away before we befell the same fate as his younger brother.

We fled down the passages to the entrance, careening off the walls and each other in our efforts to stay ahead of our undead pursuers. We made it out by the grace of Hera, bursting from the entrance and casting about wild-eyed. The sun was low on the horizon, and we still had several miles to get to the Hill of Tlachtga. I turned to run, but Bhreac blindsided me with a punch to the side of my head. I went down in a pile as the skeletons emerged from the barrow.

"You son of a bitch!" screamed Bhreac. He stood over me, his knuckles red and abraded. "My brother! You let him die! You abandoned him and let him die!"

Scrambling to my feet, I glanced beyond Bhreac at the animated dead pouring from the crypt's opening. I pointed towards them and replied, "We had no choice, and he slowed the enemy so we could escape. You can fight me later, but we have to move now!"

His eyes followed my finger to the skeletons, who were still in pursuit. We turned, sprinting the remaining length of the valley for the Samhain gathering.

We ran that accursed valley. We ran it for miles while the throng of undead pursued us. The skeletons ranged out over several hundred yards, with the Aes Sidhe and Elegis Hallow bringing up the rear. It mattered not to us, their order, nor their lineup. To fall back into that mindless horde was certain death. They loped along, slow but unrelenting. They would never tire. They would not rest. Even though we outdistanced them now, we knew that we would have to stop at some point. It was the ultimate motivation to keep going while we could, so we ran on in silence, our footfalls a peculiar harmony to the tapping of the skeletons behind us.

Bhreac gasped out, "This is madness, Dinlas. We have a horde behind us as we run into a horde in front of us. I do not care if your father is the God of War. We will never vanquish all these foes."

I huffed, "I think I know the solution. Let's just get to the festival first."

Bhreac grunted back at me but said nothing more. The last light had faded, and in the murky darkness, everything seemed eerie and surreal. Ancient Samhain festivals like this one occurred all over the countryside. They started at sunset as everyone extinguished the lights in their homes. The community then gathered and built a central bonfire, from which the whole town re-lit their hearths. This new flame symbolized a new light for the new year. According to Uncle Hades, Dala Rei's clan chose to dedicate the festival to Ankou, their God of Death. Sacrificing to him, and spreading his following, meant a downturn in souls for Hades, and he would not let that happen. So, my quest had a second purpose that benefited his standing.

We passed a few stragglers, late on their way to the festival, and ran headlong toward the renegade clan's center. Bhreac huffed and puffed as we reached the foot of the hill and scrambled up it, completely out of breath. I still carried the sword in its ancient scabbard, running past hundreds of followers and participants all dressed in makeup and face ink for the ceremony. We reached the top, and several of Dala Rei's guards immediately stopped us. One grabbed my arm and spun me around. "You can't go past this point. No admittance to the Priestess."

I glanced back at Bhreac as they wrestled him to the ground. Running for miles, with little to eat, had taken its toll on us. They forced us to our knees as Dala approached and looked at me, then Bhreac.

"Excellent, you're right on time, Lord Dinlas. I've been expecting you." She reached forward and took the sword from me as I struggled against the guards. Bhreac and I exchanged worried glances as the High Priestess chuckled and turned back to her altar. The guards roughly bound our wrists in front of us and relieved us of our weapons. I glanced back down into the valley and could see the shambling and stumbling skeleton horde approaching, but neither the High Priestess nor any of her guards seemed aware of the menace bearing down on us.

She glanced over her shoulder and laughed. "Ankou has seen your ploy. Did you really think the two of you were going to fight an entire village? Did you think you would make it past my guards? I mean, really, this is pathetic. I will spill your blood here tonight in sacrifice and reveal Ankou's power for all to see. Then he will rule these lands. I am curious what your Hades will think when another Death feasts on the soul of his favorite nephew."

I glanced again at the skeleton horde. They were much closer now, having reached the edge of the small town. Their only focus was the draw of the Sword of Perseus and their sole purpose to recover and place it back in the tomb alongside their liege, Elegis Harrow.

"Come, we've no time to waste," she said as the guards pushed Bhreac and me forward, past a line of other druids and druidesses. The last one in the row was a young woman, and one of the few with her hood down. No doubt, a newly initiated acolyte. She had red hair and blazing green eyes that seemed to bore right through me. She said nothing, but the expression of joy on her face made it clear that my bloody sacrifice would bring her much pleasure. I caught only a glimpse of her twisted delight before they hustled me past her.

It was not until we reached the stone altar that my captors became aware that something was wrong. Screams and cries, erupting from down the hill, alerted everyone that all was not well. The shambling horde was now in the crowd, maiming and killing anyone they came across as they zeroed in on the blade the priestess held.

I glanced at Bhreac and he at me as the High Priestess and her entourage paused, stunned at the swirling wave of undead cresting and breaking along the hillside below us.

"What is this?" the priestess hissed, pushing her mentees and guards toward the fray.

One of the lesser druids asked, "Where did they come from? Is this some dread magic from another clan?"

She looked at us before responding, "No doubt it's them, but it doesn't matter now. What matters now is kill or be killed." Flashes and more screaming sounded below as Elegis reached the main battle and began setting the mortals alight with his touch.

Several skeletons charged the hill and broke through the ranks. As they crashed past, one of the guards had his dagger knocked out of his hand, the weapon landing at Bhreac's feet. In his haste to protect the High Priestess, the guard ignored the dropped weapon and drew his sword. Dala Rei stood holding the Sword of Perseus, and they went straight for her. With a flash, she annihilated one with a ball of flame. Several guards tackled another and began bashing it apart.

Bhreac looked down at the dagger, then glanced at me, and I nodded. He kneeled quickly and scooped it off the ground. In just moments, he had freed us. We glanced about wildly as more skeletons made their way up the hill, including the powerful Aes Sidhe and Elegis Harrow, whom none had even touched. They crested the top where we stood at the sacrificial altar. The skeletal lich priest of Ankou prepared to square off against Dala Rei, the current priestess.

Elegis opened and closed his mouth several times, as if remembering how to talk, before he said, "Return the sword to me. I recognize you for who you are. We are not enemies here." His voice, which seemed to emanate from somewhere in his rib cage, was low and growling, and I could feel the hairs on the back of my neck stand up at his guttural tone.

Dala looked down at the sword in her hands as the lesser skeletons crowded in and encircled the hill. "So, it's true? This is the sword that killed the Gorgon?"

"It is," grated the long-dead Elegis, "and now I will reclaim it and take it back with me to the barrow." He reached out his skeletal hand as Dala looked thoughtfully at the sword. She pulled the pristine blade clear of the scabbard, held it aloft, and inspected it as the skeletons stood motionless except for a slight synchronized sway.

I motioned for Bhreac, and we slid down on the far side of the altar. I saw the look on the druidess' face and knew what was coming next. Bhreac leaned in close and whispered, "How are we going to get out of here?" In answer, I put my index finger to my lips so I could hear the next words spoken.

"This sword is mine," replied Dala flatly. "Your time has come and passed. Laying in a dusty, rat-infested tomb is a colossal waste for a weapon of such magnificence. There it is nothing more than an artifact from a bygone era."

I peered over the altar in time to see Elegis hiss at Dala and stretch both hands out towards her. Clearly, he was about to cast a spell, but Dala was not about to let that happen. With a swift downward stroke, she cut through both arms. He drew back and howled in rage as the bones below his elbows clattered to the ground. Elegis' agonizing bellow attracted the attention of everyone on the hill. A war-cry that signaled there would be no mercy or quarter given here as the remaining skeletons and the mortals clashed in combat.

The druidess slashed through a skeleton, one of the *Aes Sidhe*, then smashed another with the flat of the sword, causing it to shatter. The skeletal force occupied her retinue while all around us, a nightmarish battle raged as the living tried to kill the dead. Most of the mortals arrived unarmed and now struggled to dismember their ancient foes.

The undead throng pounced on one villager after another, ripping the flesh from their bodies with determined ease. Screams and cries for help were all around us as the dead army did their grim work with twisted hands possessing an iron grip and razor-sharp talons. It was obvious they intended to kill all the living present.

Bhreac peered from our vantage point behind the massive stone altar and whispered again, "What do we do?"

I looked at our only weapon, the small dagger he claimed earlier from the ground. "I think we sit tight for the moment. Hades told me to expect my powers restored the moment we obtained the sword, and the High Priestess was dead."

Bhreac watched as Dala and Elegis circled one another, locked in deadly combat. "We need to do something," he urged as a skeleton landed on top of a mortal nearby, disemboweled him in several bloody swipes, then lunged at another person.

I shook my head, "We need to let them kill each other."

Bhreac grimaced, then ducked behind the altar as another skeleton appeared around the other side. It lunged at us as we crouched on the ground, clawing me across the chest and ripping my leather armor. We jumped on the creature, and it went down, but with no useful weapons, we could only grab at its limbs, breaking them off at the joints while it hissed and shrieked. Bhreac removed his helmet. Using it as a club, he bludgeoned the skeleton back to death, leaving the bones scattered and motionless around us.

Bhreac raised a trembling hand to his forehead and wiped away the sweat. "We have to do something, Dinlas. We are dead if we stay here."

I peeked around the stone altar as he spoke. The din from the battle was deafening. We weren't a priority for the mob of undead, because we didn't have the sword. The only reason the mortals weren't interested in us was that they were dealing with the dead. I watched as Dala and Elegis circled one another.

"Bhreac, get ready," I said without turning to look as I lunged from our hiding spot. Dala had her back to me, but Elegis spotted me at once. He hesitated as I headed straight for the priestess. I lowered my shoulder and slammed into the small of her back at a full run. She stumbled and lurched forward, the sword flying out of her hand. Elegis and I grabbed for it, and I careened off Dala into the ancient, undead priest. My momentum knocked him backward onto the ground, and in an instant, he was clawing and ripping at me as I struggled to reach the sword. I glimpsed Bhreac, wildly swinging his helmet as a weapon at Dala. He caught her unaware, crushing the side of her head with several blows, and she sank to the ground as her blood sprayed across his face then soaked the grass.

Elegis sank his bony fingers into my neck, just above the collar of my leather. I could feel my blood running down my chest as I kicked back at him, trying to disengage. The priestess was dead, and I needed only to get the sword, grab Bhreac, and teleport away. If only I could get free of Elegis' clawing grip. I twisted in his grasp, so we were facing one another and grabbed his skull, no easy task since he was lunging and biting at me like a rabid dog. The teeth that remained in his jaws were snapping, clicking, and grinding just inches from my face. With an inhuman jerk, I pulled his head from his body and tossed it to the side.

Of all that happened that day, his disembodied head, shrieking and biting, was what stuck with me for many years. His body continued to rake and claw at me until Bhreac stepped in and smashed the skull to pieces with the flat of Perseus' sword. The moment he ruined it, the spell that bound all the undead broke. The skeletal enemies fell to the ground, now nothing more harmful than piles of old dry bones.

I struggled out from under the remains of Elegis and clambered to my feet next to Bhreac. He paused for a moment as we looked across the field. Skeletal remains were everywhere, and the mortals, unaware the threat passed, were still screaming and frantically running. Bhreac looked at me, then bowed his head slightly while offering the sword.

"Your Lordship," he murmured.

I took the sword, and my divine quest was complete. The moment my hand closed around the pommel, I felt my deified power course through me. The remaining mortals must have seen or felt the emergence of my godhood. They backed away, and many averted their eyes. I grabbed Bhreac by the shoulder to teleport back to the Underworld when a young priestess caught my eye. Or, I should say, caught it again. She was the same green-eyed ginger I had noticed when Dala held us captive, and unlike the others, her gaze bored straight through me. It was cold, angry, and brimming with hate.

How I hadn't recognized those eyes, no matter how many years later, is a mystery I still cannot understand.

THANATOS
AND THE
HOUSE
AT THE
END
OF THE WORLD

BY

MARC TIZURA

THANATOS,
GOD OF DEATH

*T*HANATOS JOURNAL ENTRY
TYPE: REMNANT WORLD ONE
NUMBER: WORLD NINETEEN
DATE: JULY 5TH, 1946

What a desolate place!

No structures stood in this place. There were no trees. No birds sang, no animals stirred, and no flies buzzed. A coat of thick black ash covered the ground. Yet I felt the pull of souls in the north, and my feet moved me in that direction like a magnet.

In the mornings, the skies were gray and overcast. Occasionally it rained water, sometimes ash, sometimes both. I alternated between flight and continuing to trek this barren landscape. At night, there was a strange luminescence under the cloud-covered sky, and lightning storms charged the air. I rested and stared off at the horizon, hearing the cry of a thousand wayward and lost souls. I felt their panic and confusion. It's a heavy sinking feeling in my heart and stomach. The back of my head tingled with static electricity as they searched for passage to the other side.

I wanted to give them the relief of that passage. It was my duty. Even though I had abdicated on my world, that didn't mean I was not still a god, let alone the God of Death.

"I am coming. I will bring you aid. I will bring sweet, blessed, and kind relief," I told the empty horizon.

The nights were cold, almost like winter minus the snow. There was nothing to burn to keep warm, so my wings would have to do the trick. They came in handy that way. I removed my trench coat. My cloak, now long discarded, was in the dark purple pouch in the backpack I carried. I unfurled my wings and wrapped them around myself to sustain my body heat. As always, they did the job well. I didn't sleep like most of my fellow gods or mortals, but entered a meditative state to rest.

At what I considered sunrise, I broke camp and started moving. The sinking sensation got stronger, which meant I was nearing the place where the souls wandered. My heart raced faster than Hermes on caffeine, which was a funny story, but that's for later. The static in the back of my head felt as if Zeus himself hit me with a lightning bolt. That's another funny story, but later.

I saw my destination on the horizon, making my nerves and hair stand on edge. It was the only structure I had found still standing in this empty world, an old, decrepit, wooden Victorian mansion. I stared in wide-eyed wonderment of this thing. Two thoughts ran through my mind. One, *how in Tartarus is this thing still standing?* Two, *where are all the gods?*

I was about to find the answers to both these questions.

Before I approached the house, I removed my pouch from my backpack. The little dark purple bag felt heavy in my hand. I'd told myself I would never don my cloak again after leaving my world, my Pantheon, behind. Not since August 9th, 1945, and yet here I am, about to drape it over myself. Honestly, what else could I do for these souls? I had a duty, and whoever was this world's version of me, had failed in his. I would bear the weight and pick up the slack.

I opened the pouch and removed the cloak. The light material weighed a ton. I stared between it and the house. The souls urged me to come in. All their voices were chattering away in my ears and filled my head like a maddening cacophony. I draped the leaden cloak over my shoulders, and it embraced me as it always had. It carried the essence of the one who wove it, my mother, Nyx. Even here and now, I heard the echo of her begging me not to go, and screaming my name as I fled. Tears threatened to run down my cheeks. I sucked it up and walked up to the house.

I climbed the creaky wooden stairs to the double doors. On my right, the porch had been extended to make an outside patio sitting area. I heard running footsteps from that direction. A child! A little girl! A soul! The first to claim. I pivoted to the right and stared into empty space. My mind raced.

Empty space? But how? I should be able to see the soul.

The creaking sound the doors made as they opened inward interrupted my thoughts. I turned slowly, the soul's cries only growing louder from the open maw. An image of a carnival performer placing his head inside a lion's mouth came to mind as I gazed into the house. I swallowed hard and audibly, then slowly exhaled to calm myself, summoning my will. My sense of duty drove me forward and over the threshold.

The doors slammed shut with a bang behind me, stirring up a small cloud of dust. I stood there, taking in the cavernous inside. It was well kept, despite the outside falling apart. I saw hardwood floors covered in expensive looking area rugs, a grand staircase, long halls that stretched forever, and multiple doorways. I stepped away from the doors and entered the drawing room.

A fire roared in the fireplace. To my right were two massive windows with a bench seat under them. In the center of the room, on the area rug, two leather high-back chairs sat with a small circular table between them. A small bar with glasses and alcohol was to the right of the fireplace, and a plant sat to its left. There were bookshelves stacked with books, and in front of me were closed sliding doors. The house went silent, still, and then...

Thump!

Thump!

Thump!

The sound was coming from my right, and my head spun in that direction. Unease filled me when I saw him. A fat, middle-aged man, balding at the back of his head. He wore black slacks and a white button-down shirt with the sleeves rolled up. He walked into the open part of the wall near the fireplace, bounced off, and walked into the wall again. I stood there, watching him do this repeatedly.

I attempted to sense him, his name, his past, so I could identify this lost soul. I reached my hand out and closed my eyes in concentration. I couldn't find him. Shocked, I opened my eyes. It was a soul. It was a dead man Death came to claim. I carefully walked over to him.

I placed my hand on his shoulder and received a large static shock. I pulled back with a hiss, shaking my now numb and throbbing palm. When the tingles stopped, I reached out and touched his shoulder again. Yes, there was a charge and a painful tingle, but I had no idea what that meant or why it was happening.

I turned the overweight man to face me so I could address him. He did not have a face, yet he screamed at my touch. It wasn't an open maw, but as if skin had grown over his face and mouth. I let the panicking soul go and took a step away. He staggered back, still screaming, and tripped as if he was lifted off his feet and thrown. Where he would have landed on his back, he fell through the floor instead. I dropped to a knee and felt the floor where he went through. One of those closed doors slid open.

I looked over my shoulder and saw a little black-haired girl in a white dress regarding me. I rose and walked to her. She smiled warmly at me, and I put on my most reassuring smile for her. I squatted down to be on eye level with the little one, my knee popping as I did. That made her giggle, and I laughed, too.

"Hello, dear one. My name is Thanatos, the God of Death. I am here to help, and there is no reason to be afraid," I said.

She nodded emphatically, causing her long black curls to bounce. Her eyes were bright and intelligent despite the black circles around them. Her smile was toothy, full of joy, and what I mistook for innocence.

"But you are wrong about one thing, God of Death who flees," she started.

My heart sank as I asked, "What did I get wrong, dear one?"

134

"You do have to be scared," she finished, giggling.

"Of what?" I asked, my throat feeling dry.

"Me!" she answered.

I gulped as she giggled. Unseen shadow tentacles rose from the ground and wrapped around my legs. I was slammed to the floor, and pulled down one of the many infinite hallways as her giggles followed.

The tentacles whipped me through the house. I careened around a corner, and my head made contact with the wall. I blacked out to the sound of the little girl's laughter.

I hung suspended in that darkness as something warm and wet ran down my face. An all-too-familiar voice called my name from what seemed a long distance.

"Thannnner! Thannnner! Get up, Thanner," the voice said.

It was Hypnos, my twin brother. *What was he doing here? He couldn't travel. Not like me.*

I opened my eyes, or rather, I tried to. They were sticky and tough to open, and my left one watered badly. Black ichor ran down from the gash in my forehead, where it had smacked into the wall.

I sat up, head throbbing. I wiped my eyes and blinked several times to clear them. Hypnos' voice spoke to me again, cutting through the ache in my head.

"Thanner? You okay, little brother?" Hypnos asked.

"Hyp? Where are you?" I asked, looking around at what appeared to be a once lavish but now dilapidated dining room.

"To your right," Hypnos answered.

I looked, but could only see a wall from where I was sitting on the floor. I chuckled and shook my head. He was having a game with me.

"That's a wall, Hyp," I told him.

"Look up, genius," Hypnos said.

I looked up, and on the wall was a mirror, and inside was the face of my twin. There were two differences between us. He'd never had wings, which I found odd. Also, I wore a beard, and he always kept his face clean-shaven. Ever keen on his looks, my dear older brother was. I touched the glass, but my hand didn't pass through. It was solid, and Hypnos's gold-black eyes followed where my fingertips met the silver surface. I looked at him, full of confusion and wonderment, and he merely shrugged in response. I knocked on it, and he took a couple of steps back.

"Hyp? How did you get in there?" I asked.

"Maybe I am not here. Maybe this is in your head. I mean, you did smack it pretty hard. The house could be messing with you. Maybe I found a way to travel, and I am just waiting until you catch up, Thanner," Hypnos said.

"That's a lot of maybes, Hyp. My head hurts real bad. I can't...can't make sense of all that," I told him.

The sound of a doorknob turning filled the empty room. Both of us looked towards the far wall. There was a door down there next to the fireplace. The knob was turning, but the door was not giving. Whatever was on the other side began to pound on it. Growling its displeasure at not gaining access to the room.

"Uh oh, that's not good. They are coming back, Thanner," Hypnos said, turning his attention back to me.

"Who is coming back, Hyp?" I asked.

"The gods of this world. I gotta run, and you should run, too. Come find me, little brother," he said.

He turned and fled from the mirror, going out a door down the hallway. I stood there, mouth agape, unable to take my eyes from where my brother once stood.

"Son of a bi...." I stared at the door at the end of the room. It gave way and finally opened.

I watched as they strolled in, a group of gods and goddesses with familiar faces. A fire ignited in the hearth as they arrived, and I could see their *offness*. The smell of cooking human flesh filled my nose. I hadn't seen it before, not until the fireplace lit up. There was a spit in there with a human torso on it.

I looked over their faces and saw that their teeth had grown large and sharp, no longer fitting entirely in their mouths. It left them with permanent toothy smiles as their cheeks and lips had eroded or ripped away to make room. They went to the center of the room, where the long dining room table sat on a worn-out area rug. I recognized them. Dinlas, Eros, Artemis, Nike, Urania, Hestia, Asteria, my mother Nyx, and sister Nemesis, plus an almost-familiar redhead at the table...Moxie.

They spoke to one another in an unintelligible garbling dialect that not even my abilities as a god could make out. I began to wonder...

Where are the rest?

My eyes fell on the torso, and I sucked in a gasp as realization sank in. They were eating themselves. They had become cannibals. Then I heard the little girl's voice. The gods at the table froze in place, as if they were statues.

"The gods of this world belong to me, coward. They are my favorite playthings," she said, her voice emanating from the walls.

"If that was the case, small one, where are the other gods?" I asked.

"Oh, yes, them. I got bored with them and put them on a permanent timeout. Look above, cowardly god," she instructed with a giggle.

I turned my gaze upward and saw them, the rest of the gods. Their heads mounted to the wall like hunter trophies. Their cannibalistic smiles forever etched upon their faces. I swallowed audibly as the walls rang out with childish laughter. The cannibal gods at the table slowly, and in unison, turned their heads to look at me. I was in trouble now. Then I heard Hypnos' voice through the walls.

"Should have run when I told you, Thanner."

They rose from their seats at the table in complete unison as I raised my empty hands. My scythe. I dropped it in the drawing room when I got yanked down the hall. I reached out, trying to move them telekinetically. It had no effect. I balled up my fist and assumed the honor stance, ready to fight as I unfurled my wings.

While my attention was on them, I did not notice the three black tentacles rise from the floor behind me. Two shot out and hit the back of my knees, forcing me to them. The third slammed into my back, pounding me into the floor. They wrapped themselves around me, two for my wrists, one for my throat. They grew taut where they had seized me, and the one around my throat lifted my face off the floor. Fresh ichor ran from my lips and nose.

The cannibal gods were on top of me with hot breath and long sticky strands of saliva falling from their mouths. Their snarling cries filled my ears. I could feel their hungry desire for my flesh. I closed my eyes, and everything in the world grew silent.

Why is it so quiet?

I opened my eyes, and the tentacles still held me fast. I looked around and knew where I was. I let out a heavy sigh. The day was April 30th, 1945. The sky was overcast, and there was a spring chill in the air. I looked around at the rubble-strewn ground. The air smelled of things burning, and dead bodies were buried under the debris. The sounds of planes and gunfire rumbled in the distance. Behind me was a bunker, and inside of it were two freshly dead souls bound for Tartarus. In front of me, the cannibal gods played in the rubble.

The cannibal Artemis stood before me, and I knew this was the spot where I proposed. This was the spot where I was rejected by duty, honor, and title. The ring I was going to give her, still worn on a chain around my neck, felt as if it weighed a ton. She had a look of greed in her eyes. A string of drool hung from her mouth as she leaned in and reached into my cloak. She grabbed the necklace and pulled it out. She stared at the ring and cried out to them, and they came with chunks of debris in hand. She pulled the chain off my neck, snapping it as she did so. She slipped it onto her finger to the applauding approval from the gods.

White-hot rage seethed up in me, and I yelled and screamed at them, "You give that back! That doesn't belong to you! It's not yours! It belongs to her! My Huntress, not you! You sick, malformed creature! Give me back what is mine!"

They all snarled and hissed. The Artemis leaned down and roared her hot breath into my face, leaving it covered in spittle. She wasn't done either. She drew her arm back and slammed her fist into and through my chest, ripping out my heart. I gasped for air and continued to pant as she held it over her head in victory. The others howled and cried out to the overcast sky. The Moxie cannibal came down and caressed my cheek before slapping a piece of rubble into the gash in my forehead, causing it to bleed again.

The Artemis took a huge bite from my heart and chewed. As if it was a cue to the others, they all lifted a piece of stone and aimed it at me. They drew their arms back, and I closed my eyes, waiting for the impact of concrete. And then, nothing.

I breathed in and out normally. I felt my heart once again beat in my chest. In my ear was the sound of tittering, high-pitched laughter. The type reserved for the loony bin or Tartarus. I opened my eyes and found myself in a dusty, musty attic with a single circular window that provided the only light source. The sound of a rocking chair moving back and forth filled the room. I recognized the voice. It was mine. It was this other-world version of me. I looked at the other me in the chair. Dust covered his cloak. A chain wrapped around his neck, the other end fastened to the wall, keeping him/me bound there. His beard was long and snow white. He had a crazed, vacant look in his obsidian eyes.

"Hello, Thanatos," he said in a high, reedy voice. "Son of Nyx, father of none. Not surprising, really. We'll never be a father, being sterile and whatnot. Brother of…"

He began to take count of my two thousand plus siblings. Between each name, the Other Thanatos broke out into that high-pitched, tittering laughter.

Down at the other end of the attic a new sound emerged, and I looked to see the cannibal Moxie on a wooden swing. She was barefoot and swinging back and forth, back and forth. She had a strange look in her eyes that I couldn't quite place. Then the walls filled with the little girl's giggles, causing them to shake.

"Oh, I am in trouble now."

The giggling stopped, the house stopped shaking, and an unnerving sense of calm filled the place. All I could hear was the other me rocking in his chair, laughing under his breath, and the Moxie cannibal swinging back and forth on the far side of the room. Then, the chair and swing stopped, adding to the uneasy silence.

"Mmm…somebody is in trouble now," the Other Than said, breaking into mad gales of laughter.

I grimaced as Moxie's own guttural chortle joined his maniacal laughter. In unison, he began to rock, and she began to swing.

This was bedlam! Madness!

"What happened here!?" I demanded of my other self.

He stopped rocking and stared vacantly at me, where I remained kneeling on the floor. I felt hot breath on my neck and turned to find the cannibal Moxie staring down at me. She panted in my ear, making low growling noises. Her touch was unexpectedly soft and tender as she reached out to caress my cheek. There was a look of desperation in her eyes. She opened her mouth and let out three short grunts. She skipped past me on bare feet to the Other Than. Sitting on the floor at his feet, she wrapped herself around his leg. He reached down and patted her head.

"Have you ever seen a creature so beautiful?" he asked, looking down at the Moxie cannibal.

They stared at each other with complete adoration and devotion. In my world, Hera had kept my version of Moxie in a child's body. Moxie had always been Hera's little Mou. The body this Moxie inhabited, I remembered, she wore it in my world as well, now dead before her time. The other me continued to stroke her hair as she hugged his leg.

How was he touching her with his bare hand and not killing the mortal vessel she inhabited?

This time I asked instead of demanded, "What happened here?"

The other me looked at me, smiled, and answered.

"Emma. Emma happened here. Her parents trapped the Goddess Hekate and attempted to make a deal for their sickly daughter's life. It backfired, obviously."

"Obviously," I agreed.

I stiffened, and a chill ran down my spine, my wings unfurling as I inhaled sharply. The Other Than and cannibal Moxie froze. His wings opened, and her gaze focused on the stairs that lead down to the main level of the house. He let loose a maddening sound.

"Aye-eeeee-eeeee!"

Cannibal Moxie growled with long strands of saliva running out of her mouth, down her chin, and onto the floor. I cast my gaze that way and saw the little girl, Emma, standing at the top of the stairs smiling at us. The Other Than hyperventilated and rocked frantically in his chair. I rose to face the little dead girl, drawing to my full height and authority.

"Emma, you've been a naughty girl, and it is time to stop!" I commanded, pointing my index finger at her.

She shot me a toothy grin, and her brown eyes lit with mischief and ill will. She approached me to the panicked sounds of both the Other Than and cannibal Moxie. I stood my ground, index finger still extended firmly in her direction. She stopped right at the tip of my outstretched finger and bit it hard. I cried out, pulling back as she flashed razor-sharp fangs at me. I held my hand to my chest and looked down at the little demon. She didn't break the skin or tear my glove, but it was enough to smart.

I looked over at the Other Than and cannibal Moxie to see he had one of his wings covering her protectively, while she peered around it snarling. I looked back at Emma. She was dead, possibly cursed by Hekate, but she was a soul, and a soul was a soul that needed reaping. She continued to bare her sharp teeth at me as I removed my glove.

I reached out quickly, catching her off guard and slamming my palm into her chest. She roared and growled like a wild beast, causing the house to shake again, bringing panicked sounds from the other me and cannibal Moxie. Emma's veins turned black, her eyes became a dead white, and her skin took on a bluish hue. She continued to scream as I began to extract the white glowing light of her soul from her chest. When it was halfway out, it spoke to me, to tell its tale, as all souls do.

"Mama, I want to go outside and play with the other kids!" she called from her bed.

"No, Em! You know not in this cold weather, baby. You wouldn't be able to breathe out there," Mama answered from the other room.

"Mama, I need friends!" she called from a wheelchair, looking out the window, watching the other children running around outside.

"We can have someone come over, but you can't get too excited. Remember your heart, my angel. And you will need to wear your mask and gloves," Mama replied.

"Are you sure we've done the right thing?" Mama whispered to Papa.

"Yes, the goddess Atë was very specific," Papa responded.

Hekate's dead body lay stretched out behind them, overlaying runes drawn on the hardwood floor. A glass beaker glowed in Papa's hand, filled with the Goddess of Magick's golden ichor and magic. They marched to Emma's room and had her drink the golden pulsing liquid. They created a monster.

The soul was nearly free of the pale blue creature. It was almost mine. Once reaped, there was hope that I could fix this nightmare they had created. Without warning, I was flung across the room. I lost my grip on the soul and it reentered the horror that was Emma. She snarled at me as the top of her head flattened, pulling back to a point, and her white eyes grew large in their sockets. Shadow tentacles danced around her aura as she lolled out a massive black tongue and ran it over her sharp teeth.

"No one was my friend in life, so they will all be my friends in death," Emma snarled and retreated down the stairs.

I did damage, and now it was time to end this, or so I thought. I would need some help. I stood up and walked over to the other me and the cannibal Moxie. Both of them stared at me in wide-eyed wonderment. I drew on my will and snapped the collar around the Other Than's neck. He rose shakily to his feet, Moxie hovering protectively close. The Other Than wobbled, and she grabbed his biceps and wrist, holding him up. He smiled a wide, lunatic smile.

"Oh, you! You are going to die!" he told me and cackled.

The cannibal Moxie joined in the laughter. I had to push down the rage I felt towards both them and the girl Emma.

"Come now. The merry chase is afoot. You do remember the merry chase, don't you?" I asked the other me.

"Oh, yes. I remember it very well," he said, letting out another round of tittering laughter.

I nodded, and he imitated me, laughing all the while.

"So serious, so stoic, my lord," the other me said with a great sweeping bow.

The Moxie cannibal applauded this show with, what I could only describe as, sounds of delight. The Other Than looked up at her from his bow and winked. She reached out and stroked his face as he rose. Taking her hand, he held it to his cheek and leaned in to kiss her. I groaned impatiently at them and gestured to the stairs. The entire house shook, and the two of them grabbed on to each other like frightened children. I raced to the stairs and down them, determined to put an end to this once and for all.

I got to the landing, then there was no landing, and into the abyss I tumbled. I flapped my wings furiously, trying to gain control and a sense of direction, but there was none to be had. Voices called to me. The gods of this world's Pantheon, the dead, and the lost. All of them screaming, crying, and begging for help that I could not give. Then Emma's voice cut through the darkness, thunderous and final.

"Silence!"

The voices went silent, and I landed on my knees in the dining room, looking directly into the eyes of the cannibal Artemis. She wore a triumphant sneer on her face, her silver bow and arrow aimed at me. She showed off the ring she wore, the one she stole from me. She let loose the arrow, and it flew, sinking deep into my shoulder.

The pain was sharp and immediate. The arrow digging itself into my flesh. I bared my teeth against it, and the Artemis cannibal laughed as she nocked another arrow. I clenched my jaw. She fired, and I rolled out of the way, the arrow whizzing past my ear.

I pulled the arrow from my shoulder. The white-hot pain I was feeling was excruciating, and fresh black ichor gushed from the wound. I rose as she was getting her bow ready to fire again. With my wing, I knocked it out of the way and out of her hands. It went sailing across the room and clattered to the ground.

She staggered back, and I caught her by her braid, pulling her close to me. With all the force I could muster, I pushed the arrow I held up through the soft skin underneath her chin, piercing the soft palate, and into her brain. The arrowhead stuck out nicely from the top of her head. The cannibal Artemis collapsed dead onto the ground as I released her. I reached down and pulled the ring from her finger. I held in front of her dead eyes, baring my teeth at her.

"This is mine!" I told the dead goddess.

Applause came from behind me, and I whipped my head around to see the Other Than and Cannibal Moxie applauding my kill. At the feet of the Other Than were two scythes, his and mine. I reached out and called mine to me. It lifted off the ground and flew into my outstretched hand. I closed my fingers around the handle as it sang its familiar song to me. I was filled with a strange sense of peace at being reunited with my scythe.

"How did you...?" I started to ask.

"We stopped at the front on our way to find you, didn't we, dearest?" he answered.

Cannibal Moxie grunted her agreement, and the two of them rubbed noses in an Eskimo kiss. I rolled my eyes. I knew from my own world, such affection was not meant for the likes of me, but how these two managed amazed me.

The house shook again as Emma loosed an animalistic scream of rage. I rose to my feet, scythe at the ready. The Other Than came to me, scythe in hand, and we stood back to back, wing to wing, the cannibal Moxie at our side.

"You killed my friend! You're a bad god! Bad, bad, bad, bad! I am coming to destroy you!" Emma raged.

There was no doubt we were in the end game now.

The house stopped shaking. It was another one of those *calm before the storm* type moments. I remained on guard and could feel the Other Than tense in the heavy silence. My senses were on hyper-drive, b*attle-ready*, as Ares would have called it. I heard my breathing, the other me breathing, cannibal Moxie breathing, and someone else was breathing in the room with us. I focused on this fourth presence and realized it was the room.

I watched the walls, and with every inhale, they drew inward. With every exhale, they pushed out just the faintest bit. I swallowed hard. It was an audible sound in the silence. My eyes drifted upward to the mounted gods' heads. They looked down on us with fresh streams of drool running from the lips of their unclosable mouths.

The floor beneath our feet bucked up and slammed down, throwing us all off balance. We staggered to regain our footing as it did it again and again and again. We rolled around, violently slamming into the walls and tables as the floor lifted and dropped.

I finally had enough and demanded, "Enough, little girl! Emma, you come stand before me, and face me!"

"Why?" she asked, giggling. "Haven't you ever played chess before, Mr. Death? Don't you know you send in the pawns before you obtain the queen?"

I looked at the Other Than, our gazes locking as I asked, "Pawns?"

Similar looks of understanding slid onto our faces, the *Oh* moment. She meant the other cannibal gods still lurking. Minus cannibal Artemis, whom I just killed, and cannibal Moxie, who was loyal to this world's Than. They would not factor into her pawns. That was when cannibal Nemesis dropped onto my back from the ceiling. Cannibals Eros and Dinlas smashed through the floorboards, grabbing the Other Than and cannibal Moxie.

I spun around and staggered about the room with the monstrous version of my older sister clinging to my back. She held fast with her knees and put me into a chokehold. I cried out in pain as her sharp, serrated teeth dug into my right shoulder. I snarled and unfurled my wings, shocking her into releasing her bite, but her stranglehold around my neck grew tighter. I flapped my wings and flew backward into the wall, slamming her into it as hard as I could. The wall was so weak we broke right through it.

We smashed through into a kitchen. Like most of the house, it was in a state of decay and ruination. I flung cannibal Nemesis from my back and skidded across the floor into the leg of a rusting metal table. She rebounded and raced at me, snarling on all fours like a beast. I was quick to recover myself, and as she lunged, I ducked, making a diagonal slice with my scythe. She sailed over me, landed on her feet, and turned to face me. I rose from my crouch and spun to confront her. I saw the deep cut I had made. It ran from her left shoulder across her top half in a diagonal line. She took a step and paused with a perplexed look on her face. The top half of her torso slid off, killing the warped version of my sister.

I stepped over her and back through the hole into the dining room to regroup with the Other Than and cannibal Moxie. I had my scythe at the ready as I came through, only to find that Other Than had disemboweled cannibal Dinlas, and cannibal Moxie held the top part of cannibal Eros' head. She playfully waved it back and forth, showing it to me like some trophy she had won.

"All right, so who is next?" I asked.

"Mother," the Other Than said weakly.

I closed my eyes and winced as I felt our mother's presence behind me. I turned and saw Nyx, Goddess of Night, snarling like a dog. Long strands of saliva hung between her massive sharpened teeth. Her wings flung open, and she lunged at me with her arms outstretched, mouth open in a growl. I retreated backward, stumbled over the body of cannibal Eros, and fell to the ground. She flew, raining hot spittle down on me. I watched the rest in slow motion. Our growling, snarling mother flew forward, and the cannibal Moxie jumped out of the way. The Other Than sidestepped and raised his scythe, bringing it down on her neck. Nyx's head hit the ground and rolled as her body hit the wall. She fell to the ground flopping like a fish, her wings flapping as the nerves died.

I rose slowly to my feet, unable to look away from our mother's dying body. The house shook again as Emma let loose another animalistic scream of rage. The three of us sprinted out of the room and down one of the infinite hallways. Emma's howls followed us as we ran past doors at a maddening pace. Similar to the breathing, the walls flexed with her cries, and the floor behind us rose in a massive wave, pursuing us as we fled.

The floor was at our heels and closing in as we dove through the nearest door. The wave rolled past us. We sat on the floor of a decaying library, catching our breath. I stood, while the Other Than gathered cannibal Moxie into his arms, hugging her close as they cowered on the floor. I went to a bookcase covered in dust and cobwebs, reached my hand through where a pane of glass should have been and touched a book. It collapsed into a pile of grayish-white ash on the warped bookshelf. I know what you're thinking, everything I touch dies, but it wasn't me this time. The books were just that old.

I wiped the book dust from my hands and turned my attention to the couple on the floor. Cannibal Moxie sat in Other Than's lap with her arms wrapped around his neck, and her head resting against his shoulder. His arms were wrapped around her waist, and they had stopped shaking. The sight of the two lovers brought a smile to my face, and I felt hope that this could be me someday. That maybe, I could find someone to touch and be close with, just as these two creatures had. I would have pursued this line of thought more, but I was interrupted.

"Peek-a-boo, I seee yoouuuu," Emma said from nowhere, the *you* became a deep, distorted growl.

The three of us tensed, and the two lovers rose to their feet as I marched over to join them in the center of the room. We stood back to back in a triangle pattern, waiting to see which of the cannibals would appear. Perhaps Emma herself would come and confront us now. I faced the doorway, Cannibal Moxie faced the window, and the Other Than faced the bookshelves. We didn't have to wait long, as what I thought were the last three cannibals came barging into the room from various directions.

Cannibal Urania crashed through the window, showering the room with broken glass. Cannibal Moxie lunged for her, and they grappled, rolling around on the floor. Cannibal Hestia came through the bookcase. The Other Than screamed and raced to meet her, which left the cannibal Asteria, the Starry One, my friend on my world. She stood in the doorway, growling low, and charged at me as I advanced on her. She fell to her knees as my shoulder rammed into her stomach. She made no further move to defend herself, simply closed her eyes as I swung my scythe, severing her head from her shoulders. Her body fell over, twitching.

It was over so quickly. It was as if these cannibal gods realized we could end them and their suffering, and they were taking us up on the offer.

"It's as if they sacrificed themselves to us," the Other Than said, looking down at the body of the cannibal Hestia.

"I had the same thought," I confessed.

Cannibal Moxie grunted her agreement while holding the top of cannibal Urania's head. She wrapped herself around the Other Than's arm, clutching her new trophy. He smiled at her, and they proceeded to Eskimo kiss, making happy humming noises.

"Was that all of them?" I asked.

As soon as the question was out of my mouth, she flew in through the open window. The cannibal Nike, Goddess of Victory. How does one beat the Goddess of Victory?

She landed in front of us, snarling with her lance in hand. The Other Than ran at her, scythe poised to attack. She dodged the swiping weapon with the grace of a dancer and, in one motion, used the lance to sweep Other Than's feet out from under him. He hit the ground hard, and the impact knocked the wind out of him. While she crouched, I believed her distracted, and I made my move. A swift booted kick to my chest defeated me. Her foot caught me center mass, and I hit the ground, sailing across the floor to the doorway.

She rose and lorded over the Other Than, raising her lance, intending to impale him. She brought it down, but he rolled out of the way. It left her kneeling, holding onto the lance which had gone deep into the floor and gotten stuck. The miss infuriated cannibal Nike. She roared and snarled, trying to pull the lance from the ground, and that's when the cannibal Moxie leaped onto her back.

Nike flailed as Moxie wrapped herself around her. Once she was securely on the back of her adversary, she threw a forearm around Nike's throat in a chokehold. Nike howled indignantly, and Moxie made her move. It was lightning quick. She thrust her free hand into her open, screaming mouth. Slipping her fingers between the spaces of cannibal Nike's teeth, Moxie got a good grip, and yanked. With a wet ripping, sucking noise, the top of Nike's head came off in her hand.

Cannibal Moxie let the body of Nike go, allowing it to fall to the floor with a thump. Golden ichor pooled on the floor. The body of cannibal Nike twitched as Moxie put one barefoot on the center of her back. Raising the top of cannibal Nike's head high, in a two-handed gesture of victory, the cannibal Moxie let loose a victory cry.

"She's gorgeous!" the Other Than proclaimed from the floor.

I merely groaned from the doorway.

That was all of her pawns. Now it was time to bring on the little monster.

I rose slowly from the doorway while cannibal Moxie discarded the top half of cannibal Nike's head and hurried to help the Other Than off the floor. They held one another, smiled, and rubbed noses. She made a little vocal sigh as he chuckled. I watched, filled with amazement and disbelief.

"How?" I asked.

"How what, my lord?" Other Than answered, not looking at me, just gazing deeply into cannibal Moxie's sea-green eyes.

"The touching. How?" I asked, feeling eager and hungry for the answer. Maybe if I knew it, the secret, I could carry it back to my world, my Pantheon.

The answer crushed me.

"Emma. She is responsible for this unexpected bit of happiness. When she altered her, my love, my Moxie, it finally gave me the ability to touch the one my heart desires. I know what you are thinking. Do you really want to bring that little monster back to your world, knowing what she did here?" the Other Than said, still gazing deeply into Moxie's eyes. They looked as if they were hypnotized.

"But with Moxie...she was always in a child's body. What of the Huntress? Now, there is a goddess to go after. There is my lov--" I began to grandstand, but he cut me off.

"The Huntress? Oh, la-de-da, the huuuuntressss! That is a child's love. A child's crush. A child's hopes and obsession. You and I are the chaste ones, loving our goddesses from afar. The only difference is my love was accepted. My love is a matured process that has blossomed over time. Then there is you, carrying that ring around your—"

There would have been more, but a black tentacle shot out, hard and fast. It separated the lovers and sent the Other Than sailing backward. The tentacle was no longer a shadow form, but a solid black skin with an inky texture and something else. Something I would discover later, and it would terrify me. The tentacle receded back into the wall, followed by the sound of Emma giggling.

We raced to him. The tentacle had cut him in two, just below the waist. I almost tripped over his legs while cannibal Moxie nimbly leaped over them. A massive pooling of black ichor stretched between his lower limbs and stomach. He coughed and laughed that high tittering cackle. Cannibal Moxie cradled him in her arms, making low keening noises in the back of her throat. My mouth hung agape. Until this moment, I was confident and assured that you could not kill the God of Death. Yet here I was, staring at my own mortality, to coin a human phrase. He smiled weakly at me and bid me close with a gesture. The cannibal Moxie's keening grew louder and mixed with heartbreaking sobbing sounds.

He panted, and though I didn't think it was possible, he looked paler. I knelt at his side, and with great effort, he thrust his scythe into my hands. He coughed, and hot ichor bubbled from his mouth and down his chin. The Moxie's cries grew louder, and I just stared on uncomprehendingly. I took his scythe with a numb hand. He noticed, chuckled, and closed his fingers over mine so I would grip it.

"You will bury it in the world of sleepwalkers," the Other Than said, laughing insanely.

"World of what?" I asked.

A mad cackle was his only answer. He was still laughing when he began to emit black smoke from every orifice. Until he was nothing but an empty cloak and a puddle of black ichor. Cannibal Moxie threw back her head and screamed, but there was no time to mourn. I felt the hackles on the back of my neck stand up. Three inky black tentacles came crashing through the walls.

Carrying the scythes with one hand, I seized the wailing Moxie's forearm and hauled her to her feet. She kept a death grip, pun intended, on the Other Than's cloak as we fled from the room.

The tentacle came bursting through, demolishing the wall and doorway as we ran down the hall. We made our way to what I believed was the front entrance and our escape into the desolate world. Far away from this child monster.

"Bastard God of Death and bitch Goddess of Metamorphosis, I am coming for you! Olly olly oxen free!" Emma called out from inside the walls.

It seemed with every room we passed along this infinite hallway, more sets of inky black tentacles came bursting through. They were snapping at our heels, coming close to tripping us as the demon giggled. She was a cat, playing with her mice before she ate them. But I would not be eaten, nor would this version of Moxie. I would see to that. Six of the appendages busted through the floorboards in front of us, stopping us dead in our tracks. This time I saw what disturbed me so greatly upon my first encounter with the physical tentacles.

Where most creatures with tentacles would have suction cups, these had faces. More specifically, the faces of the dead. Of every man, woman, and child whose life she had taken. Pale, ghost-like apparitions with black hair and black, sunken, hollowed-out eyes. All of them screaming in silent agony and horror.

I gasped, my cry caught in my throat as my skin broke out in goosebumps. I was momentarily petrified, unable to look away from their tortured faces. What's worse, I heard them screaming inside my head. I panted, trying to gather my will and thoughts while the faces swirled around inside the tentacle as if in some sort of storm. I felt cannibal Moxie hide behind me, falling to her knees and pulling my cloak in front of her like a shield.

I knew what to do. Taking both scythes, one in each hand, and crossing the blades in front of me, I severed the tentacles that stood in our way. The house screamed and shook as the appendages fell to the floor, pouring out a black sticky fluid. With a simple summoning of my will and a squeeze of my hand, I puffed the souls trapped inside out of existence. A small wisp of white smoke, a small flash of light, and there was white soul powder on the floor. I don't use this power often and usually only at the behest of Zeus, Hera, or Hades. I would use it here and now to give these trapped souls relief. I turned to cannibal Moxie, who buried her face in the cloak of the fallen Than and wept bitterly into it.

"Come now! We have to go while the coast is clear," I said, pointing forward.

She looked up at me, tears streaking her dirty cheeks. She moaned and held out the cloak while shaking her head emphatically, refusing to move, refusing to go onward. I nodded in understanding.

"Then do you seek release, to go forth to the hinterland, to be reunited with he who has passed?" I asked.

She continued to hold out the Other Than's cloak and nodded. I nodded in return and raised my scythe, steeling myself as I brought it down, taking off her head. Her lifeless body fell, and her true self exited it. Her brilliant white golden form floated inches above the floor, and I raised my scythe again to deal her the blow that would send her on. A tentacle shot through and out of the goddess' chest.

Everything froze at that moment. My heart dropped, and my arms lowered as she hung suspended by the sickly looking appendage. She gave me one final, mournful look with those sea-green eyes and sparked out of existence. The smell of ozone hung heavy in the air as the last white and gold sparks faded from view.

"Got you, you bitch!" Emma growled.

I flapped my wings and literally flew through the rest of the house and out the front door. The tentacles chased me, breaking up the house as they went. I swept down and grabbed my backpack off the front porch. I was taking my stuff with me damn it! I landed several feet from the house, and I watched it warily while I secured my pack to my back and tucked the Other Than's scythe away in my purple sack.

The house exploded.

Glass, wood, and other various items rained down all around me. I closed my wings around myself to shelter my body from most of the damage inflicted by the debris shower. When I opened them, I saw it and let out a small cry.

Where the house used to be, a black amorphous being sprouted. Its sickening form reached towards the heavens. It had thousands upon thousands of soul-screaming tentacles that writhed and danced around it. The Lovecraftian horror wore the demon child Emma's face, with hollow black eyes and sharp cannibalistic teeth. The sky above its head had turned the sickly blackish-green color of putrification.

"Oh crap," I muttered as its eyes fell upon me.

One of her massive tentacles came crashing down. And if my paralysis hadn't broken at that moment, I would not be here to tell you this tale. I dodged and rolled out of its way. It made impact with the ground, causing it to shake and crack. I reached out my will and puffed those poor souls out. The tentacle blew up in white smoke, and the Emma beast howled. The sound echoed in the barren landscape.

I took flight, dodging and evading the tentacles the best I could. One sucker-punched me in the gut, and the one above it smacked into my back, slamming me to the ground. Thankfully, adrenaline prevented me from staying still too long. As I crawled away, the tentacle that took me down pounded the ground again, leaving a crater where I would have been. With a grunt of effort, I sliced through the appendage as it came at me again. With a squeeze, I puffed those trapped souls out.

Black ichor ran from my nose, mouth, and another gash on my forehead. I staggered and ran away, unable to clear my head enough for flight. I barely dodged two of the appendages as they came from either direction to grab me. I dropped and rolled, letting my scythe go. With the use of both hands, I puffed the souls out of each tentacle.

I lay there on my back, bleeding and panting from exhaustion. Wiping these souls out en masse took a toll on my body, and I was growing weak. I watched the tentacles rise above, meaning to bear down and smash me into oblivion. I closed my eyes and awaited my fate.

The blow didn't come and the beast roared. I sat up to look. Moxie, in her true form, was darting and weaving around Emma's head. She looked like a pixie from Tartarus from this distance. Emma swung her tentacles wildly in a vain effort to strike her, but Moxie was too quick and dodged them easily. A cloud of black smoke billowed from behind the creature.

No time to figure out what that was, other than my opportunity to escape. I grabbed my scythe and willed it to take me anywhere, somewhere. The blade lit with its majestic colors. I sliced open a rift and jumped through it.

I landed on green grass under a blue sky. It was warm, and I heard people, living people, talking and laughing, children playing. I switched out of my cloak and back into my trench coat. I had a new world to explore.

SWEET DOLLY

BY

AISLING MACKAY

NEMESIS,
GODDESS OF REVENGE

I KNOW HOW YOU MORTALS LIKE YOUR SCARY STORIES. Let me tell you one of mine. It was when the world was celebrating its era of love. August 1969 found me at Woodstock, surrounded by mortals and more than a few immortals. Do I really need to mention Eros and Dionysus? Whose brainchild do you think Woodstock was?

I went mostly out of curiosity and hoping it would be a prime hunting ground for me. But everyone was *so* about peace and drugs and sex, there was no room for thoughts of revenge. Out of boredom, I allowed Dion to talk me into a *little bit of this* and a *little bit of that*. Amidst all the proclamations of brotherly love, my thoughts couldn't help but turn to my brother.

Feeling nostalgic, I ported to the Underworld. My flowing skirt flared about my knees as I turned, dancing over the desolate stretch of shore that bordered Lake Aveinos. The cottage that crouched beneath the cloud-laden sky blended into the rocky terrain, looking as if it had sprung from the ground itself. A darkly beautiful growth born from magic and ancient power.

I ran onto the porch, the grainy black sand clinging to my feet. Able to sense Thanatos within, I pushed through the door, entering onto a small landing. The magic of this realm had folded, creating a pocket of space within the cottage. The inside was much larger than what the small outer dimensions should be able to contain.

The decor could only be described as *creepy chic*. Three steps led down to the cozy main living area. Large, plush recliner chairs flanked a coffee table. The larger of the two sat next to a black, old-fashioned, wood-burning stove and a large window that overlooked the lake. A small but functional kitchen graced the back of the cottage, and a bed rested in the opposite corner.

Flashes of white, red, and purple broke up the black that would seem oppressive to most, but to me felt comforting, the shadows deep and reassuring. Shelves lined the walls of the weird maze of rooms, full of items Thanatos had collected from the shores of the River Styx. Things that had washed up from the mortal world, full of broken hopes, dreams, and promises. All was tidy and neat, everything in its place and shining with near-pristine cleanliness.

Thanatos, the God of Peaceful Death, known to mortals and immortals alike, and my youngest brother, dropped his book as I slammed my way into his home. I twirled about the room, my dark hair flying in all directions and my laughter echoing off the walls, filling the space with sound. His normally staid expression turned to shock at my unexpected arrival and my even more out-of-character behavior. He slowly stood from his chair, his lips quirking just the slightest bit, which on him was a full-out grin.

"Good gods, Nem. Where have you been, and what are you wearing?" he asked, plucking a flower from my loose black curls and taking in my flowing skirt and peasant blouse.

"You should have come, Thano! It was so much fun! Well, first it was boring, but then I found Dion, and it was so much fun after that!" I replied, dancing around him and then flopping back onto his neatly made bed, staring up at the ceiling.

"Ahh, I see," he said, stepping into the kitchen, "and what did Dion offer you that made things so much more fun?"

"Oh, I don't know. A little of this and a little of that! A nip here and a sip there! On her a lick, on him a di--"

"Nemesis!" Thanatos interrupted, horrified laughter filling his tone.

I laughed and curled up on my side. My voice trailed off as sleep dragged my eyes closed. "You should have come, Thano. Would have been more fun with you there."

"I am sure, Nem, but somehow I do not think I would have fit in."

"I didn't fit in, either. Would have been fun to not fit in together," I murmured as sleep pulled me into sweet darkness.

I woke to the smell of pancakes and sausage filling the house. I stretched on the comfortable bed, cozy beneath the soft blankets. Memories surfaced of the last few days and my arrival at Thanatos's. *Good Chaos, what had I let Dion do to me?* I closed my eyes again, mortification staining my cheeks pink. You would have thought after this many years of existence, I would know better. But then maybe I had just needed something to break up the monotony and loneliness.

I opened my eyes, and my gaze focused on an item resting on a shelf above me. My brow furrowing, I stood on the bed and reached for the brass metal urn. Black with age, the screaming face of the demon molded into the front glared malevolently back at me. I ran my fingers over the surface. Odd, this belonged to me. How had it ended up in Than's cottage?

I hopped off the bed with the vase held in my hands. "Hey, Thano?"

"Hmm?" he asked, not turning away from the stove.

"Where did you get this? This is mine."

He glanced over his shoulder. "Oh, yeah. I meant to take that back to your house. It was very odd. I came home one day, and it was sitting on my porch. I just haven't had a chance to return it."

"That is odd," I said, turning the metal over and over in my hands. "Maybe since I am here, I should stop by. It has been seventy-five years or so since I have been back to the house."

"We can go after breakfast if you would like," he offered, "and on the way, you can tell me all about this *Woodstock* you had so much fun attending."

I scowled at the devilish glint in his eyes. "I seem to recall you were none too eager to hear the *details* last night, Thano."

His cheeks flushed lightly. "Uh yeah, you can leave *those details* out, thank you very much."

161

I grinned at him and stole a piece of sausage. Wrapping a pancake around it, I took a bite, savoring the salty-sweet taste. I poured each of us a cup of coffee and, not looking at him, whispered, "I have missed you, Thano."

"Missed you, too, Nem."

After breakfast, we ported to the island I had claimed early in my existence. The trees grew high here, the bark dark, and the trunks twisted about themselves. The leaves overhead were a light green and filtered the light, creating deep pockets of shadow. A mischievous breeze blew my hair into tangles around my face, welcoming me home with soft caresses. It had been doing so since I arrived, seemingly ecstatic at my return.

The Underworld was an assault on the senses. The scents, while not all pleasant, were rich, the color of the light unique to this plane, and while the sounds would have been alien to mortal ears, they spoke of home to me. I inhaled deeply as we rounded the bend in the path, my bare feet silent on the forest floor.

We halted as my manor came into sight. It was a monument to my youth, an edifice that proclaimed my vanity and arrogance. In truth, it was a monstrosity. Gothic in design, formed of massive, cut stone blocks and elaborately carved lintels. Gargoyles stood as silent sentinels on either side of the broad stone steps that led to the large, heavy embellished front door. Spiked metal railings crowned the rooftops, and every last bit of it was black. *How very cliche and dramatic.*

It wasn't the usual flash of embarrassment that I normally felt upon seeing my house that made my brow furrow and raised both my concern and ire. "Chaos's great balls, what has happened here?" I had never kept the grounds pristine, preferring the wilder tangle of the natural flora, but like a dark English cottage garden, things always had a place. Currently, that was not the case. The exterior of the house itself had been neglected, with dark green glowing veins of what looked like moldy tendrils marbling the stone. I turned and glanced at Thanatos. His eyes were filled with concern as he stroked his chin thoughtfully.

"Have you seen anything like this before?" I asked, looking back at the house.

He didn't answer but resumed walking. I followed, my eyes scanning the surroundings. I took notice of how quiet it was. There was no bustle of activity. No movement in and out of the house, as there should be at this time of the day. There were no sounds of creatures from the forest, but most notably, no one had come to greet us. The household would have sensed and been alerted of my presence back in the Underworld, and yet no one had come to meet us. I reached out and pulled Thanatos to a stop just as the door swung open.

"Something is very wrong here, Thano," I said under my breath.

"No doubt. You should have known that if you built what looked like a haunted castle, it would someday become haunted."

"Thano. We live in the Underworld. The whole place is haunted."

He nodded and shrugged. "True. Well, let's go see what beasties lie in wait, shall we?"

I slipped by him and entered first, going preternaturally still as I stepped into the entryway. Where golden light usually filled the castle, today there was a putrid green cast to the air. Dust motes swirled past, seeming to glow in the murky light. The frayed tapestries, now drab and grey, hung precariously on the walls. The remnants of the furniture that once graced the spacious foyer littered the floor and the wide central staircase. We were accosted by the combined reek of the sickly sweet scent of rotting food and the underlying stench of unwashed clothing and bodies.

I padded silently over the stone floor, noting the paths carved through the dust and dirt that coated its surface. I felt Thanatos following silently behind me, both of us on alert, both of us sensing that the house, *my house*, was not happy we were here. Without pausing to even think about it, leather pants and a fitted black shirt replaced my flowing skirt and blouse. Between one step and the next, dark boots covered my bare feet.

I entered the main dining room and wrinkled my nose in disgust at the dishes caked with food in various stages of decomposition piled on the table. I scanned the room, searching the dark corners for any movement. Slowly, stealthily, I began to gather the shadows to me. Typically, when I called, they sprang to my bidding like well-trained pets, eager to please. These were reluctant, sullen, sluggish, and foul. The moment I had a hold on them, I released them back. Like everything in here, they were tainted and would do nothing but cause me and mine harm. They would wrap around me, then likely turn on me.

I bypassed the kitchen, really not wanting to see the condition of it considering the dining room, and moved through the doorway into the main hall. I froze, and my wings exploded from my back, hitting Thanatos across the shoulder and chest, stopping his forward momentum. I had been wrong. We were expected.

Thanatos carefully pushed my wing aside so he could see. His voice was calm and measured as always. "It's a doll."

"Nuh-uh. Nope. Nope," I denied, shaking my head.

"Hmm. Pretty sure it's a doll, Nem."

"I do *not* do dolls, Thano," I said through clenched teeth.

Thanatos raised one eyebrow but didn't look away from the room. People knelt, paying homage at the base of a makeshift throne. A large wingback chair I recognized from my library sat atop a dais built of wood and furniture. A porcelain doll was perched upon the seat. Her dark brown eyes shone with red highlights and were encircled with black. Crackle lines spider-webbed over the white of her face. Her auburn hair was sparse and sticking up, hanks of it missing, exposing the speckled scalp. She

164

wore a Victorian style dress with a high lace collar, the material yellowed and wrinkled.

My attention was so focused on that creepy little doll, I somehow missed the giant, swirling green and black dimensional hole in the ceiling until a shadowy tentacle snapped from the void and whipped towards us. I had been alive for a very long time. My brother, Thanatos? He was the God of Death. I lived in the Underworld. I knew creepy. I had seen creepy, but that doll and the malevolence pouring from that hole in my ceiling made my blood run cold.

I tipped my head to get a better look, the light emanating from that void a vile, near physical caress. "Chaos's balls…"

"What in Tartarus…?" Thanatos gaped.

I caught movement out of the corner of my eye and reluctantly looked back at the doll. I was sure she had turned towards Thanatos when he spoke. A child stepped from behind the chair, her demeanor regal, but her clothing ragged, and her hair and body unkempt. She was thin and small. The putrid green glow that filled the room only emphasized the sallow cast of her skin.

Looking at the others, she was in the best condition. I saw illness and exhaustion stamped into the lines of the bodies that held so still on the hard stone floor. Some were in nightclothes, a few wore jackets, and others still were naked. Those with no shoes had bloodied feet, the wounds infected. These were my people. They were under my care, and I thought they were safe. They should have been safe. This was my home! Their home! Many had been with me through generations.

Anger filled me, and I focused once more on the child. "What has happened here? What has happened to my people?"

The young girl lifted her chin, attempting to look down her nose at us. "I do not have to answer you. You are no longer the mistress of this house. I am! These people do what I say!"

My gaze shifted between the girl and the doll. I carefully took a step to the side, feeling Thano move a bit in the opposite direction. The girl turned towards me, and the doll's eyes tracked Thanatos.

"You think you are mistress here, little one?" I said, keeping an eye on Thanatos. He had frozen, his gaze locked on the doll and his feet rooted to the spot. His eyes were their usual ebony, but his skin had gone impossibly pale, and shock radiated from him.

"Nem," he whispered, "we might have a problem here."

His gaze flicked up towards the dimensional hole and then quickly back to the doll, as if he was loath to lose sight of it. He took another step forward, his scythe appearing in his hand, angling his head to get a look at the faces of the people on the floor. I heard him murmur, "Please, no cannibals..."

"Thano, what is happening here? What are you talking about?"

"I don't know how it can be, Nem. It doesn't make sense," he said, staying close to the edges of the room, ensuring that he didn't step beneath the swirling green mass. His gaze skipped from the people to the doll, only to flick back to the people as he tried to get a look at their lowered faces.

I reached back, my sword appearing in my hand. Drawing it forward, the blade glowed with ebony light, a physical manifestation of my power. I did not know from what direction the threat would come, but there was no doubt this was a trap. The little girl's face morphed into a sinister sneer, her eyes flashing with an unholy green.

Thanatos and I both froze as the doll suddenly stood, its gaze focused intently on him. "You have finally come to play, you coward! As always, you ran away! You killed all of my friends, took away my toys, and left me alone, trapped in the rubble of that house! But this time, I was able to find a way out." She giggled, the sound tittering and high-pitched. The eerie laughter began in the otherwise silent room, growing deeper as it echoed through the house.

"Emma?" Thanatos gasped, his eyes bulging. "Son of a bi---"

"I found my way out," she interrupted. "Did you know, you cowardly god, that the River Styx flows through many worlds? Different, but the same. You left me with no sacrifices, no meat, nothing to feed the goddess. I had to hide myself inside this shell, and step by step, make my way to you. I have been here for years, unable to get to you, unable to find you. I washed up on the shores of that river like a piece of garbage. Luckily, Amie found me and brought me here. Imagine my glee when I discovered this was the home of another goddess, and not just any goddess, but your sister! I have been using these people to sacrifice and eat, to grow strong again. I will get back to my world, and I will take you with me!"

Thanatos shook his head. I stood perplexed, watching as Amie moved closer, inch by inch. Her movements were erratic, slow one moment and then so fast my eyes barely caught it. No matter what was going on around her, her eyes remained locked on me. Every time I moved, she countered, so I began to pace back and forth along the wall. I watched as she shifted her body to keep me in full sight. My wings flared wide, and my power mantled about me. I asked into the quiet of the room, "What have you done to my people? What have you done to my house?"

The Emma doll remained fixated on Thanatos, but she answered, "They are not yours any longer, and soon you will be mine as well. Just like in my world. I will own you, and you will do what I say. You will be my friend! These mortals, even though they are of the Underworld, they are still so weak. They do not last under my spells, and they do not become strong. They just die!"

I looked over the group here and knew that she was right. There were not nearly enough, and I couldn't sense any more in the house. I glanced at Thanatos, and he nodded, able to feel the unreaped souls that filled my home. Rage ignited in me, along with anger and sorrow. "You will pay for this, you rotten little beast."

"Come play, Nemesis," Amie said in a high pitched, sing-song voice. "Don't you want to play with me and my dolly?"

I love my little dolly, sweet;
She's my best and only friend.
I bring her other kids to meet
But they don't come back again.

I suppose they just don't like me,
Though, I can't imagine why.
We're both as sweet as we can be,
'Cept when someone makes me cry.

My dolly doesn't like me sad;
That is when she's not so nice,
Bad things happen when she's mad,
So, it's best that you think twice.

Amie sang the poem, her expression never shifting from the demonic sneer. It was so at odds with the sweet, pure tones of her voice that it made my skin crawl.

"Emma, you will not hurt Nemesis, this is between you and me." Thanatos eyed the servants still kneeling on the floor. I could hear the actual fear and nervousness in his tone, and that terrified me more than anything.

Emma's laugh was a tinkling sound. "You are so concerned with your sister now, you scaredy-cat god. Did you tell her how you killed her in my world? Did you tell her how you took that scythe and chopped her right in two? You didn't even hesitate, just left her dead on the floor. You stepped over her body and left her there. You killed your sister and your mother and all the other gods as well! You ripped them apart! Did you tell her, Thanatos? Did you?!"

I glanced at Thanatos and could see by the grim set of his jaw and the tension in his body that whatever was in that doll spoke true. But I knew my brother, my faith and trust in him was absolute. If he had raised arms against me, any version of me, I was confident the action had been warranted and he had no choice. I knew it would have cost him dearly to destroy any facsimile of myself.

"Emma, be a good girl. You do not have to do this. I can help you. You can be at peace," Thanatos said, his tone strong but comforting.

Emma laughed, the doll's entire body shaking with her mirth. "You stupid coward god! I do not want to be at peace! I want to destroy and play! I was fine and happy until you came and took all my friends! I want new friends, and I will start with you!"

With the last word, shadow tentacles whipped from the ceiling, grabbed Thanatos' ankles, and pulled him towards the center of the vortex. Amie launched herself at me, her mouth opening to reveal sharp conical teeth. I reached out and caught her by the throat as I focused on Thanatos. He was twisting and slashing to cut through the darkness. No way was I going to allow this beast to use the shadows against me in my domain. I gripped them tightly with my power, not asking as I normally did, but commanding this time. They fought my hold much as Amie did, twisting and scratching, struggling to get free. I saw the veins beneath my skin go black as I poured more power into the beast, the tentacles writhing beneath my touch. My vision sharpened and I knew my eyes had gone black as I forced the tentacles to release Thanatos.

Emma screamed, and it was unnerving the amount of sound that came out of the doll. Her eyes blazed and focused intently on Thanatos as he retreated to my side, Amie still fighting in my grip. I tipped my head towards him, watching Emma rage, kicking and throwing a tantrum on her makeshift throne. "Are Amie and the others dead, Thano? What is this? What is going on?"

He shook his head. "They are not dead, not yet anyway. A few of them are very close, and once she pulls her power, they will probably die. This is an old magic, Nem. An otherworld witch goddess' magic trapped in what remains of a sad and tortured child. I have fought her before and failed in reaping that soul. She is very powerful. Or she was in her world. She feels less so here. That may be all we have going for us."

Emma spun around, seeming to remember that we were still there. She pointed and screamed, "Get them! Bring them to me. I want to go home!" The Emma doll jumped up and down on the seat of the chair, her fury radiating off of her in black slithering whips, her porcelain features cracking and oozing dark crimson.

All thirty of the remaining household staff shuffled stiffly to their feet, turning in unison to glare at us. They bared sharp teeth and lunged. I turned, wrapping my wings around both Thanatos and the still-struggling Amie, and ported us to the second floor. I ran down the hallway, intending to get Amie somewhere safe so that Than and I could deal with the horde that was already ascending the wide central staircase.

Stopping at the first set of living quarters, I threw the door open and took three steps inside before my mind registered the horror of this place. The darkened room was ravaged, the furniture and everything within lay in ruins. The only thing that was still intact was a cradle. Even in madness, whatever had raged in here would not, could not, harm what lay inside. It was neglect that had done the damage to that innocent.

Thanatos stopped as if he had slammed into a wall. His face went stark, his obsidian eyes focused on something that I could not see. He carefully leaned his scythe against the wall and walked forward, holding out his arms. I backed out of the room and opened the next door I came to. Tossing Amie inside, I slammed it shut, locking her on the other side as she launched herself at me again.

I spun and rushed back to Thanatos. Stopping in the doorway, I stood transfixed by the sorrow and the beauty. He cradled a small golden light in his arms, his face transformed by the purity of it. The glow dimmed, the tiny young soul absorbed into his safekeeping until he could release it to Charon. I placed a hand on my forehead and turned, my wings flaring wide as the first of the servants reached me. None of them would enter and this would stop here.

Emma's laughter pealed through the house, the walls vibrating with it. The sound spurred my attackers forward, leaving bloody footprints in their wake. I could not kill these people. Not only were they mine, but this many deaths in such proximity would take Thanatos down. They forced me back, biting and clawing at my flesh, the black ichor streaked my skin and sparked power into the air. I hissed and began knocking them out as quickly as I could. I was as careful as possible with their sick and weakened bodies.

Thanatos came up behind me as I pushed another man back, his broken nails scraping at my skin. "A little help here, Thano?"

I felt the scythe slice through time and space, his voice calm at my back. "Push them through, Nem. They will be safe here until we can break her hold on them." Without question, I began booting people through the rift. I tripped, shoved, and threw while Thanatos held it open.

Emma's laughter ceased. There was a moment of shocked silence as she felt the beings she controlled disappear, and then her enraged shriek echoed through the house, rattling the very foundations of it.

"You took my friends! Again!!"

Then all stopped, everything went silent, and the house stood still. Amie ceased throwing herself against the door. Thanatos and I froze. One quick glance at each other and we ran, flinging our wings wide as we launched ourselves over the railing and dropped to the first floor. Running back to the main hall, we crashed to a stop in the doorway. The green and black vortex swirled above, tentacles forming and fading as we watched, shadowy arms reaching into the room as if sensing us.

The throne sat empty and silence reigned, but not a peaceful one. This was a false calm filled with anticipation. Thanatos and I stepped into the room, bending low to look beneath furniture and rubble, keeping to the edges of the hall.

The sound of a childish giggle and the patter of small feet running through the house snapped both of us upright. We maneuvered until we were back to back, the feathers of our wings barely touching. Thanatos held his scythe ready across his body, and my sword was a familiar weight in my hand, my power rimming its ghostly edge. We turned, careful to remain away from the center of the room and the shadowy tentacles that writhed and searched.

I sent my power sweeping through the house. This was my home, and I was taking it back. No little demon doll was going to claim what was mine.

I slammed the doors around the room, one after another, until only the main entrance remained open. Thanatos and I then turned to face it. I tapped into the network of the house and the power of the land that it sat on. It had been mine for eons and responded to my touch, reluctant and unsure at first, but then more willing as it recognized my magic. My power wafted off my skin, my sword, my feathers, seeping into the very structure of the house and connecting with it. Thanatos looked at me and took up a defensive position in front of me, my ability to react hampered by the outpouring of my magic. The stone, the wood, and the land fed, demanding more growing strong off of our connection.

My voice was a low unearthly growl as I commanded, "Bring her to me now!"

The one remaining door slammed shut, and the ceiling parted, dropping the little horror in front of us. The porcelain had cracked and broken off in pieces, revealing the putrid mass beneath. Its features both frozen and yet somehow malleable, menace, hunger, and evil poured off this creature. Its desire was so great to claim him that the doll zeroed in on Thanatos, barely seeming to register me. It launched itself in a fury of tentacles, their whip-like forms barely within this existence. I stepped in front of him and caught the thing by its head, my hand wrapping over its face.

The doll screeched and fought my hold, tentacles wrapping about my hand and forearm, dark green streaks forming along my skin where they attached themselves. The magic contained within Emma was ancient and familiar, yet it held a foreignness that made it clear it was not wholly of this world. I latched onto the bit that belonged to the witch queen, the hot gold ichor that had become contaminated power, filled with rage, hatred, and despair at a life stolen. It was the catalyst that had created this monster. The final act of vengeance cast by extraordinary primal magic. Vengeance belonged to me. I was the source and balance of it. I pulled at it, plucking at the abscessed kernel of goodness walled off from the corrupted soul of the little girl.

The power that had been formed over centuries battered at my own as Emma let out a piercing shriek. My body shuddered as I absorbed this darkness, runes forming along my arm as I made it a part of myself, the pain of it making me gasp and the world tilt. I do not know where the witch queen of that realm had found this ancient language of power, but there it was, and as I made it my own, it tried to destroy me. If I gave in to it, it would claim me much as it had her, and Chaos help us then. Look at the destruction it had done in the soul of a mortal girl. Imagine what it would do in me. I threw my head back and screamed, feeling the black ichor drip from my eyes and nose. The runes crawled up my arm as the doll slowly went limp in my grip.

I shook and gasped for air. I collapsed to my knees, crushing the doll beneath my hand. Looking up, Thanatos hovered protectively over me, his wing resting over my back, his gaze focused on a spot directly in front of me.

"Emma?" he whispered.

He reached out with his other hand, and I saw the glow come into focus. The young girl, thin and sickly looking, her eyes wide as she looked up at him. Her soul appeared whole but pitted with specks of the green corruption.

I struggled to digest the foreign power dancing through my magic as I looked up at the vortex in my ceiling. Pushing against it, I forced the beast back through the hole and into its own realm. Maybe someday we would take care of that, but today it needed to return to its own time and space. My head dropped back as the words on my skin solidified and then coalesced into a dark mass. I focused my will, pushing against it experimentally, and felt it give beneath my mental touch. I concentrated and formed it into a stylized dragon over my left shoulder.

Thanatos reached out and took Emma by the hand, porting us all to the shores of the River Lethe. He assumed his deified form and picked her up in skeletal arms, walking into the eddies of the powerful current. He lowered the glowing soul into the silvery water. The waves churned and bubbled, washing away the taint of the corruption. The river absorbed the memories and freed her of their burden. Thanatos cradled Emma in his arms as he lifted her out, her soul now glowing pristine and bright. She smiled weakly and stroked his cheek.

Thanatos smiled back, his expression tender. "Come, child, it is time you rest." Slowly, gently, he dipped her beneath the waves and let the river take her, knowing she would find her way to the Styx and Charon.

He looked back at me as she disappeared, and I marveled anew at the power of him. I flopped back onto the rocks. Scratching absently at the new shadow on my shoulder, I decided to just rest there for a bit. I would go home and clean up the mess later.

FORGOTTEN
AMONG THE
FORGOTTEN

BY

DAN DOLAN

ERIS,

GOD/GODDESS OF
DISCORD & CHAOS

SOMETIMES I AM ERIS. That is the name in my head, at least. I have had so many names, but that's the one I care about. I care about so little in this thing we call life, so delegating what small amount of affection I can to a simple concept like a name seems harmless enough.

Like most things of worth, the name already belongs to someone else, and a goddess no less. A pretty lofty venue to look up to, especially from where I slept by the dumpster last night.

Not tonight, though.

"Curfew is at five," says a cheery woman, whose **Happy Helpers** name tag identifies her as *Pepper*. By her tone, she could be asking, *How do you like your eggs?*

"Is that going to be a problem...dear?" She wants to say *Miss*, but she can't quite tell. My androgynous appearance has the lovely bonus of that extra slice of awkwardness upon first meeting. I keep silent a moment longer just to draw out the tension as long as possible.

"No problems," I say, even as two dull-eyed EMTs make their way by me with a freshly filled body bag on a gurney between them, "No problems at all..."

No matter how large they make the word *Happy* on the sign outside, I usually avoid shelters for a myriad of reasons, body bags included. Still, it is getting colder, and whatever city I'm currently in has lousy exteriors.

I am fairly certain we are just getting close to Halloween. It shouldn't be *this* cold. A glance at a calendar on a nearby dartboard confirms the date as Monday, October 13th, 19...69? They couldn't even be bothered to get one from this year, nevermind this decade. The lack of detail doesn't speak highly of their level of care.

"Place your personal effects in the tray," Pepper sing-songs, waving said tray before me, her smile as warm as her eyes were cold.

I stare at her and the tray for a moment, wondering how long to allow this pregnant pause to continue. The tension of it is rather delicious.

"Nothing belongs to me." I finally shrug.

She nods, both as an answer, and I feel as a recognition that she genuinely believes that of everyone who comes through these doors. That they have nothing. That they *are* nothing.

Pepper leads me past the dark and filthy old school lockers where our *personal belongings* are kept. The zombified *employees* ravenously pilfer those storage spaces under the guise of *occupant safety*. Our safety is not a concern for anyone who would choose to work in this place. We pass a door marked *Waste Management: Employees Only*, and I think to myself that Waste Management would be a much more fitting name for this place. More honest, at the very least.

I just have to keep telling myself that all I need this place for is a roof. No, not *need*. Want. I don't *need* anything, just as no one needs me. Best to keep it that way.

I usually like a sense of danger, like that famous and infamous Eris. That goddess was all about trouble and kicking it up when things got a little too safe. But this? This is all wrong. These people don't deserve any more strife in their lives. It's no fun kicking downwards, especially when there's not much lower you can go.

This place is like so many of the others, filthy inside and out. And no one's giving anything of value away for free.

The cleanest thing in here is a woman named Caris. Her body language alone tells me she runs this place. She is sparkly clean, and she smells great to boot, which makes me dislike her on principle.

She wafts through the room, smiles, and tells you how much potential you have. And there's not even one moment where I believe she means it.

No one else can see the truth. How can I expect them to see that her brand of *help* is poisonous? They can't even see the world around them. Hell, most keep calling her Avery for some reason.

A voice in my head screams that there *is* a reason to wake up and see the world around me, but I ignore it. I don't need that kind of negativity in my life. I'd rather rest assured that I am right, and they are wrong. No matter how much of an illusion it might be.

No one sees what's really going on but me. Everyone she talks to seems to come away the worse for it. I can follow her path through this shelter by the wake of crow's feet and worry lines on those she's *helped*.

Some say I'm biased. Some say I'm mad. Most say both, but that's fine. I'll just wait for my grand moment to scream, *I told you so!* It will come. I am as sure of that as I am she'll regret wearing those white pumps into this den of filth.

I stare at her for a long time, and after she walks away, I stare at the ground where she stood. My deceptively still form conceals my overworked mind. Day soon becomes night. I notice myself shivering before I realize I'm cold.

A blanket falls from above, waking me from my reverie. Part of my mind thinks I may have just imagined it. That is far more believable than an act of charity occurring in *this* charity.

A blur of motion appears in my peripheral. I look over and see the person who apparently dropped the blanket. A middle-aged woman wearing a mix of tie-dye and hippie-style clothes sits back down beside me. Funnily enough by the look of her, she'd fit in quite well in '69…maybe this was some kind of wacky theme homeless shelter.

"I hear they call you Error," the woman whispers shyly but kindly, as she curls up to my right. Jeez, I've been here like five minutes, and I already have a nickname?

"Close enough, I suppose. Yeah, I can be Error," I say, pulling the blanket up around me. It crosses my mind to say thank you, but the words never actually pass my lips. *I have certainly been called a mistake before*, I think to myself.

"Daffodil," she says, gesturing to herself with the air of someone who knows how silly it sounds.

"Not that I'm one to judge, especially on the quality of names," I laugh, "but is that your real name?"

"Oh, no." She giggles like a girl half her age. "But when you get called *daffy* long enough, eventually you make up a reason for it. One other than being a bumbling nitwit, that is," she says, still smiling but more bittersweet than when she began.

"Sometimes," she continues, "if I try really hard, I can forget that it's not my real name. I can forget who I was altogether."

"That's easy," I say, smiling at her genuinely. "I do it all the time. Being nothing is easy. It's what everyone wants you to be anyway." But her face doesn't fall like I expect it to. Usually, after I say something depressing like that, I get some kind of rise out of them. But she just keeps smiling.

"How do you do it?" she asks, and her earnest yearning takes me briefly off guard. She *actually* wants to know.

I look at her for a long moment. If I squint, her bohemian *Age of Aquarius* garb and her soft older appearance could pass for a high priestess of old. An oracle, like we...they had back in the old Eris' days. Shouldn't she be giving *me* the answers?

My mind is throbbing.

"You know what's a good first step?" I ask at last.

"What?"

"Sleep." I hold her gaze for a moment, but then give the most minuscule of smiles.

She laughs off my curtness. "Good night, Error."

Small moments of this alien kindness are how I find myself, bit by bit, taking up space here for a while. Sticking around isn't really my style, but when you find a nice person wandering around this cynical world of monsters, it's like finding a twenty on the street. It just doesn't happen every day.

I walk around this place with a spring in my step. It even seems a little cleaner, which might be my imagination, but hey, at least they got a new calendar. It now reads October 13th, 1999, a Wednesday.

It's only been a few days, or if the seemingly fixed calendar on the wall was to be believed, a few *years*, but I think I've already got a pretty good feel for this place. The employees are the usual mix of users and abusers, but there's a special spot for the leader. That blonde, soccer-mom-looking monstrosity, Caris.

My advice notwithstanding, I notice that Daffodil seems to grow more tired the more sleep she gets. The more I notice, the more I see the staff notice me. I'd be willing to bet all the money I do not have, that Caris is *helping* her.

The employees talk and gab about those who are spending time with Avery, like it's both a good thing and a bad thing at the same time.

"I wouldn't get too attached to her, Error," a fellow *resident* named Twitch says with his titular trait in full effect, as my eyes follow Daffodil.

"Why is that?"

"She's not selling enough."

"What's going on out here?" a voice screeches from behind us. I turn to see Pepper, not nearly as friendly as she once appeared, running towards us. I turn back to Twitch with a laugh.

"What's her issue?" But my question goes unanswered. I see his white pallor and notice that, for once, he's shock-still despite his nickname.

181

"We were just talking..." I sputter as my eyes seek some trace of the life he seemed to have just moments ago.

Pepper drops to her knee, her hand going to his wrist.

"He's dead!" she gasps.

"We were just talking?" I repeat. But even as I say it, I question myself.

"Error," her eyes narrow at me, even as she furiously dials her phone, "he's clearly been dead for hours." With a sigh, she begins to ramble off the details to whatever emergency service worker is on the other end of the line.

Well, that's unfortunate.

The week of a state check, everyone seems to get remarkably more well-groomed. Shower tokens are mysteriously easy to come by, and a smile appears to be part of the employee dress code. The morning wake up procedures get more congenial, as do the pat-downs upon curfew. As an additional bonus, I notice that Caris spends less time here this week.

The man who eventually shows has *state government* written all over him. He looks around like he's in Hell but is being paid to be nice to the damned as they burn. The employees seem more on edge than you would expect, and they keep calling Caris, *Avery*. Intriguing.

The eyes on me increase, as if I am the one thing they are most afraid of going wrong. It feels like such a natural role to take, like I was born for it.

"Remember, you probably don't want any trouble yourself, right? So why not just keep your mouth shut, and we'll all come out of this like apples and cream. Okay, Error?" One particularly bold employee winks at me before it's my turn to be interviewed by *the Man*. For a moment, I think he truly believes he's doing me a favor. But like myself, he doesn't quite understand the strange thrill I get from the word *trouble*.

He walks away, and the much-ballyhooed state auditor immediately takes his place.

"What, you guys don't decorate?" He laughs in that way older men do when they're it's solely for themselves. That freedom they feel to so openly find humor in their own bland, unfunny small talk, like giving themselves a verbal pat on the back for still existing.

"Halloween's still a ways away," one worker shrugs.

"It'll be a pumpkin patch by next week," another chimes.

The man is a long grey streak in a world of sepia. He has salt and pepper hair and wears a cement colored suit. He shambles up to me, leaning greedily into my personal space, glaring down at me with perverse zeal.

"They tell me you've been here the longest. So, what do you say, kid? Anything to report?" he says, gripping my shoulder firmly with a slight pull.

"Would you believe me if I did?" I blurt, somewhat surprising even myself.

He gets a very serious look on his face and leans in even further, as if such a thing is possible.

"Believe me, young man," he falters a bit at that, but plows forward, "you may think no one out there cares what's happening in here, but we do. You have no idea the heat that could come on us if something truly scandalous happened here. With state funds, no less." An unempathetic, if honest response.

I consider him for a moment. "You want to know a problem in the making?"

"Just tell me where to look," he says in a hushed whisper.

I hook a thumb in Caris' direction, before muttering, "To the fairest."

Days go by. Sometimes it feels like years. There's still no sign of anyone coming to get to the bottom of what's going on around here. I keep to the shadowy corners and watch like the carrion bird I am. I suppose if any are to suss out what's happening, it would be someone already at the bottom.

Twitch's words still circle the squall of my mind, *She's not selling enough.*

I approach Daffodil gingerly, but despite her general malaise, she greets me with as warm a smile as she can muster.

"Keep tight to that." She points, and I notice the blanket she'd given me is laying off to the side. "A precious commodity around here."

"One of the few things that is." I laugh, and she smiles a sad smile.

I don't know what I want to say, or even what I should say, but I look at her and hope my face gets the message across, regardless. *I see her.*

After another silent second of simple recognition, which is all I have to offer, I pick up the blanket and wrap it around my waist with a wink.

She starts to respond, and her face is different. Not the sunny, positive outlook she's been trying so hard to express 24/7. This is a layer or two beneath that. This is sad and tired and real. But before a single word escapes her lips, we're interrupted.

"We have a meeting," Caris says simply, looking at Daffodil like one might at a misbehaving dog they don't like.

Daffodil rises, offering me one last smile before shambling off to follow that monster of a woman out back. Leaving me alone and, once more, unseen.

The *meetings* were scheduled, but as I look to the calendar, it is free and clear. Why would she say that? An itch at the back of my neck begins in earnest. The calendar says 1969 once more. Why would you replace an outdated calendar just to put the old one back again?

What is this place? It was time to find out. I *needed* to.

Being invisible is not a trick for me. It's like breathing. I'm nothing. It's easy for me to believe that. And when I do? I'm invisible. I slip into that nothingness, that abstract abandonment behind this world of false security and corrupted order. I notice they no longer stare at me. Instead, they allow me to slip by unnoticed. As unnoticed as any other hopeless case.

Sometimes I can be in the middle of a room, and they *still* look right past me.

"Error's been poking around again," one of the more thuggish workers scoffs to his cohort.

"She's harmless," the other replies. He is older and better at believing in his own respectability.

"Are we going with *she* these days?"

"As I was saying," he sighs, "she's harmless. She thinks Avery is some old bint who used to work here. Half the time, she thinks it is twenty years ago."

Avery is what they call Caris. I follow his eyes as he talks. He casts a wary glance at *Waste Management.*

I walk towards the door, feeling the weight of time. The past is like a riptide, and I feel it pulling me back with every step. I can almost feel the calendar pages fly off the wall. The air in the room comes down on me like a mattress. The employees blur even as they move around me.

None stop me, of course. I'm invisible.

I scent Death before I'm an inch in the room. Death is an old friend of mine. I'd recognize his aftershave anywhere. The bodies lie there around her. Posed around Caris with a sense of rest and comfort, they never quite found in life.

She stands as ever in the center of them all. As always, the contrast is quite clear, but now it is all the greater. Not just the simple difference of a working shower and a fresh pair of clothes. This is life and death.

185

The world has been programmed to think life equals goodness. The forces of light against the dark decay of Death's cold grip. But here it could not have been more different. The dead bodies draw me to them. They seem so cold and so alone, and Caris? She is *full* of life, fat like a leech on the back of a great beast. She is burning with it. The stolen energies of people who'd never known the freedom to use it.

Daffodil's skin grows even paler, cream turning to alabaster, and finally to chalk. Her veins are bright and blue in the dull lighting. They aren't just visible underneath her skin. They are coming through it. I can see them inching their way out of her body like worms as Caris looms over her.

In Caris's grip, Daffodil squirms like a fish on a dock. Her eyes bulge, and bubbles of spit churn from her gaping mouth as she fruitlessly struggles to scream. Caris's bright, beautiful veins meet Daffodil's, crawling out of their bodies and intertwining.

Hell, as I watch the women, Caris's hair itself seems to be made of them. Like a circulatory system growing from her skull or a parasitic flower in bloom, the capillaries pulse as she feeds.

"Eris," Caris says simply, acknowledging my presence without even looking up. *She sees me without looking at me. How appropriate.*

And just like that, I *am* Eris once more ...aren't I? The memory shines for a moment like a golden apple. I step forward, holding that memory in my mind like a precious treasure. I wrap it and myself in Daffodil's blanket and push forward. My eyes heat, and a part of me is aware they must now be burning with a golden light.

"That's quite enough," I hiss.

"Oh, is it?"

I take another step, feeling my size increase, just like it used to in the old days. I used to tower over the battlefield like a child over its toy soldiers.

This is not a conversation, not that we ever had those. I need to take the pulse of this interaction. I can't let her run roughshod over me.

"Let her go."

She doesn't. Instead, her cobalt tendrils expand, and the few veins Daffodil still has in her body come alive, glowing like blue Christmas lights. I see the life drain out of her. Her mouth wrenches further, her eyes bulge, and I can't seem to make it stop.

I'm no god.

I rush forward, and by instinct alone, I wrap myself around Daffodil to knock her free. All I find in my arms is a corpse. I stare into her dead eyes, and the veins still connected to her body fall around me like spiderwebs.

I only realize the veins are entering me when I see them rise out of the dead eyes glaring into mine. They crawl out like a flower in bloom. Life isn't always good.

For a moment I do nothing, I let them come, let them sink into my flesh. What the heck do I have to live for, anyway? Would this even kill me? I am a goddess, after all. Would I instead live like this forever?

"Yes, an eternal food source," Caris sighs in a melodic exhale.

At least then, my life would serve some kind of purpose.

"You won't go on like this much longer," I say simply, allowing her to envelop me.

"I will continue for the same reason your loneliness will continue, little goddess. The universe discards what is unnecessary. I'm just one of the many ways in which it does so."

I nod.

"At least now you won't be nothing anymore. Now someone wants you around. Someone *needs* you." She laughs, and it's a laugh I've heard before, from family members and even friends. That one that says in no words just how worthless I am in the eyes of others.

"Is that right?" I hiss. "How would you like to try being nothing?" I smirk as I let myself drop back into the Aether, taking Caris with me by her veiny tendrils, blood spilling from the bases of them as they pull on her skin just a little too quickly.

She screams, trying to rip her veins out from under her skin, trying to free herself, but it's too late.

There she stands, in Christ-like repose, caught between reality and gossamer phantasm. Her scream resounds throughout the layers of the world, shaking the surrounding veil before dissipating like a snowflake on water.

Then suddenly, that water becomes troubled. It churns and ripples, and she's standing before me again, but she's different. She's Avery now, and we're not alone anymore. Policemen and that man from the state are milling about. She's being led away and, once more, I am invisible. I am a ghost, able to see them properly, straight through the everyday masks they wear.

Two *Happy Helpers* look on with a laugh.

"Imagine, Avery was using these roaches to deal for her. I've been buying from a guy uptown, and it was right here under my nose the entire time."

Another laugh.

"Under my nose...get it?"

His friend stares at him, but he laughs at his own joke, regardless.

"Avery's not even getting arrested, you know?" the stone-faced man retorts.

"What? The cops..."

"They're just here to escort her off the premises. They're not filing charges. They say it'll just cause legal issues for the parent company or some shit. They're pinning it on Error since she's gone missing." He has the guts to say this while I'm standing right in front of him.

188

"Still, letting Avery go after…you know." Daffodil's body gets wheeled past. It's not her, though. It's some fresh young thing with the echo of a nice smile on her face. Daffodil would have had a hard go at it in these modern times. Even way back then, her light was fading fast.

"Victimless crime, man." The workers laugh together.

Nausea ripples through me as I head outside for what feels like the first time in decades. If I remember Daffodil's wardrobe correctly, it's been since the sixties at least, I'd look at that damn calendar, but gods know that'll be useless. This *shelter* is far too dangerous for me. I'll take my chances on the streets.

Where the monsters don't wear masks.

THE
MONSTER
WITHIN

BY

RAINBOW BRUBAKER

ATHENA,

GODDESS OF WISDOM &
WAR

I WALK SLOWLY UP TO THE ADDRESS THAT THE LOCAL PD GAVE ME. Parking is scarce in the inner-city, so I had to leave my car along the busy street. Luckily, it is after hours, and I didn't have to feed the meter. That would have added irritation to the list of what I'm feeling tonight. The crisp evening air sends chills down my spine as it whips around me. The temperatures have been unusually cold this year, and my body is revolting against it. Maybe I should move somewhere warmer. I hear that Tahiti is beautiful this time of year. The prospect of a simpler and less crime-filled life teases my mind. But who am I kidding? I would get bored and miss this.

The relaxed life of beaches and sipping Mai Tais would be nice for a little while, but it wouldn't last. Deep down, I know there is something dark within me. It craves the chase and the violence that inevitably comes with it. It's the darkness that I hide away and refuse to show anyone. It's the part of me that is the most dangerous and vulnerable. I dare not speak its name because that would bring it crashing into my reality. It would come out screaming and show everyone the monster that lives within me. You can't allow that type of darkness to be seen and not be considered evil...tainted. People fear what they don't understand. Seeing that much of the beast would scare anyone, and scared people grab their weapons and come after you. They kill what they do not understand, and I have enough people trying to kill me.

"Ms.? Ms., can I help you?" I know that someone is there, but they are eons away from my thoughts and barely hugging the edges of my consciousness. I contemplate returning to reality, but what awaits me there? More evils of the world, I suspect. More darkness to seep in and merge with my own. Feeding it, nourishing it, so it may become tangible, maybe even real.

"Ms.? Ms., can I help you?" I hear the voice again. It is closer this time, more urgent. The speaker sounds slightly panicked.

Something touches my shoulder, jarring me back to reality. Without thinking, I grab his hand and wrench it sharply behind his body. He screams in pain, and the sound alerts other officers to his distress. I stand there blankly, blinking in shock when three cops draw their guns and aim them at me. If they fire, they will hit me center mass, and it will hurt like a son-of-a-bitch. It won't kill me, but damn, healing will be hell. I may be a goddess, faster and stronger than the mortals, but wounds still hurt. If they riddle me with bullets, I will recover at a mortal pace. Slowly. I've endured extensive injuries before and do not intend to do it again. Not if I can help it.

"Let go of the officer, or we will shoot!" I hear someone yell at me. I blink and do my best to center my thoughts. *Focus, Athena. You must focus.* Forever seems to pass before I realize that I am holding a young officer hostage. If I apply any more pressure, his arm will give way and break. I immediately release him and raise my hands over my head.

"I'm sorry. You startled me, and I just reacted," I apologize as he moves away from me, cradling his injured arm. The officers do not lower their weapons and remain focused on me. The Captain asked me to come here, I remember. Impulsive actions aside, he did ask me to come.

"Turn around slowly and put your hands on your head!" another officer yells at me. I can sense their fear and anger. I am sure that the reason Renard called me here has something to do with their agitation. Of course, me assaulting one of their buddies unprovoked hasn't helped matters any. Leave it to me to fuck up the situation.

"Captain Renard asked me to come," I explain as calmly and slowly as possible. I don't want to give them any further reason to shoot me.

"The hell he did, bitch!" a different officer yells. His every word drips with venom as he spits them out. I will not gain favor from the locals today. Athena, Goddess of the Bitches. Surprisingly, I don't hate the way that sounds.

Just great. I come to help at this ridiculous hour and end up hurting an officer and pissing off multiple others. I'm off to a fantastic start. What next? I zone out and kill one of them? What in the hells is going on with me? I need to get my thoughts under control before this unpleasant situation gets worse. I am a goddess, for Zeus' sake. What would Father think? Zeus help me not to start a war with the mortals.

"Captain Renard asked me to come. Tell him Athena is here." I am not sure if it's the second mention of their superior officer or that I'm Athena that gives them pause. The officer closest to me, holsters his weapon and speaks into the mic clipped to his uniform.

"Let her through," Renard commands. Finally, a friendly voice, sweet and familiar. Maybe he can talk his people down, explain things, help me out.

"But...sir..." the officer tries to protest. He is obviously still unhappy with me for hurting his buddy. I don't blame him. I'm not very happy with me right now either. In fact, I'm downright pissed at myself. I can't imagine how they feel. Poor mortals. They are just doing their jobs, and here I come crashing in.

"Now!" Renard is angry at his subordinate's refusal to obey his order. I imagine it's either because he really thinks I can help, or because of the intimate turn our relationship has taken. Banging the boss grants you unbelievable favors. The officer lets out an audible huff of exasperation. His frustration is evident, and I understand it, but that doesn't make me any less irritated.

"You heard the Captain, let the lady through." He says *lady* like it is a vile curse word. Obviously, he would have liked to substitute many other words for *lady*. I'm sure he has a wide range of vernaculars to describe how he is feeling about me.

"Thank you, Officer. Again, I am sorry about your friend. I shouldn't have hurt him. For future notice, please tell him to watch who he puts his hands on." The officer is enraged by my comment. I really meant it as an apology. Oh hells, I guess some things you just can't come back from. I am just going to have to let this one go and deal with the ramifications later. I know that Officer Pissed-Off-At-Me will shoot me if I give him the opportunity. If he can't let this go, I'll have to return the favor. I don't want to kill one of the good guys, but I will if I have to. Goddess knows I have killed plenty before him, and there will be plenty more to come.

The officers are not happy about it, but they lower their weapons anyway and let me through. I can hear them grumbling to each other as I walk past them. There is a slew of *bitches* and *fucking the boss* comments being said. Oh hells, it will have to be a battle for another day. I have a case to assist and don't have time to play around with these mortals. Not today, anyway.

I walk past the emergency vehicles with all their obnoxious flashing lights. The scene reminds me of a rave gone terribly wrong. I almost wait for the thumping bass of the techno music and teens dancing with glow sticks to start. I blink the images away and continue to the row home in question. What in the hells is going on, and why is it so damned hard for me to focus today? I admit to being distracted occasionally...okay, often, but this is ridiculous.

The row home looks almost identical to the other dozen in this area of the city. The lights dance on the red bricks and gleam from the windows. There is another group of officers in front of the entrance, blocking the steps into the home. I approach, and this time everyone is careful not to touch me. Look at that. They *do* learn. They part like water and let me through. Captain Renard appears and ushers me in, pulling me to a stop just inside the entrance.

"Athena, thank you for coming. I'm sorry for the incident outside. We are lucky that you can assist us with this case. I have seen some gruesome scenes in my time, but this one…I don't know…I am at a loss on this one." Something flashes within his eyes. It's fear. This must be bad for him to be reacting this way. It's the first time that I have seen him off his game. The man will rush headfirst into a sea of gunfire without blinking, and this has him scared. That's not a good sign. I have a feeling that things are going to go from bad to worse, fast.

"It's no problem, Captain. I'll do what I can to help you. I'm sorry about your officer. I really hope that I didn't hurt him too badly. I don't think I broke anything." I give him a small smile to reassure him. I have gotten to know him very well, both professionally and personally, these last few months. I have seen the man cooking eggs buck-naked for goddess' sake. I want to say something comforting, but I don't know what I am walking into. I have no words to make him feel better, to make any of this better. I doubt there can be a better right now.

"Okay, Renard, show me, and let's see if I can help." I meet his eyes, and we share a moment of understanding. He nods and turns on his heel, walking through the living room. I follow silently, taking in the large space and all its neatly placed furniture. The stench hits me the moment we enter the dining room. It is a putrid punch to the face. You never forget the pungent smell of death. Not that of rotting corpses, but the sweet metallic scent of blood and the unique horror of punctured bowels. It's the smell of fresh death. There is something terrible underlying the odor, and I can promise you it is something you remember. I am more accustomed to it now, but it still makes me feel slightly nauseous.

This is a typical dining room with a large oak table, matching chairs, and a cabinet with gleaming china saved for special occasions that would no longer come. The room is pristine except for the bodies. Sitting at the table is what is left of a large man. He looks like he was gutted as he sat down for dinner. His face is frozen in agony and fear, but free of blood. Both hands hang limply at his sides. His stomach has a huge gaping hole as if someone took a giant ice-cream scoop to it. Blood still drips from his ravaged torso and pools around the base of the chair. His legs are untouched, and only his vital organs are missing.

Walking over to what is left of his corpse, I am careful not to step in the blood. It's beyond difficult to remove from shoes. Usually, I bring a go-bag with everything that I need for two days, but I don't remember loading it into my car. I will have to drive home in nothing but my underwear if I mess up these clothes. I can only imagine the awkward conversation between me and the local PD if I was seen or pulled over. No, I think I'll leave that gem to my nightmares. It's equivalent to the dream of being naked in class.

"If he was alive when the killer gutted him, he wasn't for long. With these wounds, he would have bled out quickly. It would have been painful but fast. It appears as if someone removed all his vital organs and bowels. Seemingly scooped out with a large tool, or perhaps..." I lean in closer to look at the wound.

"No, there are tear marks in the wound. Whatever did this, did it with its claws. It literally dug the innards out of him."

Renard swallows audibly. "It...not he or she...it?" He is worried about the answer because if it isn't human, we are dealing with a monster. Some form of humanoid that literally ate out his heart and everything else. Standing up straight so I can examine the rest of the man, I walk around him. There is nothing else significant that I can tell him. I leave him there, glazed over eyes staring at the ceiling, crying for help that will always be too late.

Next is the wife. She looks as if she had tried to climb across the table to get away from whatever attacked her. She hadn't made it far before it got her. The upper half of her body is still on the table, clutching it for dear life. Her cold, dead eyes stare off into the distance. Her face forever frozen in a silent scream.

196

"Her death was quicker than his. She would have bled out in seconds. At first glance, hers seems to be more violent, but I don't think that's it. These killings don't look premeditated or for the sake of torture. Whatever did this, did it for the sole purpose of eating them. They were a meal and nothing more."

"How do you know?" The Captain is gazing intently at me. As if he can forget the scene or make it disappear altogether if he stares at me hard enough. Unfortunately, no amount of redirection will make this go away. I doubt a truckload of bleach and cleaning solvent will erase this. This house will be a bitch to sell.

"If this were about anything more than eating the people, there would be more carnage, more destruction. Nothing else is out of place. It's only the people who have been torn apart."

I'll never forget the look of pure terror frozen on this woman's face. I scan the rest of the scene, as cold and impartial as possible, before examining her body closer. I walk around, seeing if the lower part of her is still there. Sure enough, it has been ripped off and pulled beneath the table.

"It dragged her under the table. Most likely so it would feel covered while it finished eating her," I say, indicating the bloody streaks.

"Are these the only two bodies?" I ask without looking at Renard. I know he is still there, waiting for my assessment, and trying to ignore the stench of the corpses.

"Yes, there are no other victims in the home." Something about the way he says it sounds odd.

"In the home? Does that mean there are victims somewhere else?" I can feel the lump rise in my throat, and I hope that I am wrong about his tone. Gods, please don't let there be any half-eaten children. I can't handle the mangled bodies of kids right now. I close my eyes and pray for anything else but children.

"Family dog outside is pretty chewed up."

"Shit." Dogs, well, any animals really, are right there on the list with children for me. Poor pooch. I walk closer to the edge of the table. Crouching down to get a better look at the body only makes the smell stronger. *I will not vomit,* I recite silently to myself on repeat.

"Rigor mortis is just beginning to set in, so this is a fresh kill. No more than a few hours. Is it okay if I disturb the scene to examine the remains?" It's easier to think of them as remains, instead of people. If you don't take it personally, don't think of them as someone's family, it almost makes it easier. Almost.

"Yes, the scene is all yours," he says and hands me a pair of blue medical gloves, anticipating my need. We have worked together on many cases and have found that we make a great team. I quickly put them on and lean in closer to what is left of the lower part of the woman's body. I'm careful not to let any of the tepid, cooling blood drip on me. That is the last thing I want, and I grimace at the thought.

"What is it?" he asks, noticing the look on my face.

"Nothing pertaining to the case."

"Tell me, anyway." Being the always considerate man that he is, he wants to know what I was thinking regardless of relevance.

"I was thinking that I have to be careful, so I don't get blood on me. You told me it's bad to strip in front of your officers because it distracts them." I give him a wicked smile that promises more once we are far away from this place. He lets out a small chuckle in response.

"Yes, that is a privilege that I am hoping to reserve just for me." He is slightly possessive, how cute. He has no idea what he is asking. Silly man. My smile widens at the thought.

"So, what are your thoughts on the woman?" He changes the subject quickly. Very smart man. Can't have us having sex in the crime scene. I stifle any further thoughts and focus on the task at hand.

"The left femur, patella, fibula, and tibia are stripped almost to the bone. Both feet and phalanges seem to be intact. However, I will have to remove the right shoe to be sure. Her right leg was relatively spared. The UNSUB must have been disturbed during his kill or had its fill and left the rest." I carefully remove the black and pink flats. "Both feet are completely intact and have no visible wounds. Are there any witnesses?"

"Yes, the neighbor reported hearing screams and what she described as a large dog in the home. She came to check on them and could see the woman's upper half still on the table. She screamed and called 911. Apparently, the UNSUB fled immediately after."

I crawl back to the woman's lower body and legs.

"Something is odd about these leg bones." I pick up what is left of the woman's eaten leg, and it immediately pulls free from the other flesh. I hadn't pulled hard, but the unexpected release made me tilt backward.

"Shit...the leg pulled free. I'd speculate that it was torn off but had not completely detached during the struggle. The slight force of me picking it up caused it to detach the rest of the way." Pulling it closer, I examine the markings on the bones. I try not to look embarrassed at my fumble.

"This doesn't look like it was made from a weapon. The edges are too erratic. These marks...they look like teeth marks."

I could hear Renard swallow behind me.

"The killer ate them both, like a cannibal?" He sounds as if he is going to vomit. He still doesn't want to accept that this isn't a murder committed by an average human and that whatever did this, literally ate the evidence.

"No, these marks are not consistent with human bite marks. Honestly, it looks like canine teeth."

"A dog did this? What kind of dog could do this much damage?" His voice holds a hint of hysteria. I hope that he can keep it together. I can't figure out what happened here *and* help him.

"A large dog could have possibly done this, but it would have to be massive to inflict this much damage. What kind of dog did the victims own?" I am hoping it is a behemoth of a dog. That would make life so much easier if their pooch had eaten them. Who knows? Maybe they deserved it. What can I say? I usually prefer dogs to people. They are more loyal and trustworthy. I have never had a dog lie to me about kibble.

"A Chihuahua."

Shit, so much for it being the family pooch. Unless the tiny pup can morph into something much larger, it wasn't the dog.

"The only thing left of him is his bloody collar and his hind legs. People are one thing, but pets are right there with kids for me. I have a hell of a time with cases involving them." I silently correct him with *hells* instead of hell. Oh, there is so much the mortals don't yet understand.

"I can assure you that a Chihuahua did not do this. Whatever did this was much bigger." Placing the leg back, I stand and walk around the table again. There must be something here. Some clue that can tell us what happened. That's when I spot it. There are two neat prints in the blood and a host of them going towards the kitchen. Canine, except they are the equivalent to a men's size ten shoe, and the strides between them are too wide. There is a good three feet between each one. The long strides explain why I had not noticed them sooner. That and that I was too focused on what was left of the couple.

"Is this some sort of sick joke? These prints are huge and far to spread out to be a dog of any breed." I feel anger bubble inside of me. This is so not fucking funny.

"No, Athena, I wouldn't have called you out if we had any other explanation. We are stumped, and you are the only one who seems to be able to solve the unsolvable." The anger fades as quickly as it arrived. He is right. They call me in when they come up empty. I am sort of their *oh shit* handle that gets pulled in dire emergencies. Consultant or not, the locals are not fans of outsiders mucking up their scenes or investigations. Since I am not human, I am about as outsider as it gets. Renard knows the truth about me. It's probably a huge factor in why he trusts me, well that and my ridiculously high crime solve rate. I don't like to boast, but I am damn good at what I do. Of course, getting to shag a goddess doesn't hurt. I'm damn good at that, too.

"Okay, I think I have learned all that I can for now. I will have to do some research to give you any further form of...explanation for all of this." I spread my arms out to encompass the scene.

"I will call you as soon as I know anything. I have a theory, but it's based on urban legends and lore. I want to be sure before I start implicating anything."

"Okay. Thank you for coming out. I will wait to hear from you before releasing anything official."

"Don't thank me yet. I don't have any real answers for what happened here." I don't have a realistic answer, at least not yet. I can't go around yelling *werewolf* without enough proof.

"What you have told me will help. Just call me when you know more. I pray that this is a one-time thing and not the beginning of something worse."

I suppose the only thing that could be worse than this is a lot more of this. More half-eaten bodies would be much worse. Gods, I hope this isn't the start of a killing spree. If it is, Tahiti is looking better and better.

I say my goodbyes and exit the home. As soon as I am outside, I draw in a deep breath and inhale the fresh air. It is great to get away from the stench of fresh death and disemboweled bodies. Leaving the scene, I can't help but be thankful for the simple things like city air. It may not smell great, but it is far better than the air in that place.

The officer that I had injured and his comrades seem to have left, or they just didn't want to run into me again, so they made themselves scarce. Either way, it doesn't bother me. I have had enough for one night. I quickly walk to my car. The thought of jogging there crosses my mind, but I don't want to give off the wrong impression. I am thankful to get far away from the half-eaten bodies but don't want to seem desperate to get away. Big, bad goddess that I am...right? Honestly, if I never see a half-eaten corpse for the rest of my life, it will still be too soon.

I won't be able to draw in a breath of relief until I am on my way home. As I approach my car, the small hairs stand at attention on the back of my neck, and goosebumps raise on my arms. Someone is following me, watching me. Watching and waiting.

I turn around, but no one is there. Paranoid? No, not me. I quicken my pace, nearly running to my car. I fumble with the keys and drop them. Cursing at myself for acting like a scared child, I bend to retrieve them. *This is ridiculous! You are a goddess and shouldn't be so freaked out right now.* I am fishing around, looking for the keys, when something crashes into me. It's huge and heavy, knocking me completely off my feet and onto my back.

I slam against the sidewalk with such force that I can hear the concrete crack underneath my body. It is echoed by the sickening sound of my bones breaking. All the air leaves me, and I gasp wildly, struggling to breathe. I have multiple broken bones, some of which are my ribs. I can't get the air to go into my lungs, and I feel like I am drowning. Within a heartbeat, a blur of blood-soaked fur is on top of me, huge jaws snapping at my face. The putrid breath fills what little of my lungs are still operational and gags me. I put my hands up and desperately try to keep its fangs from tearing off my face. With everything that I have, I push against the massive creature.

I struggle to get free, but the animal is so large that I can't get away. Its massive paws are pinning my stomach and chest to the ground. I can feel its claws digging deep into my skin, tender flesh giving way and tearing, blood pouring from the wounds. Trying to shove the beast off only angers it more. It raises a huge paw and violently slashes at me. My torso and face split open like the peeling of an orange. My vision goes red as blood obscures my eyes. I know there isn't anything left of my face or chest. Nothing recognizable, not anymore.

Screaming in pain is all that I can do as I sink heavily into oblivion. I guess my suspicions about what had killed those two people were correct, and it will keep killing. The massacres will not end with me. It won't stop feeding its bloodlust. Not until someone is able to put it down. I can still feel the tugging of the beast as it shreds me into pieces and disembowels me. It consumes me, and I am left helpless as it does. Thankfully, the pain is gone now. I am numb and drifting. I guess I am not the one to stop this monster. I am not the goddess of legend that I thought I was. The Goddess of Wisdom and War, killed by a werewolf. Instead of stopping it, I have become one with it. I want to laugh at the irony. I tried so hard to keep my inner monster at bay, only to be eaten by this one.

Thick blackness covers everything. It is sticky like tar. I can't move. I feel myself sinking deeper and deeper into the icky, gooey sludge. It sucks me under, and I want to panic, to scream, to cry for help. I can't do anything. And who will even hear me? Who will even care? I am all alone. My heart aches as despair fills me. The blackness envelopes me, filling me with its darkness. I feel it taking over, tainting everything it touches. Will anyone even notice that I am gone? Probably not. I have never felt so alone, so helpless, so sad. All the love and joy that once was, is gone. All that is left is the blackness. I don't even care anymore. Everyone has someone who loves them, and who do I have? I don't even have a cat to come home to. I start to give up and let the dark have me.

"Don't you *dare* give up!" I hear a woman's voice say, and she sounds pissed.

"If I have to go to the very depths of Tartarus and drag your sorry ass back here, there will be hell to pay." The voice is so familiar. Then I hear sobbing. Someone is crying. Why are they so sad? After what seems like forever has passed, my own sobs join theirs. We all cry together. The voices and I.

Then, something is lifting me, or maybe someone. The blackness tries to hold on to me, wants to suck me deeper. To finish what it started and take me into eternal oblivion. Whatever is pulling me free does not yield. It continues to yank me out. The more I rise from the darkness, the more the black sludge falls away, melting into nothing. I can breathe again and don't feel so hopeless. I lay there and watch as I float toward a warm, bright light. I can feel it cleansing me. I am so close to the light. I can almost touch it.

My eyes open as the scream erupts from my lips. I am sitting, clutching my chest where the beast had torn through my body. The skin is unharmed, and I am safe in my bed. I fall back onto my comfortable, memory foam, aloe-cooled mattress, and focus all my efforts on re-learning how to breathe. During my dream…no, nightmare, I had kicked all the blankets off and somehow tossed my pillows across the room. I am drenched in sweat and need a shower. Slowly I sit up, deciding that a shower sounds like a wonderful idea. Honestly, who in the hells would want to go back to sleep after a nightmare like that? No, thank you.

Rubbing the last remnants of sleep from my eyes, I stumble to the master bath and turn on the light. Gods, it is bright. Looking at my reflection in the large oval mirrors, all I can think is, *Damn, you look terrible.* I slowly undress and turn on the shower. Everything aches, and my muscles scream at me every time I move. Every single inch hurts like hells. Suddenly, the idea of trying to go back to sleep doesn't seem so bad. No, I can't do that. I must get moving and figure out what is going on. I step under the hot water and let it wash over my body, rinsing the nightmare down the drain. If only it were that easy.

After thoroughly scrubbing every part of me until my skin is bright pink and then conditioning my hair, I turn off the water and step out of the shower into the steam-filled room. I dry off and brush my hair and teeth. Normally, I wrap a towel around me before exiting back into my room to get dressed, but I don't care today. Besides, it's not like anyone will see me anyway. I walk nude into my bedroom and don a pair of comfortable jeans and a red silk shirt. I slip on flats and look at them on my feet. They look so familiar. Not because they are my shoes…it's something else. Staring at them, I finally place the memory. They are the same flats that the dead woman was wearing. Nope, not doing that. Hells no.

I immediately remove them and walk out of my bedroom and into the kitchen. I go to the trash can and throw them away. I will have to buy new comfortable shoes. Today, I will wear boots. The first order of business is coffee. I need coffee. Then I will get new shoes and find out what the nightmare really means. I suspect that it has something to do with the growing darkness that I feel inside of me. It's there every day. I can't outrun it or get rid of it. Maybe this is my mind's way of telling me I must face it. I rub my temples and let out my breath. I can feel a migraine coming on. I am going to need coffee…lots of it.

TIME
TO
FLY

BY

GEORGIA MOODY

HESTIA,
GODDESS OF THE HEARTH
& HOME

O *NE SOUL LIES ANXIOUS, WIDE AWAKE...CRUEL AND COLD, LIKE WINDS FROM THE SEA...*
The floor shook, and more water poured in around me. The sky was torn to shreds with lightning, and stones were falling from the ceilings and walls. They were coming, and I was the last one left. First and Last, always.

Too pigheaded to leave, too terrified to stay, I sat with my brazier on my lap and sheltered the fire from the rain. I didn't have a weapon, and even if I did, it wouldn't have done any good.

I am so desperately tired. They don't need me anymore. They've forgotten me.

My siblings had fled, leaving me alone to guard the fire. I could practically hear Hera sniggering about me being the *sacrificial offering.* I squinted into the rain, but I couldn't see anything.

Another chunk of the sky fell down, landing with a thunderous roar, its impact spider-webbing the once-white marble floors into jagged shards. Orion's bow skittered away across the room, taking out a column, while the three stars of his belt fizzled down to nothingness. The Scales fell next, crashing into the rubble and beginning to corrode, their brilliant gold melting under the rain, peeling away to crumbling clay.

I should just...let...go.

A peacock screamed, cut off mid-shriek. Bloody feathers blew in, plastering the crumbling walls with iridescent eyes weeping ruby tears. Bulls bellowed, then the wind carried the acrid stink of burning hair and smoldering fat. My boars, set free as the invaders came, roared challenges and died squealing, joining the sacred bulls on the roasting spit.

Golden horses whinnied and reared, kicking away their traces, biting and stomping at the invaders. They were cruelly subdued, with iron bits that burned soft mouths used to the finest ambrosia, and their gleaming coats turned dull brown in the mud and rain.

Wolves tore at man-flesh, but for each invader killed, they lost a dozen or more. The hinds, harmless things of beauty and moonlight, crashed away down the mountain. They died when grabbed by greedy hands, like a too-eager child that crushes the butterfly that lands on their palm.

Their boots could be felt through the floor now. Their torches, undaunted by the wind and rain, made shadows cavort like the former residents of these halls. I clutched my brazier even tighter and closed my eyes.

Who does a goddess pray to, when she is faced with oblivion?

Don't forget me. Someone light a fire, say my name!

I felt a new sensation, one I had never felt before, and dropped my brazier, spilling the coals into the swirling waters. They died in a hiss of steam as I looked at my hands. For the first time, blisters rose from where my fingers and arms had touched the bronze that cradled the fire.

I pushed myself to my feet, and the water swirled around my ankles, cold as death. I turned my back on my hearth and home and began to run for my life. The hounds bayed as the storm rose further, and I ran faster. Artemis' hounds never lost their quarry, even now in the hands of another. They were too well trained for that.

Olympus was falling, and I was the only one left. Everywhere there was cold and darkness and oblivion, stinking of fear, burning blood, and the harsh metallic reek of ozone from the lightning striking all around me. The forge had fallen, and the stables were being pillaged. Sacred animals and beloved companions alike were being fed to the fires that raged even in the rain.

"There's one left! Quickly, get her! It's that virgin bitch!"

"She won't be a virgin for long after we catch her!"

One of Hephaestus' arrows slammed into my shoulder, the beautifully filigreed arrowhead protruding through my chest. The swirls and swooping curves were dark with blood, the ivory shaft stained crimson in the stormlight, as my dress began to darken.

Blood? I don't bleed...

I scrambled up to the heights behind the remains of the forge, not sure where I was going, but knowing that to go backwards was to hasten my demise. A trail of torches followed my footsteps, the eternal braziers being knocked over or kicked aside as they came. Great plumes of steam rose, and as the bronze basins cooled, I saw men pick them up. Those beauties wrought by the skilled hands of Hephaestus' automatons were more perfect than any man could create. They slung them across the backs of looters, careless and irreverent, plunder from the halls of the gods.

I was running out of places to go, and my shoulder hurt so much. I staggered and fell, my knees and palms bloodied against the stone. My tears of pain and confusion mixed with the rain as I realized there was nowhere else to flee.

I stood next to one of the obelisks that marked the borders of Olympus. Ahead of me was empty air, all the way to the stone thousands of feet below.

Behind me, the hunters grew closer. Paws scrabbled on rocks, and I heard the snarling of dogs I had fed from my table for centuries. A cat screamed, high and sharp over the rumbling thunder, and I knew Dionysus' leopards had met their end. I took a step back, holding my bleeding hands out towards the beasts I had petted and spoiled for millennia.

"Easy, easy," I said, and my voice was shaking. "Good girls, easy...you know me."

One of the big boarhounds lunged at me, ivory teeth slamming closed millimeters from my hand. I yanked it back, taking another step backwards. I stumbled as my heel came down on a pebble and barely caught myself from going over the precipice.

The dogs surged forward, and I moved back as far as I could. My sandals were barely keeping a grip on the edge of the gaping abyss of nothingness behind me.

I had a choice to make.

Die here, being torn apart by animals, despoiled by humans. Take the risk of being left worse than dead, or take my life into my own hands, in a last act of defiance.

I had always wondered what it was like to fly. Time I found out.

I expected dying would hurt, so when I woke up, the fact that I wasn't in shrieking agony and splattered across the basalt of Mount Olympus was surprising. That I woke up on Olympus at all was shocking, if I am honest. I had expected to wake up in Tartarus, probably with Charon prodding at me with a boat oar, if the invaders hadn't killed him as well.

I was still cold and wet, but the storm was gone, and I was under unfamiliar stars, with something sharp digging into my spine. I hadn't seen too much of Tartarus, but I didn't think there were pine trees there.

I heard screaming, which checked with Tartarus, and smelled fresh blood, which didn't. Whatever I had landed on wasn't happy about it and wriggled away. I heard snorting and growling. I pushed myself upright and looked around, seeing a grey-and-black furry mass disappearing under a huge fallen tree.

Well enough, then. Where in the name of Hades was I?

Hoofbeats, and screaming, and crying children—wherever I was, I needed to do something about it, since the Fates had decided that I was to live. I stood up, wobble-kneed as a fresh lamb, and took a breath of this strange, cold air. Out of habit, I snapped my fingers, hoping to conjure a ball of flame.

Nothing except a stinging sensation and a tiny, almost invisible, spark that vanished like a breath.

210

All right, I couldn't use my fire, but I could go try to help. They had to have spared me for *something*. I staggered down the slope towards the screaming. I heard the distinct scrape of flint against steel, and my ears perked. Someone was trying to start a fire.

"Lady of Flames, help me, help us, please!" Scrape, scrape, scrape.

"Mama, they're coming, they're coming!"

"Lady, *please!*" Scrape, scrape, the sound of metal hitting rocks. "Mama!"

I snapped my fingers again. A tiny ball of fire appeared, pale and weak, but still, flame. I would forgive the mortals the informal address this time. I felt warm breath on my back and turned. Nothing there, but I decided to start running, just in case. I cradled my little flame close to my breast and headed to where I was needed.

I slid down the end of a scree and landed in a tangle. I immediately clenched my fist around the flame and felt it grow. The scrapes and bruises seared into my skin, but healed.

I smelled burning wool on the damp air and heard whispered prayers underneath the screaming of children coming from a small hollow in the rock. The night wind was cold on my face, but I ran as quick as I could.

Dark shapes of men and dogs were advancing on the hollow, and fitful light was rising, throwing ghastly shadows onto all the trees. I saw bodies on the ground, goat-legged and human alike, and beasts tearing at the flesh. An altar was tossed aside, and a brazier spilled into the damp bracken—a brazier bearing the horns of my own symbol. A woman's body was draped grotesquely over the remains of the altar stone, her clothing torn apart. In the starlight, the bloody streaks were dark on her pale flesh, cold and still as marble. A satyr lay dead at her feet, his hand still clutching her ankle, weapon in his other hand, and cold steel protruding from his chest.

I was not a goddess of battle, but these mortals were *mine*, and I would protect them.

I screamed with all the power of a vengeful goddess, and in that moment, I felt the warmth course through me. The fire roared high, and leapt from its cradle of wool, rising and blossoming into a great blazing nova of white-hot death, searing invader flesh from bone and on to crumbling ash in the space between heartbeats.

The flames sank back to a small blaze, warm and comforting, and I approached the mortals. Two women, three children, were huddling close against the rock wall. I knelt by the fire and held my hands over it. It was far larger than the twist of wool should support, and I smiled. Flames licked at my fingers, soft as kitten fur. This was *my* fire. The new scars were bright against my skin, and I was glad they were there. They would make sure I never forgot this night.

The older of the two women clutched her son close. I could see that he had cloven hooves, and she had flowers growing throughout her hair. Nymphs? But why would nymphs fear me?

The younger one held her two girls, but she didn't cower. "Lady of Flames? You came..."

"Of course I came, my dear. I always come to those who ask my aid," I said, the urge to hunt down those who desecrated this place riding high under my skin. "Where are the rest of you?"

"The pack tried to lead them off, but we got separated," she answered. "We came to the shrine, thinking they would respect that, but..."

"I saw. I will personally see that their shades go to Elysia," I vowed. She closed her eyes, holding her girls. They were looking at me, eyes bright as new pennies in the firelight. The blossoms in their hair were just beginning to bud, hard little green lumps amid the tangled curls.

They were just babies.

"I'm going to go find your mates," I said, and pushed myself to my feet. "Stay by the fire. It will keep you safe. My fire will always keep you safe." I unpinned my cloak from my shoulders and draped it around the five of them. "I will go find your pack."

I did not know this place, but I knew satyrs. They would be where the fighting was thickest, especially if their girls were in danger. They would have led the invaders away from this place, so...follow the trail of carnage. The satyrs would have the advantage amongst the trees, so no doubt the humans would try to shift the fight to a clearing.

I found them, or what was left of them. There was a clearing, all right, and it was choked with bodies of man, beast, and satyr alike. Old bucks wielding axes, young bucks fighting with bare hands and stolen swords, humans gutted and shredded, faces twisted in death agonies as they attempted to hold their guts in.

Across the clearing, a few survivors huddled in the deeper darkness under the trees - pine trees, sacred to Pan. I heard faint prayers, gasped phrases that ended in bubbling wheezes. Moving as quickly as I could, I knelt among the wounded. Most of these here would survive, given time and just a bit of luck. Satyrs had a keen instinct when death was nearby, and would likely have granted as much mercy as they could to those who had fallen on the field.

"Come on, boys, your girls need you," I said, lifting a young warrior to his feet. He had a nasty gash into the deep muscle of his shoulder, but it was already clotted. "What's your name, handsome?"

"Hector, my lady," he grunted, trying to get his feet under him. "I'm all right. Help my brothers."

He stood guard while I did so, but there wasn't much for me to do. They were pulling themselves up, hasty bandages applied, water and wine offered.

As they all managed to stand, I looked around the area under the tree. There had been a shrine of a different sort here, horned skulls

213

and antlers scattered about, and shards of amphorae in the distinct red-brown of Greek clay. I saw a smiling face holding grapes before a large cloven hoof came down on it, grinding it to dust.

"He didn't come for us, my lady, but you came for our does and our kids. For that, we swear our service to you," Hector said, and knelt. One by one, the survivors joined him, the worst of the wounded bowing their heads.

"Lady of Flames, Goddess of Hearth and Home, we are in your debt for coming to the aid of our wives and children. We are yours to command."

The faith was palpable, and I shivered.

"Let's go find the rest of your pack," I said, leading the way across the battlefield. I stopped at every satyr's corpse and laid drachma over their eyes, praying that Charon would give them swift passage to Elysia.

Once I had gotten them on the path back to the girls, I turned and faced the stinking clearing once again. I sent my newly renewed flame to burn the satyrs' bodies, leaving their attackers to rot slowly and be devoured by scavengers.

I heard the happy shrieks of children and lovers being reunited behind me as the braver does came looking for their bucks. There were cries of anguish and weeping as well. A couple of the nymphs came to stand beside me, mute with grief. I put my arms around them and hugged gently.

I will protect them, I swore to the heavens. *These are my people now.*

214

DARKNESS FALLS

BY

JENNIFER MORTON

MEDUSA,

THE MORTAL GORGON

I KNEW I WAS SLEEPING. I remembered going to bed, remembered tossing and turning until sleep finally claimed me. The black mist surrounding me was definitely the stuff of nightmares, but this wasn't like any dream I'd ever had.

As I walked, the mist coalesced around me. There was a malevolence hiding within the darkness that made my skin crawl. The air felt suffocating, and I struggled to keep my breathing under control.

I noticed a constant soft hissing and realized with a start that I was in full Gorgon mode. For the first time, I was thankful for the protection and didn't try to force the monster down to hide within my skin.

I tried to look past the inky fog, but there was nothing. Not that I couldn't see past the darkness, there was just nothing to see. I kept walking, trying to wake up or at least get beyond the black mist. Several times I turned, feeling as if someone was about to jump me from behind. There was never anything there but more black mist. It moved and swirled as if it were alive, radiating feelings of dread. I wanted to recoil, to get beyond its reach, but it was everywhere.

I was trapped in a dream that wasn't a dream and tried to keep myself from panicking. I closed my eyes and concentrated, willing myself to wake up.

"Closed eyes to see through the darkness?" a grave voice asked with a laugh.

My eyes flew open, and my snakes went wild. I spun around, looking for the source of the voice, and found only darkness and shadows. I fought the urge to run, mostly because I didn't think there was anywhere *to* run. I stood with my feet frozen in place. Okay, so I probably couldn't have run even if I wanted to. The feeling of dread washing over me was crippling.

I felt something slither over my foot and looked down. The mist was wriggling over the ground and crawling up my legs.

"What do you want from me?" I yelled as I tried to kick the fog away.

"It isn't just what I want, but what must be done."

"I don't know what that means, stop playing games!" I ground out through gritted teeth.

"The requirement is a hunt. Dire it is, a taunt it is not. The balance hangs. If the balance falls, darkness wins, and the light will fade."

"Oh, what fresh hell is this?" I couldn't keep the comment from slipping out.

"Hell, it is, fresh, it is not."

I whirled around and stomped off, but the grave voice continued, "Run, you may try, circles you will do until the darkness is found."

The voice sounded further and further away the more it spoke. Before I could reply, there was a blinding flash of light. I found myself thrown out of the void and into the sunshine of an autumn morning. I blinked several times, trying to adjust to the sudden brightness. My snakes writhed in anger and fear, and I reached up to calm them as I pushed the Gorgon down. I glanced around, frantically trying to figure out where I was. I was definitely in a cemetery, that much was obvious considering the mausoleums surrounding me.

Well, no way was I going to stay here. I tried to teleport out, but nothing happened. Absolutely nothing. Weird. I pulled the Gorgon closer to the surface and looked at my hand. Yep, that still worked. Fine, if I couldn't leave the easy way, I could walk. At least to a phone. Then I'd get as far from wherever this was as I could.

The graveyard was massive. Hmm, is graveyard the right term, or is it cemetery? There were rows and rows of mausoleums, so I followed the path towards what I hoped was the gate. As I walked, I noticed the dates that time hadn't worn away. I was still learning, but I guessed them to be from the Civil War era. Under other circumstances, I might have enjoyed exploring.

The sun was low, so I knew it was still early, but I would have expected to see someone visiting a grave. Or maybe a groundskeeper. But there was no one. It didn't matter, and I wasn't staying. I didn't care what the nightmare voice said. This wasn't my circus, and I was leaving before the clowns showed up.

The gate finally came into view. It was closed, so I pushed on it, expecting it to swing open. It didn't because I couldn't actually make contact with the iron bars. I moved a few feet over and put my hands up, reaching out slowly. There seemed to be some kind of invisible barrier keeping me in. I experimented, walking with my hand out, trailing my fingers over it as I went. I was trapped in an empty graveyard, the day before Halloween. If this was someone's idea of a joke, I would turn them into stone and use the statue as a coat rack.

I turned to walk towards the opposite end of the cemetery and caught movement from the corner of my eye. I spun around, but there was no one there. My skin crawled like I was being watched. I could feel the touch of eyes, and a sensation of complete disgust rolled over me. I shivered and gave myself a mental slap to help me focus.

Then, I noticed the mist. There was a thin layer spreading over the nearest crypt, and it carried the night within it. The darkness overpowered everything, pushing back the light wherever it touched. It was hard to look at directly, so I hurried away, feeling my hopes of this being a prank float away on the chill breeze. I didn't want to be anywhere near that evil fog.

I gave up looking for a way out and concentrated on finding where the black mist was coming from. The more I walked, the more my skin crawled, and the feeling that I was being watched intensified. I could feel eyes on me, but every time I looked, there was no one there. Just the mist coming out from under more and more crypts the farther into the cemetery I walked. It pooled and swirled along the ground, and sometimes even sent tendrils up like it was looking around. It was getting almost impossible to walk without wading into it.

I didn't want that fog to touch me. I remembered how it felt clinging to my skin in the dream that wasn't a dream. I wanted to avoid letting that happen again. If the mist touched me here, I wasn't sure what would happen. I turned to circle around the misty darkness. Panic rose as it countered and cut me off. It moved with my steps with an intelligence I hadn't noticed before. Someone, or something, had to be controlling it.

I spun in a circle, looking for an escape, and the mist shot forward from every direction. I screamed, and my Gorgon roared to the surface just before the fog could touch me. This form, always so repulsive to me, became unexpected armor. I could feel the fog trying to force its way in, pushing and pulsing. But it rolled right off when it came in contact with my skin. I didn't even want to think about what could have happened if it got past.

I let out a breath and felt the tension leave my shoulders. It couldn't hurt me. Now, I needed to find out if I could damage it.

With a renewed sense of purpose, I headed toward the heart of the old cemetery. Several pumpkins sitting at the door of an unusually large mausoleum caught my eye. They seemed to laugh at me with their crooked smiles. The fog was pouring from under the door at an alarming rate. It had to have a source somewhere. Unfortunately for me, it seemed to be underground.

My snakes were hissing furiously as the darkness crawled around my ankles. Even though the sun was still rising, the inky fog absorbed the light. Taking a breath, I pushed as hard as I could, inching the door of the mausoleum open enough for me to squeeze through. Inside, the light barely penetrated the shadows. With a last look behind me, I pushed further inside. The musty smell of death was overpowering, and I could feel anger radiating from the mist. I edged my way along the interior and was disappointed to see the floor slope deeper into the earth.

Resigned, I followed the path, keeping one hand on the wall to guide my way. The narrow tunnel opened into a massive room with torches hanging along the walls. The darkness was so absolute that the firelight dancing over the stone almost hurt my eyes. A huge mass of black energy swirled in the center of the room. It was more than just mist or fog. It was alive. Waves of blackness rolled from it in an endless stream.

The air around the mass shimmered and pulsed, and I had to resist the urge to reach out to it. Instead, I leaned in to get a closer look. There were even darker shapes moving under the surface. It was almost mesmerizing, like I was looking into shadows that kept swirling around each other. Red eyes peered back at me from deep within the darkness. I screamed and scrambled away, slamming against the wall. The fog slid up my back and over my shoulders, circling my neck. I pressed my lips together and clenched my jaw, afraid whatever this thing was would continue its exploration and cover my face.

I spun away from the wall and clawed at the darkness over my throat. My snakes hissed and bit at it. It finally retreated just enough for me to pull it away. Instead of feeling like fog and dissipating with my struggles, it was solid and resisted. Then all at once, it fell away, and I got the distinct impression that it was just playing with me.

I was suddenly aware of a cacophony of voices. My gaze flew around the room, looking for their source. The fog climbed over the walls like a stain, eating the light from the torches.

My mind flashed back to the feeling of being watched earlier, and I wondered if something had been hiding in the fog then. No wonder it seemed alive. There was something sentient within it. I had no idea how to fight darkness or the mysterious creatures that lived within it.

More and more eyes were coming to the surface to watch me. I had walked right into a trap. The dark mist was spreading out and covering the room, hiding the way out. The tunnel I had followed in was utterly swallowed by darkness.

The voices that had only moments before seemed like hundreds had coalesced into one. It sounded like rocks being ground together, and it made my skin crawl. I couldn't focus on the words, so instead, I turned my attention to the eyes. If I could look at enough of them at once, maybe I could turn the center to stone and stop the spread of the mist.

Everywhere I looked, eyes peered at me through the curtain of shadows. There were too many, in too large of an area. I couldn't look everywhere fast enough. Sensing my panic, my snakes went wild, trying to lash out. My mind raced to come up with a way to turn the heart of the darkness to stone.

I was cycling through my options, when I realized the rasping voice was saying something about a veil.

"We are the Darkness, and we have come to take the light and make this world ours. The veil between dimensions is thin. It weakens and tears to make way for us," the Darkness boomed out in a voice that seemed to come from inside my head.

I instinctively covered my ears to keep the sound out, even as I knew it wouldn't do any good. "This isn't your world, and I won't let you have it!" I yelled, my hands still over my ears.

"Let us? Little snake girl, don't you see? It's already ours. We are covering this land, eating the light until all that's left is darkness. The veil between worlds is falling, and darkness is rising."

I was almost out of time. There had to be something I could do. Someone brought me here for a reason. I was a Gorgon, damn it. I had to be able to use that. Why else was I chosen?

I was finally ready to embrace who I am, and now I'd never get the chance. I wiped angrily at the tears running freely down my face. I didn't want it to end like this. I wasn't ready for it to end at all. I had so much life left to live. Everyone did. It wasn't fair for a monster from another world to take everything away from us.

There had to be a way. I paced within the darkness, frantically looking for some way to hurt it, or even just slow it down to buy me time to think. If only I could think. The voices had spread out again, and I gave up trying to make sense of the sounds.

The thought of my new life being taken from me, just as I was starting to live, filled me with so much pain and grief it was crippling. Instead of giving in and letting it consume me, I was determined to fight. I'd never give up. Life was a gift, and I didn't want to let it go. I wouldn't. If it wasn't worth fighting for, it wouldn't be worth living.

I screamed in frustration, then watched as every set of eyes tracked my movement. Before I could think it through, I pushed my way into the center of the mass of darkness. I could feel it pushing against me, but there was nothing but emptiness inside. The shadows recoiled, but they weren't fast enough, and I was able to catch them in my furious gaze. The mist that kept them protected didn't do them any good when I was inside it with them.

As I looked from one evil, distorted face to the next, they turned to stone while the mist crumbled into sand. I stood, shaking with fury, and watched as the fog that had surrounded me rushed to get away before it too was nothing more than dust blowing in the breeze.

I sank to my knees, exhausted. My snakes hung limply at my shoulders. It was over. Relief coursed through me as I struggled to get my breathing under control. I had never used so much energy at once before. I could feel the Gorgon slide down to hide under my skin. My snakes gave one last weak hiss, and I was human again. At least on the outside.

I put my hands on the cold dirt of the catacomb floor and pushed to my feet. I ignored the fresh piles of sand as I made my way through the tunnel. When I stepped out into the afternoon sun, I had to shield my eyes while they adjusted to the brightness. The sand was everywhere. It covered tombs, headstones, and piled like snowdrifts along the walkways.

I picked a direction and walked, putting the mist, the darkness, and the evil that was hiding within it, behind me.

THE WEAVER

BY

ALICE CALLISTO

CLIO,

MUSE OF HISTORY

September 2019

A FEW MONTHS AGO, HERMES, THE GOD OF TRAVEL, THIEVES, AND TRADE, SHOWED UP AT MY DOOR WITH A LETTER FROM MY FATHER, ZEUS. I decided once I finished working at the archeological dig site in Cairo, Egypt, I would head home. We were working at the Luxor Temple, where the mortals were about to make an amazing discovery. I couldn't wait to see the excitement on their faces. Being the Muse of History, I already knew what they were about to discover, but I couldn't tell them. The mortals had to learn about the past on their own without an immortal's interference. It was more meaningful that way.

Sadly, the digging process had stopped. There was a rumour going around about one of the mines. Apparently, there had been echoes of laughter coming from inside. The townspeople knew the area was not safe around the autumn season. They said that if you go inside after dark, you would never be seen again. Of course, I knew that was an old wives' tale, but mortals find these stories scary.

A week passed, and I became more suspicious. A few of the mortals from the site had disappeared. I thought that maybe they went into town to get a few things, but they had been gone way too long. That was why I was making my way to the mine tunnel at two in the morning.

The moon was high in the sky, and it lit our way as we walked to the entrance. With me, I had my mortal assistant, Ali. He had traveled with me for the last four archaeological digs, and I found his company enjoyable. I met him at a coffee shop in DC, close to the National Museum of Natural History. We got along well, and it was a surprise to learn that we were both headed to the same dig site. During those weeks, I got close to the mortal. I offered him a job for the next few projects. At our last exploration, he accepted my offer to be my assistant, and the rest is history.

"Are you sure about this, Clio?" Ali asked.

"Yes, Ali. I am sure," I said, handing him my bag. "Just stay here. It shouldn't take me too long."

I gave him one last smile, although he didn't return it. He continued to look at me, worry furrowing his brow. If only he knew I was an immortal, and there was nothing to fear.

I stepped into the mine, and a cold wind blew by me. The darkness was complete, so I lit a torch, the light illuminating the tunnel. I shivered, something about this cave was eerie. I couldn't tell if it was the cool breeze or the shadows from the rocks that spooked me.

I made my way cautiously through the mine, lighting up the wall torches as I went. Along with the musty cave odor, the smell of rotting bodies tingled my nose, and I felt the urge to vomit. Yes, I was a goddess, and yes, I had lived forty thousand years, but the smell still bothered me. I covered my nose with my scarf, lowering the light closer to the ground. Footprints led into the right tunnel. I followed the path, trailing my hand on the stone wall. In the distance, I could see cobwebs hanging from the ceiling. As I continued, they became thicker, and I couldn't help but wonder about the creatures that created them.

Looking up, I forgot to pay attention to the ground. I tripped over something and landed on my stomach with a groan. The torch rolled away from me, illuminating the floor of the tunnel. Dead bodies littered the cavern I had stumbled into. I scrambled to my feet, dusting off my pants. I turned to see what I had tripped on. My jaw dropped as I recognized one of the researchers from the site, his body a crumpled shell on the ground. I grabbed my torch, shining the light over him. I had seen him the other day, just before he said he was going to town. No one knew he was missing…

I studied his corpse. Thick white webs wrapped his body. His face was ghostly white, and little puncture wounds covered his arms and neck. I ran my fingers over his eyelids, closing them before I stood.

Strange, what kind of creature did this?

Two bodies looked fresh, while the others were beginning to decompose. All had sticky white webs wrapped tightly around them. The ones that still had flesh had matching puncture wounds on their skin. I shivered, there was definitely something in this cave, and I no longer doubted the mortal's fears.

I heard female laughter and spun to look behind me. *Yeah... I think it is time to go.* Although I was a goddess, I was still allowed to be creeped out by this situation. Being immortal, didn't mean I could evade death. If I wasn't careful, I could die. I also had no weapons other than the torch. I was vulnerable.

I started back down the tunnel towards the exit, but only made it a couple of steps before a large spider web stopped me. Within the delicate strands were words written in Mesopotamian. Luckily for me, I could translate the language.

You who has lived more than one life,
Will soon learn the truth to the past you once knew.

I squinted at the words. *What could that mean? Was someone else in the cave?* Looking around, I noticed nothing out of the ordinary. Other than the dead bodies. The laughter echoed through the tunnels once more, and I felt my entire body shiver. I turned to leave the mine, but jerked to a halt. Thousands of spiders were crawling towards me. The sound of their feet hitting the rocky floor created a sickening clicking. My heart pounded hard in my chest, and I was frozen on the spot. I mean, I was okay with one or two spiders, but thousands? Coming right at me?

I ran the opposite way from the exit, hoping there would be another way out of this place. The pathway led me to another opening where skeletons scattered the floor. Perched in the middle of the room was another spider. It was much bigger than the rest, its body nearly filling the entire cavern. The hairs on the back of my neck stood up as I took a step away from it. *That explains the missing people.*

The spider turned around to face me. Its eight eyes surveyed the room in every direction before it focused on me its gaze piercing deep into my soul. The creature abandoned its victim, fangs dripping blood, and crawled towards me. I took a step back, and something crunched. Looking down, I saw smaller spiders surrounding me. Some attempted to climb my leg, the hairs on their feet tickling me. I jumped up and down, dancing to shake off the little beasts.

"Muse of History," a voice called out in my mind. My attention turned back to the bigger spider. *"Fancy seeing you here."*

"Who are you?" I asked her.

"Forgotten me?" she hissed. *"I thought you, out of all the muses, would remember me."*

I focused on the spider, my eyes glowing as I searched my mind for historic events involving the creature. Only one story came to mind.

"Arachne?" I muttered.

"Correct, Muse," she sang.

"What do you want?" I asked her.

"What do I want?" She paused, walking closer to me. *"I want the mortals of this world to remember my story, but they seem to have forgotten. I want you to remind them."*

I thought back on Arachne's story before nodding.

"All right," I said, "but you must leave these mortals alone. Find another feeding ground. If I hear you have returned, our deal is off."

If a spider could smile, Arachne would be doing that right now. Drool dripped from her mouth onto a carcass below.

"You have my word, Muse. And if you break yours, I will be sure to return. There will not be a mortal left in this region once I finish feeding."

I nodded. "Deal."

Arachne stared at me for a few more seconds before letting out a high-pitched squeal. The rest of the spiders chattered and crawled around me. The noise would have probably made most people shiver, but I was unaffected. They didn't scare me like they did others.

Once the spiders were out of sight, I made my way out of the cave. Ali was still waiting at the entrance. His eyes were wide, and his face was as white as a ghost.

"What's wrong?" I asked him.

He pointed his finger to the ground. In the sand, there were millions of tiny footprints. I sighed. At least I knew they were gone. I waved for Ali to follow me.

"Come, Ali. I need to pack my bags. It is time for me to head home."

After a month of being back at Olympus, I had kept my promise to Arachne to remind others of her story. After a few days of reviewing, I had finally written it down.

I proudly present to you, the story of Arachne:

Arachne was a beautiful mortal, with long flowing black hair and piercing brown eyes. But it wasn't her beauty that was the most extraordinary thing about her. It was her talent. Arachne was a masterful weaver. The best mortal weaver one could find. She practiced day in and day out, perfecting her art.

One day, she ventured to Athena's temple to challenge the Goddess of War, Handicraft, and Practical Reason to see which of the two was the more talented weaver. Athena accepted the challenge, and both got to work on their tapestry. The goddess wove hers to depict the gods in majesty, while Arachne's showed the gods in their adventures.

229

The beauty of Arachne's tapestry enraged Athena. Before their work was to be judged, the goddess tore Arachne's to pieces. Arachne was so heartbroken that she hung herself with the remaining threads. Athena saw this, and out of pity, she loosened the rope that wrapped around the mortal's neck, astounded when it turned into spider silk. Arachne, herself, was transformed into a spider and was never seen again.

FROZEN SOUL

BY

EMBER SAVAGE

PERSEPHONE,

GODDESS OF SPRING

S ITTING BOLT UPRIGHT IN BED WITH MY HEART BEATING RAPIDLY, I SCANNED THE ROOM FOR THE NOISE THAT AWOKE ME. All I heard was my own ragged breathing. This was not the first time. It had been happening more and more over the last week. Each night something jolted me awake. Last night, I finally pinpointed that it was not natural to the environment. Living in the Underworld for half the year, I was accustomed to the natural sounds and the wailing of the souls being punished in their eternity. The distant murmur of the River Styx, and the low-level hum that existed in the Underworld, were constant. This sound was different. There was a hollowness to it, and something below the noise that cut me deep.

In one fluid motion, I swung out of bed, my bare feet sinking into the plush rug of my apartment. A cup of tea would settle my nerves so I could get back to sleep. As I crossed the threshold into the kitchen, I heard it again. This time I was awake. A low bass sound I could feel through the stone floor, echoed in a darkness broken only by a small sliver of light. The eerie sound crawled up my spine with the small prickles of spider legs, freezing me in place.

Before I could stop my impulse, I headed for the door of my apartment. The hallways were dark, lights flickered out along the corridor, leaving an inky, suffocating blackness that surrounded me.

My breathing was too loud in the hall, and each step took me farther from my room and comfort. I stopped, bare feet on the floor, and centered myself using the techniques I learned when I was younger. I needed calm breathing, soft footfalls, and to move with purpose and determination. Though I never became as proficient as some of my sisters, I still had base knowledge. Muted sounds reached my ears, a low drone that reverberated through my bones. The stone beneath my soles felt cold and sent shivers up my spine as I moved around a corner. The hallway stretched out before me, shadows dancing along the walls like creatures with their own agenda. Hesitantly, I took a step forward, my eyes tracking the corners for danger even though I knew I was perfectly safe within my home.

The scratching came next. With each of my steps, I heard the skitter clacking of something dragging along the stone. I froze, and the noise stopped. Like the howls, I thought they were a figment of my imagination. It was only when they repeated over and over I became certain they were real. It was the sound of something sharp along the rock. Dagger or claws that promised grooves in the floor if only they pressed harder.

I caught a brief glimpse out of the corner of my eye when I reached the end of the hallway. A fluid movement of white so quick, I was not sure if I had seen it. Everything had become suspect in the darkness. I could not trust my senses to tell me the truth of my surroundings.

There was no way to keep the door quiet as I pushed it open. The slight sound reverberated like a foghorn. I moved into the courtyard where hazy mist crawled along the ground. Smoky tendrils extended, searching the land for its victims. Outside of the penthouse, the ambient noises amplified. I could not follow my quarry by sound, so I would need to rely on my eyes. It was not as easy as a mortal might think. This realm was not all shades of blacks and greys, and the white I was chasing would not stand out. The Underworld was as full of color and variance as the mortal world.

I regretted the impulse that sent me scurrying out without shoes or slippers. The ground was painful on my bare feet. A shiver ran up my spine as I continued through the courtyard, trying to catch sight of the creature that eluded me.

Though my sister Artemis taught me to track my quarry years ago, I had never been good at it, and tonight proved nothing had changed. I spent hours searching the grounds around the apartments before I returned to my home, the hem of my pajamas damp from the fog. I would try again the next night, hopefully with more luck.

All was quiet for a few nights before it happened again. The scream snapped me out of a deep sleep, my heart trying to beat out of my chest in fright. The cry was not of pain or loss, but of fear and terror. It cut through the other sounds like a knife, drilling into my heart. I could feel every bit of horror that the soul howled into the night. Tears stung my eyes as the panic of that scream rose, clawing at my throat.

The hall was chillier that night, and my breath puffed as grey clouds. I shivered, pulling my shawl tight around my shoulders. Better prepared this time, I remembered to slip my feet into sandals before heading out of the apartment.

Moving down the hallway was a repeat of the first night. The sounds reaching my ears were the same howls and scratching noises against the stone. I caught the same glimpses of white, and apprehension made my skin crawl as I moved at a pace that made it feel like time had stopped. The sound of my heartbeat was a rapid staccato that amplified with each step I took away from the safety of my room.

I saw the shade of white dash past the end of the corridor, angling towards the long flights of stairs. Ignoring the fear rising in my throat, I sped forward, slamming through the doors with a boom to wake the dead. But this was the Underworld, and the dead were already awake. Peering over the railing, I searched the descending stairs for a glimpse of my quarry. A touch of white floated along the dark and little used stairs.

My nightdress tangled around my calves as I hurried down those steps, the sounds of my slippers against the stone like whispers of the forlorn. Reaching the bottom landing, I pushed the door open and peered into the basement.

The sounds of machinery caressed my ears like mechanical giants breathing in their sleep, a rhythmic whooshing of air as it pumped through the apartment building. I searched the room, weaving through the pipes, glancing under the large water receptacle and other critical systems. For hours, I combed every nook and cranny of the subterranean world beneath my home to only once again come up empty-handed.

This had been a different path than previously taken. Before, I ended in the courtyard, watching the fog crawl across the ground. Whatever haunted the building was intelligent. It knew to alter its course and change its direction of flight to avoid discovery. Whatever it was, it had not come for judgment, and it had not passed through the traditional routes. Thanatos had not gathered its soul, and Charon had not ferried it across the River Styx. This was an entity that should not be here, should not be loose within our world. Yet nightly, its howls of pain and suffering woke me with an icy grip around my heart and sent me on a hunt through the twists and turns of the Underworld.

Exhausted, I returned to my apartments, unsuccessful yet again. I set the kettle on for a hot cup of tea. My mind wandered, replaying the pitiful noises that had been waking me, and what they might mean. So lost in my thoughts, I did not register the whistle of the boiling water, thinking it yet another of the cries. The piercing pitch rose, shattering my focus and ripping me back to the moment.

"I only hear the sounds at night, when I sleep," I muttered as I poured hot water over the diffuser, the scent of the rich tea filling my nose. "The cries, they are full of pain and suffering. There is terror behind that. It is not an angry or violent sound. But one of pain." Blowing across the rising steam, I took the delicate cup with me back to my bed, the scent of flowers mingling with the tea to enhance the aroma. "That is a soul in torment. But yet, so different."

235

I had duties to attend to as the queen, things that could not be put off. And so I spent the day going about my tasks with only half of my mind focused. I dispatched each responsibility with minimum attention. I was intent on returning to the high rise as soon as possible, to begin my hunt again. That night, I sat upon my bed, anticipation sending my heart racing. I listened for each sound in the darkness, waiting for that tormented wail that signaled my direction.

Like the claxon of an alarm, I heard the cry. I was up and dashing towards the door before my mind registered the movement. This time, as I entered the hall, I saw the movement clearer. It was lower to the ground than I had assumed. Whatever I chased was squat and small. I retraced my steps from the night before, following the cries through the stairwell into the basement. The scrabbling of what sounded like claws on the stairs drew me until I again stood deep in the lower reaches of the building. Each step I took, I saw that subtle movement, like a spirit that was half there. I clung to the wisps in my vision. It darted this way and that, looking for a place to hide. This time, I entered the basement armed with new information. I dropped to my knees, looking underneath things and low to the ground.

Crawling on hands and knees in the direction I had seen the specter flee, I saw the glint for a moment, a flash of light to my left. Beneath a large metal cabinet full of equipment, I saw two nearly clear, pale blue eyes peering back at me. A fearful growl emanated from the darkened hiding spot, and it was then that it struck me. The sounds, the growls and whines, the speed at which my quarry had moved. The specter had not come for judgment because it was not human.

"Hello there," I whispered, trying to keep my voice calm and soothing. This was not a human soul that ran in fear. This was a hurt and pained animal, a creature that did not understand where it had found itself, nor how it had gotten here. As if it understood, it shifted in the darkness. A muzzle of white with curled lips growled at me, baring teeth to ward me off.

"Shhhhh. You are safe."

I reached my hand towards the animal cowering beneath the metal structure, trying to coax it out. Okay, so it wasn't the smartest thing I had ever done. But in my defense, I did spend time with Cerberus on a regular basis, and he was one of the most feared creatures in the Underworld. What could this small thing do to me?

Between one blink and the next, the cornered animal clamped its jaws down on my hand, the teeth tearing into my flesh. Ruby ichor ran in rivulets and pooled on the concrete floor. I sucked my breath between my teeth, but held fast against the pain, keeping my gaze locked on the piercing blue eyes.

"You are safe," I repeated, the edge in my voice wavering some from the pain. The growl that answered me was conveying a simple message. It wanted to be left alone. We sat there, locked in a stalemate. The animal kept its jaws clenched on my hand, and I crouched on my knees, facing it off. After what seemed like an eternity, it released its grip, and I pulled my bleeding hand back. In that flash, I got a better look at what I was dealing with. The white muzzle ended in a pink nose, blue eyes flashing in fear, and two folded over ears on the top of its wide head. Though it looked much different from Cerberus, what haunted the apartments of the Underworld was very much a dog.

Cradling my hand, I wrapped the hem of my dress around it to staunch the bleeding. I spent the whole night sitting on the cold concrete floor, whispering softly to calm the poor frightened creature. As the Underworld night ended, the specter of the dog faded away, the white fur becoming translucent before it drifted off like smoke on the wind. The last visage to leave my sight was the haunted blue eyes, staring at me in terror and pain.

Thus, my nights became the same. I waited up for the howls that signaled the ghost dog's arrival. I slipped out of my apartment to repeat the same walk along the hall, down the stairs, and to the basement. I always found the poor terrified creature cowering beneath the metal giants. Each night, I would sit on the floor, coaxing the frightened thing to me with whispers and soft words. At the end of the night, the specter would dissipate like spent smoke. My heart grew heavier with each trip back up the stairs to my apartment. Witnessing the pain this poor ghost dog relived every night was agonizing. The fear I saw in its eyes became etched on my soul.

I waited until my hand had healed before I tried to touch the dog again. This time, though it snapped and bit, the damage was not as thorough as before. I wrapped my injured hand and speculated why it seemed the dog, though insubstantial with the Underworld morning, could still be solid and painful to me in the night. Was it because I was of the Underworld at this time? Because it was manifesting in a place of great power? I repeated these questions with each attempt to calm the beast.

Long sleepless nights were taking their toll. I slept in short bursts throughout the day, my duties as Queen becoming less and less focused. But I refused to give up. This was a war of attrition, and I was going to conquer the ghost dog's fears, if for no other reason but to give the poor creature its rest.

Weeks stretched on in this manner, one night bleeding into the next. My hand was wrapped in bandages less and less. I used every bit of patience I had, repeating the same night over and over.

Joy finally came the night I reached for the hidden dog, and not only did it not bite my hand in fear, but let me softly brush its cold fur. I stamped down the urge to laugh with happiness, knowing that my voice raised in such jubilation would set the dog back, and I would lose the ground we had gained. This breakthrough became the new benchmark. Now, after trailing in its wake to the basement each night, it rewarded my patience with more and more trust. Until, shaking in terror and slinking low to the ground, the dog crawled from its hiding place. With the terrified movements of an animal that had felt the anger of a bad owner leveraged upon it, he lay his head down on my upturned hand.

Tears flowed freely in that moment, as the lonely queen and forgotten animal bonded in the basement of the Underworld. The soul of a dog, frozen in time, abandoned and forgotten. It had crawled the depths of the afterlife until it found its way to a heart just as frozen and lonely. I stared into its blue eyes. He looked up at me as his body began to dissipate, the tail turning into smoke and rolling away with the breeze. I held his triangular head in my hands, bent to press a kiss to it, and whispered, "You will never be alone again."

My powers welled within me as I called to them. My body hummed with the gift of life. Mine to bestow on a spirit that begged to return. I had granted this gift only a few times before. But there had never been a soul more worthy of the kiss of life than the one I held in my hands at this moment.

"Breathe," I whispered as the tears rolled down my cheeks. "You will not have to leave again. You will live in joy and happiness. You will be loved and cared for. You will be by my side, and I will guard and protect you." Like the fog rolling in from the sea, the smoke of his spirit recoiled, forming the solid body once again. Soul became flesh and bone, blood and heartbeat. Warmth returned to his body and silky fur beneath my fingers. "With your new life, I will give you a new name. Snow, for you are soft, pure, and beautiful."

Snow peered up at me with his large blue eyes. His mouth opened in what I could only describe as a smile. His tongue lolled out, and he darted it out to lick my hand. I knew though the road had been long, we still had a long way to go. But he would never have to hide in fear again. The thawing of winter had begun, and Snow would be forever cherished.

RELIVING THE NIGHTMARE

BY

MOXIE MALONE

MOXIE,

GODDESS OF

METAMORPHOSIS

CAN YOU FEEL IT, TOO?

It's barely perceptible, but it's there. It's the sense that summer is giving way to the fall, and soon darkness will have its way with the light. From light to dim to dark.

It's instinctual, I think. At least, it has always been that way for me and my kind. I can only presume that mortals, too, sense the veil thinning. The barrier between this world and the other side. At the apex of Samhain, it is stretched to its thinnest. Liminal. It continues to soften and thin right up to All Hallows Eve.

Some believe that passing between the veil only happens on October 31st. That's not true. That's just when even the weakest can pass through to this plane unhindered. Stronger spirits and entities can cross much sooner, especially if they find a weak spot or if something else damages part of the barrier. The nastier creatures are always seeking ways through those defenses. They breach the veil more often than you may think—more often than you may care to know and still sleep well at night. Take heart in the knowledge that your Gods are vigilant.

Perhaps that's why our minds turn to dark things, spooky things, creepy things. Maybe we can sense them among us.

Without the benefit or need of a clock or calendar, I know this time approaches when a nagging little poem begins to whisper in my head.

> *Beneath ancient bearded sentinels, fires burn.*
> *Mark the liminal end and beginning;*
> *This time of the veil thinning,*
> *When those who left, return.*

I've been hearing it for weeks now. That means many of the human spirits from my past will soon visit me. I both welcome and dread it. This year, foreboding hangs heavy on me, even though there are some humans I look forward to seeing again, if only briefly.

It is no secret that I love mortals. One of my mothers was a mortal. Alcina, my second mother, carried me beneath her heart for nine months. When she gave birth to her own daughter, it was me who occupied the child's human form. It wasn't until many years later that Gaia, my first mother, drew me from the mortal child. Of course, I love them.

I've even foolishly fallen *in* love with a few, though it is heart-wrenching to lose them when they die. My love can add many years to their natural lives, but it always remains the same. They will grow old. Their spirit will leave their bodies. They will be fetched by Thanatos. They will become property of Hades.

The last time I was in love with a mortal, I watched as he was dragged to the other side. We had a very long life together by the way you measure time. He lived nearly 150 of your years. Still, he was not ready to give up his human form.

I don't envy Thanatos, who came to fetch him. It seems like it would be a soul-crushing job. As the God of Death, Than, as most of the family calls him, seems to thrive in his work. Even though most mortals fear him, he is a remarkably cheerful and kind deity. Did you know that he likes black peppermints and owns a chain of Mr. T's Sweet and Sundae shops? I'm rambling, aren't I? Be patient. I will get to the point of my tale eventually.

Since Zeus commanded my return to Olympus, we've had many other family members come home. I will begrudgingly admit that I am happy to see them. It would be so much better if everything wasn't colored with the sense of disquiet that comes with the season. The permeating ripples of fear I feel, from recent escapes and vicious attacks by wild packs of nightgoyles. A dread I feel in knowing I will once again see Calantha, the mortal who died a gruesome, horrible death because of me so long ago.

When I was young, a mere two or three hundred years old, a certain god captured my heart quite by accident. He did not set out with any intention. In fact, he hardly noticed me at all. Rather, it was I who noticed him. There was something in his manner, something that few others ever saw beyond his darkness. I saw a tenderness, a lightness of spirit that glowed through his obsidian eyes. He wanted to be seen, to be known, and mostly he wanted to love and be loved. I suppose that could be said about any god, or mortal. But in this case, it was so easy to overlook given his charge. And he was ever vigilant in the execution of his duties. In truth, it seemed he thought of nothing else.

I can hear your question. The answer is—No, I will not say which god.

To this day, he doesn't even know the whole of this story. I don't know that he ever will. Perhaps, in time, I will tell him, but not today.

Today, I will tell you about my brutal encounter with nightgoyles, and how the unnamed god unwittingly played a role in the demise of Calantha, the mortal whom I took into danger's path.

I became so enamored with him that I'd often go out of my way to linger nearby when he would visit. I knew where I could find him most times and would sneak away to see him. Not that he paid much attention to my lurking about, mind you. Still, I liked being around him, even if he remained oblivious to my presence.

You see, when I shed a mortal body, it is easy to travel quickly, though I typically go unnoticed. I am most often mistaken for a wandering lost soul, a ghost. I suppose my natural form can be off-putting to the beautiful deities that are my family. It is only when I take a human body that I am ever noticed by most.

I thought he might like me better if I wore a human's face. A more adult human than the ones that Hera, my third and foster mother, insisted I wear. That's why I chose Calantha. Truly, she was

244

a rare, incomparable flower among the most beautiful young women in her time. Surely then, he would notice her and, by extension, me. And he did notice that fateful night, though it didn't happen in the way I hoped.

I spoke of him to Mamá, Hera, but she would not hear of it. "You are too young, Mou," she said. She often called me by that nickname. "You have eternity to grow up. Don't rush your youth. It is something you never get back."

Of course, it was ridiculous in my mind. *Too young?* I thought. *I'd already outlived generations of mortals who I watched come into this world. I'd seen my mortal mother give birth to more children. I followed and watched over them, and her grandchildren, and even her great-grandchildren, as they lived, loved, mated, and died. How could I be too young?*

When I argued my case, she heaped on more of her reasons for denying my heart's desire. "More importantly, you are not ready," she told me. "You have not fully grown into your powers and do not understand the consequences of wielding them. The answer is no."

Again, I thought her argument was absurd. I helped Zeus win the battle with the Titans and helped rescue *her*. Who was *she* to tell me of my powers?

Gaia likewise ignored my pleas. I thought she would understand my desire to bond with another. She did not argue my age or maturity. Instead, she told me it was a bad match and could not happen—The Fates would not allow it. I won't go into her reasons, lest I give away too much of his identity. But she was equally adamant. "This pairing will not happen."

But the heart wants what it wants, and that led to me embodying Calantha that night. I was determined to turn his head. I wanted him to notice me. Neither of my mothers could stop me if he wanted me in return.

For weeks, our family worked to contain the nightgoyles behind the veil. It was a constant struggle to keep them in Tartarus, and they breached the protective layer with unnerving regularity.

As a rule, the horrendous beasts were more of a nuisance than a threat to immortals. However, they were deadly to humans. Tales were still told of the times they massacred entire villages. For a while, Thanatos was nearly overwhelmed with the numbers he had to bring to the shores of the Underworld. Charon surely delighted at the volume of coins he gathered in those bloody days.

I was well aware that many of those foul creatures had escaped Tartarus. I knew, too, that our family would be busy hunting them down and dealing with the aftermath of their destruction that night. It would provide a marvelous diversion for my plan. No one would notice that I wasn't still playing in the gardens, wearing the pigtails that Hera loved so much.

If I cloaked Calantha, I could slip right past my family while they stalked the monsters. I could make my way to him and reveal her beauty. Perhaps for once, he would see me. He would see my eyes and my soul through her visage. Maybe his heart would feel for me what my heart felt for him. I could see his light. Would he see mine?

I intended to find out.

I had little to fear of the creatures that my family was pursuing. When I'd stumbled upon them in my deified form, I went unnoticed. At best, I was a blur, a flash of light to them. Even if they could catch me, they could not hold me. In hindsight, it was folly to think I could move past them in human form.

The next part of this story is not for the faint of heart. You can stop now and surmise the rest. If you continue, you enter my nightmare at your own risk. I should give you fair warning. What I am about to tell you is not a pretty tale. Except for one moment of pure bliss, it is horrible, grisly, and heartbreaking. It is also a shame that I've carried for thousands of years.

Don't think I'm telling you this to unburden myself. I am not. It does not work that way. When you are immortal, you remember everything for eternity. The fortunate ones make peace with the things they've done. And, of course, some have no compunction or remorse at all. Neither is the case for me. I bury my guilt under thousands of years of other memories until something brings it back to the surface again. In this case, the perfect storm of my return home to Olympus, the nightgoyles breaking free from Tartarus, and the proximity to Samhain triggered my memory. The time when I may once again see Calantha.

Now, to the story you came to hear.

That night, as planned, I left my mortal child body in the gardens of Olympus and sped towards the village. Slipping into Calantha's family home, I took over her body and wrestled her consciousness to sleep. Rouging soft lips and cheeks and adorning with the finest clothes, I spared no detail to present Calantha as a goddess-like beauty. Finally satisfied that she was ready to be seen, I pulled the hood over her glorious auburn hair and set off to find my love.

Moving along the shadows with only the moon and stars to light my way, I headed to a farm on the outskirts of the village. That was where the nightgoyles last attacked. I knew many of my family would be there to deal with the aftermath and hunt, which meant that my secret love would be there as well.

I reached the edge of the village and only stopped when a voice called out, "Calantha!" I turned to see a handsome young man bearing a torch. He dashed towards me. "What are you doing out here? Have you not heard that the nightgoyles are loose? It is not safe!"

Startled, I quickly scanned her mind and discovered who he was. Fílos. Erastís. He was her sweetheart. His name, Spiros. Spirit. He was a night guardian for the village. In a flash, I saw how they walked together, kissed near the woods, laughed, and made plans for their future. I saw their lives together, her hopes, her dreams, and I felt the warmth of her love for him spread into my belly.

I didn't look at him as I struggled for words, not knowing what to say or how to explain her presence at that hour, so near the site of carnage. "Spiros, I am fine. I am carrying a message for a friend to a loved one. I will return soon. I must run now."

I turned to leave, but he took my arm and pulled me to him. "No. It is not safe. There is no message so important that you risk this danger."

That is when our eyes met.

I inhaled a sharp gasp as a rush exploded through me. For the first time, I felt seen. I knew what love looked like in another's eyes. Of course, the love was for her. It must have been for her, but it was me he looked into. I watched his pupils expand impossibly wide until only a light brown sliver encircled the black. In that moment, I saw into his soul, and he into mine.

I have lived that moment thousands upon thousands of times since. We transcended time. Eternity stretched out and enfolded us as we gazed into and upon each other. He seemed dumbfounded, confused. It was as if he didn't quite recognize her or was seeing her for the very first time. He drew me to him and kissed me, first tenderly. Then he kissed deeper, passionately. I could not breathe. I had the urge to leave her body and merge with his, wanting to be closer than was possible between two mortal forms.

I reached into his mind. He felt it, too. He saw us entwined, but we were not the mortal forms of Calantha and Spiros. He saw me as I am. We were twin pillars of white gold light forged in flames. Undulating swirls of colors spun around us and expanded into infinity. We were vibrations and light and star matter. And for the first time, I felt a part of everything. Whole. Complete.

Somewhere, a voice broke through our endless revery. *"Moxie!"* It was Mamá. *"Moxie, wake up!"* I knew that she had found my child-form in the garden. If I didn't move swiftly, I would be found out.

Primal rhythms pulsed through my being, urging me to stay right there with Spiros until the stars fell from the heavens. *"Mou! Wake up!"* Hera's voice again, this time with more urgency. It snapped me out of my rapture.

No. No. Stop this. He thinks I'm Calantha. It's not you that he wants. It's just not possible, I told myself as I pushed softly against his chest and turned to leave. "I must go, Spiros. I will be back with you soon."

Time was wasting, and though I felt a pull in my belly to stay with this beautiful mortal, my intended was nearby. I needed to see him. More importantly, I needed him to see me. I needed us to look into each other's eyes and find the same power that just passed between the mortal and me. To know. To be whole. To be eternal.

My feet carried me swiftly down the cobbled steps, giving way to a flat, well-beaten path that exited the border of the village. Far ahead, through the shadowed treeline, I could see torchlights blazing in the darkness. That was where my family and any survivors would be. I ran as fast as I could, but found the burden of Calantha's mortal form slowed me considerably.

To the right, I heard rustling in the brush as I made my way past the dense woods. Low growls and snarls came from the field to my left, the creatures closing in from each side. I kept moving, pushing on harder, taxing her mortal muscles for speed.

Each step brought me closer to the lights. *Faster, girl, faster,* I repeated over and over in my head, the pounding of her heart beating wildly in my ears.

A screeching howl pierced the night air, and a dark blur sped by my peripheral vision. I pressed on. We were so close to the circle of flames that would provide protection. It wouldn't be long before I could uncloak the mortal, Calantha, for his godly eyes to behold.

"Calantha! Stop!"

It was Spiros. The damned fool followed me. Followed *her*.

"*No, no, no!*" my mind screamed. I looked back. "Spiros, No! Go—"

Suddenly the weight and force of a building slammed into her, sending us crashing to the ground. Searing pain shot through her body, and my vision blurred with blinding flashes of multi-colored lights bursting from behind her eyes. No breath would enter our lungs. I pushed us back to our feet, gasping for air.

My vision cleared, and I saw Spiros standing only feet away, holding his torch. Between us was a beast. A nightgoyle. And he was hungry.

I could have made it, you know. I *would* have made it to the safety of my family, if I could have kept running. I was only a hundred yards away from the bright flames and the immortals who would have protected us. Only one hundred yards away from my intended.

I was so very close to finally realizing my heart's desire, but the damned mortal had to be a hero. Now my plans had come entirely unraveled. So, there we were, five or six feet apart, with a death machine between us.

It seemed like an eternity passed while Spiros and I stood frozen, looking at each other with the beast growling, crouched and ready to spring. I didn't blink or breathe, knowing that any movement would set destruction in motion. We both knew it. Even the nightgoyle knew it.

My mind went in a hundred directions, playing out probable scenarios. If I moved Calantha, the nightgoyle would come for her, and Spiros could run. But would he? The witless fool already demonstrated that he needed to be a hero more than he needed to

250

be alive. I considered the possibility of reaching into his mind and planting the idea for him to run. But from a dead stop, and at such close proximity, I doubted that I could outrun the creature while wearing Calantha's mortal form. So she would likely be sacrificed.

What would it take for both of them to survive this?

I considered manipulating the nightgoyle. They seemed like simple-minded creatures. Could I control its mind enough to put it to sleep, or make it turn away while I still embodied Calantha? Would that buy us enough time to run before the rest of the pack descended upon us? It was doubtful, but so far, it was also the best plan.

What other weapons did I have? The vines and foliage. Perhaps I could ensnare the beast, allowing us time to escape. Still, the other night creatures would be here quickly. How many were still lurking in the shadows? Could I ensnare them all? My vines were already slithering towards us, but were there enough of them to hold back these powerful monsters? Was there enough time?

If only I wasn't limited by this mortal body.

Then I hit upon the best possible scenario. I would leave Calantha's body and distract the creature and its brethren. The fiends would give chase to my deified form, and that would allow Spiros and Calantha enough time to escape. Surely, I could distract the creatures long enough for the two to run the one hundred yards to safety.

I made the decision and prepared to leave Calantha's body as I sent a simple thought to Spiros, *"Run!"*

At the same moment, I heard the whisper of Spiros' voice in my head, "Se agapó." *I love you.*

But he didn't run. Instead, he lurched forward, waving the torch at the nightgoyle and yelled, "Run, my love. Run!"

I watched in horror as the beast leapt from its crouching position and hurled itself full force into Spiros. In the blink of an eye, Spiros was flung to the ground, immobilized, with the creature squatting upon his stomach, growling hungrily.

"Dammit, no!" I screamed as I stepped towards them. The beast turned back to look at me. Its mouth pulled back into a heinous grin, exposing multiple rows of dagger-sharp teeth designed to rip flesh from bone.

Now, what? my mind screamed as I gazed into the inky black eyes of the demon. *"Don't move,"* I thought to myself and Spiros simultaneously. *"Stay perfectly still."*

If I dropped Calantha's body, would it give chase? Highly doubtful. Why would it when it had one of us already in its clutches? I needed the vines. I could hear rustling coming from the woods. Was it the vines creeping their way to us, or was it the other nightgoyles?

The beast snarled at me, then began to chitter and laugh. It was a garbled, guttural, hissing noise that sent chills into my soul. It was the sound of pure evil. But why was it laughing? I didn't have to wait long to find out.

"To the woods, my love, go now!" Spiros yelled out as he struck the beast on the head with his torch. The creature screeched in pain and anger as the flame lit its flesh.

I glanced at the woods and took a single step towards them when I heard Spiros' agonizing scream. It was the last sound I would ever hear from him. I looked back to see the beast sit back on its haunches, triumphant, with a mangled, bloody mass clenched in its teeth. Spiros' body lay beneath it, twitching as blood pumped through the gaping hole in his neck.

The creature jerked its head, tossing the flesh into the air, then caught it, chomping and chewing noisily, growling in satisfaction. I closed my eyes as it leaned forward to take another bite. I couldn't watch, and there was nothing I could do to save Spiros now.

That was when I heard the sound behind me. A deep rumbling growl. I knew then why the other creature was laughing. The same reason Spiros suddenly lashed out and told me to run to the woods. But it was too late to run. I'd have to fight. And her mortal flesh was no match for these murderous fiends.

Everything moved so quickly and so painfully slow at the same time. Even now, I can remember every movement in meticulous, horrifying detail, as if it played out on a movie reel. Frame by frame, I can relive the nightmare. I can even fast forward through those last moments and stop to zoom in on the smallest detail: The deep crimson that hemorrhaged from the mortal wound in Spiros' neck as his body twitched in its death throes, his words of love in my head only seconds before that, the stomach turning sound of the beast as he ravenously devoured the man who tried to save my life, *her life,* and the stench of the creature that crept up behind me.

I called forth the vines that had been snaking their way to me, and I turned to face certain death, but not without a fight.

The torch lights flared and flickered in the distance, bouncing through the trees as my family and the villagers made their way towards me. Undoubtedly, they heard Spiros' scream. I just needed to keep the creatures at bay until they arrived.

I sensed Ares in the group and sent him a thought. "Ares. Over here! It's Moxie. Nightgoyles. Hurry!"

Behind me, I heard the beast growl with gluttonous satisfaction as it tore another piece of flesh from Spiros and devoured it. The sound made my skin crawl and my stomach churn in revulsion.

"That will be you next, goddess," the creature in front of me cackled and chittered in its obscure, guttural dialect. It sounded more like someone drowning in their own vomit than an actual language.

The last thing I wanted to do was talk to this thing, but every moment of conversation bought precious time. Time for help to arrive. "Ah. So, you can see me in her. Then you know that you cannot kill me, demon spawn. My family draws near. You will die slowly and painfully. Run now, and you might escape."

"I know no such thing," it replied. "I am bored with human flesh. I always wondered what a goddess would taste like." It ran its long, thick tongue across its muzzle and smiled widely, exposing its gnarled, yellowed fangs.

"Keep it talking. Keep it distracted."

I opened my mouth to reply, but without any warning, the beast lunged at me, snarling and spraying me with spittle. Startled, I stumbled backward and out of its reach. My vines ensnared the creature, yanking it to the ground. At last, I saw the opening I needed. As the beast struggled with the writhing plants, it spat curses at me, vowing to eat me slowly. I wasted no time and took off running towards the torch lights and to safety.

I'd only gotten a few steps away before another nightgoyle hurtled into us. Its razor-sharp claws sliced deeply down my back as I pitched forward and landed face-first onto the dirt path. Searing, exquisite pain burned in each open gash. Her flesh torn open from shoulder to hip. I scrambled to my knees and dug my nails into the ground, pulling myself forward. It hit me again, this time in the back of the head. I could feel the warm blood oozing from the wounds left by its talons.

The blow knocked me down again, and I rolled to my side to get away from the beast. My heart started racing in a double beat, and I realized that Calantha had awakened to this nightmare. The pain snapped her from her sleep, and she became aware of the danger she was in. Seeing Spiros' slaughtered body only feet away, she screamed out in blood-curdling anguish and fear, trying to rush to his side.

"No, no, no! Not now," my mind cried as I wrangled her consciousness back to sleep while trying to get up. Failing, I fell

back, landing hard on my ass. I saw that the one I'd ensnared was now rushing towards me, broken vines trailing behind.

I scrambled backward to get away from it and backed into another one that growled viciously. I heard a third one creep closer. They chittered in their own tongue, speaking of making a meal of me...of her. They argued over which pieces each would eat.

I could hear Hephaestus. "Over there! Over there!" he yelled. And Ares called to me, "Moxie! Moxie! We are coming!"

"Almost. They are almost here."

I hissed for the nightgoyles to get away and used all of my power to bring forth the vines. The vibrating tentacles lashed out and wrapped themselves around two of the beasts. I found myself suddenly on my back, shoulders pegged to the ground by the one I'd ensnared earlier. Its face was inches away, and its foul, hot breath filled my nostrils. I struggled beneath it, trying to free myself, but it was so heavy and so strong, and her mortal body so weak.

Time seemed to speed up. Everything around me became a blur of movement, punctuated with snarls and howls and excruciating agony.

I yelled out as a horrific pain ripped into my calf. One of them bit me, taking a chunk of flesh with it. I felt teeth sink into my foot while the other loomed over me, laughing. And for the second time that night, I felt Calantha awaken.

If only I could leave her body, I could create a diversion, a distraction, and my powers would be so much stronger. But I knew if I did, she would stay awake and feel everything. Pinned beneath the beast, the most I could do was force her back to sleep, fight, and hope that my brothers could reach me in time.

I sent a thought into the beast's mind, distracting it for a second, and smashed my forehead into its snout, startling it enough to free my hands. I beat at it and kicked at the other. It was a futile effort. They became frenzied with bloodlust, tearing at her flesh.

255

There were too many to fend off and still keep her asleep, while trying to control the vines and enter their minds. I felt every bite, every rip of tendon and muscle, as they tore her beautiful form to pieces.

I heard the sickening, wet crack of skulls being smashed as Hephaestus swung his hammer.

"Die, you bastard," Ares yelled as they battled the winged vermin.

My brothers had finally come, but it was too late to save her.

I stayed there with her until the end. The metallic taste of blood filled my mouth, and I stared into the night as her life force flowed from her shredded veins onto the ground. Trickles of blood slid from a gash on her forehead, blurring my vision. Everything turned red, especially the moon that hung large against the pitch-black sky.

So, this is what it is like to die, I thought, as numbness and cold seeped into her body, overtaking the piercing pain that throbbed there only moments before. My vision faded, and her heartbeat stuttered and slowed.

I ached at my core, knowing that her last memory would be of Spiros lying lifeless, his body wrecked and mangled. Ever so gently, now that the pain was gone, I woke her with the image of them lying together in an open field. Their fingers entwined as they stared at the stars and the peculiar red moon.

Her lips curved at the edges, and we whispered to him, *"S 'agapó, Spýros."*

At that final moment, when she inhaled her last breath, we were floating in a sweet delirium and we heard Spiros reply, *"An éprepe na zíso ti zoí mu xaná, tha se évriska norítera."* If I were to live my life again, I'd find you sooner.

Torchlights surrounded us as the last of the beasts were killed or ran off into the shadows. I drew myself out of her and looked at the carnage. Her body was ripped to pieces and strewn across the path.

Hera's warning echoed in my mind, *"You are not ready. You have not fully grown into your powers and do not understand the consequences of wielding them."*

"I caused this," I whispered. "All of this is my fault."

Thanatos arrived swiftly. He reached into her chest and pulled her soul from her body. It was whole, unlike her corporeal form lying scattered on the ground. He glanced at Spiros' body and furrowed his brows questioningly. "Hmmm. Where'd the other one go?"

Thanatos looked back and regarded me for a moment. Shaking his head and sighing, his brow knitted ever so slightly. "It was not her time," he said flatly before he turned and walked away, cradling her in his arms.

His words were a dagger in my chest. I could not breathe. I couldn't stand the way he looked at me. Not *him*.

Thanatos was right, though. It wasn't her time, nor her sweetheart's. Calantha and Spiros should have been off stealing kisses from one another tonight, not butchered and turned into feed for monsters. All of her hopes and dreams were gone. No marriage. No children. No wonderful, simple life spent with the one she loved. Why? Because I wanted what I could not have, and I was willing to use her to get it. I stole their lives...and for what?

Nothing.

Ares stood close and surveyed the scene. He spoke softly, "Moxie, you shouldn't be here. Now go home. Do not come back here."

I nodded numbly as I took one last look at them. The lovers. The innocents. The victims of my willful folly. Two beautiful humans were dead, and there was nothing that I could do to bring them back, to give back what I'd taken from them. They were dead, but I would have an eternity to remember what I did.

It's strange. I can remember every detail of that night, but can't recall how I got back home. All I remember is falling into Mamá's arms, broken.

She held me close while I sobbed, spilling out my pain and grief over what I had wrought. In the morning, she caressed my cheek and sighed. "Now you are ready."

I left Olympus that day. And now you know how I came to leave my home.

SHAKE IT OFF

BY

TAMMY DAVIS

PANACEA,

GODDESS OF HEALING

SALUTING THE SUN WITH MY FIRST CUP OF COFFEE, I GO ON TO QUERY MY COMPUTER. Setting the background to pictures of sugar skulls, I then push the green "Go-Live" button and tap out a morning salutation to my audience.

Panacea: *We are live on THE Panacea TV today! How is everyone this morning? Are you ready to celebrate Halloween tonight? How do you celebrate the Harvest season?*

This feels so *fawkward—fake and awkward*. Haha, now that's funny! I do amuse myself. But, hey, at least my audience of one appreciates my humor. Here I am, talking to myself as…Wait a minute! What's this? Names? Comments? It's showtime!

Panacea: *Thank you for tuning in! Because many of you like to ask questions and make comments, I thought, why not chat in real-time? What do you have for me on this All Hallows Eve?*

LilyB: *I love your style! Where can I buy your outfit?*

Panacea: *That's a great compliment, and you can't. All of my clothes are custom made for me.*

sparkyphd: *Damn gurl you HOT!!! Let me holla at you a minute. My gurl needs a dress like that hotness 4 Halloween. You know what I am saying?*

Panacea: *What's up, sparkyphd? Let me just say, I dig your name! I'm not sure I understand your point. You think my dress is THE hot look your girlfriend needs for Halloween? Hot? Who wears dresses to be hot? I wear a dress like this to be cool.*

I scroll through more comments until one catches my attention. "Uh-oh. Here we go."

Princessghoshi: *How dare you appropriate someone else's culture...have you no shame!? You should be ashamed of yourself! People like you are what's wrong with society and you make me sick!!*

Deep breath...

Panacea: *Hey there, Princessghoshi! It's rare to find a princess online. Nice to meet you. I admire your spirit. What do you mean that I'm appropriating someone else's culture? Most modern culture evolved from my kind. I can hardly appropriate something that I pre-date, can I?*

Oh boy. She's still typing. I will type faster!

Panacea: *But how would you even know? We just met! I bet you've never met a thousand-year-old goddess before either.*

Princessghoshi: *Right! So you are just delusional as well. A thousand years? And a goddess? This is just you trying to get followers! Some stupid Halloween prank to up your numbers!*

Oh great. Now, I've opened up Pandora's box.

DoubleOh7: *Goddess???? Wtf?*

EanieMeanie: *You don't look a day over 999. LOL!*

de_k: *You poor lost soul. May the blessing of the most holy find and heal you. I will be praying for you, God bless!*

Sarah K: *This message is from the blessing angel who has visited you today. Send this to 100 followers and the Lord will grant your prayers! God bless!*

Robort13: Girls! Girls! Girls! Click the link to see more Girls!

Tom: *"Oh my beautiful one please to marry me. I know I good for you. I rich and make you rich too. Think about it oh my beautiful one!"*

Nawty1: *Beautiful? She looks like an aging hippie in that outfit.*

Ugh. This is not going as planned.

Panacea: *Look, mortals. I was summoned here to teach you. I'm here to help. The idea is to help others, not shame them. Let's get back on track! I am going to a Halloween party and was thinking I would dress up with a sugar skull and celebrate Dia de los Muertos at the same time.*

sparkyphd: *No shame in this game. I asked about the outfit. This time of year the ghosts & zombies walk around scaring people,* *looking for brains, while we all celebrate Day of the Dead baby. But you got nothin' to worry about gurl...I am gonna protect ya!*

Tommy2005: *Don't 4get the candy! Trix & treets!*

sparkyphd: *Ahh hell yeah!*

I think I've lost them. Shaking my head in dismay, I have to wonder if they even know. Maybe now is the time to instruct and to teach them the lessons I have learned.

Panacea: *Is that what you really think this time of year is about? Outfits and candy? You mortals and your love of sugar...*

de_k: *Halloween is the Devil's day! Turn away from sin and the empty lies of Satan and follow Christ, the true Savior and Redeemer!*

Princessghoshi: *Day of the Dead, so more cultural theft! You are the worst sort of human being! Get your own culture to steal from!*

Princessghoshi has exited the chat

I stop reading the comments and turn on the record feature, activating the red blinking microphone icon. I think it is time to record a history lesson. The mortals should like this. I settle into my chair, arrange my dress, and look directly into the camera.

Greetings, mortals! It appears that some of you misunderstand or are determined to twist the traditions of sacred holidays. Maybe you have just forgotten the old ways. The ways that had meaning, and regardless of the fickle nature of humans, have carried on through centuries.

I must admit that I was not sure about returning to the mortal realm after so many years away, but I think I now understand why we are back. I think you have forgotten much of your roots. I believe that mortals are in desperate need of healing, and I hope to remedy that.

I was summoned here to teach people how to raise their frequency and activate their ability to heal themselves and others. These beliefs and behaviors are a big part of what's at the root of your diseases and disorders, and now you're in jeopardy. So, let's call this lesson a tonic for the mind, a remedy for the soul, a healing of the heart, and a reconnection to your roots.

In many ways, your ancestors were more connected to each other and to those that came before than you are today, even with the marvelous technology available at your fingertips. They came together as communities. They worked the land and were grateful when an abundant harvest fed their family. Gratitude, by the way, is a key to healing and happiness.

They recognized that they shared this realm with other kinds who had the same right to be here—animals, mystical creatures, other tribes, and even deities like myself. They felt the rhythms of the seasons in their bones and celebrated both life and afterlife. They honored their departed, and yes, some feared them as well. Whether they feared or embraced death was really a matter of perspective. It remains the same to this very day. Your poet, Anaïs Nin, said it best, "We don't see the world as it is, we see it as we are."

Mortals struggle with forming their own perspectives and beliefs, even within this *enlightened age.* You claim you have them, but you are resistant to seeing anyone else's. Sometimes, we have to work through the discomfort, not be controlled by the underlying emotions, and that's all I see you mortals do. You use laughter as a mask, and you hide behind screens. Not unlike the masks that people wear for Halloween or Day of the Dead. Speaking of which, do you even know why you dress up and wear masks these days? Do you understand the origins of these traditions?

On the night of Samhain, it was believed that ghosts passed through to this earthly realm. People feared encountering these spirits and the other creatures that may venture beyond the thinned veil. To avoid being recognized, they would wear masks when they left their homes after dark so that they would be mistaken for a fellow spirit. But there is more to it than that that I'll discuss shortly.

Halloween is deeply rooted in the traditions of Samhain, a Celtic festival of the harvest. It ushered in the dark half of the year when brown replaces green, and dead leaves fall from the trees, all symbols of death and dying. So, it became partially a celebration of the harvest and partially fear-based rituals to deal with the notion of death that was all around. Nature's transition from bounty to scarcity reminded humans of their own fragile mortality. This set the tone for how they viewed and reacted to the season. They adopted traditions to help them deal with the terror of the unknown.

That's not to say there weren't other terrors during Samhain that caused the mortal to bar their doors and huddle close during the long cold dark nights. There was the belief that the fae or Sidhes would kidnap them, so food was left outside the fields or villages to appease the fairy folken. There were the shape-shifting trickster spirits known as Pukah. Yes, just like Harvey, the rabbit. Do you even know who that is? Nevermind, but you should look it up. The Pukah, like the fae, were left an offering of food outside the fields and villages.

Why, they even had Lady Gwyn, a headless maiden dressed all in white who chases the night accompanied by a black pig...I am rambling...

But that does remind me of another lady figure, the Grande Dame of Death, La Catrina. Often portrayed as a tall, elegantly attired female skeleton sporting an extravagantly plumed hat. She symbolizes the Mexican willingness to laugh at death itself, and we all know what powerful medicine laughter can be! Catrina was originally portrayed as a wealthy and well-dressed woman, reminding everyone that all are equal in the end. She is beloved within a culture that treats death with familiarity and hospitality. The grande dame and her marigold wreaths are tied to the Day of the Dead festivities celebrated in Mexico.

Day of the Dead or Dia de los Muertos is celebrated on November 1st, and for the same reason that Samhain is recognized. It is the time of the year when the veil between the living and the dead is blurred. The difference? This tradition is not rooted in fear. It is a time to honor and celebrate those that have traveled to the next life. The holiday involves family and friends gathering to pray for and remember their loved ones who have died. Those living helping to support the dead in their spiritual journey, much as they supported them in life. In Mexican culture, death is viewed as a natural part of the human cycle. It is not a day of sadness or fear, but a day of celebration because their loved ones awaken and celebrate with them.

Their joy of life in the face of its inevitable end is evident in their festivals. From altars, picnics, parades, and the irreverent writings of the Calaveras—a satirical poem that people write about one another, which includes the way the subject dies. That reminds me! I have copies of ones that my friend Gwen and I wrote last year at a Day of the Dead art opening! Let me find them...Ah! Here they are:

When la muerta came knocking on her door,
Gwen sought refuge under the floor.
While patiently waiting for death to move on,
She began scrolling Facebook, averting a yawn.
When minutes turned to hours and hours turned to sleep,
Gwen never noticed the weight of the mete.

That was the one that I wrote for Gwen. Here is the one that she wrote for me. Irreverent, indeed! But we did have a laugh.

Summoned to work here by Zeus,
Panacea consistently has an excuse.
Because she loves risas, and baila, and food,

265

She's always looking for something else to do.
Today she chose to celebrate the Day of the Dead,
Pretending to be La Catrina, it all went to her head.
Drinking tequila and eating tamales,
Panacea was truly feeling her jollies.
Laying down for a tic, she shouts cheerio,
Not realizing she is about to be the sacrificio.

What a fun night that was! Both of us more than a little tipsy and wearing marigold crowns.

And here is where the lesson exists. This modern culture has adopted many of the traditions of those ancient Celts, huddling behind their masks. You hide behind words and computers in the ultimate disguise. Trying to fit in with the very things that terrify you, and in the process, you become what you fear. You become one of the monsters in the dark that others shy from.

Consider also the ways of other cultures. Learn the lessons they have to share. Embrace others, reach out, finding the joy and laughter in the moments that you do have. Mortal lives are so very short. Why not choose to be happy and grateful? So lovely mortals, what do you think about this season now?

LilyB: *So cool. It's so much more than what I thought, wish they would've taught that in school.*

LilyB has exited the chat

sparkyphd: *Ahhh that's a helluva story, but we cool. I can't vibe with the whole death thing though it gives me the heebie jeebies... real talk, yo. Peace. Ama bounce.*

de_k: *God so loved the world he sent his only begotten son, go to the light of Christ...John 3:16...*

sparkyphd has exited the chat
de_k has exited the chat

Welp. It looks like I have my work cut out for me. As your mortal singer says, "Shake it off." Teaching these mortals is going to be tougher than I thought, but I'm up to the task…
Princessghoshi has entered the chat

Maybe I'll start fresh tomorrow.
Panacea has exited the chat

STAR-CROSSED

BY

MELODY WINGFIELD

ASTERIA,

TITANESS OF THE STARS

ANDREA HAS AN AGELESS SORT OF BEAUTY. She's not young anymore by current mortal standards, but the flow of years seems to have worn her smooth. Every morning before dawn, she stops on the way to the patisserie where she works and orders her usual, Cafe au lait, two sugars, on the house. Her brown hair is straight and glossy, not its natural state. By the time she drops off treats for Rigel on her way home in the afternoon, her Creole is on full display, with hair that would make a Gorgon weep for its beauty.

Louis has a sense of agelessness about him, too. He hasn't changed since his heart gave out in a brothel a hundred or so years ago. His dark hair and fair face would cause whiplash all up and down Royal Street, if anyone could see him. Then again, so would his typical coat, tails, and top hat. Out of place both in time and in this miserable heat. Every morning before dawn, he strolls in like he's just left the opera, lays his gloves on the bar, and orders a coffee he can only taste in memory.

I remember the first morning they met.

Louis had just learned that Darkstar operates outside the normal metaphysical bounds of this world. He had been watching from the street corner for a week. Other spirits came in and drank their fill of things dead tongues can't taste, content with the mummery of living, happy to be seen. He waited until Darkstar was nearly empty, near to the Dead Hours, before walking up to the bar and asking Rigel for black coffee. He was three sips into the first cup he'd had in a century when Andrea swept in and hopped onto the barstool next to him.

She smiled at him and said she wasn't aware that street performers stayed out this late.

He smiled at her and said nothing. The curve of her lips had tied up his tongue.

That's how it's been for weeks. Every morning, Louis is sitting at the bar when she comes in. She never questions why he wears the same thing day in and day out. Even though New Orleans is eccentric, believing he's a character actor on Bourbon Street will be easier for her to handle than the truth.

Their morning meetings stretch longer and longer. Andrea pushes the clock for a few extra minutes at the bar with the quiet and perpetually overdressed Louis. Louis forces himself to let her go without asking for more. What began as an August happenstance is now an October love affair. The star-crossed kind.

She loves him. He loves her. In any other story, this would be enough.

But outside the bounds of Darkstar Coffee Bar, their love can't draw breath.

Because Louis is dead, and Andrea is not. Ain't Fate a corpse-cold bitch?

I'm behind the bar with Rigel, counting back the till for the morning deposit. That's my excuse, anyway. Andrea and Louis have moved their mornings from the bar to a table in the corner. I'm really back here to watch the lovebirds skewer themselves on the things they aren't saying to each other.

Louis has the harder part. Imagine telling a woman you love her before you tell her you're dead. But I get it. Sitting here, drinking his coffee, he's as real as he will ever be again. And when a woman like Andrea looks at you with eyes the color of Spanish moss in the moonlight, he probably doesn't feel dead. I'm sure it slipped his mind.

If Louis is silenced by death, Andrea is silenced by life. Every time I think mankind has evolved, all I have to do is watch the way women act with men they find attractive. She's sweet and coy, and indirect as all fuck. She doesn't try to nail him down for dinner or ask him about the ring on his finger, lest he tell her that he's married. Ignorance is bliss for as long as it lasts.

As far as I'm concerned, it's lasted long enough.

The only other patron throws a ten spot on the bar top and leaves. Now's as good a time as any. I walk over to their table with a plate of scones and jam. Andrea looks up and smiles as I approach. Louis has no eyes for me, a goddess. He only sees Andrea. That's one seriously lovestruck spirit.

I reach across their clasped hands and set the plate between them on the table. "On the house."

"Thank you, Asteria," Andrea says. She notices there's no flatware on the table. "Do you have a knife?"

"Yes, of course."

I reach over and take a butter knife from a place setting on a nearby table, grab it by the weighted hilt, and plunge the blunt blade right down through the back of Louis' wrist.

"Christ!" Andrea screams, jumping back from the table.

Then, she notices that Louis jumps back from the table, too. With his hand. There's no blood in sight. No wound in his flesh.

The vertical knife wobbles back and forth with a metallic hum. It falls with a clatter onto the plate, splattering raspberry preserves where blood should be.

I give Louis an apologetic look. He's too shocked to be mad. Andrea's too shocked to be anything but shocked.

"Tell her, Louis."

And he does.

TO:	Thanatos
FROM:	Asteria
CC/BC:	admin@darkstarcoffeebar.com
RE:	I think this needs your special touch

It's been a long time, dear friend, and I'm sure you are busy with your appointed tasks, especially this time of year.

I have a rather strange situation here in New Orleans and wondered if you would have time to stop by tomorrow in the wee hours of morning, maybe around 3 a.m. I can explain more then, but for now, let's say that someone needs killing.

Temporarily, of course.

Love like stars,

Asteria

Death and a ghost walked into an empty coffee bar...

Sounds like the start of a grim joke, does it not? But tonight, it's the truth. Louis is long-since dead. Darkstar might as well be for the lack of customers. And Death is sitting with us at the table, trying to displace the coffee in his cup with sugar.

I've missed Thanatos. He's still easy on the eyes—same dark hair and goatee, eyes sharp as an obsidian blade in the moonlight. The trench coat is new, though. It really sets off his shoulders. I was partial to the cloak, but I could get used to the upgrade.

Louis hasn't taken a single drink from his cup since Thanatos poured it for him. The coffee is probably as cold as his buried bones by now. He keeps looking at Thanatos, sussing him out, trying to place where he's seen him before.

Thanatos reaches in his pocket and pulls out a handful of black peppermints. He slides them across the table toward Louis with an encouraging smile.

Louis looks at me. I can't tell if he's asking permission or gauging what might happen if he refuses my guest's hospitality.

"You should try one," I tell him as I snag one for myself, tucking it away to enjoy later. "Special recipe."

I'm not sure if it was what I said or how I said it, but Louis reaches for a peppermint like I've pointed a gun to his head.

Unwrapping it, he dutifully puts it in his mouth. I watch him shift it from one cheek to another, back and forth across his pointless tongue.

Then his eyes go wide. Because he can *taste* it.

I take a sip of my espresso. "Told you they were special."

Louis leans back in his chair and tries to relax. He puts on a good show except for the constant tumble of that mint in his mouth. Every time Louis' nerves waver, the bottles of liquor behind the bar begin to tinkle like chimes in a breeze. You think mortal anxiety is bad? Ghost anxiety is like a poltergeist amateur hour.

Can't say I blame him. For the first time in Darkstar's existence, Andrea's late. And everyone at the table knows it's no coincidence.

Apart from his clumsy start, Louis handled telling her well. Her reaction isn't his fault. No woman wants to be on the other end of any conversation that begins with, *"I haven't been entirely honest with you."* But to Andrea's credit, she didn't run.

Or maybe she did, I think, as I look at the clock.

Louis jumps up, nearly knocking over his chair at the sight of Andrea in the doorway. Lack of sleep has smudged dark crescents beneath her red-rimmed eyes. Just by looking at her face, I can tell her emotions are as tangled as her hair.

Thanatos swivels in his seat, gives her a smile, and then stands up to pull a chair out for her. Andrea looks over her shoulder, staring at the mist-shrouded street behind her. I can hear her arguing with her fear. Her fear seems to be winning.

"Andrea."

The desperation in Louis' voice settles like a leaden feather on the scales in her heart, tipping them. She sits down beside me, releasing the breath I know she's been holding since she walked in.

I give Thanatos an apologetic look. Tonight isn't even going to be the hard part. Thanatos sips the sweet sludge in his cup and winks at me. He knows how mortals are, both the ones still attached to their bodies and those that aren't.

"I'm glad you came," I say as Vega drops off Andrea's usual order. "I was beginning to worry."

Andrea runs her fingers around the edge of her cup. "I almost didn't. I mean, what's the point?"

Louis gives her a look that touches even my jaded heart, but to his credit, he says nothing.

"What do you mean?" I ask.

"He's *dead*," Andrea says with a bitter laugh. "I mean, I knew I was good at falling for unattainable men, but this is a whole new level of stupid. Even for me."

I put my cup down and wait until the weight of my silence forces her to look at me. "You can't help who you love, Andrea. True love, like yours and Louis', exists on a soul level. It transcends everything that seeks to contain it, including time, distance, and flesh."

Andrea pushes her chair away from the table. "I don't even know why I'm here. I certainly didn't come for some New Age bullshit consolation prize! So, if that's all you have to offer—"

"What if I told you there was a way you and Louis could be together?"

Andrea looks at Louis and back at me. I can see the wheels turning in her mind.

"Can you bring him back to life?"

The hope in her voice makes me regret the words on my tongue. Thanatos beats me to it, though, and I'm glad. It sounds better coming from him.

"I'm sorry, my dear. Death is a one-way street, I'm afraid. Most certainly for the long-departed."

"Then, if you can't bring him back, that only leaves..."

The color drains from Andrea's face as she fills in the blanks. She presses a hand to her chest, weighing out the choice before her in forfeited breaths, thirty-two years of them, to be exact. Not that she knows that's how much time she has left.

"So I would be...a gh-ghost?" Her eyes are fear-filled and curious, a good sign.

"For a time, yes," I say, nodding at Thanatos. "He is due to collect you, but not for a while. There is no law saying that you have to finish your incarnation attached to your body. If you choose, Thanatos can separate your soul from your flesh, releasing you from the prison that keeps you parted from Louis. And from that moment until your appointed time, you can be together."

Aware now that Death sits beside her, Andrea stares at Thanatos. His kind smile seems to unnerve her even more, but she doesn't flinch when he covers her hand with his.

Andrea looks longingly at Louis and asks the obvious question, "How much time will I have?"

Though Thanatos and I know the answer, we agreed that her choice has to be made blind. No mortal knows the hour Thanatos will come calling. All human decisions are made in the shadow of Death. That's why they have power.

"We can't tell you," I say. "You must still make your choice within the limits of your existence, weighing its worth and its costs. But given the unusual nature of your choice, there is *one* thing we can do to help you decide."

I nod to Thanatos, letting him take over.

"With your permission, I can draw forth your soul and set it free to wander for a single night. Come dawn, you will have to return to your body. But for a short while, you can experience what waits on the other side."

Andrea smiles at me. "He can really do that? But what about my body?"

"I will keep your body here. You will not come to harm," I assure her.

Louis leans forward and looks her in the eyes. "You don't have to do this, Andrea. I will meet you here every night for the rest of your life if that's all we can have."

"No, I want to see. If this is the only way, I have to know." Andrea turns to Thanatos. "Go ahead. Do it. I'm ready."

Thanatos may be the only person who can laugh at someone and not make them feel a fool. He grins at me across the table as I shake my head and smile.

"Not tonight," he explains. "You would only have two hours before sunrise."

"Tomorrow then! I mean, tonight! I'll come back tonight."

"Very well," I say, drawing her attention back to me. "Be here when the sun goes down. Eat nothing this day, drink nothing but water. It will make the reaping…easier."

"I'll be here!" Andrea dashes a tear from her cheek and gives Louis a dazzling smile before darting out the door.

Louis notices she's headed in the opposite direction of the patisserie. "Where is she going? I'll be right back."

He chases her into the street, calling her name. She turns around, mist swirling about her like a dissolving cloak. Thanatos and I don't listen to their conversation. It's tempting, but we're going to be interfering enough as it is by nightfall. I watch Louis brush Andrea's cheek with a hand she can hardly feel before she rushes off into the night.

Louis wanders back in and sits down. He looks bewildered, hopeful, and perched on the edge of potential devastation.

"Everything okay?" I ask.

Louis nods. He picks up another peppermint and pops it in his mouth. "She's gone home. Said she has no intention of spending her last day on earth covered in flour."

"Rooftop's closed tonight, Rigel. No one comes up. Not even servers."

Rigel gives me a casual salute and wipes down the bar. He knows what's going on, having witnessed everything this morning. I wouldn't be surprised to discover he's guessed who Thanatos is, either. Rigel grew up on the streets. In the hood, Death hits doorsteps like the morning paper, and everyone is yesterday's news.

I wend my way through the crowded bar and head upstairs where they're waiting for me. Death, the Dead, and the Soon-To-Be.

I step out onto the rooftop and lock the door behind me. Louis and Andrea are standing face to face, whispering, making plans. Louis is telling her all the things he wants to show her. His face holds all the excitement of a hundred years' haunt made new again. Can't say I blame him.

I close my eyes, feeling for the moment the sun slips below the horizon. A few seconds later, night thrums through my immortal body. It's time.

"Are you ready to go into the Between, Andrea?" I ask.

She steps forward with a nervous smile. "As ready as I'll be, I guess."

I point towards a chaise lounge tucked behind a folding screen at the far corner of the patio. Andrea goes first, followed by Louis, then me. Thanatos brings up the rear. He's a gentleman like that.

"You should lie down," Thanatos says. "A deadweight fall means nothing to a corpse. The dead are done with their bodies. You aren't. This will be hard enough without a broken leg as a homecoming present."

Worry overtakes the anticipation on Andrea's face as she lies down. "Hard how? Is it going to hurt?"

Thanatos arches an eyebrow at me, making sure one last time that I meant what I said. I nod. I meant every word. I *want* this to hurt.

"Yes, it will hurt," I say, owning it. "It doesn't have to. Thanatos can reap souls as softly as Morpheus weaves dreams. But I've asked him to make sure it does."

"Why on earth would you do such a thing?" Louis gives me an angry look. Not that I care.

"Because dying is painful. If Andrea is going to make a choice to kill herself for love, then she needs to know that the pain she feels departing her flesh is nothing compared to the pain she leaves behind her." I turn to Andrea. "Do not be under any illusion. The choice you are considering is the most selfish you can make."

Andrea unwraps the words I've spoken and swallows the truth inside. Eyes glassy with tears, she nods. "I understand."

"Very well, then. Once Thanatos has removed your soul, your body will remain here at rest, under my protection. You must be back at dawn, no exceptions."

"Or Cinderella becomes a zombie?" Andrea grins.

I stare at her so hard she presses herself back into the chaise cushions. "Or Thanatos will hunt you down and shove you back in your corpse, and the choice to live out the rest of your incarnation at Louis' side will be off the table."

Andrea glances up at Louis, who refuses to look at me. He's still mad at me. I suspect that won't change until the moment his phantom arms wrap around her newly spectral flesh. Andrea motions for Louis to kneel beside her, which he does.

"Are you ready?" Thanatos brushes a lock of wildly curling hair away from Andrea's face.

Andrea takes a deep breath and presses her lips together. I watch her knuckles whiten as she grips the sides of the chair.

"Do it."

"As she said, this will hurt." His night-hued eyes soften. "For that, I am sorry."

Thanatos traces the crescent of her ear and the arterial line of her neck, then trails his hand down the open front of her shirt. With a grace I find myself envying, his fingertips splay over her heart. Andrea looks at Thanatos and gasps, or tries to, but there's no air left for her to breathe. Like gossamer clouds racing across a moonlit sky, the whites of Thanatos's eyes recede, leaving nothing but the void all mortals must face at the end.

Stark light blooms beneath his hand as Andrea's soul rises to his silent call. With a cry of pain, she arches her back and thrusts her chest towards his gentle, summoning hand.

I sigh. Mortals always create more pain than they're meant to feel. "Don't fight him, Andrea. Surrender."

Tears leak from the corners of Andrea's eyes. Her hands let go of the chair as her body lets loose of her soul. She slumps back, muscles slack. Life miraculously paused.

Thanatos lifts his hand from her chest. Cradled in his palm is an amorphous ball of shimmering white light, glowing like a newborn star. He steps away from Andrea's body and releases the life he has reaped. Her soul-orb hovers for a moment, wavering, then begins to unfold itself into something Andrea-shaped.

As her bare feet touch the cold tiles of the roof, a spectral solidity ripples up her body, fixing the details in place. Louis clambers to his feet and watches her take form from the tips of her pink-polished nails to the spiraling ends of her chestnut hair. Emerging from her coma of flesh, Andrea opens her eyes and stares in wonder at a world her living eyes have never seen.

She gasps when she looks at Thanatos, at me. Unbound by the limits of her mortal body and the mortal disbelief that comes with it, Andrea sees us as all the Dead do, terrible and shining. When she can pull her eyes away, her gaze lands on Louis, and she chokes back a sob of joy.

Thanatos steps aside, clearing a path between the lovers. Louis crosses the rooftop to stand in front of his love. He reaches up to brush her cheek with the back of his fingertips. Gasping at his touch, Andrea's hand flies up to cover his. She presses the side of her face into his palm and kisses his wrist. Louis loses what little control he had and buries his hands in Andrea's hair, claiming her lips for the first time.

I feel a stab of jealousy watching Andrea coming to life in Louis' arms. Five thousand years and nothing is new for me anymore. But for Louis and Andrea, the world in which the dead reside has never been more wondrous, never been more alive.

It's a myth that spirits cannot feel, or hunger, or any of a hundred other things reserved for the flesh. Souls are simply less dense, less tethered, less…physical. Every whisper-like touch that Andrea could barely feel while connected to her body hits like a hammer here. Thanatos and I give the lovers their space, not that they know we are here. All that exists in their world right now is them.

Thanatos sees the look on my face and leans closer. "Should I arrange for Eros to pay a little visit?"

I huff a laugh. "Not unless you want to test the theory about whether Death can die. So, when she comes back, what will you need to do?"

"Nothing." Thanatos smiles at the sight of Louis swinging Andrea around. It's a movie moment if ever there was one. "As long as you're keeping her body in stasis, her soul will stitch itself back to her flesh the moment she lies down."

"And if she decides she wants to make this…condition permanent?"

Thanatos leans over to brush a kiss across my cheek. "You know where to find me."

As Thanatos passes the couple, Andrea's hand snakes out and grabs his wrist.

"Thank you," she says, tucking her head under Louis' chin.

Thanatos smiles at the couple. "I hope you have a wonderful evening."

And three steps later, Death has left the building.

I whisper a quick spell of cloaking over Andrea's interrupted body, then head for the door leading into the bar. "Come, you two. The night is young, but it will be over quicker than you think."

Andrea marvels at the way the moonlight seems to glow from inside her skin as she and Louis follow me inside. Things have picked up in the short time we've been upstairs. I cast my eyes about the room, looking for Spica.

Hmmm...no Spica. Vega will have to do it.

I catch sight of Vega's ponytail weaving through the crowd and send out a silent message. She looks up as though I've called her name aloud and heads my direction. She waves at Louis and Andrea. Inside Darkstar, they look like regular patrons. Outside, though...

"I need you to do me a favor," I say, pulling a pendant from thin air behind my back. It's a rectangular lozenge of bright silver, stamped with sigils no one has seen in three thousand years. That's ok. She doesn't need to know what it does. I do.

"Sure."

Vega sets down her tray and pulls Antares over to ask him to cash out a tab on table 9. Antares gives her a surly look but agrees.

"Alright, what do you need?"

"You know Louis here. And Andrea. I just need you to wander around with them tonight. Show them around, give them their space, but make sure they're back by dawn."

The intensity of that last request sends a chill up Vega's spine. She crosses herself. Like *that's* going to do anything.

"Sure," she agrees, pulling off her apron.

I loop the necklace over her head.

"What's this for?"

"Just a charm. Something to help you see better in the dark. Make sure you keep it on."

Vega raises an eyebrow, then shrugs and tucks the pendant inside her shirt. "You two ready?"

Louis breaks away from nibbling on Andrea's ear and clears his throat. "Yes. I'm sorry, yes."

Andrea hugs me tightly and whispers in my ear, "Thank you. So much."

"Don't thank me just yet," I say, as she pulls away and retakes Louis' hand. "Go on. Live a little."

They laugh at my joke as I shoo them out into the night. I watch from the promenade as they weave a love-drunk path down Royal Street and turn toward the river.

"On second thought," I whisper, "live a lot."

"Andrea..."

I've never understood long goodbyes. Andrea and Louis are playing chicken with the rising sun, torturing themselves for just five more minutes. I probably do need Eros to make a pincushion of my ass. I've gotten jaded.

Andrea kisses Louis one last time. Okaaaay, maybe not. She's kissing him again.

"The sun is rising," I say, nodding at the eastern sky. It's as rosy as Andrea's flesh, which I've kept warm for her.

With a pained expression on his face, Louis finally does the gentlemanly thing and pushes her away. But he keeps hold of her hand, and together they walk toward the chaise where Andrea's body rests. She leans her forehead against his, eyes closed.

"Thank you for a wonderful evening," she says.

I'm not sure if she's talking to me or Louis. I decide to let it be him.

She looks at me. "How do I…?"

"Pretend your body isn't there," I tell her. "Lie down like you are going to sleep. Your soul will do the rest. It knows the way."

Andrea sits on the edge of the chaise and sinks back against her mortal shell, still holding tight to Louis' hand. She gasps as her flesh begins to knit itself back to her spirit.

It hurts, coming home. Ankle to knee to hip, her legs begin to burn as they come back to life. All pins and needles, like her whole body has been dead asleep, because it has. The moment the reattachment process reaches the base of her spine, her body rips Andrea's ghostly hand from Louis' grip and slams her soul home.

Louis recoils as the veil of Andrea's flesh comes down hard between them. She groans like a woman on a birthing bed and rolls over to vomit a yellow stream of bile on my white-tiled rooftop. Louis watches her with a look of concern that sets my teeth on edge. Something isn't right.

Louis looks down at his left hand, watching it fade as the rising sun turns the Mississippi into a mirror of fire. His voice is a grave whisper, and not long for this world.

"Andi."

Andrea swipes her mouth with the back of her hand and looks up and through him. Realizing they are out of time, she jumps up on deadened legs and immediately comes crashing down. Her bloodied knees add a splash of red to the tiles.

As she pulls herself to her feet, I scan her body to make sure nothing is broken. She's fine, but that's going to hurt like hell when her nerves come back online.

A golden sunbeam pierces the clouds as Helios steers his chariot toward the heights. Shadows solidify. Louis does the opposite. Andrea whimpers as the sun begins to burn away the man she loves like so much fog. He lifts his hand to her cheek. His fingertips pass through her tears.

"Three weeks," Andrea whispers. "Then, forever."

Louis brushes an ephemeral kiss across her forehead.

His broken eyes are on me as his lost soul goes to ground.

The querent sitting across from me is nursing a broken heart. And it's my job to stomp on it. For his own good.

"Three of Swords. Pain all around. You, him, your relationship."

He flinches at my words. He knows he fucked up. I flip another card.

"Two of Cups. The soulmate card. Your hope and your fear."

When I'm done telling him that he's an idiot for letting go of the best man he's ever going to meet, I'll send him downstairs to nurse a Mai Tai or two. Maybe have Spica slip a coin in his pocket to help him clean up the mess he's made of things. This love shit has to work out for someone.

I flip over the final card. "Judgment."

The twentieth trump snatches the words from my tongue. It's been twenty days since I've seen Andrea, since I had Rigel walk her home after her little out-of-body experience. I haven't seen Louis since that night, either. It's his absence that has me on edge. The look on his face the last time I saw him has been haunting me for weeks. You'd think he was a ghost or something.

"It's all on you, Ross," I say, pushing the card across the table. "Is this the life you want? Always denying the thing that could make you happy, just to avoid the possibility it won't?"

"But what if it doesn't work out?" Ross says, gnawing at his nails.

"Then it doesn't work out." I shrug and gather up the cards. "I can tell you this, though. Acting like everything is a matter of life-and-death is killing your chances of having a life at all."

284

"What if…" Ross stumbles over his words, "what if Ethan won't take me back?"

I slip the cards back into the velvet-lined box. "Then you do what you do with any loss. You move on. Or don't you believe in life after love?"

"Did you just quote a fucking Cher song?" Ross laughs until he cries, fanning his face. "Oh, honey! I'm so proud!"

He rounds the table and pulls me into the kind of disjointed hug that avoids my breasts entirely. I stop him when he reaches for his wallet.

"I'm working pro bono tonight," I tell him with a smile. "Now, go on. Tell Rigel I said your drink's on me. A little liquid courage will do you some good."

A little luck won't hurt, either.

He drops an air-kiss beside my cheek and heads for the stairs. I reach out to Spica with my mind and slip a coin in her pocket. She'll know what to do.

It's two in the morning. The lovers should be arriving soon. Thanatos, too. I lean back in my chair and stare up at the night sky, grateful for the magical dome that blocks out all the light pollution from the city. The Orionids have already peaked for the year, but my attention seems to coax a few more falling stars from the sky.

The door to the rooftop opens. I smell Spica before I see her and turn. She stops a couple of paces away from me, clutching an envelope in her hand. Even upside down, the flowing handwriting makes Andrea's name easy to read. I sit up straight as she places the letter on the table and heads back downstairs.

The envelope is sealed. I run my fingertips along the seal, heating the glue. It's a pointless curiosity. I don't have to read the words to know how the story ends. I unfold the letter and sigh.

My dearest love,

When you asked me about the ring on my finger, I told you it was a tale for another time. That time is now.

Madeleine was my wife, a golden and delicate flower that bloomed in the sun of my affections. Her family hailed from New York, where I had traveled for business. I loved her on sight. That seems to be the only way my heart knows to move.

She was as different from you in every way it is possible to be—except one: she left her life behind to be with me. Her family, her charity work, her social circles. I crooked my finger, and she followed, believing she could survive anywhere in the light of my love.

But swamps make wet graves, and dead places never seem dead when you're wrapped around a lover.

It wasn't long before she began to fade, my sweet Maddie. The stifling heat wilted her, and her grounded spirit could find no purchase in the silted soil of New Orleans. When the resentment first set in, she clung to me, as sweet and thorny as the climbing roses scaling the arbor.

But then, like a mildewy haze, her despair overtook her spirit, draping her in a shroud of death I did not see until I found her dead in the garden, empty bottle in hand. The belladonna she'd been taking to help her sleep had closed her bright eyes forever.

Despite the love my heart bears for you, I cannot bring myself to rip another flower from the living world to plant it in my dead one. The way you spoke of your mother, your sister, the dreams you were willing to leave unfulfilled to be at my side...your life is more precious to you than you know.

I hope that you will never read this letter. That you will have heard your living heart as clearly as I did when you held my hand and told me all the things you were willing to sacrifice for me. But if not, I can only pray you will accept my decision. My sacrifice for love.

It is only by letting you go that I can keep you alive and blooming in the salted ground of my heart. Forever.

Live well, my love.

- L

Goddamn it, Louis. I fold his knife of a letter and return it to its sheath. I'm not angry. I'm...moved. The gods know I've dealt harder blows than this one and flinched less, so it's not that.

It's that selfless mortal shit that's got me twisted. Gods don't do that. What we want, we get. And if we don't get it, we burn down the world until we do. The only sacrifices we're concerned with are the ones on our altars, in our beds.

The sound of the rooftop door opening makes me flinch. I instinctively tuck Louis' letter out of sight beneath me. Good thing, too, because Andrea is headed toward me.

"You're early," I say with a smile I don't feel. "Never seen someone so eager to die."

Andrea sits down beside me. Her hand drifts to the tiny vase of rosebuds, her fingertips tracing their silky, spiraling hearts.

"I love roses," she whispers. "I can't seem to grow them for shit, but Mom has a garden full of them."

I say nothing. Not because I have nothing to say, the letter burning a hole in my ass has that covered, but it's considered bad form to talk at a funeral.

"It was surreal, knowing today was my last day. I mean, who gets that? I spent the morning in the garden with my mom. We had coffee and biscuits. My sister had to cancel. I'm usually the one doing that. Always thinking I'll see them next time. Oops."

Her laugh is bittersweet. Or sweetbitter. I can't make out the predominant flavor in her tone.

"Did you tell them?" I ask, curious.

Talk about a whole lot of pain for nothing, I think, knowing I'm going to have to deal the blow, and the sooner, the better.

Andrea blinks back tears and shakes her head. "The only thing I'm worse at than love is goodbyes, Asteria."

I'm reaching for Louis' letter when Andrea slides an envelope of her own across the table. Her bubbly, rounded script is so different from Louis' flowing hand. And there's a circle of pale blue ink where a teardrop has washed out the first letter of his name.

I'm still processing the convergence of fate on my rooftop when Andrea stands up. Like a woman who's afraid she'll change her mind, she hurries to the door in a walk that desperately wants to be a run. The hollow gong of the rooftop door gives way to the scudding squeal of Thanatos pulling a chair up to the table.

"Was that my blushing corpse-to-be?" he asks.

I drum my fingers once on Andrea's letter, then set Louis' letter beside hers. Thanatos' eyebrows shoot up.

"And you can keep that comment about pulling things out of my ass to yourself," I warn him.

He smiles, which makes me smile, which I don't realize I need until it happens. I wave my hand over the table and magic us up some coffee, beignets, and a full bowl of sugar.

"I'm sorry you came all this way for nothing," I tell him, dotting a lump of powdered sugar with my finger and transferring it to my tongue.

Smiling, he sets to emptying the sugar bowl into his cup, a spoonful at a time. "Don't be. Nothing makes me happier than showing up for a potential suicide and finding my services are no longer required."

We sit there for a long time, enjoying the bittersweetness of dark things, both the coffee and everything that has happened tonight. He doesn't ask what happened, and I don't tell him. Gods have little use for reasons *why*. For beings like us, mortal lives are sparks rising from a fire, stars falling from the sky. We blink, and you are gone.

"Than?"

He pulls his gaze away from the night sky and looks at me.

"Promise me something."

"If I can."

I lay my hand on top of his, on top of the love letters. "Next time, remind me to leave the whole star-crossed lovers thing to Eros."

Thanatos chuckles and turns his hand over in mine.

"Agreed," he says, giving my hand a squeeze. "But just between you and me, you did alright."

A Soul For A Soul

BY

RASHMI MENON

ARTEMIS,
GODDESS OF THE HUNT

F OR THE HUNDREDTH TIME TODAY, I HEARD KARA, MY SECRETARY, EXPLAIN TO YET ANOTHER MORTAL PLANNING TO VISIT THE OLYMPUS NATIONAL PARK THAT THERE WAS NO GIANT SHADOW HARVESTING THE HIKERS.

"Yes, ma'am! We are open. Yes, the park is safe. Nothing to worry about," Kara said to the woman on the phone. "No, that's a silly rumor the kids started...You know, it's just the season...I assure you," she said, smiling before hanging up.

"Another dark shadow inquiry?" I asked, getting up to pour myself a cup of coffee. "Who makes up these rumors?"

Hyale, my nymph, walked into my office. "People seem to enjoy linking everything to Halloween. Their creative juices flow during this season, and they cook up one spooky tale after another," she answered.

"Are these rumors created because of the people reported to have gone missing from the park?" I asked, reaching for the files on my desk and flipping through its contents. "I thought the investigations proved they were abducted by some mortal mafia and had nothing to do with the park!" I said, frustrated by the lack of details in the folder.

"I've been taking the shorter route through the woods going home, and I haven't seen or heard anything out of the ordinary. I wouldn't worry much, ma'am," Kara reassured me. "After all, who would dare disturb the peace in Artemis' park?" She winked at me with a knowing smile.

Kara, a mortal, knew she was working for the immortals of the Greek Pantheon. Specifically for me, a wild huntress, but she never once suspected or questioned our motives for returning to live among the mortals. That's what I loved about Kara. She knew how to stick to her business.

But it wouldn't hurt to be cautious, even if it is only a rumor.

"I am sure it's only mortal imaginations running wild, but let's keep an eye out for any oddball events," I said.

Jamie, the satyr, and head of security at the park, got up from his seat at the reception desk of the visitor center. "I will amp up the security if required," he said, walking into my chamber.

"Thank you, Jamie. Perhaps an additional guard or two."

"If that is all, ma'am, I'd like to take my leave," Kara said.

"Yes, of course, it's late. You should've been out of here a couple of hours ago, Kara. Go home and spend time with your family." Normally, I wouldn't have worried about Kara walking alone through the woods. But tonight, I felt it was better that she had company.

"Hyale, please walk with Kara. It's late, and I think she could use the company. Jamie will join you as well."

Kara protested, "I will be fine. It's just a fifteen-minute walk from here, ten if I hurry. There's no need to bother Hyale or Jamie."

"Kara, I wasn't asking. Hyale and Jamie will accompany you," I said and waved goodbye as they left.

I summoned my dragon, Sayeh, deciding to fly to the waterfall near my temple in the deepest part of the woods. To mortal eyes, she appeared as a large hound. But every time I needed her, she would transform into her original dragon shape. I climbed onto her scaly green back and held her by her thick horns. She nuzzled against my foot, and I rubbed her head. After casting a spell to hide us from mortal view, I tapped her gently. With a flap of her massive wings, she took off into the air. The aerial view of the park would provide me with an advantage to spot anything unusual.

I reached my temple and noticed someone waiting at the entrance of the cave. The 6' 5" muscular frame was familiar. His long dark hair was pulled back into a ponytail, and he carried a bow in his right hand with a quiver slung across his shoulders. I dismounted from Sayeh and walked to the entrance.

"Orion! It's been long since we last met," I greeted him, pleasantly surprised by his visit.

"Artemis…yes, a long time, indeed. But I could see you from up there." He pointed towards the night sky. I smiled, following his gaze.

"Can we talk?" he asked, taking my hands. "There's something I need to tell you about the park."

"Of course, come on in." I had barely completed my sentence when a shrill scream pierced the cloudy air. I recognized that voice.

"That's Hyale! I must go!" I said and took off in the direction of the scream, Orion following at my heels.

My feet slapped the velvet flesh of the forest ground as I sprinted in the direction of the commotion. Tracking my way through the trees, I found them not too far from the outskirts of the woods. Hyale was unconscious on the floor with a flustered Jamie trying to tend to her.

"Jamie!" I called out. "What happened? I heard her scream."

"The shadow…the dark shadow, it's real! We saw it!" he stammered.

"Shadow? What shadow?" Orion asked, catching up.

"Where's Kara?" I asked, noticing her absence.

"She wouldn't stop. I asked her to, but she just kept following the shadow. I begged her to stop!" Jamie replied. "Hyale suddenly screamed and collapsed. I had to help her," he said, lowering his eyes.

"What shadow?" Orion asked again, his voice laced with a tinge of irritation.

"There were whispers among the mortals about a dark presence in our park. Something about a cloud-like shadow that left them disoriented and some even dead. A few cases of missing persons were reported as well. The local authorities investigated these disappearances, and the missing people either turned up dead outside of the park boundaries or were never found. There was no evidence or eyewitnesses to link these disappearances directly to the park, and nobody suspected anything unnatural. Most believed they were just rumors. That is, until now..." Jamie trailed off.

I looked at them with a grim expression and said, "Please take Hyale back to the temple and tend to her there. I am going after Kara."

"I am coming with you," Orion said. I wanted to protest. Orion was here on a visit, and I didn't want to drag him with me into danger. "This is why I am here. I heard whispers about a breakout from the Underworld. Something about a sorceress and her dark energy during Samhain," he insisted.

"You knew about the dark shadow?" I asked. The slight tremor in my voice betrayed my concern. "And what is this about a sorceress, now?"

"Unfortunately, I don't have more information. I came as soon as I heard," he replied, lowering his eyes. He raised a balled fist and placed it against his chest as he lowered to one knee. "I won't be in your way, Huntress! Please allow me to accompany you."

A hunter's promise.

With the rumors, Jamie's statement, and the information from Orion, it seemed I had a major dark shadow problem in the park. Exhaling a long gust of air, I nodded and signaled for Sayeh. She flew in and scooped both of us onto her back.

We didn't have to go far before we found Kara walking towards the edge of a cliff near the waterfall, following something shaped like a dense, low-lying dark cloud. The fog impeded my vision from whatever captivated her. I called out, asking her to turn around, but my pleas fell on deaf ears.

We drew closer, and Orion jumped off the dragon, running towards Kara while I followed the shadowy figure amidst the fog. Its thick hide, chiseled from stones, supported droopy bat-like wings.

Bright red eyes flared like molten lava in a dark recess, casting an irresistible allure. Its body was infused with pure darkness, giving the figure an aura of desecration. Here was the dark shadow many had witnessed. Yet, it was no mere shadow. This was an immortal creature.

The beast locked its eyes onto mine, and scorching heat coursed through my body, leaving small bumps on my skin. It was trying to keep me from helping Kara. I, Goddess of the Wild and Creatures, recognized every animal existing in my woods, yet here was one I could not control.

The dark shadow whispered something to Kara before it jumped across the cliff towards the waterfall. Kara ran to the edge, following the creature. Her eyes rolled back into her skull in a state of hypnosis. There was no way Orion would be able to catch her in time. His calls to her remained unanswered, and she jumped into the waterfall.

"Sayeh, dive!" I yelled, watching Kara fall towards the whooshing vortex below. Sayeh dove head-on, full speed, towards her. The winds scraped my skin as the pressure of our descent pushed against me. I held onto Sayeh's horn with one hand and swooped up Kara just before she hit the rocky bed beneath the falls. Sayeh pulled up, landing on the cliff. The creature gave us a death glare before disappearing into the mist.

With an unconscious Kara in my arms, Orion and I made our way back to the temple. A diffused silvery-bluish light beamed through the dome of the temple. The fragrance of incense filled the air as Iphigenia, the temple priestess, tended to Hyale's injuries. Jamie paced the pillared halls, awaiting news of Kara. They rushed forward to help us lay her at the base of the shrine. I sprinkled some water on her and whispered a healing spell to wake her up.

Kara jolted, sitting upright in a quick motion. She opened her eyes, staring blankly ahead. They were a bottomless void, lifeless

295

and lacking emotions. The spark that existed in them had vanished. Her lips were drained of color and cracked. Deep scratches appeared on her chocolate brown skin, but there was no hint of blood. She tipped her head slightly to one side and continued to stare with a blank expression. Either thoughts ravaged her mind, or the shock had rendered her unresponsive.

Before I could say anything, Kara broke out in a high-pitched cackle. She looked around the room and said, "You're next." The guttural voice reverberated, bouncing off the chamber walls, but it sounded nothing like Kara.

With a heavy heart, I realized the creature had reaped Kara's soul. She was at this moment an undead corpse. I had about five days to help her. If I did not restore Kara's soul within this period, she would become a soulless monster and lost to us forever.

Only five days.

My chest felt tight as the heaviness of this knowledge weighed on my heart. I stood there, contemplating my next steps.

Hyale and Iphigenia looked at me, eyes wide with fear and concern. Kara used their distraction to push them away and jumped off the shrine, landing on Jamie. With a low-pitched snarl, she dug her fingernails into his eyes, trying to gouge them out. Jamie held onto Kara's hands, trying to push her off, yet Kara possessed an abnormal strength that was impossible for a mere mortal. I gasped, watching the scene unfold. Kara, a mortal, had Jamie subdued.

Orion ran to the duo and held Kara from behind. He tried to pull her off Jamie, but she struggled against him and growled, kicking into the air. It took both Orion and Jamie to restrain and lay her down on the marble altar beneath the shrine. With a quick prayer to my sister, Hekate, I cast a spell that brought forth a set of magical vines. We bound her to the altar with the plants holding her in place.

"Jamie, I need you to guard the temple while Iphigenia and Hyale tend to Kara. Do not worry. She will not be able to break free from the vines. I must find a way to return Kara's soul," I said, getting ready to go back into the woods in search of the dark shadow.

"Her soul?" my nymphs asked in unison.

"Yes, the dark shadow has sucked out Kara's soul. If not brought back to her soon, Kara, as we know her, will be lost to us forever."

With sad eyes, Hyale looked down at Kara restrained by the spell and the vines.

I changed into my hunting gear, but instead of my beloved bow and arrow, I took my hunting sword and silver blade—a gift from my father, Zeus. Forged using celestial minerals, my magically enhanced silver blade could fatally wound any living creature, mortal or immortal.

Something sinister was going on in my park. Samhain or not, I was going to hunt it down. All those dark shadow inquiries, and I dismissed them as mere rumors. Now Kara was paying the price. I could not let her bear the brunt of my neglect. Deciding to close the park until we fixed the dark shadow problem, I called one of my nymphs who had remained in the park's office. I left her with instructions to close Olympus National Park to the public until after Samhain. There was no way I would allow that creature to capture any more innocent souls. I wondered how many it had already reaped.

Orion insisted on joining me for the hunt again. This time I did not resist. I could use a trained hunter like him. Leaving Sayeh behind to guard the temple with Jamie, we set out towards the waterfall where the dark shadow had disappeared.

A fresh batch of leaves had fallen, covering the damp floor of the woods. Like a whispering audience, they crunched under my feet. The cold breeze played with a few strands of hair that had escaped from my braid. A whiff of earthy, woody incense wafted on the air. The deeper we walked into the woods, the darker it became. The moonlight partially blocked by majestic trees cast an eerie glow, accentuated by the illumination from the mildewed floor. Low-hanging branches from giant oak trees creaked as the autumn winds continued their assault. I held the sword in my right hand and the silver blade in my left. Taking small strides, we combed the woods looking for the creature. All my senses signaled to the dangers of following this beast, but I shut them out.

I did not know how to summon the creature, but hoped it would sense my presence. The sound of twigs cracking to my right caught my attention, and I turned to investigate. Orion waited, crouching into position, expecting a blitz attack. A blanket of grey mist descended upon us, veiling our vision. A silhouette moved swiftly, darting back and forth in the darkened maze. There it was again, the coruscating glow of its dazzling red eyes and the smoky haze of its dark flaky wings. The shadow had an enchanting presence, beckoning us into its pulsing heart.

The further we went, the more mystical and spellbinding the magnetism became. There was no way any mortal could withstand this attraction. I quietly followed the shadow with Orion in tow. Compelled by this external force, we continued to walk deeper into the woods. As we drew closer to the creature, the burning sensation I had during our earlier encounter coursed through my body. My heart rate increased as an extreme urge to dip into the cold water filled my senses. I walked in a trance, following Orion and closing my eyes as we marched onwards to the dark shadow.

The sound of water grew louder as it plummeted into the whooshing vortex at the bottom of the waterfall. Cold droplets grazed my face, bringing me back to the present. I opened my eyes just in time to stop Orion from jumping off the cliff. I only needed to see the creature once under the moonlight to realize it was no ordinary beast. This was a nightgoyle. The kind that only existed in Tartarus. Orion was right about the breakout from the Underworld.

What were they doing in my woods? How did they escape from Tartarus?

Before we could do anything, the nightgoyle jumped into the waterfall and disappeared in the mist as it had the last time. I cursed my luck and kicked the dirt under my feet. In the darkness of the night, there was no way to figure out exactly where the creature had disappeared. Orion wanted to follow it, but I stopped him. We needed more information before attacking its lair. Reluctantly, we made our way back to the temple.

At least now, I knew it was a nightgoyle. But how many of them were there?

Two days passed without another sighting of the dark shadow. Orion and I took different routes, hunting the beast in the woods, but it didn't appear again. Kara's body was showing signs of decay. I could use another healing spell on her, but it would only delay the inevitable by a slight margin. There was nothing I could do without her soul. The creature had disappeared from my grasp yet again. At least this time, it hadn't taken a soul with it. However, that did not make me feel any better. A nightgoyle was claiming mortals in my woods. Was it just the one? Or were there others?

Why did the nightgoyle need mortal souls? Were they working for someone?

The fact that it was leaving behind the mortal bodies after collecting the souls perplexed me. Clearly, it was not hunting for sustenance.

Who was the sorceress Orion mentioned?

There was something larger at play, and it was happening right under my nose. Yet, I was no closer to solving the mystery now than when I first laid eyes on the nightgoyle. There were more unanswered questions than I liked to admit.

"It's not your fault," Orion said, handing me a bowl of medicinal herbs ground into a paste.

I took the bowl. "You and I both know this is not going to help Kara. What kind of a goddess am I if I can't help the ones I'm sworn to protect?"

"Don't do that. This is not the time for you to brood," Orion said, looking at me.

I shook my head in disappointment.

"Come on, Artemis. You cannot do this to yourself. That's equivalent to giving up, and I know you're much better than that."

"I. Am. *Not*. Giving. Up," I said each word slowly through gritted teeth. "I am worried about time. The clock is running out on Kara."

"I know, and that's exactly why we need to hunt the nightgoyle instead of waiting for it to show up."

I took a deep breath and walked towards Kara. She remained restrained with the magically enhanced vines. Orion followed me. I handed the bowl to one of my nymphs and turned to face him. "How do you suppose we hunt the nightgoyle when I have nothing to track it?"

"These are creatures of the Underworld. There must be someone you know who can help."

Kara screamed the moment Hyale applied the linctus on her body. Her screams now sounded more like low-pitched growls. Her eyes remained dark and lifeless. It hurt me to see her in pain. Perhaps it was Kara's dark eyes or Orion's mention of the Underworld, but it triggered a name into my mind.

"Thanatos! He can help. The nightgoyle is a creature of the Underworld, and Thanatos can track them anywhere in the universe."

"Why would he be willing to help?" Orion asked. "I mean, he's the God of Death. He may want to claim her soul for the Underworld."

"He may be the God of Death, but I know he has principles. He would never want a mortal to suffer like this."

Kara growled and pulled at the vines with such force that I was sure it would sever her arms. She was turning more into a zombie with every minute that passed. Although my nymphs tended to her, I noticed the fear in their eyes every time she growled. I walked to the corner of the shrine and picked up a talisman that Thanatos had given me. I traced my hands through it, repeating his name and a chant.

Despite Kara's growls and the resulting chaos, the flicker of light as heavy wings unfurled behind me was hard to miss. I turned around to see the hooded and cloaked figure holding a scythe with a gloved hand. His dark wings closed against his back when our eyes met.

"Than, you came, and so soon!" I walked towards him, and we hugged.

He gave me his awkward smile. "Of course, Arty! I heard your call and knew this had to be serious."

"Come," I said, leading him to the altar so he could observe Kara.

"This is pointless! We should all be out hunting the creature," Orion said, stomping his feet.

"We will most certainly hunt the beast, Orion," Thanatos replied. "But I need a sense of it, and that can only come from Kara. I need to study her for a moment."

He walked towards Kara, who was getting stronger despite her decaying body. Some evil force was transmitting its energy into her. The magical vines wouldn't restrain her much longer, especially with the dark energy nourishing her. My nymphs took a few steps back, and I wondered if the fear in their eyes was due to Kara or Thanatos. He held his hand out to Kara. She took it after only a moment's hesitation. Kara's empty, lifeless eyes rolled back and forth until they fixed on Thanatos. Orion sighed and walked away, murmuring to himself about wasting time.

301

"Oh, dear Lord of Death, take me with you. I am ready," Kara said in ecstasy.

"In due time, dear one, just focus on my eyes," Thanatos instructed.

"Yes, my lord." She obeyed.

I watched with admiration as Thanatos calmed Kara's growls. Positioning himself into a comfortable stance, he cupped her face, looking into a fragment of her aura left behind. Within a few minutes, he established a spiritual connection with Kara's soul and through her to the nightgoyle that reaped it. Everything seemed to be okay until Kara began snarling again. Her eyes rolled back, and a sneer appeared on her face. Licking her lips, she jumped forward, opening her mouth wide, trying to take a bite of Thanatos' face. The vines pulled at her, holding her in place.

Thanatos smiled and turned to face me. "I am ready whenever you are, Arty," he said.

I asked Thanatos to lead the way, much to Orion's chagrin. He smirked and motioned Thanatos to move ahead. I took my beloved silver blade and hunting sword, while Orion switched to a broadsword.

"Good choice," I said, looking at him.

We followed a shrouded Thanatos as he led us into the woods. I squinted my eyes to adjust to the darkness of the forest. The leaves rustled in the cool breeze. The sound of dried twigs snapping under our feet echoed in the air. A fog descended upon us, and the mist touched my skin ever so lightly. Concentrating on the rustling of leaves on treetops, we marched ahead. The nightgoyle wasn't far from us. Multiple high-pitched growls emanated from the shadows. We looked at each other. The hunters were now the hunted.

"It's here. Be ready to strike," Thanatos whispered.

Breathing hard, I tried to focus on the sounds of the forest—*my* forest that was a part of my soul. I had to tune out every familiar noise of these woods and concentrate on the sound I normally wouldn't expect. That would be the one I was hunting. The rustling from the treetops continued. Wings flapped to my left. I spun, swinging my sword through the air, slicing into empty space.

A blood-curdling screech echoed from above as a nightgoyle descended directly upon Thanatos. He stood firm, gripping his scythe, ready for the creature. Another high-pitched growl and the flapping of wings grabbed my attention. The same bright-red eyes bored into me as the nightgoyle lunged, pushing off its strong hind legs. I slid sideways to slice my sword through the creature's abdomen. The beast rose, anticipating my moves, and perched on the tree branch above. It sat there, glaring into my eyes as the dark fog wrapped around me. The nightgoyle was trying to enchant me as it had Kara. It tightened the hold on my body as heat emanated from my pores, causing me to keel over in pain. I looked away from the branch into the distance and saw Thanatos and Orion battling the other nightgoyle. My distraction gave the nightgoyle above me enough time to attack again. This time, the beast wrapped me in its wings and jumped back onto the branch, carrying me with it.

"Arty!" Thanatos yelled.

His voice only made the nightgoyle tighten its grip. Despite its leathery appearance, it was chiseled from rough stone. The weight of its wings crushed into my ribs. It squeezed harder, trapping my movements. I could not get a hold of the blade that lay flat against my chest. The creature's eyes shone brighter, and the burning in my body peaked. I screamed as my skin melted.

Thanatos left Orion to battle the other nightgoyle and ran towards me. He unfurled his wings and rose to meet the beast, ready to strike it down with his scythe. The creature knew that Thanatos' scythe meant certain death. It jumped out of his reach, loosening its grip over my body, giving me enough space to free my left hand. The nightgoyle did not see the strike coming. I brought down my silver blade and plunged it into its chest. It felt like cutting through stone. The creature released me, its wings shrinking back and falling limp. Thanatos decapitated it. The moment his scythe touched it, the nightgoyle stiffened and burst into a puff of dust.

"Arty, are you alright?" Thanatos asked. "What were you doing? You know better than to allow the creature to wrap you in its wings!"

"Sometimes, to capture a predator, we need to become the prey, Than," I said, running in the direction where Orion battled the other nightgoyle. Thanatos followed me, mumbling something.

By the time we got to Orion, he had the creature restrained and hung from a tree branch. He had brought the magical vines from the temple.

"Good call bringing the vines," I said.

"Unlike you, my dear, I like to be prepared." I rolled my eyes at him.

Thanatos brought his scythe up to the nightgoyle, but I stopped him. "We still don't know where Kara's soul is, and we'll need this one to find out."

He nodded in response and approached the beast. Its eyes fixed on Thanatos with a smirk meant to manipulate him, aware that Thanatos was a creature of the Underworld, just like them.

The nightgoyle spoke first, "Hail, Thanatos, Lord of Death, Son of Nyx, Father of None."

Thanatos unfurled his wings, hearing the nightgoyle address him in its guttural, low bass tongue. With a quick look towards us, Thanatos said, "Bondsman, I command you to speak the truth. Where have you led the soul of the mortal Kara? I sense it is not in you."

A throaty laugh that sounded like stones in a grinder escaped from the nightgoyle, mocking the God of Death. Thanatos's face turned a shade darker than his current form. The nightgoyle sputtered, "Kara's soul? I am afraid I do not know what my lord seeks. Perhaps the lord must ask your mother, Lady Nyx. Unless she's busy servicing the Olympian in Tartarus," it said with a loud croaky laugh.

Thanatos gritted his teeth, his expression grim. I balled my hands into a fist at the audacity of the nightgoyle. Orion moved to strike, but Thanatos stopped him. He slammed the creature against the tree and laid his hand on its chest. Murmuring a spell, Thanatos pulled the soul of the nightgoyle out of its body. Black ichor ran from its nose and mouth as it screeched in pain. Yet, it would not give the answer Thanatos sought.

"You will not take my mother's name in that manner again," Thanatos said as he pulled the ghostly-looking soul out of the creature. It shrieked in response.

"My lord...I have not the mortal's soul."

"Then, where is it? I command you, fiend, speak now!"

The nightgoyle looked at me with lust-filled eyes. "Give me the flesh of the Goddess of the Hunt and the eyes of the Hunter Orion, and I shall tell all, my lord."

Thanatos and Orion tensed at the creature's contemptuous words. I raised my blade and struck the nightgoyle's right eye, popping it out of its socket. The beast howled as thick black ichor flowed down its face. Thanatos pulled the soul out of its body entirely and slammed it back several times. Losing one's soul is a painful process, and Thanatos made the nightgoyle endure it continuously until it begged for mercy.

"Where is the soul? And tell me, who have you bonded to?" Thanatos yelled.

"Zakar, Zakar, my lord. Zakar has the souls," the nightgoyle howled in agony.

"Where is it?"

"At the cave. Behind...behind the waterfall."

305

Thanatos slammed the soul back into the nightgoyle and brought his scythe forward. Sensing its doom, the creature yelled, "I will be free! I will capture the Huntress and her companion. I will drag you, all of you, to my master! To Zakar, the Demon Lord!"

Without waiting to hear the rest, Thanatos decapitated the nightgoyle with his scythe. Turning to face us, he gestured towards the waterfall. We left the creature as it dissipated in a thick cloud of black smoke. Thanatos smirked. He had sent the creature's soul into Lady Nyx's void, evident by the vapor it left behind. There was no way the nightgoyle would ever escape from the eternal realm.

Thanatos held a grim expression. "It is not the nightgoyle that has been collecting the souls," he said, falling in step with me.

"Zakar, the Demon Lord?" I asked.

Thanatos nodded before replying, "Yes, the nightgoyles were working for Zakar, the demon who escaped from the dungeons of Tartarus. I do not know why he needs the souls, but I can tell you it probably isn't for anything good."

A demon trespassed into my woods, and I had no idea! I rubbed my face hard, unable to come to terms with the fact.

The three of us gathered our weapons and ran to the waterfall. We stood at the edge of the cliff, looking for the cave the nightgoyle mentioned. The water from the river split into two as it plunged over the edge. One part crashed to the bottom, while the other seemed to disappear into mist. As we walked along the bank, Orion reached out to stop us, his hunter's eyes focused intently. He crouched and tugged on my hand, pulling me down beside him. I gasped, seeing what I had missed so many times before. The water fell into a cave, its entrance nearly obscured.

I dove in, followed by Orion and Thanatos. We landed in the depths of the cave, dry with no river in sight. The water flowing in simply disappeared. The cavern wormed its way half a mile ahead, its general shape ovoid. The walls below the ridge smoothly curved to the floor, while the ceiling above arched another hundred feet up to giant stalactites. Small, loose stones littered the floor leading to multiple minor alcoves, guarded by jagged rocks stacked one over another. Lanterns lit the cave, casting an eerie glow, and shone a path into the innards. We walked in slowly, taking step after step, weapons in hand. The cries of captured souls reverberated, bouncing off the cave walls. Closing my eyes for a brief moment, I took a deep breath. An unintelligible rhythmic chanting echoed from an inner chamber, the voice hauntingly hypnotic. We were getting closer.

Inside, Zakar sat cross-legged at the center of an elaborate pentagram. A cluster of crystals was placed at each of its corners. The incessant howling of the captured souls beat against the sparkling walls and pulsated in the air. Zakar was in genuine prayer, apparently to the King of Demons. His devotion and austerity were so intense he did not see us coming.

Orion raised his broadsword, ready to strike. Without opening his eyes, Zakar flicked his hand in the hunter's direction. The gesture sent him flying to the wall. I helped Orion to his feet while Thanatos approached the demon.

"Zakar, these souls belong to the Underworld. You have no business with them. Hand them over now, and I may show you mercy," he said.

Zakar smirked and looked at the trio of us. "Here to make a deal with the devil, are you?" he asked, attempting to strike up a Faustian bargain. He rose from the pentagram and walked towards me. His leathery wings unfurled, the sharp edges of horns rising above his brows curled and pointed upwards. He stared at me with blazing crimson eyes. Putting his index finger under my chin, he raised my face to meet his. His sharp nails cut into my skin, drawing silver ichor. "The Dark Lord would love to have you, beautiful Huntress!"

I pushed his hand away and wiped the ichor from my chin. Stepping away, I looked him up and down, sizing him up. "I am sure he'd be wonderful as my lackey. He'd have to wait his turn, though. I need to be done with you first."

Orion and Thanatos chuckled at my response. Zakar turned, revealing his immortal form in all his glory. The color on his face and body changed to a fiery red, matching his eyes, as his horns burst into flames. A furious sneer adorned his face as he marched towards me.

I smiled at his feeble attempt. "Intimidation is the oldest trick in the book, Zakar. Thanatos here will be happy to tutor you. Perhaps you'll learn to do it better," I said, placing the tip of my silver blade on his abdomen. He raised his hand, attempting to strike me.

Thanatos stepped forward, putting his scythe on Zakar's neck. "I wouldn't do that if I were you."

Orion positioned himself beside Thanatos, his sword drawn. "Enough with the games, Zakar. We know you have been collecting the mortal souls," he said, looking at the crystals.

"Who are you doing it for?" I asked, applying a light pressure on the silver blade pressed against his abdomen. "Think before you speak. You will be suspended in the eternal void forever if Thanatos' scythe meets your neck. Is that what you want?"

"What makes you think I am working for someone else?" he retorted.

I shook my head and looked at Thanatos. "I don't have the patience for this! Send him to the void."

"No, no, don't do that! I did not say I won't cooperate!" Zakar shouted. I smirked at his horror of being suspended in eternal limbo.

"Alright, spill it. Now!" I wanted this charade to be over so I could return to help Kara.

"The mortal souls you seek are caged in those crystals. They are at the pentacle," he said, pointing towards them.

I walked over to the crystals and searched for the one with Kara's soul, astonished by the sheer number that lay in the pentagram. I knew most of them belonged to the Underworld, which meant Thanatos would have to take them back. I looked at him with worried eyes. He understood my concern. I did not have to say the words.

"Do not worry, Arty. While most of these souls belong to the Underworld, some were reaped before their time. I will return such souls, and that includes Kara. Once freed from the crystal, her soul will be rejoined with her body," he explained.

I nodded, feeling better, but at the back of my mind, I was still trying to figure out why Zakar needed the souls in the first place.

"Why?" I asked, looking at Zakar. "Why have you been collecting them? And what were you doing in the pentagram?"

"Speak, fiend," Thanatos said, his tone flat and hard as he used the scythe to make a shallow slice into Zakar's neck.

Zakar cowered into a corner, trying to get away from the scythe. He was left with no doubts that Thanatos would easily use it to end his immortal existence. He took a deep breath before explaining, "Souls are the source of one of the strongest forms of energy, the energy of an eternal spirit. The more we collect, the more energy we have for our mistress."

"Your mistress?"

"Yes. The mistress has plans for you gods," he spat.

"What plans?" I asked.

"I don't know anything about her plans!"

"Who is she?" I shouted, pushing my blade into his ribs. He screamed out in agony as my sword burned through his body.

"I only know her as the sorceress. I don't know where she is or what her plans are exactly. My job is only to send her the spirit energy through a portal using this pentagram," he said, keeling over in pain.

Zakar was speaking the truth. There was no point in wasting further time here. We needed to get him and the mortal souls back into the Underworld. Thanatos plucked three black feathers from his wings and brought it to his lips. Chanting something, he flung them into the air. The dust from the cave's floor swirled into a twister as three cloned versions of Thanatos rose from the ground. He nodded at the clones, and they approached Zakar. Unfurling their wings in unison, they wrapped him from all sides.

Orion destroyed the pentagram while I collected the crystals. I handed the bags to Thanatos. He decided to leave immediately to the Underworld. Promising to be back at first light to help Kara, he teleported from the cave with his clones and the restrained Zakar in tow.

Zakar did not know the name or the location of the sorceress. I wondered if she was also a part of the Underworld. Either way, we had to find her and throw her into the lowest dungeon in Tartarus. With a wave of his hand, Orion opened a portal to my temple in the woods. He stepped through and held his hand out to me. A flash of light with a low-pitched growl caught my attention, and I turned away to investigate. Loud rumbling echoed within the cavern. The walls vibrated, loosening the stalactites. The portal began shredding in places, and I hurried back to it. Orion pulled his hand back just as it collapsed before me, leaving him on the other side.

That was a first! A portal closing on its own?

Dusting my hands, I readied to open another portal. Concentrating on the temple, I centered my energy and swirled my hand in a circular motion. But nothing happened. I tried again, but nothing!

"There is no escape, goddess!" a rough, throaty voice said.

310

"Fidelis? Fidelis Drabek?" I asked, turning to face her. A light gasp escaped my lips, unable to fathom her changed form since our last encounter. The all-powerful witch I had known in Olympus four thousand years ago was not the one who stood before me tonight. The sheen of her once glossy hair now looked like the remains of a bird's nest, crowned with a diadem of thorny twigs. Her skin was gnarled like the bark of woodland trees. A bumpy collection of warts on the tip of her nose fell heavily against her large leathery lips, and her eyes narrowed to a squint so close it was impossible to tell their color. The sorceress who once graced almost six-foot, a giant amongst the young witches, now had a pronounced hunch-back.

"Fidelis, you're the sorceress controlling Zakar and the nightgoyles?" I asked, surprised by her demeanor.

"Nice to see you again, lovely Huntress," she said in a croaky voice. "You have not aged a day since our last meeting. When was it? Four thousand years ago?"

"Aged? You know aging is not a part of my immortal life, Fidelis."

"Immortal," she spat with disgust.

"So, that's what this was all about? Immortality?"

Fidelis smirked, taking a few steps towards me. I clutched my sword tighter and shook my head. "Does my form disgust you, Huntress?" she yelled. "I have been living with this for thousands of years!"

"Hekate is not going to be pleased by your actions, Fidelis, neither will Lord Hades," I said with contempt.

"I worked hard to gain her favor, to gain Circe's and Hades' favor! And what? They did nothing for me, nothing! All I asked for was immortality, and they gave me this instead!" she said, looking down at herself.

"Clearly, you didn't deserve their favor," I retorted, pointing to the cave.

"I don't need them now. I will use the spirit energy to win over the Underworld. Hades will beg me for mercy as I take his crown."

"Sorry to break it to you, but you're no longer getting the spirit energy. Thanatos took care of that," I said with a smirk.

Fidelis' tiny eyes burned with rage at my words. The sharply pointed crown on her head sliced the air as she levitated and stayed airborne. With a wave of her hands, she sent an array of glassy shards my way. I fell onto my right knee and ducked, getting out of their way. I rushed towards her with my silver blade drawn, but she soared out of my reach, sending shards of steel. A few of them tore at my arms and abdomen. A steady stream of silver ichor trickled from my injuries.

Fidelis smirked. "Your mortal form makes you weak, Huntress."

I stood up and swung my sword at her, but she soared higher, my sword only managing to slice air. She cackled at my attempts to fight her, taunting me.

"Enough is enough, Fidelis. Give this up now!" I screamed. "Your game is over! We have the souls, and Zakar is back where he belongs. There's nothing you can do."

"Zakar, pfft," she said. "I don't care for him. If not him, then some other demon. There's no dearth of demons with a grudge against you gods that I can use."

"What makes you think you are getting out of here alive?"

"What are you going to do, Huntress? You cannot even catch poor old me," she mocked.

I ducked for cover and chanted, calling for my bow and arrow, but the dark energy emanating from Fidelis interrupted my spells. I took a deep breath. With a silent prayer to Hekate, I spoke the words again, this time successfully materializing my bow and arrow. Fidelis may be a powerful witch, but her four thousand years of power wasn't enough to defeat the name of Hekate, the Queen of Witches.

Sitting down on one knee, I took a bolt out of the quiver and aimed at her. "Wanna say that again, Fidelis?"

Fidelis wiped the grin off her face the moment my trusted bow and arrow appeared in my hands. Yet, she didn't give up.

"Surrender now, and I will let you live!"

"Live? Where? In the dungeons of Tartarus? I'd rather die," she screamed, sending streaks of poisoned shafts my way. They hit me on my ribs and legs, weakening my body. I held my bow steady in my left hand despite the onslaught and pulled the string back. Keeping my elbow parallel to the ground, my back straight, I drew the line a notch further before releasing the arrow. It whizzed by, slicing the air, and slammed into her neck. She collapsed immediately, unable to utter her spells as dark blood pooled around her.

I walked to her, pulling out my silver blade from the horizontal scabbard tied to my torso. Uttering a prayer to Lord Hades to collect her soul in Tartarus, I plunged the knife deep between her ribs and into her heart.

"Forgive me for killing you, my old friend," I whispered. "But this was the only way to release you from your agony. May your soul find purpose again," I said as the light went out of her tiny eyes. Her mortal remains dissipated into a thick black cloud, disappearing into the Underworld.

As the sun rose over the cliff, I teleported out of the cave back to my temple. Thanatos had returned after delivering Zakar into the dungeons and the souls back to their mortal hosts or to the River Styx. My injuries were beginning to heal, but were still visible. The nymphs rushed to me when they saw me stumble into the temple, wounded and bleeding.

"Artemis, what happened?" Orion asked. "I couldn't open the portal again."

"Long story! I will tell you some other time. For now, just know that the sorceress is no longer an issue. She paid her dues with her soul," I said, walking towards Thanatos, who was still working over Kara. I wanted to know if she was back to her usual chirpy self. Thanatos mumbled something and pulled off the vines that restrained her. Jamie stepped back, unsure of her reaction, but her eyes remained closed.

I kept a hand on Thanatos's shoulder, hoping we were not too late. He patted my back. "She'll be fine. Don't worry."

A tiny glint of light flashed through Kara, and she slowly opened her eyes. She looked at her surroundings, and a smile crept onto her lips. "Ma'am!" Kara cried. Getting off the altar, she ran into my arms. I stroked her back as she hugged me. "You came for me, and you brought me back. Thank you!"

"Kara, I am sworn to protect every woman and child of the mortal realm. That's why I am here. And for you, I'd go to the end of this world. Besides, I had help from the best," I said, mouthing a *thank you* to Orion and Thanatos.

MERMAID'S TALE

BY

NIKKI CRUMP-HANSTED

NIKE, GODDESS OF VICTORY

I FOLLOWED MY UNCLE OUT OF THE BAR. "Thank you, Victory. I can't tell you how much I appreciate that you'll watch over things here for me."

"Sure thing, Uncle," I said as we arrived at his car.

"I've left you a note on my desk with instructions for the bar. Most of the renovations are handled, and supplies are ordered for the grand reopening. There really isn't much left to do. It should go off without a hitch."

"How long will you be away?"

"I hope to be back in time for the opening, but can't be certain."

"Do you really think you can find her?"

"I have a new lead. It is the first true clue I have had in centuries in the search for my consort. I know the timing is bad, but I have to follow this thread and see where it leads."

Pulling a long golden feather from my pocket, I handed it to him. "Here, Uncle, I know you would never ask me for this, so I give it to you freely. I wish for you to have the victory you seek. The power it holds will release at the very moment it is needed."

He pulled me into a great hug and whispered against my hair, "Thank you, little one. Two last things. Remember what I told you about sea-witches and don't let Brian get under your skin. He's rough, but his food is better than that of the gods."

I pulled away and nodded, counting off each item on my fingers. "One. There's a note on your desk. Two. It should go without a hitch. Three. No sea-witches in the bar. And four, don't let Brian bug me. Got it."

I stood on the pier, waving and putting on a brave smile as I watched Poseidon drive away.

Why did I say yes to doing this?

I walked back into the Mermaid's Tale. Waiting there was the chef, Brian, the two bartenders, Martina and Deja, and four of the wait staff.

Well, now, this is going to be fun.

"Hi, everyone. As my uncle pointed out, I'm just here to oversee things while he...while he's away," I said as I looked at each person.

"How long will that son of a bitch be gone?" Brian, the chef, demanded.

My eyebrows rose in surprise, hearing him speak of Poseidon in such a way. "He didn't say. So you're stuck with me until his return."

"Fucking, sea dog! That's fine by me. Are you even old enough to be here, much less run the place? Just stay the fuck out of my kitchen, fucking newbie!" Brian shouted as he stormed off to the kitchen.

"Don't mind him, Nike, he's always like that," Martina said.

"My uncle warned me about him," I said with a small smile. "So, what happens around here? I know what Poseidon told me, but I want to know what exactly you all do here."

We gathered around a table, and they filled me in, each one giving me their perspective on how things worked here at the Mermaid's Tale. Poseidon was a bit of a hard ass about certain things. He insisted that the booze always be stocked and was very strict on who was not allowed in his establishment—namely, witches.

The mortal staff was nervous and on edge after the new upgrades and the swim-thru window bar that brought in various residents of the deep. Their feelings of stress were increased by this being the week of their grand reopening. They knew how meticulous Poseidon was and wanted everything to go smoothly. No one wanted to face his wrath. The staff headed back to work, and I went to the office.

Fall in Olympus had a way of becoming unpredictable. We were days from Samhain, when the veils were at their thinnest. In all of his wisdom, Uncle Poseidon decided that this was the perfect time to reopen his bar. At this time of year, anything can happen, and most times, it's not for good. It was when mortals could see magic at its strongest, and with the gods having returned to the world in the last months, the realm was already in turmoil. Who knew what chaos could be unleashed?

What have I gotten myself into?

I read over Poseidon's instructions, making a few notes and then picked up my phone. I needed to call in some favors. My sister, Athena, was first on my list. I asked her if she would make me a black sheer curtain woven from strands of Lady Nyx's stardust. With the right enchantments, stardust threads protect the wearer, or in this case, the space, from harmful intent. I wanted to drape the cloth throughout the restaurant. It would create the illusion of a night sky and give us a little added security.

I figured if I were going to be *in charge,* I would go all out. I didn't want to put up the usual decor that mortals tend towards, like fake witches and ghost cutouts. Instead, I ordered pumpkins in varying sizes, candles to decorate each table, and creepy old sea artifacts. I put a rush on the orders, and things began arriving later that day. The staff loved it, and I could feel some of the tension in the bar ease.

Over the next few days, I added some fall foods and drinks to the menu. Chef Brian wasn't keen on me making changes, but they don't call me Victory for nothing. I soon had him believing that it was all his idea, and the bad-tempered mortal might have actually smiled, or was it a smirk? Either way, I called it a win.

Finally, I called in a favor from an old friend who offered his expertise in interior design. With his tips and tricks, my uncle's dive bar was brought up to the level of a fancy bar and grill on the wharf. I hoped that Uncle liked the changes I had made. I know that I was pleased.

Everything looked grand, and it had only taken me three days to pull it all together. It was the afternoon of our big reopening, and excitement filled the bar. I had called my sister, Bia, and my brothers in to help with greeting and security. They each chose an area to cover. Bia decided to be on the door. Through telepathy, she could read minds and would hopefully stop trouble before it started. Zelus would be with the wait staff, although he refused to wear the uniform. I thought they looked great in their white button-down shirts, mermaid print bowtie, black pants, and long black aprons. Kratos looked like he owned the place, and that suited me just fine.

I stopped at the bottom of the stairs and looked around the restaurant. Candlelight bathed the rustic space, forming shadows in the corners. The mermaid figurehead resembled Amphitrite in her youth, and the trunks in the corner overflowed with treasures from the deep. We draped some of the fabric that Athena wove through the beams overhead, and it mimicked the clear night sky. My mouth watered at the scents wafting from the kitchen. The cheerful sound of ice hitting glass drew my gaze. The bar was stocked with everything from the expensive top-shelf liquor, like Japanese whiskey that cost $100 a glass, to plenty of inexpensive alcohol for well drinks. I had added a pumpkin spice slider and a pumpkin martini for the season.

The new Mermaid's Tale was now officially open. There was a line outside for the restaurant, and the bar was filling up. We had valet parking, an outside patio, and dancing. My favorite was the sea-level dining. You felt like you were sitting inside an aquarium, able to watch the sea life, and interact with the merfolk when they approached the swim-thru window.

A couple of hours in and the staff and my family were working like a team that had been together for years. All areas were moving like clockwork. I looked around at the crowded bar and the flurry of organized chaos. I could hear Chef Brian in the kitchen. He was his usual *jovial* self, shouting at the cooks and using every profane word in three languages.

Hmm, this is easier than I thought.

I knew better than even to think that. It just kind of slipped out. Deja tapped me on the shoulder. "Nike, I need your help."

"Yes, what's up?" I asked.

"We have a problem with a guy at the bar. He won't pay for his drinks."

"Oh, can you ask my brother to help you?"

"He's busy at the door. Something's happening out there."

"Okay," I said with a sigh and headed to the bar. "Where is this customer?"

I really shouldn't jinx myself by thinking this would be easy.

I followed Deja back to the bar. As I got closer, I heard people ordering different types of drinks: tequilas and margaritas, bourbon neat, black opals. A man leaned over the bar and yelled at Martina, and I turned to look at him.

"I am not going to pay for drinks that have been watered down!" he shouted.

"What seems to be the problem here?" I said as I stepped up next to Martina.

"Nike, he is refusing to pay for the three glasses of the Hibiki Harmony he and his friends ordered," Martina said calmly.

"And why won't you pay for what you ordered?" I asked, meeting his gaze.

"Because your girl here watered down the drinks."

I looked over at Deja. "How much is this...?"

"Hibiki. And it cost $100 a glass, and he ordered it neat, so there is chilled spring *water* and no *ice*."

"Did he order this?"

"Yes, he did."

"And was he made aware of the cost of the drink he ordered?"

"Yes, Nike, he knew," Martina said sarcastically, directing her words and their tone to the man.

"Very well. Sir, you will pay what you owe."

"I will not! Do you know who I am?"

"No, do you know who *I* am?" I felt my wings ache, wanting to burst free, my deity form pushing against my skin at the challenge.

"Nike!" Zelus's voice whispered across the room. Pulling me back from the edge of going full goddess. My eyes snapped in his direction, and he pointed to the ceiling.

The woven stardust drape shimmered and waved in the still air. They were signaling that supernatural beings with ill intent were approaching or in the bar.

"Nike, come to the door, we need your help," I heard my sister's voice say in my head.

"Alright, I'll be right there." Turning back to the belligerent customer, I caught his gaze. I felt my eyes change to a fiery blaze, and said, "You will pay what you owe, and you will leave this bar right *after!*"

The man's eyes shone with fear, and he pulled out his wallet. I turned and headed to the door.

"What else can go wrong?" I whispered to myself. I was about to find out.

I heard Bia in my mind, *"Nike, it's witches."*

"Oh no, why witches?" I said with a sigh, rolling my eyes.

"You can't deny us entry. It is against the law," a cold, arrogant female voice said.

"Ladies, there are plenty of other establishments," my brother said soothingly.

"We will put a curse on you," another of the three exclaimed, her body taut with outrage.

"Whoa there, ladies, it's fine," I said as I walked outside. I recalled what my uncle had said about the types of people he allowed in his bar.

"Nike, no matter what, don't let a sea witch in here."

"But, Uncle, surely you can't..."

He didn't say another word. It was the look of an ice-cold chill, a frosted stare that any child who has ever angered their parents knew. I took a step back, lowering my head. He grabbed my hand and lifted my chin with his other. "Little one, you can do this. Please. This is my only rule."

I raised my head to meet his eyes. I knew my uncle's pain, and I knew that while this might seem unfair, he had his reasons. I nodded, and he wrapped me up in a big hug. "Thank you, little Nike."

"As you wish, Uncle."

"Ladies, please..." Thinking quickly, I asked, "Are you here to eat, or did you want to go to the bar?"

"We have the right to be here!" the first witch said again, her eyes flashing with anger.

Whispering to the three, I said, "Look, my uncle, he has been burned by witches."

"How do you know we are witches?"

"Let's just say I know," I said, my voice soft and calm.

"Fine, and?" the witch said, crossing her arms over her chest.

"If you promise not to cause any trouble or curse my uncle's bar, I'll let you in."

"We only wanted to eat here. We wanted to try the Tuxedo Sam Pasta we heard about," the third witch said, speaking up for the first time.

"Alright," I said with a nod and a smile, my instincts telling me that this was the path to victory for tonight.

"Nike, you can't. What will Poseidon say?" Bia sent the thought to me.

"I know, Bia, I know. Search their minds. Do they mean us any harm?"

Bia took a moment to scan their minds. She glanced at me, and her voice filled my head, *"They mean us no harm, Nike. They are just mortals with skills in witchcraft. They have some power, and that is probably why the stardust strands reacted."*

I looked up and spotted Zelus, motioning him over. "Very good. Zelus, will you take care of our guests?" I breathed a sigh of relief that they accepted my apologies. Zelus escorted the ladies to their table and waited on them personally. He gave them his most charming smile and brought them a bottle of Dionysos's wine. My tensions eased, seeing that they were happy and in good hands.

I decided to take a few minutes for myself and went to my Uncle's office to kick back behind his desk and enjoy the victory of the grand reopening.

"*Not bad*," I thought, "*Two minor crises averted. All in all, it is going off without a hitch.*"

Once again, I spoke, or thought, too soon.

Ear-piercing screams echoed through the walls, and I immediately dashed the door. Pushing through the fleeing crowd and into the dining room, I stopped in stunned disbelief at the chaos. The tables were being tossed about, glasses and dishes crashing to the floor, and the stardust cloth was flapping wildly in alert.

Bia ran up to me. *"Where have you been?"*

"What happened?" I cried, taking in the destruction.

"Look." She pointed to the ceiling.

I looked above the bar and saw them. Nightgoyles, vicious, and destructive human killers. "What the Hades are they doing here?!" I only saw one, but they traveled in packs. "*Samhain. They must have slipped through the veil.*"

Bia handed me my sword.

"Where is Zelus?" I said over the screams.

"I am here," Zelus said, running up to us.

"Get them out! Get all the mortals out of here," I ordered.

"I'm on it," Zelus said as he released his wings and rose, helping to shepherd the mortals out. Bia went airborne with a little hop, rising to meet a nightgoyle in combat. I could see Martina and Deja hiding behind the bar and screamed for them to get out of there. They moved to obey, and my breath caught in horror when a nightgoyle landed before them, blocking their way. Before I could intervene, Bia threw her sword, pinning the creature to the wall.

Martina and Deja slipped out the door just as the kitchen erupted. Pots and pans hit the wall, followed by Chef Brian screaming the most profane words. They were so bad I can't even write them down, but it might have had something to do with donkeys. With a somewhat impressed look on his face and the chef's creativity, Kratos went to check on those in the kitchen.

"Hetty the first, Hetty the first, you bring the blessing and not a curse.
Hetty the first, Hetty the first, we summon you to help us.
Hetty the first, Hetty the first, bind these shadows for us.
Hetty the first, Hetty the first, you bring the blessing and not a curse."

I heard the chant above the noise in the bar, my head spinning in that direction. The three mortal witches were holding hands, their eyes glowing.

With a snap, the curtains released from the hooks and whipped around the restaurant. It grabbed up the four nightgoyles and wrapped them tightly. I could see the stardust strands constrict, the creatures screaming as the fabric pulled tighter and tighter. With a loud *pop*, there was silence, and the beasts were gone. My siblings and I stood in stunned surprise, watching the fabric float back into place. The three witches looked at us, smiled, and vanished.

"Nike, what the...?"

"Where'd they go?"

I had no answers, and we all just looked at each other and then at the mess. I opened my mouth to say something, but stopped when I heard in my head, *"Thank you for your kindness, goddess. You tell Poseidon his bar will not be cursed by any of our covens. You have proven yourself worthy. You are pure of heart."*

Bia looked over at me, her eyes wide. *"Did you hear that?"*

324

I nodded.

"Well, this was one hell of an opening!" Lucas, one of the wait staff, yelled. "Man, I knew it! What do you all have planned for tomorrow?"

We all burst into laughter, the sound ringing through the restaurant and easing the lingering fear and tension.

The next day the paper gave us a review, and the highlight read: **The new Mermaid's Tale Bar and Grill offered the best Halloween show I've ever seen. With realistic Greek mythology showmanship. I wonder how they will top themselves for Christmas.**

HAIR TODAY, GONE

TOMORROW

BY

MELISSA STODDART

EREBUS,

PRIMORDIAL OF

DARKNESS

Cabbage Night, Moving Night, Mischief Night, or Devil's Night, even Goosey Night, but where my mortal scribe comes from, they refer to it as Gate Night. The night when young mortals engage and play pranks, creating all sorts of general mayhem. As you can imagine, this sparked my interest. Who doesn't love a good prank? I've sometimes been told these evenings can get out of hand, but I, Erebus, God of Darkness, have no intention of getting out of hand. Insert evil gif picture here, if you will.

After being trapped in Melinoë's nightmare realm, my reality has been but a nightmare. Even if it wasn't that bad of a dream and the blonde bombshell with the spiky hair still consumes my thoughts. With Nyx and I having our falling out as an indirect result of my absence and three months of no bookings for Erebus After Dark, my life is in chaos. I'm rambling. What's done is done.

Wringing my hands together, I let my thoughts carry me away. Melinoë has a thing or two coming her way, even though my imprisonment wasn't entirely her doing. I found it too easy for Melinoë to pass the buck onto Atë, a goddess who conveniently disappeared from Olympus. It was Melinoë's facilities that kept me locked away. Therefore, I feel that a little retribution should come her way. I mean, I can't have other gods or goddesses thinking they can just lock up the mighty Erebus. I'm the freaking God of Darkness and Shadows. They're supposed to fear me. At least the mortals are.

I decide it is an excellent time to drop in and see my good friend Eros. If anyone knows a thing or two about mischief and causing chaos, it is him. Eros's flat is one floor above Erebus After Dark Bookings. I walk in, just dodging an arrow to the head.

"Yow! Watch it!" I jump to the side.

"Oh, hey, E!" Eros jumps off his perch from the arm of the chair. "What brings you here? Have you finally given up on Tinder? Come to get struck by one of my lovely arrows?" Eros holds an arrow up to his mouth and kisses it. "I've got this one here, just waiting for you."

I snort at Eros. Ever since my separation, he's been itching to hit me with one of his love darts. That is the last thing I want right now.

"Not exactly." I push the arrow aside. As I do so, I notice my name written on the shaft. He isn't kidding.

Eros slaps an arm around my shoulders and leads me further into his domain.

"Are you familiar with Gate Night?" I ask.

"Come again, what's that now?"

"Gate Night? Mischief Night?" I raise a brow at him.

"Fuck yeah! Atë may have founded Mischief Night, but I've made it a legend in some parts of the world."

"What are your plans for this upcoming Mischief Night? Care to join me in a harmless prank?"

Eros rubs his hands together, a devilish smile spreading across his face. "Whatdja have in mind? Ohhh, did you want to steal all the peacocks?"

"Peacocks?" I say, confused.

"Hera's peacocks."

I give him a funny look. "Err no, something a little more badass than that, my friend."

Eros and I arrive at Hekate's apartment. It is a little underwhelming, to say the least. Vials and jars cover every countertop. Hekate looks as though she is in the middle of an incantation when we casually waltz in. She looks over at us, seemingly annoyed.

"The God of Darkness is hanging around with Eros. Well, this is a sight I'd never thought I'd see. What are you two up to?"

"We need your help," Eros smiles.

I can feel my dark shadows slowly creeping around from corner to corner of the small apartment, investigating. My eyes close in on her, and the room feels heavy. "Someone has wronged me."

"Inadvertently," Eros says.

I shoot him a quick look. Like it matters, Hekate doesn't need to know the details of why we are here. All I want from her is a potion or a spell, something to torture Melinoë for her involvement in my temporary capture.

"Is this about Nyxie? Because I am not about to help—"

"No. I'm over that," I say harshly.

Hekate gives me a cockeyed look from over her spell, and I can feel Eros' eyes burning a hole in the back of my head.

"Just a little something to pay back someone for—"

"He wants revenge on Melinoë for putting him in the nightmare realm for three months."

I turn on my heel and tightly wrap my shadows around Eros. Squeezing him gently, not enough to hurt him, but enough that he can barely shrug sorry. I've forgotten how much energy and impatience the young god has.

"Just something to scare her, I don't want to hurt her."

Hekate grabs a leafy green plant and some clear liquid. She mashes them together, all the while mumbling to herself. Eros and I sit back and watch, unsure if we should speak. When she is finished, she hands me a small vial.

"What is it?" I ask, looking at it. Unsure if this tiny little vial will do the trick.

"Atropa belladonna, with a little extra something I made up myself. Just put a little into whatever it is Melinoë is drinking and voila! Let the fun begin."

I look at Hekate doubtfully. "Not meaning to judge you, but do you think this will get by her? She does know a thing or two about spells."

"Trust me, you're good. You just have to get close enough to put it in her drink."

Releasing my shadows from Eros and grabbing him by the shoulders, I say, "Why do you think I brought him along?"

I had received word that Melinoë had picked up a job working for Nyx at Whole Latte Love since the last time I'd seen her. Go figure, the little goddess ran to safety. While it might not be the best place for her to take the potion, it was our only option.

I send Eros ahead to make sure Nyx isn't in. I don't want a war to break out. This is just a harmless prank. No need to involve Ares.

When I get the all-clear from Eros, I saunter in slowly. The plan is for me to distract Melinoë long enough for Eros to slip the potion into her water. It won't suffice for me to just watch from the sidelines. No, I desire to witness Hekate's handy work in action. Otherwise, what is the point?

Melinoë is sitting at a small table at the back of the room, away from the little mortal critters.

Perfect.

As I walk closer to her, I see her eyes dilate. Immediately, she throws up a wall of defense. Smart goddess, but it will be of no use. Not against Hekate's concoction, which Eros has safely tucked in the palm of his hand.

"What can I help you with, Erebus?" Her voice, soft and cautious, holds a distinct darkness.

"Well, I think we got off on the wrong foot. I've had some time to mull things over, and I'm willing to forgive and forget." I flash her a quick smile, hoping she is buying what I am selling.

"I may have been south for the last few decades or maybe a hundred, but I'm not stupid." Melinoë side glances at Eros. "If you're traveling with him these days, Hades help us all."

I look at Eros, who is spinning an arrow between his fingers like a drumstick. "I don't know...he's kind of rubbing off on me. Who doesn't like a little fun and chaos every now and again? I don't always have to be doom and gloom."

Eros *accidentally* lets the arrow slip from his grasp, and it ricochets across the room, buzzing a little too close to a germ-bag's head.

"Oh, shit!" he exclaims. "Melinoë, I'm so sorry."

Melinoë jumps up from the table and runs over to the child to make sure he isn't hurt.

I lean against the table, blocking her view of Eros while he casually pours the potion into her water.

"Just great, Eros! Nyx will have my head if any of these children are hurt. Are you two trying to get me fired?" Melinoë fusses over the little human and makes sure he is okay before returning her focus to us.

"On the contrary, I am here to offer you a job." Eros pulls out another arrow and begins twirling it around.

She pauses, squinting at him for so long of a moment that I think she might actually be interested. With a swift and subtle shake of her head, though, the expression vanishes. "If you haven't noticed, I already have one."

"A better one," he adds, stroking the fletching.

Melinoë stands up and crosses the room to us. "Will you put that away?" she growls, grabs the arrow from Eros' hand, and snaps it in two.

Eros is the best god to involve in this form of trickery. He knows just how to push everyone's buttons.

Pushing myself off the table, I nonchalantly nudge her glass of water towards her. She absentmindedly picks it up and chugs it back. A devious smile spreads across my face. I count in my head as each second passes, waiting for the potion to kick in.

"Come on, Melinoë. Don't you want to be on the hottest reality dating show? It will be even better than The *Bachelor.* I'll let you have first crack at the dating pool. I mean, of course, you would have to interview beforehand, and get a background check. The network insists." Eros rolls his eyes dramatically.

Melinoë looks at the two of us like we are crazy. I can't help but smile. Oh, sister, you have no idea the amount of crazy that's about to start.

"No, I think I'll pass. When I'm ready for grotesque things like love, I'll ask Aphrodite." Melinoë sits back down and resumes mindlessly making shadow puppets again. "Is that all?"

I take a step back, all the while whistling. My patience is growing thin. When would this blasted potion kick in? We are running out of time. Eros looks to me. It is up to me to stall. I have nothing, and my mind draws a blank. I have been so wrapped up in this revenge scheme I can't see straight. I need to come up with something...anything.

"Err...How about you and I go out? For coffee...or something?" Oh, that was awkward.

"You two?" Eros can't hold back his laughter. "Actually, I can ship that," he says, pulling out yet another arrow.

Melinoë waves her hands in protest. "Stop. Get out!"

I look to Eros and shrug. Now what?

Just then, a chunk of black hair falls from Melinoë's head and settles across the table in front of her. All eyes go to her missing hair. Her hands fly to her head.

"What—"

Like ghosts, her fingers float to her scalp. They tap hesitantly, searching for a bald spot. When she runs them through her hair and pulls them in front of her face, she is staring back at entire chunks of hair, black in one hand and white in the other.

Without her help, it continues falling out in chunks. Eros and I back up, inching our way towards the exit. Melinoë stands from the table again, frantically calling for the other childcare provider to come over. When her coworker arrives, she looks just as perplexed as she does.

I stifle a laugh.

The noise catches Melinoë's attention. She glares and points a finger in my direction. "You did this!"

"Me? I don't know what you're referring to. I can't make your hair disappear. Perhaps it was something you drank?" I say with a chuckle.

She snaps her attention to the glass of water, her cheeks flushing red. She roars, clutching her head as if it would protect what little hair she has left. "How could you do this?"

"How? No, why would I do such a thing? I couldn't possibly harm a single hair on your head." Eros and I burst into laughter. Revenge is sweet.

Despite her best efforts, her long, luxurious hair continues drifting to the ground. "It—it keeps falling out," she utters, her eyes wide with terror. Her legs crumble beneath her as she begins rocking.

For a split second, I feel something deep within my gut...Regret? Nah...

With every groan and whimper, Melinoë becomes louder. The children in the room take notice of the commotion and come to see what is wrong. I expect them to run away in fear, but to my surprise, they sit down beside her. One of the little rugrats takes Melinoë's hand in hers and holds it gently. They are looking up to her with admiration and concern.

"What's wrong, Miss Mellie?"

Melinoë looks up to the small thing, pulling at her remaining hair. "I...my hair...it won't stop falling. I'm going to be bald."

The spawnlings look up at her head, confusion plain in all of their expressions. What appears to be the youngest of the group reaches up and gently runs its hands around Melinoë's head, as if its

333

fingers are running through hair. "You have beeaaauuteefwal hair, Miss Melwie."

Eros and I look at one another, puzzled. Could they not see that her hair has fallen out? What exactly did Hekate's potion do?

"I wish I had hair like you, Miss Mellie," says the first one.

The remaining hell-spawns circle her, giving her a group hug. Life returns to Melinoë's eyes as she smiles at the children surrounding her.

As the room quiets, Eros and I duck out into the street, puzzled by what happened.

"Well, that was weird." Eros scratches his head with an arrow.

I spin to face him. "You saw her hair come out, right?"

"Totally. She looked like an old crone." Eros laughs at the visualization.

I look back inside through the windows, but Melinoë has disappeared. Probably to the washroom to collect herself and what was left of her hair. I am still smiling at the memory of Melinoë's face when she realized her hair was falling out. I wonder why the little gremlins weren't afraid of her? Maybe they are protected somehow? Nyx would have thought of everything to make sure her little humans wouldn't get hurt while in her care. Either way, I would say it was a successful Mischief Night.

Turning away from Whole Latte Love, Eros and I walk down the street. I can tell Eros is itching to pull another prank. My phone vibrates, alerting me to a text message. I stop to pull the mobile from my pants pocket. Eros is ahead of me, scoping a couple outside of a bar. Surely his trigger finger is itching. I look at the message from Hekate.

Hope you enjoyed the show. The illusion should wear off soon enough. Of course, I couldn't really make her hair fall out. Hope you understand. Xoxo.

SACRIFICE TO THE DARK ELVES

BY

JEANETTE ROSE

EROS,
GOD OF LOVE & SEX

BANG! BANG!

I groan, reaching blindly for the alarm clock I assume to be going off, hoping to stop the obnoxious sounds disturbing me. Slitting my eyes open when my hand slams down on my empty bedside table, I belatedly remember I have never owned an alarm clock in my entire immortal life. *I must be dreaming.*

I shift in the Cal King sized bed I had delivered a week ago. All my other possessions from Los Angeles are slowly making their way to Olympus. The black silk sheets slide across my skin, allowing me to settle back into my feather pillow. After a two-thousand-year absence, I've been back home with my family for less than a month, and am already regretting the decision. Within a couple seconds of blissful silence, I start drifting off to sleep.

Bang! Bang! Bang!

This time I groan out loud. Propping myself up on my elbows, I glare at the door that leads to the rest of my floor in the God Complex, the monstrosity my grandfather, Zeus—yes, *that* Zeus—created to house everyone when he summoned us back to Greece.

I pray that whoever has decided to bang on my door at this gods-forsaken-hour will give up and allow me to go back to sleep. It's probably Hermes, trying to get in for some ridiculously formal message, or my brother, Dinlas, God of Hate and Jealousy, realizing I stole all the soles out of his left shoes. Both of them could fuck off at the moment and allow me to go back to sleep.

Bang! Bang! Bang! Bang!

They were clearly getting more annoyed that I still have not answered the door. The sound awakens my two white tigers, who were passed out on the floor next to my bed. They were gifted to me by the Goddess of Mischief, Atë, over two thousand years ago. I named them Din and Las as a joke to irk my brother. I mean, can you imagine Dinlas's face when he realized I'd named two pussy cats after him? To say I wish the camera existed when he found out is an understatement.

Din stretches his massive body on the floor, his claws making marks, before resting his large head on his paws, eyeing the door passively.

Neither tiger bothers to get up to investigate the disturbance. Hate and Jealousy would be pawing at the door, prowling in front of it if someone were to interrupt my brother's sleep like this. Din and Las are the opposite of my brother's wolves. More lackadaisical, only leaping to my side if they think I am in immediate danger. *Very immediate danger.* Otherwise, they barely acknowledge me.

They say that pets take on the personalities of their owners. Maybe I should be *less* surprised at their attitude.

Climbing out of bed when the pounding begins again, I dance around Din and Las. Snatching the red silk robe from a nearby chair, I pull it over my naked form, and tie it loosely at my waist. Whoever is pounding on my door is just going to have to endure my barely dressed state. It's their fault for waking me up in the first place.

When the banging starts again, I reach for the door and throw it open. Preparing to throat punch whoever is on the other side, just like my grandmother taught me.

I don't get the chance.

"Coooooopppppppp!" my visitor bellows.

A smile stretches across my face at the sight of my uncle, Dionysus. My irritation at the interruption of my sleep immediately dissipates. He's probably the only person I would allow to pull me out of bed in such a manner. Mostly because I have done the same to him numerous times in the past. I keep telling people, mischief is a full-time gig, and you have to be awake to every opportunity. Being close with the God of Wine and Ritual Madness is a trickster rite of passage.

He pulls me into a boisterous hug, the smile lighting my face growing even wider at my uncle's exuberance. There's something about him that always cheers me up. Still grinning like a fool, I slap him hard on the back, before pulling away to fully take him in.

"Dion! Finally finished your tour of all the bars in the Middle East?"

Without waiting for permission, my uncle swans past me into my residence. Dion isn't what most people expect of the God of Wine. He's not the short, portly man of some myth depictions. He is a *god*, after all. Have you ever seen a *fat* god? Except for Silenus, which is who mortals picture when they think of Dion now.

Assessing him objectively, I snicker at his attire. It is just so *Dion*. He always dresses like a cross between *you have to be rich to look this poor,* and *I'm missing from a psychiatric ward somewhere.* He's currently wearing a white tuxedo jacket with a white bow tie hanging askew around his neck, and no sign of a shirt. His white pants are covered in sand from mid-thigh down. He is barefoot, though he doesn't seem to notice, and there appears to be half of a pair of handcuffs dangling around one of his ankles.

"I missed you, Coop," Dion remarks, his nickname for me, short for Cupid. The only person ever allowed to call me that.

He dances nimbly around me, pouring himself a drink from my sidebar. He shoots back the first before filling two more glasses, offering one to me.

I accept it from his hand and take a large swig, not even raising a brow that Dion has filled the glass to the rim, rather than the typical finger or two. Dion is not a god who believes in half measures. Chugging the rest with a gulp, I idly smirk, but then, *neither am I.*

Dion assesses me from head to toe as I finish my drink, placing the empty glass back on the bar. With slightly narrowed eyes, he asks skeptically, "Is that what you're wearing?"

"Currently? Yes," I quip easily, bringing a smile to his jovial face.

"Coop, always such an asshole, no wonder you're my favorite nephew. I *meant*, is that what you're going to wear for SDE?"

My eyebrows come down in confusion. "SDE?"

Dion moves to flop down on an armchair I had flown in from my house in Malibu, resting his shoeless feet on the sleeping Las's back. The tiger doesn't even bat an eye.

"S.D.E., or Sacrifice to the Dark Elves, is the rave we are having on Halloween," Dion announces, using his sand-covered toe to scratch Las' side, the tiger's chuff echoing loudly throughout the room. I should probably care that Dion has dragged sand of unknown origin across my floor, but I'm so happy to see him, I ignore it.

I stroll towards the massive walk-in closet I've erected in my new residence, filled with all the latest styles. Unlike the rest of my family, I've spent the last two thousand years among mortals, and I've kept up to date on the current fashion.

Do you know how boring always wearing a tailored black suit is? Yes, that is directed at you, Brother.

For years, I've had a staff of mortals taking care of me, from a chef to a driver. I strong-armed them into relocating here, and they've been arriving sporadically for the last couple weeks. My personal shopper was initially reluctant to relocate from Los Angeles to Greece, but tripling her salary finally convinced her. If I have to move to rejoin my family, I will take the comfort I'm used to with me.

"We're having a rave?" I call out to Dion, rifling through my clothes. The last time I saw my uncle was a little more than a decade ago in Los Angeles.

Dion is the exception to the rest of my family. He's the only person who knew where I was for the last two thousand years, because I knew Dion would never ask. He would never ask where

339

my wings were, why I was alone. All the questions I dodge from my family now.

Because he is running, too.

"Of course we're having a rave! I've just returned, it's almost Halloween, and you've finally come home. We absolutely require a rave under the circumstances."

"Required now, is it?"

I pull on a pair of sweatpants and a T-shirt. I've long grown out of my *cherubic* appearance, towering over most mortals at a couple inches over six feet. I spent hours every week in the gym to rid myself of the baby fat that once made me famous. Heading back out, I see Dion filling his glass again. Dion could drink enough to take down three gods with minimal effect.

"Required. It is our obligation as gods to have SDE. I mean, can you even call yourself a mischief-maker if we don't?"

Ruffling my hands through my hair, I dispel the lingering signs of my interrupted sleep. I smile at the sight of Dion trying to antagonize Din. The tiger still refused to rise to the bait.

"You're right, like always. So, where are we holding this rave?" I ask, already imagining the kind of trouble I could cause with Dion home.

"The forest, of course," Dion answers, wiggling his eyebrows at me. "The more places to sneak off for *illicit* activities."

"I'm in." My smile stretches wickedly across my face, anticipating the event.

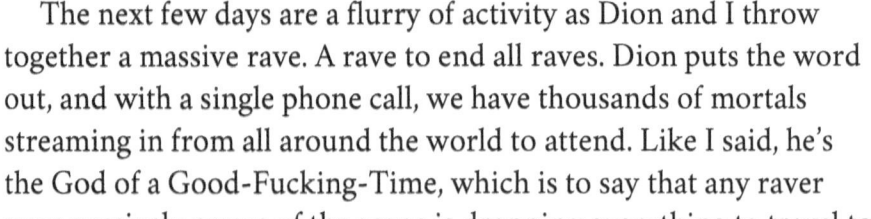

The next few days are a flurry of activity as Dion and I throw together a massive rave. A rave to end all raves. Dion puts the word out, and with a single phone call, we have thousands of mortals streaming in from all around the world to attend. Like I said, he's the God of a Good-Fucking-Time, which is to say that any raver even passively aware of the scene is dropping everything to travel to

Greece. The fear of missing out is a strong motivator for most mortals, and people will talk about this rave for years to come. I only contributed the funds for the event. Well, rather, Dinlas did, via the credit card I stole from him the night before.

What's Halloween without a little mischief?

With Dion's touch and my desire for a distraction from my own thoughts, we completely transform the clearing in Olympus National Park into a massive rave. The trees surrounding the open meadow allow for mortals to sneak off and hook up. *God of Love and Sex, remember?* It's kind of my job to make sure people are getting it on.

Standing in the DJ booth, I glance at Erebus who woke from a long nap just to spin for the occasion. Surveying the mass of mortals partying in front of me, I even spot Nemesis coming out to cause some trouble. It is a party for the record books. Mortals will talk about it for years to come. It will be the standard by which they will measure all parties. I should feel some satisfaction at the event coming together so flawlessly.

So why do I feel ambivalent?

Where is the usual feeling of gratification I get from causing mischief on such a massive scale? Maybe it would be better if I could get rid of these nightmares that keep plaguing me. Inwardly, I scoff at my own thoughts.

You've had the same nightmare every time you sleep for the last two thousand years. Do you really expect them to suddenly just disappear?

Dion comes to my side, slapping me hard on the back and shouting over the noise, "You don't look like you're enjoying yourself, Coop."

My lips twitch into a small smile, despite my mood. "Nonsense. Of course, I am!"

Dion raises a skeptical dark brow, holding an offended hand to his chest. "You forget who I am, I'm the God of *Merriment.*"

341

So he knows I'm only going through the motions, one of his many powers. With a huff, I confess to him, "I don't know. Something is different. Maybe I should never have come back."

Slinging his arm around my shoulders, he pulls me into his side affectionately. "I didn't ask for your fucking life story. You need something to make you not be such a baby."

A chuckle actually breaks from my throat. This is why Dion will always be my favorite uncle. "And you have the means for such a change?"

I recognize the wicked smile that spreads across Dion's face, and I know no good will come from it. Dion reaches into his pants pocket, pulling out a bag with *Mr. T's Sweets* labeled on the side.

Okay, was definitely not expecting that.

"Candy? Your solution to my mood is candy?"

"You know, I've really missed your snark. Open your mouth, Coop."

I do, about to make some crude comment about the last time someone said such a thing to me, but Dion takes his chance and shoves four of the candies into my mouth. I swallow reflexively, and they slowly slide down my throat.

"What the fuck was that, Dion?" I snap, coughing slightly.

My uncle smirks, popping several of the candies into his own mouth. "It's called knowing you well, Coop. Would you have taken them if I told you they were hallucinogens?"

Dion turns away, but I grab his arm to stop him, shouting over the music, "Hallucinogens?!"

His smile returns, this time glinting in the rave lights, displaying its evil upturn. "Yep. You won't be able to be such a baby when you're fighting the dragon guarding the fridge. Have funnnnnn."

Dion plops several more into his mouth, disappearing down the stairs and into the crowd, leaving me behind. He has to be at the heart of the event, so he's heading for the very center of the depravity. I'm frozen on the DJ stage, trying to figure out my next steps.

Alright, shit. Hallucinogens. Fuck, Dion level hallucinogens.

If Dion owned them, they would be powerful enough to incapacitate several mortals, and knock most gods on their ass.

And Dion shoved four in my mouth.

Fuck. Fuck. *Fuck.* Maybe I should head home to devolve in private, instead of surrounded by mortals, all of them in their own varying levels of intoxication. I'm enough to handle when I'm sober. I can't imagine what kind of problem I'm going to be drunk *and* high. Fucking Dion. Why didn't I remember *why* I don't party with him more often?

Yeah, I got to get my ass home before this hits.

I stumble down the steps from the DJ stage and pull my phone out of my pocket. My eyes nearly cross as I attempt to focus my fingers and input the right number. I am *already* pretty trashed. Dion and I have been drinking steadily since he showed up several days ago, and I'm not exactly sure when I was last sober. As I scroll, I can't even remember which contact I'm actually trying to find. I press one of the names saved, holding it up to my ear, having no idea who will answer.

I breathe a slight sigh of relief when I hear Tory, what I call Nike, the Goddess of Victory.

"Nephew?" she asks. I can barely hear her over the blaring music.

"Tory!" I shout. Fuck, why did I call her again?

"Where are you? It's so loud!"

"The woods. Come." I'm not sure if I make any sense, and I fumble my phone, accidentally hanging up on her. Shit, I have to call her back. Dropping to my hands and knees, I scramble on the forest floor for my phone. I barely grasp it before a mortal stomps on it. Clutching the device, I struggle to stand, disoriented from having lost my uncle somewhere in the crowd. I was looking for him, right? Or was I calling someone?

Like I said, I was already more than a little drunk, probably hovering more in the absolute trashed area.

Glancing up from my phone for a moment, I notice the lights seem really, *really* bright. And was the music that loud a minute ago?

Shit, are these drugs hitting *already?*

I have to get out of here. Immediately. Focusing on the outline of the God Complex headquarters in the distance, I force my feet to head in that general direction.

One foot in front of the other, Eros.

My path is blocked several times when wasted mortals fall into my path. Can't they tell I'm in a hurry? Do they have an idea what will happen if I'm here when these drugs hit?

Do I?

When the next couple blocks my path, their limbs and lips intertwined, I realize I'm too late. A shiver shoots down my spine, goosebumps form over every inch of my skin, and my hair stands on end. The music suddenly fades. I can still sense the pounding bass of the music, but I can't hear anything.

I'm going to kill Dion. In fact, I will kill him right now. I can totally kill my uncle and make it back to God Complex before these drugs hit. I mean, I am a *god* after all.

I whirl around on my heel, and the sudden movement disorients me for a moment. My vision flickers, and I wait for it to clear before taking a step in the direction I think I saw Dion head.

Another mortal bumps my shoulder hard, turning me in another direction. *Did we really need to have this many guests?* It seems excessive. In my state, I'm completely at the whims of the jostling bodies around me. Another slams into my side, spinning me. I manage to stop myself from falling, and I send an annoyed growl at the culprit.

Which is when I first see her.

At the edge of the dance area, the farthest possible location from me, the outline of a female snags my attention. Her back is facing me, and I'm not sure what it is about her that ensnares me so immediately. There are women all around me, yet I'm focused only on this one.

It's like the thread of Fate is looped from my soul to hers, linking us across the entire rave.

Sable locks cascade down her back, falling like a midnight wave. I'm a *sucker* for brunettes. My brother and father have a strange affinity for redheads, but it's dark hair that fascinates me. I love the way it wraps around my fist when I hold them, their bodies submitting to my will, like a midnight tie between us.

She's facing away from me, with no idea that she is now the sole focus of the God of Love. Like a youth in the first blush of lust, I take several stumbling steps towards the mysterious woman.

I lose sight of her temporarily when I'm hit in the side by another mortal. Rounding on the offender, a snarl of rage rips from me. I snatch him by the throat, suspending him midair. It takes a beat for me to come to my senses, allowing me to drop the terrified man. I watch as he hits the ground and scrambles away from me.

What was that?

I don't react like that. I'm not my father. I'm not my brothers. There's only one person who's ever invoked that kind of reaction in me. A single being in my entire immortal life.

Snapping my head back toward the mysterious female, I catch sight of her again. She's even farther away, lingering on the edge of the clearing. Narrowing my eyes on her, I try to figure out what it is about her that's calling to me.

Most of the mortals came in some kind of costume or other, and the strange female is dressed like a fairy, complete with a set of wings. From here, I can tell that they're not feathered like mine used to be. They appear delicate, translucent, and iridescent, like the wings of a butterfly, but with a soft glow.

My stomach rolls again. There's only one woman who has wings like that, hair like that.

Frantically shoving the mortals aside, I push through the crowd, trying to keep her in sight at the same time. Every time I catch a glimpse of her, it looks like she's farther away instead of closer.

I force my way through the mortals and reach the edge of the dance area, my jaw grinding when I see her standing near a copse of trees. If she makes it into the forest, I will lose her.

Can't lose her, not again.

She's balancing on the balls of her feet, still facing away from me, and I pause for a second. My breath catches as desire punches me in the gut, raging through me, making every inch of my body hard. *Achingly* hard and desperate for release. I haven't felt this kind of immediate lust since *her.*

*But it can't be her. No fucking way. It's been two thousand years. It's not her. It's simply **not**.*

I stand captivated as she turns her head slightly, looking at me over her shoulder. Her face is pale, shining in the mix of moon and rave lights, allowing me to catch sight of a straight nose, and full, dark red lips. But it's her eyes which hold me spellbound. A swirling kaleidoscope of colors, as if an entire rainbow lives in her eyes. Eyes that I know better than my own, they've been the star of my nightmares for the last two millennia.

It's her.

She turns away from me, heading deeper into the forest, and like the fool I am, I resume stumbling after her.

How could I not?

346

She's my wife.

I push forward, unsteady under the effects of the copious amounts of alcohol and the hallucinogens Dion tricked me into taking. Reaching the edge of the trees, where she stood only a moment before, I rest my hand against the trunk, forcing some steadying breaths through my mouth. I need to get my shit together before I follow her.

Stepping into the forest, I see no sign of her passing. I blindly go straight, hoping to stumble across her.

Tyche, you little minx, I could do with some luck right about now.

Keeping to my course as much as possible in my inebriated state, I search the dark between the trees. A slash of sudden pain forces me to a stop, my breath coming in short pants at the intensity. I glance down at myself, and my eyes shoot wide when I see blood spilling down my chest from lash marks. My hands shake, coming up to touch the injury. I blink, and before I make contact, they're gone.

Maybe I should rest for a moment, you know, gather my wits, just for a moment. Then I can continue after her.

My back hits the closest tree, and I slide against the rough trunk until I'm sprawled on the ground at its base. I sit, trying to focus and hoping this will give me a moment of clarity so I can resume my pursuit. Out of the corner of my eye, a flash of red hair flies by, the sounds of whispering chants echoing through my head, making it spin. Yet when I turn, trying to narrow down the source, there's nothing.

This is not the time for your usual inattention, Eros! Where is she?

My vision continues to blur, so I close my eyes, hoping that will help. The sound of chanting and cackling dims, and the lingering phantom burn across my chest disappears.

Taking a marshaling breath, forcing my mind to focus on the task at hand, I pull open my eyes. The air I just gained immediately rushes out of me.

Because she's right in front of me.

She's just as beautiful as I remember. More so. My heart thuds hard at the sight of her, beating a painful rhythm against my ribs, as if it's about to jump from my chest. I'm completely spellbound by her. Like I always am.

Her perfect face comes into full focus after a moment, and it tears at me how beautiful she is. It's not just her form, but her soul. It *shines* from within her. The familiar scent of lemons washes over me, invoking the memories I've repressed for so long. The memories I've spent two thousand years running from.

Kneeling at my side, she tilts her head at me, evaluating me. My breath catches as I wait for her to disappear before my eyes.

"I'm hallucinating," I announce shakily, hoping I never come down from this high.

Whatever you gave me, Dion, I need a life's supply.

A small smile stretches across her red lips, and I recall the feeling of them running across my skin, pressing against mine. The shape of them telling me she loves me, that she wants to marry me.

"Does that make this any less real?" she asks, stroking her elegant fingers along my cheek. Her voice is lyrical, and again, the tides of memories surge.

Reaching up, I cover her hand with mine, pressing it against my cheek. Turning my face towards it, I place a reverent kiss to the palm. I look back to her, resting my cheek into her touch, my fingers tightening on hers.

"I've missed you so much," I whisper, my voice almost lost in the sounds of the rave continuing nearby.

"Then why haven't you come to find me? Why can't you forgive me?" she whispers back, her voice catching slightly, choking on emotion.

"*Princissika...*" I begin, swallowing my agony. I never want this moment to end.

"Princess? I love you like a nephew. But I draw the line there," Dion calls, making me take my eyes off her and turn my head towards my uncle. When had he gotten here?

My brow furrows at my uncle, but I dismiss him after a momentary confusion. Snapping my head back to her, I find my hand touching nothing but my own cheek. My heart drops to the realm of my toes with the realization that she was nothing but a figment of my imagination. She was never there. It was all in my head. Because of the drugs.

Dion's drugs.

Struggling to a stand, I grab two fistfuls of Dion's jacket, throwing him against another tree, lifting him several inches off the ground.

"What did you give me!?" I scream, rage coloring my vision.

Dion's eyes go wide, shocked at my violent outburst. "Nothing! It was just candy!"

"You said hallucinogens! Not just candy!"

Still holding him suspended, my rage giving me an unprecedented amount of strength and my anger muting all the other emotions. The devastation I'm feeling. All a hallucination, because of the god I grip in my fists.

"I was just fucking with you, Coop! Why? Did you see something?"

Dion would have owned up to it by now. If he drugged me, he would have admitted to it.

Dion's face turns curious instead of frightened as I lower him back to the ground. Glancing around, I drop my hands from where they gripped my uncle. If it wasn't him, what just happened?

"Dion, please, you need to tell me the truth because if you didn't drug me, then how did I just see..." I trail off, thinking back on the small interaction with her.

If Dion didn't drug me, what in the name of Rhea just happened?!

Dion shakes his head ruefully, slapping my shoulder affectionately. "Come back to the party, Coop. Stop hiding in the woods like a pussy."

I nod my head absently, murmuring, "Yeah, I... I'll catch up with you."

Dion leaves me alone in the woods, popping more of the candies into his mouth as he strolls away, heading back to the rave. I'm tempted for a moment to follow him, to forget what I just saw, to grab some mortal female, or two, and lose myself in them for a couple hours. Gods aren't incapable of moving on, and we're not bound by the idea of monogamy, at least most of us aren't. Why do I have this hang-up?

Closing my eyes, I picture it in my mind. Two gorgeous women approaching me in bed, maybe a blonde and a redhead? Laying back on my sheets, I notice their eyes fire with excitement as they stroll closer to me. And why shouldn't they be excited? I mean, have you *seen* me? When they reach the sides of the bed, my hackles rise, yanking me out of my fantasy.

I still can't make myself stray, even in my mind. Opening my eyes, I slam my fist into a tree, barely feeling the pain as my knuckles split from the strike.

Why does she still have such a hold over me? Two thousand years and I can't forget her. Will I never be able to move on?

Heaving a short, unsteady breath, I look down at my fist to assess my injuries, blood covering my knuckles. Wincing, I wipe my hand

SACRIFICE TO THE DARK ELVES

off on my pants. As I do, my sleeve rides up, and my eyes shoot wide with confusion. Along my wrist is a deep burn, as if I was bound for days without reprieve.

Okay, what the fuck? That was definitely not there a moment ago.

I yank my other hand up, and an identical burn marks that wrist, too. Trailing a shaking finger along the wounds, I gape as the injury heals, closing before my very eyes.

What the hell is happening to me?

Grabbing the tree, I steady myself as my vision spins and spots form. I am suddenly on the verge of passing out. After a moment, my mind clears, and I breathe a sigh of relief. A blinding, searing pain breaks across my chest. Whip marks cut into my flesh, trailing down my forearms, and dripping blood. The excruciating pain forces me to my knees. Pressing a shaking hand to my chest, I watch as the wounds heal and fade almost as quickly as they appeared.

My eyesight wavers consistently, seeing the ghosts of people I don't recognize pass by me. My arm comes up in reflex when an unseen enemy swings a sword at me, aiming for my head. The hallucination vanishes into a wisp of smoke a moment before it hits. Voices pound through my head, screaming and whispering at the same time, calling for me, begging me, but I can't focus on a single one long enough to decipher it.

Collapsing to my knees, my hands grip the side of my head, forcing unsteady breaths out of my mouth, trying to get a grasp on what's happening. With the cacophony in my head, I can barely think, barely see, but there's one thing I know.

I need to talk to Dinlas.

This isn't the drugs, Dion would have fessed up if it was. He was never a god to refuse to take credit for a well-done prank, so this is something else. If anyone can help me figure this out, it will be my brother. Closing my eyes, I reach out through my link to locate him. One of my special abilities is the link to another's emotions. I may

351

not be close to my brother, but he's still my brother. That tie of blood allows me to track him, to sense his emotions and location from a greater distance than any other.

I don't immediately sense the bitterness, so I focus more intently. I wait to feel my brother so I can track him down. I need him to help me figure out what's happening. There's a moment of complete silence.

Then another.

My stomach drops, and I'm sure my entire face drains of all color.

There's nothing.

I can't feel my brother. I should feel his heart tied to mine, but I can't. There's no heartbreak, no pain, no longing.

Just nothing.

I don't even open my eyes before popping to my brother's warehouse. I hope to find him lounging in his office, pissed at me for suddenly appearing without warning. There's an eerie, oppressive silence, and I know in my gut that something is wrong.

"Dinlas?" I call shakily, praying he'll answer.

"Back here!" an unfamiliar female voice answers.

I follow it, my gut clenching. I am still not picking up any trace of Dinlas in the vicinity. I refuse to acknowledge the bright, flashing reason why I can't feel my brother's heart.

There's some other reason I can't feel him. There has to be.

Still, I prepare myself, tracking the voice to my brother's bedroom, my heart steeling itself to take on yet another loss.

Can I survive this one? I barely survived losing her, and I don't think I will make it if Dinlas is...

Holding my breath, I step into the room. Artemis and an unknown mortal woman are sawing away at ropes binding my brother's wrists. Hurrying forward, I reach down to yank away the ties around his feet, horrified at the sight of him. He's been whipped so brutally. There are slashes criss crossing his whole body, the wounds forming some sick pattern. Whoever did this *enjoyed* the pain they dealt him.

Once she frees him of the bindings, my aunt steps away. She pulls out her phone as she walks out of the room, undoubtedly summoning help. The mortal woman and I are left behind with the ravaged remains of my brother.

"W-what happened to him?" I stutter out, moving to the side of the bed and gazing at the mess of wounds that lay across his body.

"That *thing* over there," the mortal woman gestured to the residue of what looked like a woman lying on the floor, "is what happened to him. I hazard a guess it's some wild Wiccan, but I imagine you gods will dig up more information when the others show up."

Passively, I take in the decomposing body and Dinlas' wolves tearing at what looks to be some kind of white reptile. None of that matters now, not when I still can't feel my brother's heart.

Kneeling beside Dinlas, a shaky breath of relief slips past my lips when I catch the slow rise and fall of his chest. *He's alive, looks like he went ten rounds with a Prime, but he's alive.*

I can hear Artemis and the mortal in the adjacent room, making frantic calls on their cellphones, summoning my family. I take the opportunity to whisper to my unconscious brother, "Don't you dare leave me, Din. I...I can't do this without you."

Gods, he's in bad shape. With a shaking hand, I begin to assess his injuries, and the more I find, the more horrified I become.

How could he survive this?

My eyes catch on his wrists. Carefully so as not to cause him further pain, if that is even possible at this point, I turn his hand over.

This is exactly the mark I saw on mine. The burns on his wrists from the ropes that held him are what I saw on my own wrists in the woods, and what drove me to the warehouse. My shaking hand hovers over his injuries, assessing them with new eyes. Those lash marks appeared on my forearms, on my chest, identical to the wounds on my brother. But his aren't disappearing.

The visions, the injuries, they were him.

Everything I saw at the rave, it was a warning, a warning about how close to death my brother is. Even *her*, all trying to tell me of my brother's need for me, and I didn't listen, couldn't understand. *I failed him* again. I failed him when I didn't speak up when he was sent to Tartarus by our parents. I failed him every single day when I remained silent about his treatment at our family's hands. He is *dying*, and all I saw was my own torment, instead of his message.

So fucking selfish, just like always. The cruel son of Aphrodite, who played with hearts for his own amusement.

Even this close to him, I can't feel his heart, but he is here, his chest rising with shallow, unsteady breaths. So he can't be, I *refuse*—

There's a sudden commotion as gods begin popping into the warehouse, no doubt alerted by Artemis and the mortal. Still kneeling beside my brother, I glance up at the sound of high heels running along iron. It is strangely loud in the eerie silence of a moment before.

My mother grips the doorway, and from the look of her, it is the only thing keeping her from collapsing. She appears wild and unkempt. Her normally perfect blonde locks are in complete disarray, and her bright blue eyes, identical to mine, are filled with turmoil.

Her heart links to mine, the horror and agony she is experiencing now coursing through me as well.

Without a word to me, she strides to the other side of Din's bed, collapsing to her knees. Tears stream down her face as she reaches out a shaking hand to push back the lock of hair from his face.

"My baby boy, who did this to you?" she murmurs, her entire body shaking as she assessed his injuries.

More gods shuffle in, and soon both *Miteras* and I are pulled away from him. My mother is comforted by another god, and my father grabs me for a rare hug. Their hearts link with mine, and I take on my family's heartaches and pain. But for the first time, it doesn't cripple me because it's nothing compared to the fear coursing through me at the idea that my brother might not make it.

I-I need air. I half stagger, half stumble, out the warehouse door, taking heaving breaths as I do, unable to cope with the possibility of a world without Dinlas. Sliding down the wall, I pull my legs to my chest, trying unsuccessfully to steady my breathing.

The door to the warehouse opens and closes next to me. I don't have to look up to know it's my mother.

She slides down beside me, and silently we link hands feeding each other support.

"*Miteras?*" I murmur, staring off in the distance.

"Hmm?"

"Something strange happened tonight. I think it's related to what Din went through." Rubbing my palms against my pants, I glance at her, finding her eyes locked on my face. "I knew something was wrong. No one had to call me. I felt an echo of his injuries." I rub my wrist absently, remembering the feeling of pain ripping through me, and again, I wonder at how Dinlas survived what he had. "*Miteras,* they formed on my skin."

My mother lets out a short gasp of shock. I turn to connect with her eyes, and there's a flash of knowledge in them an instant before she manages to hide it.

"I don't know why that would happen, Eros. Samhain is a strange night steeped in mystery. I'm sure it's nothing. I wouldn't worry about it."

She's lying.

There's only one other time I can recall my mother lying to me, and that led to one of the most traumatic experiences of my life. I may not be as good as Dinlas or Uncle Hades at sniffing out a lie, but I *know* my mother. My grip on her hand turns painful. It's hard for me to cause her even slight pain, but this is *Dinlas*. When it comes to my brother, all bets are off.

"Eros! You're hurting me," she yelps in pain, yet I refuse to release her.

"You're lying. What do you know?" I demand, my voice whipping harshly against the otherwise quiet atmosphere.

"Eros! Let me go!"

My grip only tightens. "What. Do. You. Know?"

"You're twins! Alright? You're twins."

PIECE
OF
CAKE

BY

AMBER ALBRIGHT

ATË,

GODDESS OF MISCHIEF & RUIN

I t has been a while since I have been home and free from my prison cell. Being the Goddess of Ruin and coming back to destroy Olympus didn't exactly go as planned. My father, Zeus, had tossed me out and erased the memories of all who knew me, and I had planned revenge for centuries. Sure, coming back and releasing the Titans wasn't the best idea, but hey what's a goddess to do? Trust me, if you felt that much hate, loss, and abandonment, you would do some crazy shit too. But alas, that is neither here nor there. I have done my time. A thousand years of it in the pits of Tartarus. Now I am home and slowly trying to make amends with the family I once lost.

The Jeep bumps on the old hidden dirt road, shaking me from my thoughts. I am in a convoy with a driver and three other guys who all smell like sweat and the overuse of cheap cologne. They remind me of the bootleg version of old action heroes. One is tattooed, the other bearded, and the last looks like he has seen his fair share of the world.

Trees snap and hit the side of the Jeep as we truck further away from civilizations and off the beaten path. They may try to hide their sudden fear, but you can practically feel it radiate from them. I have paid a pretty penny for these three knuckleheads to find the certain ruin I am looking for.

Tons of places have been wiped off the mortal map, and with my latest attempt to overthrow Olympus, I have lost my touch with the mortal world, so to speak. The Jeep lurches forward once more and hits a deeper hole in the road, slinging mud along the side. We are deep in the forests of Honduras, Mexico. A recent Mayan ruin was discovered, and just as quickly covered up by the media. Which, to be honest, only perks my interest more. The locals call it *maldito*, which means cursed. The name alone means no mortal will set foot here. Another win for me, given I am immortal.

The Jeep comes to a stop, the road we are on ending. The driver in front whistles, speaking in his native tongue.

"This is as far as I go. I can wait until half-past dusk, but no longer. The woods surrounding this place--"

"Cursed? Yeah, I got the gist," I reply in the same language.

He nods once before turning to the other three men. Their gazes meet mine, and I roll my eyes before hopping out. I wear cargo pants with a pair of thick black commando boots, a black tank top, and my hair pulled away from my face. When I first showed up asking for their assistance, they laughed, calling me a barbie with a mental illness for trying to go deep in the jungle dressed like this. I have no equipment, but little do they know I am Ruin personified. After flashing some major cash, they soon swallowed their remarks and led me here. Except now, they seem to be second-guessing their previous investment.

The three men jump out, heading for the back of the Jeep. They throw a large green tarp over the side and pick up weapons. They load themselves down with a couple of backpacks and what looks like automatics and a machetes. They catch my expression, and one rolls his eyes as the other tries to hand me a knife. I shake my head, and the other two laugh.

"Your funeral," one remarks.

I cock an eyebrow. "And how so?"

Another points to the endless line of jungle and back to me. "This place is full of jaguars and plenty of things that would eat a girl like you."

His comment gets a laugh and snicker from the others, even the driver, but if he is trying to throw a jab with an innuendo, he should probably try harder. After all, I am best friends with Eros, which makes his comment lackluster at best.

I grin and lift one shoulder in a shrug, ready to get what I came for. "Shall we get moving?"

The machetes come in handy for the mortals as they slice and dice their way through the overgrown bush. I guess I could just use my power to dematerialize and find it myself, but like I said, not too familiar with the area. What feels like hours later, we finally reach a clearing. Pushing more overgrown branches from my view, the old temple looms ahead. It has to be at least a couple hundred feet tall. The parts that can be seen are overgrown with vegetation trying to reclaim the area. I quicken my pace, eager to reach it, when a hand grabs my arm. I spin around, controlling my temper, so my eyes don't flash and scare the mortals.

"Are you crazy? It's almost sundown. Hosta will leave us here if we don't turn back," one of the men said.

Hosta? Oh, so that was the driver's name. I am terrible at remembering mortals' names. I shrug from his grip.

"If you are scared. Go home. I came here for a reason. Besides, do you really want to turn back and let a girl go on when you were too afraid?" I jab.

The three of them look at each other. They grumble and curse under their breaths before one of them nods and steps forward to lead the way.

"Crazy ass woman," another mumbles.

We trek onward, getting closer to the temple. I can see what looks like tape has been used to section parts of this place off. It seems they started, and something spooked them and made them quit. We stop at the base of the roughly hewn stone steps, looking up at the task before us. The sun is setting off in the distance, and the smell of fear is rising. Shuffling from behind me tells me they are looking through their backpacks. The encroaching gloom is pushed back as one by one they turn on flashlights. I feel the cold metal touch the side of my arm as one guy hands me a spare. I want to shake my head, saying I don't need it since Tartarus itself is darker than this place, but I also need to keep up appearances. Smiling briefly, I take it as the bearded guy steps forward, trying to lead the way.

We take the stone steps two at a time, overgrowth crunching beneath our boots. Darkness falls quickly, the stars above the only light besides the flashlights. We make it to the top, pausing to catch our breath before a huge stone door. Two of the men behind me start whispering to themselves, and it takes me a minute to catch what they are saying. I turn as the color drains from their face.

"What are you two going on about?" I snap.

A tap on my shoulder has me turning back around as the bearded man, damn I really have to get better at names, shines his flashlight at the words carved above the door. I squint, deciphering the language.

DAMNATI OMNES QUI INGREDIUNTUR BEATI RELINQUUNT
DAMNED ARE ALL WHO ENTER, BLESSED ARE THOSE WHO LEAVE.

Shrugging, I look at him. "Okay?"

He seems to choke on his spit. "And? You know what that means?"

The two men behind us continue to chant, but I wave my hand, ignoring them. "Yeah, it means I paid you, so let's keep going."

He shakes his head at me, lowering his flashlight. "No, chica. The devil owns this place. We go no further."

Exasperated, I place my hands on my hips, sighing before tilting my head back then looking at him. "Seriously? A few words etched on an ancient building, and suddenly you are pissing your pants?"

He says nothing else, just steps back, staring at the door and its warning. I turn, ignoring them, and approach the door. I push against the weathered stone, expecting resistance with the edges calcified by time, but it moves like butter for me. A hollow sound escapes as air held too long in the temple is released. The wail of high-pitched screams and feet descending stairs tell me my guides have left. Rolling my eyes, I toss the flashlight to the side. I don't need it anymore. My vision is immaculate. Besides, the darkness doesn't scare me. Being trapped in it for a thousand years and then screwing the one who controls it kind of makes you numb to the eerie chill the mortals experience.

I step inside, taking a look around. Where the forest hadn't tried to reclaim this temple, spider webs hung. I move my hands through most of it as I get further inside. Ancient battles are depicted on some of the stone walls as other parts look to be crumbling. Honestly, it is beautiful. I love ruins in every shape. Where others see horror or disgust, I see what once was. Ruins fill me with joy. I don't know how else to explain it. They remind me of myself at times. Before I came home. They were once beautiful prestige. Then something happened, and they were left unattended. Abandoned, they survived every harsh obstacle thrown at them. Sure, they are chipped and dirty from it, but they remain, claiming their place in the world.

I gather my thoughts. I am here for a reason, and nostalgia isn't it. I turn a corner, heading deeper into the temple when suddenly the ground beneath me gives way. I don't have much time to react as I fall a few hundred feet, hitting rock bottom. And I mean that literally. I look up, rubbing my already sore ass, and catch the sight of more debris heading my way. Dissipating into a black mist, I move out from beneath the falling rock and dirt, reforming on the other side of the room. Sure, it won't kill me, but it would still hurt like shit.

Once I am solid again, I take a look around the room, coughing up dust. Bingo. I have found what I came looking for. The room is an old, abandoned place of worship. Probably an ancient civilization lost once more. Statues, missing limbs and heads, line most of the space while a strange coffin rests in the middle. I walk closer to it, noticing how much it has aged. A side of it has been torn away like someone, or something, tried to get in.

Hmm, strange.

Upon further inspection, I notice the coffin has engravings on the side. Double bingo. Grabbing both sides, I yank upwards, ripping the lid straight off. I toss it to the side, swatting away the dust that follows. Peering over the edge, I see the skeletal remains of a man wearing an ancient crown. The inside of his coffin is lined with ancient jewels and cloths. My eyes flicker over them momentarily until I see what he is holding. Both of his skeletal hands are wrapped around a large weathered book. Reaching over, I grab it, breaking the bones that held it.

Yahtzee. Clio is going to love this.

Paris, A few days later.

I shimmy to the music filling the kitchen as I make breakfast in my Paris apartment. Tiny wings flap over my head as my imp circles, copying my movements. I saved him from the King of Titans, who thought after he served him in his plans for freedom, he could just discard him. I held a special place in my cold heart for the little creature. He had no one, like I hadn't.

"If you put your tiny clawed hands on that stove, and spill those eggs, you will not get any of them," I call over my shoulder as I look through the spice rack.

He mumbles under his breath and grins a wide, sharp-toothed smile as I turn and squint at him. Shaking my head, I finish cooking and we sit on the couch, watching the news. Normal reports of stupid crap mortals worry about fills the airwaves, but I am looking for something in particular. I split my bagel in half, offering a piece to Ebhot, who happily takes it and devours the whole thing. The next story to flash across the screen is the Grand Museum opening in Paris this evening. I smile as I continue to watch. They talk about

Clio and how this is supposed to be an amazing elegant event. Celebrities are flying in for the show, along with elites from across the world. All are humming and buzzing about the artifacts that will be presented. Chloe Amors' name appears at the bottom of the screen as they continue to discuss the details of the upcoming evening.

It is funny to me, the alias she goes by. After all, she is married to the God of Love. She is Chloe Amor to the world, but to us immortals, she is Clio, the Muse of History. There is no point in time that she does not remember. Even the stories the mortals tried to hide or change. Speaking of which...

I hop up from the sofa, sliding my plate over to Ebhot, giving him the rest of my breakfast. He happily devours it, making a mess that I will have to clean up later. I head to the kitchen looking for my phone. I find it on the counter next to the book I stole for Clio. I dial Clio's number and as it rings, I think to myself, *If I have enough time, maybe I can make her a cake as a happy opening day present.*

The sound of a high-pitched cry echoes from the receiver as she picks up. "Hello?"

I tilt my head away from the phone, grimacing at the shrill sound. One eye still closed, I respond, "Clio? Can you hear me? Is this a bad time?"

I hear shuffling in the background before she answers, "Yes, Atë. I can hear you. What's up?"

I pace the kitchen slowly as I glance at the book. "Oh, nothing really." I pause. "The opening is still at eight tonight, correct?"

"Yes, it is. Thank you for reminding me," she groans into the receiver.

Lately, the little muse seems to have her hands full. I mean, I don't blame her. She recently had twins, so it seems pretty normal for her to be so busy. Not that I can relate. I have no children and plan to keep it that way for the rest of my existence.

"Reminding you?" I snort. "I was just watching them talk about your grand opening on the news, Mrs. Amor."

The sound of a plate breaking in the living room cuts off her response. I shake my head at Ebhot. The little imp had dropped the plate, shattering it everywhere, and is now grinning at me like a scolded child. He squawks before flying into the kitchen and circling me overhead.

I turn back to the phone in my hand. "You are still going, right?"

I pace, chewing on my thumbnail as I wait for her response. I eye the book and its old rustic leather binding nervously. If she doesn't go, this will all have been a waste.

"Yes, I am still going! I will ask Hedone to watch the twins."

Ahh Hedone. Their other daughter. Although I am still not too keen on the logistics, given my time away from Olympus and my later incarceration. I know that they have a daughter in her late teens.

"Okay, good. I may or may not have gotten you something for your opening. I know you've been busy with family and I just..."

I stop as Ebhot makes a weird face at me, confused. I wave a hand, shushing him. It isn't like me to admit that I care about anything, but it is a new improvement. Well, I have tried to make it one.

I hear her call out to her husband, and more shuffling and muffled voices before she returns to the phone. "Atë, you didn't have to get me anything." She pauses. "Wait. You didn't steal this, did you?"

I tuck a strand of hair behind my ear as I play it cool. Well, I try. "Steal? What me? Define steal?"

"Atë," her voice warned.

"Sorry, what was that?" I fake static over the phone. "I can't hear you. You are breaking up."

She starts to comment, but I quickly hang up and turn to Ebhot.

"Okay, eight o'clock she said, which means I have plenty of time to do one more thing. I am going to change clothes and run to the store." I head for my room, and then stop, turning around. "That means no touching anything. Understood?"

He bounces his little horned head up and down as I shake mine. With a deep sigh, I go to get ready. I have a few hours to kill and want to bake her something for the event. I mean, granted I stole a book, but this would make up for that, right? And yes, I know I am trying too hard. But you come back home, kidnap your best friend, cause a mass prison outbreak, and try to kill your father. Then tell me what you wouldn't be willing to do to make amends to the ones that matter.

The shopping doesn't take long. I already have the list of ingredients I need and just went by that. Also, I may or may not have cut in line to get back faster. I just don't trust Ebhot alone that long, and entering the apartment, I remember why.

The inside of my home looks like a tornado went through it. Broken glasses on the floor, torn paper everywhere, the TV louder than normal. Sighing, I drop the groceries on the nearby table and survey the mess. I start to clean it up when I stop, frozen in horror as I stare at the paper in my hands. Papers? *Oh fuck.* I run to the counter, looking for the book. Not finding it, I drop to the floor, frantically searching on my hands and knees. As I round the corner, I see it lying under the kitchen table. Picking it up, I stand, looking it over with care. Making sure my blasted imp has not destroyed the one relic I have for Clio's museum tonight. I sigh in relief when the book appears to be intact and unharmed.

"Ebhot!" I scream.

I hear the clicking of tiny nails as his horned head pops out from behind the door. Another smile dances across his little face.

"What did you do?" I ask through clenched teeth.

He hops out of the room, rubbing his hands over each other nervously. "You left. Don't know if you would come back. Got scared," he speaks in the same broken English he always does.

I pinch the bridge of my nose, controlling my growing temper. Okay, fair. The last time I had left the little dude, I ended up in Tartarus. So, he has a reason to have a little anxiety.

"It's fine," I say, looking at him. "You didn't touch this book though, did you?"

He shakes his head from side to side. Nodding, I turn back to the mess and start to clean. What I thought would be a small endeavor turns out to take longer than expected. He made more of a mess than I previously thought. Once everything is back in order, I call him over to help me cook. He seems to be less stressed when he has something to do. So, like this morning, I turn on the music and get to work.

The oven is preheating while I have Ebhot read off the ingredients and instructions to me. He sits on the counter with his tiny imp legs folded beneath him. It is almost cute how he flips the pages with his tail. He is helping, which means he isn't being destructive. He calls off a few more things that I add to my mixing bowl as I hold it to my side, stirring the ingredients. The apron I wear, along with the rest of me, is covered in flour. Okay, and most of the kitchen. And counters.

Hey, it's not like I am the Goddess of Baking, okay?

I spin in a slow circle, humming to myself as he drones on. Most of the ingredients I added fit, so I don't know why he keeps murmuring. Although, half the time, I can't differentiate between what is English or gibberish. I stop, facing him as I tilt my head.

"What are you going on about? There is no way I need more ingredients. Give me that."

I place the bowl down, reaching for the cookbook. He gladly hands it over, smiling.

367

Strange. Why is this page more worn than the others? This isn't even French anymore.

I squint, holding the book closer to my face as I read over the text. It really is strange. Given my immortality and stay among the mortals, I am fluent in all languages. I have learned it all. So why is this giving me such difficulty? Some of the words look like ancient Romanian, where others seem almost Sumerian with a dash of Latin mixed in. The text does seem familiar, like I have seen it before and recently. I mull over the words, whispering them out as I try to make sense of them. I stop mid-sentence, my eyes going wide as it hits me. I meet Ebhot's gaze and he cowers from me, tucking himself between the toaster and the wall. I know where I have seen this text. Inside the fucking temple. That is the last thought I have before my kitchen erupts in fire.

I am thrown back several feet by what feels like a small nuclear bomb. I sit up, rubbing the side of my head, a loud siren ringing through the entire apartment building. Opening my eyes, they adjust quickly to the new scene. But a couple of things stick out. One, my entire apartment is ruined and not in the fun, *I just had crazy sex with my primordial boyfriend* ruined. No, more that every surface is singed and currently aflame. Two, I am somewhat still on fire. Three, a giant horned man stands in the middle of my once gorgeous living room, with his arms outstretched, saying something. And four, I cannot hear what is being said given my newly developed tinnitus. I see Ebhot hiding behind the counter and wave for him to escape. He looks between me and the demon in the living room and flies out the front door. Good. One less thing to worry about.

I rub my ears repeatedly as the sound starts to come back to my ruptured eardrums. I pick up his voice at the very end.

"....not been listening to a thing I said?"

368

I prop myself up on my elbows. "Oh, I am sorry. My eardrums ruptured from whatever the fuck you just did entering my kitchen."

The horns protruding from his skull slowly make their way back into his head as he walks forward, adjusting a suit that seems to appear out of nowhere. Okay, that was a cute party trick. He stops in front of me, picking me up by my arms, which is his first mistake.

I. Do. Not. Like. To. Be. Touched.

Blame it on my own special brand of PTSD from being tossed off Olympus against my wishes. My expression must change because his red eyes suddenly glisten with excitement.

"Oh," his deep throaty voice echoes, "you are not human."

"No, I am not." I shrug out of his grip. "Now, if you could explain to me how the fuck you got into my kitchen, I would appreciate it."

He tilts his head back and releases a deep laugh before spinning around the room again. What the fuck is up with the theatrics?

"I am Chareth, and you, goddess, have summoned me," he responds.

I think he wants to sound intimidating, but the moment the dramatic proclamation leaves his lips, the sprinklers go off. I stand there, my arms crossed as the water extinguishes the flames still clinging to me and those licking at the living room furniture. He stares at me as steam billows and rolls off of him.

I raise a single finger, pointing at him and his smoke show. "Oh, so you're like Hephaestus?"

His nose curls for a second. "Who?"

Shrugging, I respond, "You know the God of Fire? Forges all cool Olympian weapons?"

I immediately regret my words. His eyes take on a different shine as his original scaly form returns. I guess he is over the small talk.

"Olympian, you say? The Old Gods?"

"Whoa, whoa, whoa, let's watch it on the old part, okay?" I say, holding my hands up.

"Summoned by an Olympian Goddess? You will be my ticket to every layer of Hell." He smiles, his teeth suddenly overgrown.

I take a small step back as the water from the sprinklers cuts off. "I will be your ticket to nothing. I think you need to crawl back into whatever hole you escaped from."

He steps forward, not caring about my messy threat. "Here I thought I could plague the earth like the olden days, but you have given me so much more purpose, a beautiful one. I will make a queen of you!" He reaches out, grabbing my arms again and pulling me to him.

Okay, that's it. Now I'm pissed.

His eyes widen and I see the reflection of my amber gaze in his as I let loose my power. The room shakes violently, distracting him as I use that leverage to headbutt him. He flies back, hitting the wall, and leaving a massive hole in it. Great, more damage. The floor still shakes as he levitates to his feet. What I thought was shock turns into maniacal laughter.

"Oh, I am so going to keep you."

I lift my hands to slam them together and crush him in this building. I stop. No. This isn't me anymore. I'd destroy this building, killing the innocent lives below me, and my family would regard me all the same. As Atë the Bringer of Ruin. Guess I can do this the old-fashioned way. Now, don't get me wrong, I am no Goddess of War, but that doesn't mean I don't know how to fight.

"You want me? Come and get me," I taunt.

He takes my invitation without hesitation and charges me. I anticipate his move, dissipating into a shard of black mist and reappearing behind him. I kick the back of his knees, sending him flying headfirst into the cabinets below. He roars as his anger grows, using the horns on his head to rip his way free. He turns to me, smoke flowing from his nostrils, looking every bit demonic and pissed.

I shrug and grin at him. "What? I never said I would play fair."

He shakes his head. "No, you didn't. But if you won't, neither will I."

He rubs his hands together, creating a fine orange glow that slowly builds in intensity. I have a moment to register that he just summoned a fireball before he throws it at me. The core of it hits my abdomen, sending me sailing backward. I land with a thud in the hallway outside my apartment as people to my right scream and run towards the exit. I nod, thinking that is probably a smart thing to do as I sit up, patting at the flames singing what is left of my clothes.

Heavy footsteps echo, drawing my gaze upwards. He towers over me with hungry, blood-red eyes.

"You will be my queen. Either willingly or by force. Your choice."

"Hold that thought," I say, winking at the demon, and vanish into a cloud of black smoke.

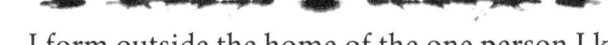

I form outside the home of the one person I know has a chance of getting rid of whoever the fuck he said his name was. My sister, the Witch Queen herself, Hekate. My bare feet tap on the concrete stairs as I reach the door and raise my hand to knock. I pause, knowing Hekate may not be inclined to help me. Given the whole releasing the Titans thing that may or may not have caused damage to not only her place and her people, but also herself. My clothes still smoke in some places as I absently slap the lingering flames to ash, thinking I should probably just leave. But I stop myself. I have been trying, *in my own way,* to regain the sister I once lost. I just still have a hard time letting anyone completely in. Sighing, I raise my hand again and knock. Loudly.

371

A voice rings out from inside without the door being opened, "No, Atë."

I place my hands on my hips and tap my foot before I yell, "Oh, come on, Hekate! Let me in! Unless you want me just to stand out here yelling in front of all the mortals?"

The air shifts as she materializes behind me. I turn, smiling as innocently as I can. She folds her arms, not buying it for a second. "I said no."

"But. You didn't even hear the question."

One dark eyebrow arches, regarding me as she takes in my appearance. I'm sure my singed clothing does not help. "From what I can see, it looks like a pretty normal day for you." She pauses. "Then again, you don't usually willingly come to me for anything. Which means this has to be good."

She waits for my rebuttal, staring intently at me. It is unnerving how well she knows me. She hit the nail on the head with her words.

Sighing, I say, "Okay, very valid points, I'll give you that, but I need your help." I stop, taking a deep breath, and forcing the words out through gritted teeth. "You're the only one that can help me at this point."

Hekate throws up her hands and rolls her eyes. "Oh, fuck. There goes the world. What did you do?" She demands, meeting my gaze, her voice turning stern.

I look down, fiddling with my hands for a second. "I may or may not have accidentally summoned a demon."

Hekate pauses, her eyes narrowing. "Say that again?"

"And by demon, I mean actual demon. He said something about making me his queen, but I honestly didn't get a lot before he firebombed the kitchen when I said no...you know, with my fist."

"Goddammit, Atë!" She pushes past me and through the front door, moving fast. The doors burst forward from her speed, and I roll my eyes following behind her. I mean, really, why was she mad?

I would have to cover up the inferno of the damned apartment. Plus, I don't even know if the clothes I have are ruined.

"What?" I ask as I close the door behind us.

The inside of Hekate's apartment isn't what I expect for the Witch Queen. What I expect to be shades of dark were more creams, whites, and purples. A few white chairs sit to the side, and a large set of drawers are against the wall. A hallway leads off to a different room, but she doesn't head that way. She stops by a nearby bookshelf, grabbing a few items, and then moves to the dresser and opens it. She pulls out a satchel and starts tossing things in. From here, I can make out some of the contents which range from salt, weird looking water, and various herbs.

She whirls on me, pointing a stern finger. "First of all, you can't *accidentally* summon a demon which means you did something on purpose. Stupidly. Second of all, doing so is no laughing matter."

Rolling my eyes, I place my hands on my hips as I stare at her frantic movements. "Technically, I didn't know I was summoning anything. I was actually trying to bake a cake when Ebhot kept giving me directions and herbs. He just got this stupid book I stole mixed up with my cookbook."

I honestly think Hekate stops breathing for a moment.

"For fuck's sake! You really are an idiot! How could you possibly not recognize the difference between Betty Crocker and Beelzebub? Brown sugar and brimstone?"

I scratch the side of my head. "I don't think he said that was his name. Oh wait, you are being facetious." I shake my head. "Listen, I just wanted to make Clio a *congratulations-on-the-new-museum* cake."

Sighing, she closes up the satchel with ingredients before continuing, "I gotta think."

She moves past me, heading for a small bar towards the entrance, and pours herself a drink. She takes a second glass and waves me over, and I gladly comply. We both stand silently for a moment, drinking as she contemplates my recent endeavor. I would be lying if I said I don't feel a semblance of guilt for dragging her into this with me.

"Listen," she finally says, the bottle near empty, "he's a demon that you called forth from a text used to summon him. Governed by the laws of nature, that is a contract of sorts."

I shoot the last of my drink back with a grimace. "Wait...there is a contract?"

She looks at me puzzled for a second. "You summoned a demon, Atë."

"I didn't mean to!" I lean forward, lightly touching her arm. "I mean, there has to be a get out of Hell free clause?"

"Contracts are contracts, and infernal contracts are especially infuriating. You can't tear them up. You can only..." She pauses, eyes flashing. Whatever she is considering is good, but it isn't going to be easy. She is having to think too long about it. "You remember how mortals went through a frenzy back in the latter part of the last century about playing records backward and hearing demonic messages and shit?"

I nod, waving my hand in a *go on* gesture. "Yeah. Their weird obsession with subliminal messages? What about it?"

"Well, it's a bunch of nonsense. Except You-Know-Who downstairs decided he liked the idea and started using that as his escape hatch. One of those things where it wasn't real to start with, but then it became an urban legend, and now it's a real thing."

My mind mulls over the information she is giving me until a lightbulb clicks in my head.

"Saying something backward, hmm? Like, say a certain contract I may have spoken?"

She grins at me. "Precisely. The reason it works so well is that it's in movies and such, so no one thinks it actually works. But it does.

Reading backward is a bitch and a half, though. And if you get one thing wrong, you have to start over." She thinks for a minute. "Probably another reason people think it doesn't work."

I reach over to pour the last of the bottle for us before downing it and slamming my glass down.

"Hekate, I am going to say this once and only once. You may be the smartest witch I know….Actually...Yeah, no, you are."

She grins at me. "No, if I was smart, I'd tell you to deal with it your own damn self and leave me, quite literally, the hell out of it."

I hop to my feet, a new plan formulating in my mind. Hekate doesn't even realize what she did, but she just gave me a perfect get out of Hell free clause. I move faster than she can catch and I place a kiss on the top of her head. I hop back and smile at her shocked expression before heading for the door.

"Atë, where the fuck are you going?" I hear her call as I rush out the door.

I don't respond as the door slams behind me. My form dissipates and I jet through the sky, back towards my apartment. Hekate gave me enough ammunition to send this demon back to Hell, and I don't need any potion, herb, or magic water. Oh no. I may have summoned this hell beast, but he is about to learn it was a big mistake on his part. I may be the Goddess of Ruin, but I am the Goddess of Mischief too, and he is about to learn that the hard way.

I form in the hallway of my apartment after sneaking past all the firefighters and police officers downstairs. It seems my little blowout shook the very foundation of the building.

I make my way to the spot where my door used to be, glass shards crunching under my feet. I peek in and I am shocked to see not only the demon I summoned but what looks like a group of his friends. Multiple heads turn in my direction as I enter with a sheepish grin on my face.

The apartment is still a mess, but no longer on fire. All the furniture and appliances are charred, soggy lumps. I swallow as I look around the room. Chareth is the only one that even resembles some sort of human. The other four beings remind me of something out of a mortal horror movie. Their blackened skin seems to drip hot sulfur and they stand straight up with no hint of a slouch. Like oozing toy soldiers.

Chareth leans over the counter, a large devilish smile greeting my return.

"Ahh there she is. I knew you would be back."

I stop a few feet away, not getting to close. I am not here for a fight. No, not this time.

"What can I say? I had time to think and reflect. I mean, we can talk this out, can't we? Like we both know this is a mishap...a mistake. Like I make a cake, and you get summoned from Hell."

He chuckles to himself, rising once more. "Oh, goddess, you are funny. I like funny."

"I can see that. So, what's with the entourage?" I ask, gesturing to the inky creatures with him.

He turns his head slightly before meeting my gaze. "Oh, these guys? Well, they are my...what would you call them? Leverage."

I scoff, "Leverage? You're telling me the all-powerful demon I summoned needs leverage?"

His smile is cold and full of an emotion I don't want to decipher. "Oh, sweetie, they are not for me. No, they are here because of you."

"Me?" I ask, a little surprised.

"Yes." He stops, straightening to his full height as he tries to round the counter. I instinctively move, keeping that space between us. He notices, and it only makes him chuckle more.

"Yes, you. See, while you were away, I did a bit of research. You are Atë. Goddess of Ruin. Firstborn of Zeus. Chaos born. And you know what that means?"

"No," I snap the words out, trying to maintain my cool.

"The price for you just went up." He winks.

"What the fuck does that mean?"

"Do you have any idea how fast they will follow me with you as my queen? There will be no world or dimension we cannot have."

"So that's what this is now? A popularity contest?"

"Oh no. It's so much more than that," He says as we continue to dance slowly around the kitchen island. "Think about it. You will have a place to rule. They don't appreciate you here. They never have. We have been here for what? Hours? And I haven't even heard the phone ring."

I would be lying if I said his words did not hit a small nerve. After Tartarus and what I had done, I am insecure, to say the least, about my family. I know it sounds stupid, but that dark empty pit I feel in my chest never really goes away. I know I can survive alone. Shit, I have been alone most of my mortal life, but it still stings.

"So that's it? I either say yes or what?" I remark, my voice dripping with sarcasm.

His smile drops. "Here is how this is going to work. You either come to Hell to be my queen, or I open a Hellgate and suck this miserable world and all its occupants into it."

I stop myself from rolling my eyes at his attempt at a threat. I mean, I guess if he had come to me sooner with this whole *end the world* scenario, I might have been all for it. But dammit, I am a recently reformed bad guy.

For my plan to work, I will need to play along. I move closer to him, walking to the opposite side of the burned kitchen. I tilt my head like I am weighing the options as I slide a single finger across the blackened countertop. While I portray this false image, I scan for the page I used to summon him. I figure Hell demon books are flame resistant. As I get closer, I see what looks like the remains behind him.

Okay, time for Plan B.

Sighing, I stop and shrug my shoulders in false defeat. "Okay. I mean, you drive a hard bargain, but Ruler of Hell seems like a pretty cool gig compared to what I am doing."

His eyes roam over me as if he just won a brand new car. It makes me feel sick. He moves closer to me, but I don't walk the opposite way this time. If I want to sell this and send him back to Hell, I need to play along. He reaches me, and it takes all I have not to curl my lip at the smell of sulfur wafting off of him.

Is that what demons smell like when they get excited?

He reaches for my face, cupping it with his newly clawed hands, and draws my lips to his. I have to commend myself on the insane willpower it takes not to barf in his face. He tastes like stone, metal, and ash. I pull away as he turns and throws one arm to the center of the living room. A bright orange ring forms and then an inferno bursts through the portal.

He looks at me, no longer hiding the creature he is. "Now, we leave."

"Wait!" I cry, louder than I mean to. I place a hand on the middle of his chest, trying to keep up my ruse.

He watches me, slightly annoyed at first, but I know if I want this to work, I need him on this plane. I shake my head as seductively as I can and gaze up at him.

"I want my immortal ceremony to be on earth. Besides, you already brought guests, and like you said, no one is coming to check on me. So why not here?"

What I can only assume is an eyebrow, given he looks like a horned rock creature, raises as he asks, "Here?"

He stops, looking around in disdain at the blackened apartment, and the fire pit still circling in the middle of the living room. I follow his gaze, shrugging my shoulders.

"Why not? You are this badass demon. Can't you fix this with a wave of your hand?"

Come on, Atë. You can do better than that.

His face doesn't change much, as if my offer is the last thing his rock brain would ever consider. Fuck. Okay, plan C. He may be a demon from Hell and made of rock, but he is still male. Sort of.

I clear my throat, standing on my tiptoes so I am close to whatever the fuck he has that resembles an ear. "Besides, I like to be wine, dined, and sixty-nined."

He pulls back, and the spinning fire ring of death in the living room disappears. I give him a seductive smile and head to my room, so glad that worked and I can move away from him. Pretending to pick up some of the mess, I grab the page from the book. I turn back, playing it off like I wasn't looking for that all along, and wave my hand at him.

"There, I cleaned up some, now hurry up. I am going to get ready. Don't keep your queen waiting." I smirk.

I don't wait for a response as I slip into the bedroom, shutting the door behind me. I lean against the wood, letting out a breath I didn't realize I was holding, and clutch the papers to my chest. I look down, unfolding the piece, and nearly scream to see it is the one I need. Hope to Hekate this fucking works. I open my closet to get ready for a living room wedding from literal Hell.

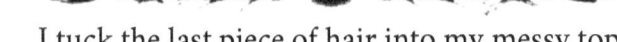

I tuck the last piece of hair into my messy top bun. I'd finished my makeup, going for my usual sultry look with red lips. I figure if my plan works, at least I will be ready for Clio's big night. I look in the mirror and smooth my hands over the short, strapless, black cocktail dress that lands just past mid-thigh. The long black feathered train that dances around me as I walk, a playful twist. It is perfect. I picked it out weeks ago and am excited to wear it out. I am just worried I won't get a chance. I really do get myself in the most trouble.

I turn from my reflection, grabbing the page I had prepared. I close the door behind me, face the room, and almost gasp. It is different from what it was five minutes ago. Actually, it is completely different. Strands of red lights hang from my ceiling, the ends gathered into a chandelier over the table in what used to be the living room. I feel like I stepped into an upscale New York restaurant instead of my Paris residence. The inky creatures wear butler attire as they stand close to my future, not husband. I guess he decided to put the horns away for dinner as he is wearing a red-assin suit. He leans back casually in his chair, one hand resting on his chin and the other tapping the table impatiently. He isn't terrible to look at in his human form, but alas, my heart belongs to the Primordial God of Darkness, and I am no longer evil. We have no chance.

He stands as I enter, smoothing the front of his suit, his eyes raking over me possessively. "You look--"

I raise my hand, cutting him off. "Gorgeous. I know."

I look around the apartment with its new decorations and say, "You did well."

He chuckles to himself and pulls my chair out for me. I make my way over and sit down. He retakes his seat, looking from the room and then back to me.

"Well, you did say wine, dine, and what was that last part again?"

I plaster a smile on my face as his inky buddies put plates of food in front of us, along with a wine I had been saving, and two glasses. I steal the wine, pouring my own and offering it back with a forced smile. I don't even want to know what they prepared, given they keep leaking all over. I place the folded paper on the table, sliding it towards him. His eyes dart from it, to me, and back again.

"What's this?" he asks, meeting my gaze.

I clear my throat, leaning forward on the table. "I have a few rules, too. If you really want this whole Queen of Hell thing to work."

Scoffing, he shakes his head. "Rules?"

"Just read them over."

I can tell he is mulling over the options, and given as he has already won, I am hoping he will take the bait. His eyes bore into mine for a solid minute before he shrugs and lifts the paper. He looks to be scanning it, but I want him to read it out loud. I need to make sure it works.

Clearing my throat, I get his attention. "Speak up, please. I can't hear you, dear."

He arches a brow at me and I ask, "You sure you want to be attached to me for eternity?"

"Very well." He focuses on the page, drawing it closer as he reads, "I, Atë, promise to be your devoted consort for eternity to come, only if you agree to the following demands." He stops for a moment, looking at me before proceeding, "One: Promise to not hurt my family when we leave this plane." He nods, agreeing to that one. "Two: If you take me to a Hell dimension that smells of pig shit, this deal is off. Been there, done that." His lips quirk. "Three: I request to come back every few hundred years to check up on the latest fashion trends. Four: I would like my own personal castle on the days you annoy me and I want peace." He scoffs. "Five: I think minions who only answer to my beck and call would be a great idea and Six…"

His voice changes as he reads the same language I had hours earlier. I had written the page used to summon him, hoping that Hekate was right and that it would send him back. My hopes die in my chest after he finishes reading it, and his eyes meet mine. A red ring appears around his irises as he finishes the last words, the recognition clicking.

"You bitch!" he roars as horns spring from his head. But it is too late.

The page he holds goes up in flames and his hands and arms follow. He stands from the table, almost knocking it over as the fire spreads. I sit where I am, unbothered as a slow sadistic smile lights my face. The inky black creatures he came with echo his hollow scream. He moves from side to side, trying to extinguish the flames as he curses me in every language.

I take a sip of the wine and sit back, watching the light show. "Oh, you probably should've remembered in your little history lesson about me. I am the Goddess of Mischief, too."

I smile behind my glass as he stops, still engulfed in flames, and lets out a roar of rage. The floor erupts and sucks in him and his minions. The portal closes, and the room goes dead silent. I sigh, leaning back in my chair as I finally relax, my nerves not on edge for the first time in the last eight hours. I need to thank Hekate.

My peace is interrupted when my newly repaired-by-a-demon door bursts open, sending shards flying everywhere.

"What the fuck!" I yell, turning to see Erebus.

The Primordial God of Darkness stands in my ruined front door with Ebhot hiding behind his feet. We coordinated our clothing for Clio's event, and he is wearing an all-black suit. He looks like he is ready to rip the heads off of anything moving, which always makes him a little bit hotter in my eyes.

"Ebhot said you were in trouble," he snaps before looking at me, then the room and back at the imp. "I can see he was wrong."

"Yeah, I took care of that a few minutes ago."

He comes to my side, grabbing my arms and looking me over. He is the only living creature I will let touch me and not immediately try to rip to pieces. He runs his hands over me, making sure I'm not broken, but I feel like it is more to make me laugh. And I do, playfully swatting his hands away.

"Okay, okay, I'm fine." I smile, brushing a piece of hair from my face.

He leans down to kiss me before pulling back and making a face. "What have you been eating?"

My eyes widen for a split second before I change the subject. "Uhhhhhh, we should head out to Clio's event. Don't want to be late."

He gives me an odd look but shrugs, turning and grabbing the cursed book from the counter. "Hey, we can't leave your book."

"Burn it!" I yell at him as I all but scurry to the door. Ebhot squawks as he flies out first, I grab my small clutch purse and follow.

DIMINISHING RETURNS

BY

MICHAEL Z. RYAN

ZEUS,

KING OF THE GODS

I t was always a cool 67 degrees in the office. Even in winter, it was the same temperature. Zeus promised torture, the likes of which even Sisyphus and Prometheus had never known, to anyone who approached the thermostat.

Today was different. It felt like the inside of Hephaestus's forge.

The American stock market was tanking. Down 800 points, it looked to erase an entire year's worth of gains in a single afternoon. The President, a fool so adept at losing money that he bankrupted a casino, addressed global climate change concerns by offering to purchase Greenland. How buying a landmass of melting ice, just to have it eventually flood Florida solved rising tides, was an issue for another day. Zeus was angry, and not in his usual way. This was anger not seen by Olympus since the betrayal of Constantine. Zeus had seen many administrations rise and fall over the millennia, but this American administration angered him in a way only equaled by the Romans.

"If I could smite him, I would have done it before he started a trade war with Asia," Zeus screamed at the speakerphone on his desk. A mood bordering on palpable hate filled the office. "Your Excellency," replied the box, "Denmark doesn't take him seriously, and neither should we. The land grants we have secured by the Danish government are still valid." The disembodied voice was calm, measured, and in stark contrast to the God of Storms.

"You are lucky you're family, God of Commerce." Sarcasm was heavy on Zeus's lips. "What are our options? We have at least six temples in the planning stages on this Greenland deal. If this idiot American gets anyone to actually make a move, how do we beat them to it?"

"We have numerous ventures in place. Our fishing fleet and shipyards handle nearly two-thirds of the Greenland shrimping economy. The Danes may own the physical land, Father, but

Olympus owns their ability to generate revenue. Their economy lives and dies by our hand. We could threaten to license our fisheries and vessels to America to increase our leverage," the God of Commerce explained. "The American President, in all his folly, may have simply been speaking nonsense. Still, we have the Arctic under control." He paused momentarily. A hesitation picked up on immediately by Zeus, who moved to speak but was cut off. "Unless the Norse Administration intervenes."

"The Vikings!" Zeus erupted. His muscles tensed and coiled in such a way that he looked to snap himself in half. A ball of light emerged from his right hand and flew to the far wall of his office. It exploded upon impact, leaving a gaping hole.

"This is *not* their time! If the one-eyed bastard wants to play war, I will give him war," Zeus fumed. His skin turned a bright shade of red as anger boiled inside him. His blue eyes became even more electric, and sparks shot across his face.

"I'll see who we have in the trickster's office. Give me a few days," came the reply.

"You have the weekend, Hermes. I know how fast you can be. Monday morning. My office. Personally."

The simple *click* ending the call sounded like thunder. Not some far off rumble, but a tangible and visceral shaking inside the room. Zeus stood motionless for what felt like an eternity, until his daughter and personal assistant, Hebe, entered through the hole he had just created.

"Shall I contact the interior designers? You do so love open floor plans."

Zeus, seemingly despite himself, chuckled lightly and turned to greet her directly. "What do I have next?"

"I moved your nine o'clock to ten. You have a visitor."

Zeus, puzzled by the vague statement, looked behind Hebe into the lobby. A man stood silent, but in all manner, a king and a god in his own right.

"Perseus."

The office hung in silence for many moments. Zeus stood, in all regality and power, eye to eye with an equal. Perseus was a legend. A hero and a king. More importantly, a son of Zeus.

"Hello, Father," Perseus said finally. "It has been too long."

Zeus moved like a flash across the room and embraced his son with his massive frame. Perseus, to his credit, held fast, and warmly returned the gesture. A lesser man, a lesser god, would have collapsed.

"What brings you here, my boy? Is Andromeda with you? Is everything all right at home?" Zeus asked, with concern heavy on his lips.

Perseus smiled and held his hands out in an effort to calm his father. "The family is fine. I am here on business, and you will want to sit down."

Still standing next to the hole in the waiting room Zeus had just created, Hebe hopped into action. "I'll make your ten a.m. wait until after lunch. The floor will be empty. Good to see you, Brother," she said as she bowed, then exited.

Zeus held his expression. Not anxious, nor angry, only a hint of curiosity that registered in his sparkling blue eyes. He bid Perseus to sit at the conference table.

"The bullion storage facilities are being invaded," Perseus stated matter-of-factly. "My reserve forces have been overrun. Two full legions, gone. Security has collapsed, and our engagement zone continues to get pushed back by a kilometer or so every day." He paused, unblinking and determined.

Zeus sat firm, unmoving. "Trojans? Russians? For the love of Olympus, is it the gods damned Vikings?" he said, growing only slightly agitated at the mention of his northern rivals.

"My intelligence assets have confirmed the invaders as nightgoyles."

Zeus said nothing. Not a hint of movement or a twitch of a muscle. Perseus continued, "Why they are attacking those facilities is unknown. It is not out of character for those creatures to want wealth and financial gains, but never on this level. They usually attack for trinkets and petty materials. That is why we believe this to be a targeted, planned event."

"Nightgoyles? Dammit. They made an appearance here not too long ago. During my discussion with Moxie about…" Zeus paused, seeing that he had lost Perseus in his explanation. "Other business meetings. Anyhow, a whole damned flock flew over the city a few weeks back. Still looking for an answer on who, or what, may have let them out. Hades would never be so stupid. He knows those things are like vermin up here. We have various other hostile elements who could have opened a door on their rookery."

"We haven't been able to get a view inside the facilities as of yet. We've been focused on containment. Is there anyone who would have an immediate motive to attack a hard target like this?" Perseus asked.

More silence from Zeus. A tangible air of tension and a slight crackling of sparks trickled from the eyes of the King of Olympus. He finally spoke, "It does not matter who right now. That will be discovered upon your return. You will have the full resources of Olympus behind you. Hebe!" Zeus called, "I need transport to Mycenae set up ASAP. Use the helipad on the roof, please."

Hebe appeared from behind the hole in the wall at a start. "Yes, Father. Shall I contact Ares or Athena?"

"No," Zeus replied sharply, catching both Hebe and Perseus off guard. "Get the Wards, have them gathered on the helipad in an hour."

"All of them?" Hebe asked.

"Yes, with all speed."

"Nike is not available. I believe she is off campus with Nyx and Eros. Should I place a call?"

"Unnecessary. The others will do."

Hebe spun away and disappeared behind the wall. Perseus stood and made for the door, Zeus held up a hand, causing him to pause.

"Who else do we have in the field? Anyone who could scramble on short notice?"

Perseus considered for a long moment. "The only agent in the region would be Ajax."

Zeus' eyes opened wide at the name. "Ah, great-grandson. A perfect defender. Go with speed to contact Ajax and await my arrival on the helipad. Hebe, cancel all meetings today and tomorrow. Reschedule the face to face with the Prime Minister of Denmark. Tell him I'll cut a check for Greenland if he waits a week. Jackass loves our wineries anyway," Zeus called to his assistant.

"You're coming personally? I appreciate the resources, Father. You needn't waste time and energy on a minor incursion yourself."

Zeus smiled. "For one thing, dealing with real estate in Greenland is tedious, and the dumb shit the idiot American President vomits out bores me. Second, when's the last time we fought side by side? Gibraltar? Rome? The good old days, my boy. Makes me feel young again." Zeus closed his laptop and clapped the lights off in the room before heading towards the door. "Third," he said with all seriousness and purpose, "no one fucks with my money."

The Wards, as Zeus called them, were not his children. Many, though Zeus had. These three, of the total four, were his foster children from the days of the Titanomachy. The Winged Victory

389

was Nike. Mortals were enamored with her, but she was absent this day. Standing before Zeus and Perseus on the helipad were Kratos, God of Strength, Zelus, the God of Zeal, and the silent Bia, Goddess of Force. These three were powerful, and always at the side of Zeus. By promise and oath, Zeus favored these young deities and wished them higher station upon Olympus.

"Good," Zeus said. "We mustn't delay any longer. Perseus, you remember my wards?" Perseus clasped the forearm of each in succession as a show of respect.

"Memories flood the mind of victories shared by all. Good to see you again," Perseus said as he entered the waiting helicopter.

Zeus stood in front of his gathered children, silently taking a moment. Power, strength, and righteousness permeated the group. Finally, a smile from the King of Skies broke the quiet. The three entered the helo and strapped themselves in, and Zeus motioned to the pilot to take off.

They flew south, to the Kingdom of Mycenae, the ancient domain of Tiryns and the site of the Labours of Hercules. These places of great historical significance had stayed active in the years of the Olympians' absence. The mines in the region boasted riches upon which the Olympus Administration was built. Modern gold bullion depositories occupied the landscape. They were bolstered by the still lucrative tourism and vacation industries that had supported the OA since the economy of Rome evaporated.

"Why do they attack my money?" Zeus bellowed, with no need for a microphone to communicate.

Perseus, unable to match the power and volume of the King of Storms, used the available headset. "We don't know. They appeared a week ago, and it felt like nothing more than a random skirmish. We know nightgoyles steal and covet minor baubles and trinkets. But when enough of them invaded a major installation and wiped out two full legions, we had reason to believe a bigger player was behind this."

For the first time, another spoke. "Who, or what, can bend a swarm of nightgoyles to their will?" Zelus asked.

The question hung in the air, unanswered. Perseus provided more in the way of intelligence.

"That's what I had hoped to discover with your deployed resources, Father. The last word from those inside the facility claimed to hear music. Sounds over the comms were not clear, but the legionnaires said they heard a lament in an old tongue. Nothing our mortal soldiers could identify."

The pilot interrupted their discussion to provide a status update. They would arrive in less than ten minutes, but the skies were darkening. It was barely midday, yet the horizon was so dark even Nyx would feel at home.

As if in response to the scene, the helo began to rock violently back and forth. "Lord Zeus, swarm inbound, intercept course, two o'clock," the pilot explained.

Zeus made a fist with his right hand, electricity charging and sparkling into a ball of powerful energy. Zelus casually touched his foster father's arm to stop him. "Let us, milord," Zelus said. Zeus immediately dissolved the lightning and nodded to the three young gods.

Each gestured a sign of excitement toward Zeus as they leaped headlong into the swarm of nightgoyles. They flew like angels of destruction amongst the creatures. Zelus cried out an oath to Zeus for strength as he tore the wings from the nearest gray skinned nightmare. Its body fell lifeless to the earth as he moved to the next.

Kratos swung his fists wildly. Red and orange auras surrounded him in his vicious attacks, and a nightgoyle is dispatched and dead with each rage fueled strike.

Bia floated into the middle of the swarm, eyes closed as if she were the most at peace she had ever been. In a flash, she awoke, a visible globe of force extended out from her body. A wave of devastation tore through the remaining handful of nightgoyles. Their bodies shuddered and contorted as her power hit them. Like leaves on an autumn breeze, they gently fell out of the sky.

"A tempest against wayward ships," Zeus said, clearly proud of the fashion in which his foster children performed.

Perseus was on comms with someone on the ground. "Excellent, let him get a foothold at the gates, and we will meet him there." He turned to Zeus. "Ajax brought Myrmidons. Fifty. Well seasoned and ready to engage at the main vault."

Zeus only nodded lightly in acknowledgment, eyes still fixed on the display of his wards. The helicopter slowly made its descent towards the waiting Trojan War hero, Ajax.

As Zeus calmly exited the craft, Perseus was off in a flurry of reports and requests from his soldiers. Zeus had been too long away from the fields of battle. Men were carved into legend here, and the King of Storms looked to recognize any soldier worthy of attention. Above him, the skies cleared of the winged beasts who had insulted Zeus so by attempting to steal his amassed wealth. One by one, the Wards landed on the fields ahead of him, their power evident in the ripples of electricity that radiated around him. "Worthy of legend, indeed," Zeus said softly.

"Father, the swarms have moved. They have consolidated over the main vault," Perseus yelled. "We may yet take control this day."

Perseus rallied with Ajax and his Myrmidons. Lines formed and weapons drawn. The hulking beast of a man walked directly to the Lord of Olympus. "Great-grandfather, it has been too long," he said, clasping the forearms of his patriarch. "Would that we could drink to adventures long complete, but I fear we still have ground to claim. What say you, King? Dare we attack the front or solidify our defense?"

A glimmer of light emerged from the vault. The front door was wide open. Its many-inches-thick doors collapsed and distorted off to each side. A man stood at the entrance, not the hunched over and winged figure of a nightgoyle. No, this was the leader and the power behind the hordes.

"Ajax and Perseus, take the fight to the nightgoyles on the outside. I want this area clear and ready to retrieve the dead or wounded. Wards, to me. We take our assault to the doorstep of the thief." Zelus, Kratos, and Bia formed a V-shaped wedge in front of their King. They all walked slowly but deliberately towards the entrance to the main vault. "No one fucks with my money."

Zeus stood behind his adopted children. There was no fear, no hesitation. Just power. The nightgoyles at the fringes of the fighting continued to scatter. Ajax swung his mighty war hammer and crushed the horrid beasts. Perseus displayed an expertise with his swords that could only be described as epic. All the kin of Zeus were warriors.

They were all legend.

Until they weren't…

The Wards charged forward in a blur. Zelus to the right, Kratos left, Bia center. The target, the man in the doorway, stood unmoved. In unison, they struck first. Red-orange streaks flashed from Kratos' fists, directed at the man. Zelus cried for strength and slammed down into the doorway. Bia, the irresistible force, rushed and exploded her wall of power at the threat.

They failed.

In succession, the young gods were hurled backward and away from the door. They flew, lifeless, and landed directly at the feet of a stunned Zeus. A purple haze of magic encapsulated each of them. They seemed paralyzed and caught inside a blanket of energy. Their eyes were open and frantically looking to their father for help. They were afraid, and they were in pain, but made no sounds at all. They just writhed in silent agony.

"Mother Gaia, what is this?" Zeus asked the universe.

A song floated on the air, breaking the silence. The words were old, very old. Zeus knew the language but hadn't spoken it in at least 3,000 years.

"No," Zeus whispered. Shock and surprise claiming his thoughts.

The man slowly walked forward. No rush, no urgency. Draped in a dark violet orb of magical energy, this mysterious sorcerer became clear. Still, the song grew louder. It was a lament, exactly as Perseus reported it. A song of loss. Of pain. Of anguish. The ancient words hit Zeus with a power he couldn't identify. His mind lost its grip on the present as he was forced into a flashback. Louder and louder, it grew in his mind. He had heard this song before.

"Orpheus," Zeus unconsciously blurted out loud. "How?"

The mind of the King of Storms raced. He was losing strength. His knees buckled, and his stomach churned to the point Zeus could no longer keep his legs under him. He fell to one knee, nearly collapsing completely.

"How are you even alive?" Zeus asked.

The man, Orpheus, drew closer. He was a poet of old, even a hero of legend, having traveled as an Argonaut. This figure of antiquity came upon Zeus and spoke to him, this time in the common tongue.

"Good to see you too, *King*," he said, heavy sarcasm on the mention of the title. "Been some time. Apparently, this is the only way I could get your attention."

Orpheus stalked around the still-kneeling Zeus.

"I once tried to appeal to your compassion, to your kindness. You refused me." Orpheus stood behind him, as a slight purple haze crawled across Zeus' body. The sorcerer put a hand to the wilting shoulder of the Lord of Olympus. "If only I knew to just take from you the thing you love the most."

Orpheus struck Zeus in the back of the head, causing him to fall flat on his face on the dusty ground.

"Three thousand years is a long time to regret something. Or do you *have* regrets? Given your notable tales, probably not." Orpheus continued to slowly and methodically circle Zeus, who was now fully covered in a web of dancing purple energy. It jumped and snapped into a cocoon that trapped the Lord of Skies.

"I hope you understand the lengths I've gone to for you to be here. Nightgoyles are an absolute pain in the ass to negotiate with. They really are just stupid creatures. They lack nuance and subtlety." Orpheus paused, crouching down to look at the prone Zeus and whispered, "I think a bunch of them shit in your vault. Accessible bathrooms, boss. Think about them." The poet stood up, turned his back, and walked toward the depository. His song began again.

"Eurydice would never have wanted this," Zeus struggled to cough out the words.

Orpheus immediately stopped and spun back to Zeus.

"Do not presume to speak to me about my wife!" he screamed. A ball of violent flame grew from the right hand of the sorcerer. He lifted it high, ready to cast its power down upon the vulnerable Zeus. "You lied to me, you coward!!" Orpheus threw his arm down to release his assault, but was tackled to the ground mid-swing.

"Father, get up!" Perseus bellowed. The two struggled on the ground, fists reaching the face of the caught-off-guard poet. Blow after blow connected, leaving Orpheus reeling and distracted. The assault allowed the Wards and Zeus the opportunity to break free. They moved to rise and orient themselves. Perseus kept up the furious attack against Orpheus, keeping him occupied long enough for Bia and Kratos to join the fray. Zelus took to his father.

"Lord Zeus, are you alright?"

Seeing the leader of their horde in distress, the last remaining nightgoyles descended upon Perseus, Bia, and Kratos. Claws and teeth gnashed and scraped the Olympians. The melee became a dust storm of punches, kicks, and furious shots, making it difficult to see who was winning.

"I'm fine, boy. Where is my phone?" Zeus asked.

"What? Your phone? I don't know. Is that important right now, Father?" Zelus replied, incredulous.

Zeus stood patting his pockets, looking like an old man searching for his lost reading glasses. "Yes, yes, it is...AHA! Here, I found it. Go be with your siblings. I need but a few moments."

Zelus, confused but never able to refuse his father, turned and ran back to the brawl. Zeus took a moment to catch his breath. He opened his Razr flip phone, found the one contact he needed, and dialed.

"Voicemail. Motherfu..." The line opened, and Zeus began immediately, "It's your father. If you want it, it's yours, but I need you *now*. I'm texting you the coordinates. Get here."

Zeus hung up, texted his message and put the phone away. He focused on the battle. The tide was shifting, and his children were losing. The nightgoyles had given Orpheus the time he needed to regain composure. On the air, the song began again. Zeus felt the melody grasping for his mind, and he steeled himself and focused on resisting its beauty. Zeus extended his right arm wide, and a five-foot-long bolt of light appeared in his hand. Tightly he grasped it, aimed directly at Orpheus, and let it loose.

The bolt collided home in the wall of nightgoyles, protecting their benefactor. They burned to ash without a sound. A cloud of dust and debris hung in the air. The smell of flesh and burnt stone violated the olfactory senses of the Lord of Lightning.

Zeus readied another bolt.

When the scene settled, all the nightgoyles were either dead or soot under the boots of Zeus' children. Perseus stood off to the Zeus' right, while the Wards once again made a wedge formation in front of their father.

"You are beaten, Orpheus. Your hordes are gone, you are outnumbered, lay down your arms." Perseus commanded the sorcerer who was now kneeling, his face to the ground.

"Beaten? You morons, I'm just getting warmed up." Orpheus snapped his head up, eyes now a deep and electric violet. He threw out his right arm and let loose a stream of power at the Wards. Caught by an immeasurably fast rope of purple energy, they could not move fast enough to escape the now tightening noose. Their bodies convulsed as they were electrocuted and thrown casually aside. Zeus acted too late and threw his bolt. Orpheus called up a shield of energy that surrounded and protected him. The force of the bolt was simply absorbed, and it vanished.

Zeus stood dumbfounded, unable to move. Perseus was under no such spell and charged towards Orpheus. The sorcerer looked the King of Storms directly in the eye, winked, and turned towards the onrushing king. What sounded like a gun echoed throughout the valley, yet it wasn't any mortal weapon. It was the bolt of lightning Zeus had thrown. Its energy was redirected somehow, and it struck Perseus, favored son of Zeus, square in the chest. The resulting discharge launched him over a hundred feet away.

Silence hung over the battlefield like a tangible cloud. All life had been drained from the area, and Zeus was lost in a daze. He just saw his son be hurled away by a bolt of power that wasn't meant for him. How was this happening? This was not the same Orpheus who came to him 3,000 years ago, was it? He was but a bard, a storyteller. Rumors of his demise were widely reported, but Zeus hadn't needed to look for a body. He didn't care. It was below him to be concerned about trivial things like that. *Where did you get this power?* Zeus

397

thought. The one question allowed to sneak through his speeding mind.

"How many more of your bastards do I need to kill before you give me what you promised?" The question cut into Zeus' mind, crashing him back to reality. "The young ones count, don't they? Or since they aren't yours, do you even care?" Orpheus was taunting Zeus now, baiting him for something.

"Eurydice was not mine to return to you. The Underworld is not my domain," Zeus replied.

The sorcerer did not take the statement lightly. A sudden and heavy bolt of purple energy cracked into Zeus' shoulder. Fast. Incredibly fast. A match for Hermes, even. Zeus fell back a step and cried out in pain. Pain? He was hurt. Taking a quick look at his shoulder, Zeus saw something that he had thought never to see again. He was bleeding.

"Oh, I'm so sorry. My bad. Well, I guess this was all just a misunderstanding. I'm so embarrassed." Orpheus feigned shock and held his hands to his cheeks to mimic concern. "I've only been planning this for three millennia, you stupid prick. Hades will get his, but this is your call, big boy. You had the power then, you have the power now, and you promised me. I want her back."

Orpheus stood in front of Zeus now. No fear. No pleading. This was a demand. This was a collection of payment. The King of Storms was used to being the aggressor in situations like this. In fact, it was Zeus and his rigid policies on hospitality that made the demand he was being given now so alarming. Orpheus was right. Ignoring the pain in his shoulder as much as he could, he squared himself to meet the partner in this duel.

"I am sorry, Orpheus. I promised you something I could never give you," Zeus said.

This caught the poet off guard. Apparently, honesty was not an anticipated response. Orpheus shuffled slightly on his feet, a sign of insecurity.

"No. I sang for you. You said that you were moved. You allowed her to follow me from Tartarus. Why did you take her back when we made it out?" Orpheus asked. A tinge of emotion building in the question.

Zeus forced himself to ignore the fire in his shoulder and looked his foe directly in the eye.

"I lied to you. It was a trick," Zeus began, unsure why he thought he could just talk his way out of what was to come. "Eurydice was never behind you. It wasn't real. I wanted to teach you a lesson. We couldn't, I mean, I couldn't let someone beg me to get a soul back when it's gone. I'd have mortals lined up from here to Troy trying to cheat the ferryman."

Zeus felt a buzzing in his pocket, took his eyes away from Orpheus for just a moment. Instant regret washed over the King of Storms. Orpheus darted forward with speed Zeus could barely comprehend. A feeble attempt to block the sorcerer failed as the pair tumbled to the ground. Orpheus now had what looked like a magical knife of energy in his hand. He stabbed again and again. Cuts and lacerations appeared over Zeus' arms, blood coloring the ground beneath them.

"Why? Why? Why?" The repeated word from Orpheus came at the end of every strike. "Why?" There would never be a good enough answer to that question, but he kept asking it as the tip of the knife dug into flesh. Zeus finally caught the wrist of the man on top of him and grabbed tight. With the mighty strength of Olympus, he twisted it backwards until the knife vanished. They fought for control, and Zeus was gaining the advantage. Orpheus was crying the word over and over again, even in the fight for his life. "Why? Why?" Zeus finally got into position behind the now sobbing poet.

He clutched him in a bear hug, hands clamped on Orpheus' wrists, pulling them across his chest.

"I am sorry. Orpheus, listen to me. Listen." The man struggled against Zeus in a way that no one had in thousands of years.

"I can take you to her. Orpheus. I can. I can let you talk to Eurydice again," Zeus said loudly, hoping to pierce the grieving man's emotional wall. "I can take you to Eurydice." Orpheus stopped struggling. He sank into Zeus' arms, and both collapsed onto the ground, still tangled together. Zeus chanced a glance around him. The scene filled with legionnaires securing the perimeter, and Ajax, his great-grandson. They all stood a generous distance away, but weapons ready. Zeus took a moment to breathe and calm himself, figuring out what to do with the now silent poet still locked in his arms.

Zeus never loosened his grip as he used his considerable power to lift Orpheus from the ground. He made eye contact with Ajax, who recognized that as permission to move. Legionnaires and Myrmidons alike came forward in a rush to secure the quarry. Zeus heard rumbling, like horses charging, or the rapid succession of explosive charges being set off. He let go of Orpheus and turned to watch his depository blow up in front of him. Gold, coin, the backbone of the Olympus Administration economy, was housed in that facility. And it was being ripped apart from the inside. Immediately realizing his mistake, he looked back at the silent sorcerer. He held out a hand with a remote detonator, red light flashing to show it had been activated.

"Fuck you, old man." Orpheus created a large dagger of purple electricity and lunged at the Lord of Olympus, gutting him completely. The magical blade plunged so deep into Zeus' stomach that the tip nearly poked out his back. Orpheus quickly restored his orb of shielding, this time including Zeus inside the sphere. The soldiers caught in the field as it extended were shredded by the force of the energy. Body parts flew about the field as cries of agony and alarm filled the air. Orpheus closed his eyes, savoring the chaos he had created.

"You almost had me, you clever sonofabitch," he said. "You should get credit for being the salesman that you are. But you blew it. You said you could *take me to her*. That's where you went wrong, because I want her *here*. With me. On *this* plane. You take me to her...that means I'm dead. And that, you slippery prick, simply will not do."

Zeus crumpled into a ball. On his knees, he held his stomach from falling out of his body. The amount of blood soaking his clothes and pooling on the ground was astonishing. He had only ever been this wounded once in his life, and it took a monster of legend and myth to carve him into pieces. That had been the work of Typhon, for crimes against Gaia and how he had failed as a ruler. This...this was different. This was a man who wanted his wife back and somehow came into a power that could leave Zeus at the brink of death. Death? Was that even possible? He'd been alive somewhere in the neighborhood of 55,000 years, and the thought of actually dying had never been as close as it was right now. A darkness bordered his vision. Slowly, it tunneled. An end was near. He could feel his breathing slow. His heart pumped, but most of the blood it pushed was exiting through the gaping wound he couldn't keep closed.

"Now, before I get caught monologuing here, I should really mention that this is just step one," Orpheus said. "I wanted to take you out first, because it's personal. That wasn't...entirely the plan. Hey, we make adjustments on the fly sometimes, right? Anyway, before you bleed out and finally take the fucking dirt nap you're overdue for, let me tell you one thing...your dad says hi."

Zeus looked up into the eyes of his tormentor. Vision cloudy and fading, he caught a glimpse of a shadow behind Orpheus, gliding down towards the barrier. Zeus gathered the last vestiges of energy he had and created a bolt, tossing it straight up. Startled, Orpheus cried out. Just as it had before, the lightning bolt crashed into the shield, dissolved, and redirected back to Orpheus.

"You know, Jesus Christ said you were an idiot," Orpheus said as the energy collected back into the poet. He took his right hand and made a finger gun right at Zeus' forehead.

"Bang." The word didn't come from Orpheus. The poet was too busy staring at the gauntleted arm that was protruding from his chest. Blood dripped from a hand that did not belong to him.

"Tell your wife I said *heeeey*." The voice was female, and belonged to the owner of the arm that was removing itself from the chest of the now dead Orpheus, sorcerer, poet, Argonaut, husband.

The body fell to the ground in a heap, purple energy faded and gone. The only thing left was the figure of a battle-armored woman, cleaning the blood and entrails from the gauntlet on her right hand. She was a daughter of Zeus, and a God of War. Enyo.

"Hi, Daddy. You get my text?" she said as Zeus lost consciousness and fell over.

The world went dark.

It was still dark, but he felt the cold slab of concrete on his back. His muscles strained, but they moved with a bit of encouragement. How? It must have been no more than a minute ago he was holding his innards in his hands, trying not to bleed out on the fields of Mycenae. Quickly he patted his stomach. All was intact. He shot to his feet with a speed and agility he thought he shouldn't have.

"What in the hells is going on?" he said to no one. His eyes scanned his immediate surroundings, only to find a gray scene before him. Concrete slab, walls, a ceiling, again, concrete. He was in a structure that he wasn't in moments ago. He rubbed his eyes, thinking they betrayed him somehow. "Nope," he said.

There was a doorway, but no door. He stepped through and found himself in what his mind would have called *outside*, but this exterior area had no color. No sun. Just gray. Everywhere. The street he stood on could have been from any old archaeological dig. The buildings were their base forms, but no decoration. No paint. Nothing. He followed the alley to his left, only to see more of the same. There were no indications of life. No plants, animals, or other people he could talk to. It was all empty, perhaps abandoned, unused for a very long time. What struck Zeus was the lack of any kind of color. Sure, there was shadow, but that only made the gray seem black. It was as if he found himself inside a black and white television from the golden days of mortal entertainment.

Around a corner, he saw the makings of a street. There was a sidewalk, unoccupied shops, and what looked like a sandwich stand. They were all signs of normal mortal civilization, except there were no mortals. He stopped when he came to the first intersection.

"Ah shit," he said, defeated. Ahead of him, he saw a large domed building. It was a grandiose facility, even by the standards of Zeus. It had to be twenty, thirty stories tall, and all around it were windows that reflected no light. Because there wasn't any.

This was a station, the greatest one in the known cosmos. Above it in all directions were elevated lanes of traffic. These were not roads for vehicles, but transit lanes for another type of transport. Zeus was familiar with the stories. He was a voracious reader of ancient texts, and to be honest, the gossip columns of modern tabloids. The King of the Gods was painfully aware of *where* he was, even if the *how* was not quite making sense. This was the Ethereal Realm. The Grand Central Station for all recently departed, lost, and wayward souls traveling to wherever their AfterWorld was.

"You've gotta be shitting me. How did I get to the Ethereal plane?" he said aloud, again to no one. The only option left was to walk towards the building. Zeus knew his answers were inside. So, he did what any good tourist would do and went to the ticket booth. When he approached, the booth seemed empty. When he was ten feet from the window, a form appeared out of what looked like smoke. An attendant sat behind the glass, looking all manner of professional, if a bit lifeless. He greeted Zeus in a flat monotone that somehow matched the drab, gray realm.

"Tickets to the AfterWorld. Please present your soul for routing. No exchanges. No transfers. No refunds."

"Uh..." Zeus stammered. "See, here's the thing. I don't have..." He was interrupted by the monotoned booth agent.

"Vessels without proper authorization must speak to the Lucifer. Please use the door to the right." With that, the agent vanished. A simple puff of smoke and the booth was empty again. Zeus stood motionless for a time until he heard a large metal door open in front of him. The sound of old rusted metal grinding on hinges echoed in the vast, empty courtyard in front of the Ethereal Station. Zeus entered slowly, not at all certain of what he was walking into.

"Welcome to The Ethereal Station, Gateway to the AfterWorld. Passengers, please keep your immortal soul on your person at all times. Enjoy your journey. Mind the gap."

Inside the station, Zeus' senses were completely bombarded. While the outside was devoid of all color, inside was a total shift in palette. The interior of the station was a powerful sapphire. It was as if a mountain of the azure stone was carved into the representation of a major transit hub. Zeus could find no light source, but the sparkle and shine assaulted his visual senses. He looked down at his own body, shocked to see he had turned blue himself. A sort of translucent, crystalline hue that he could almost see through.

"What in the bleeding eye of Odin is going on!" Zeus roared, causing a group of wandering souls to turn slightly to regard him, only to turn back quickly, focusing on their wait for some sort of transport to wherever it was they were going. Zeus hardly cared.

Seeing no one make any moves to assist him, or even acknowledge him, he stormed toward what appeared to be an eatery. He looked at the small arrangement of tables and chairs, seeking someone in charge.

"Who is the authority here?" Zeus called to anyone who would listen. "Where is Lucifer? Someone find me Morningstar," he said, voice heavy with impatience.

The patrons, such as they were, looked up at Zeus, stared for a few seconds, and looked away almost in unison. "Someone answer me! Have you all had your tongues cut out?" he yelled, anger simmering and burning brighter in his gut. There was a commotion behind the tables, and what appeared to be a kitchen door swung open. A tall woman strode into the room. Her black hair was up in a bun and her skin solid blue, but not the translucent color Zeus currently wore. She had four very muscled arms and approached Zeus with a very unhappy look on her face.

"Listen, big boy. You're upsetting my customers. I can't have that. So, is there some way I can help you, or do I need to punch you in your mouth, so you shut up?" The woman crossed all four arms across her chest.

"Big boy?" Zeus shuffled his stance, caught off guard by the act of intimidation. "Do you know who I am?" Zeus said, throwing his right arm out wide, fingers spread, ready to call a lightning bolt to his hand.

Nothing.

Zeus turned and looked at his hand, betrayal in his eyes as his most famous method of retribution failed to materialize at his call. The woman who insulted Zeus stood with a slight smirk on her face.

"Performance issues?" she said. "Or are you always show with no go?" This statement garnered some light laughter from the patrons of the eatery. "You want to actually do something, or just yell like an idiot and disrupt my customers?"

Zeus stood dumbfounded, still looking at his empty hand. "I...don't know why the bolt didn't work. That always works," he said.

"We don't allow weapons here," the woman said. "We are beyond those concerns in this place. Best you can do is throw a punch, which I am still willing to do. Or is there something you want?"

Zeus did not make eye contact, still looking at his hand. "I need Lucifer. Where is he?"

"Oh honey, that ain't how it works. You're gonna need to make an appointment, and the office don't open until sunrise," the woman said, taking a file to the nails on one of her right hands. "You can either wait here, in the Ether Pit, or find a room at the hotel. Your choice, big boy."

Zeus was feeling defeated. He'd tried to throw his weight around, and it fell flat. He had no power to call his lightning bolt. "You have any whiskey?" he asked.

A smile worked its way onto the blue woman's face. "You got it, honey. Name's Kali. I'd be happy to serve you at the bar." She turned and pointed towards the back of the restaurant.

He walked to the bar, sat down, and watched Kali expertly pour a three-fingered whiskey. "Trying to get me to divulge my bank account numbers?" He grabbed the glass and examined it, realizing it had the same translucent blue coloring. "This should be enough to get even a god tipsy."

Kali snorted. "Typical upper crust. Coming in here thinking you're something big, special. A soul is just a soul, big boy. Everyone is equal here." She put the bottle back on the rack. "Besides, this will only get you tipsy if you want it to. If your soul isn't in it, it'll just be water. Did no one explain the rules to you, or are you one of those types that never thought you'd die?"

Zeus had the glass right to his lips when he heard the word *die*. "Wait, so am I actually dead? Like these people?" He nodded towards the patrons behind him. Kali looked at him without blinking.

"There are only three types of souls who end up at my bar. The departed, the transcendent, and the disconnected," Kali said. "It seems to me, with your piss poor attitude, that you're disconnected."

Zeus emptied the glass quickly, only to discover it tasted just like water. Exactly as Kali had said.

"Water?" she asked.

"Water."

"Well, the good news is I don't charge for water," Kali said, wiping a glass with her bottom arms.

"And the bad news?" Zeus asked, irritated.

"Bad news is that you need the Lucifer, and he's not in his office."

Zeus sat the glass down on the bar and pushed it away. He leaned back against the back of the barstool, taking in the information she had provided. "You mean to tell me that the Morningstar is the manager of the AfterWorld transit hub? Isn't that a bit out of character for someone who likes to torture souls? He runs a bus station?"

Kali laughed loudly in Zeus' face. She laughed so hard she had to use her top two arms to cover her mouth while resting her body against the bar with the bottom two. The patrons closest to the bar turned in their slight way, said nothing, and turned back to their business.

"You are so damned adorable." Kali stifled another laughing fit. "You're Greek, right? You're tall enough, the long beard and the whole...bolt thing sorta gave you away." She made a crude gesture with her top hands in the same way Zeus did when he tried to summon his bolt. "Wrong Lucifer, big boy. The guy you're talking about runs a bar somewhere on the Prime Material Plane."

Zeus looked confused. His mind was reeling at the simple mistake of language he just made. He let his face fall into his hands, letting out a loud groan of disappointment.

"You mean the literal Lucifer, the Dawn Bringer. Phosphorus." Zeus dragged his hands down his sapphire face. "He's going to be so pissed at me."

Kali's expression changed quickly. No longer did she laugh. Suddenly, she seemed very concerned. "I don't know what name you just called him by, but that's not what we call him here. You have history?"

"You could say that. I uh, well, I'm probably the reason he goes by Lucifer down here." Zeus slid off of the stool and stood. "I fired him and gave his job to someone else."

Zeus turned away from the bar and walked towards the hotel Kali mentioned before. She called after him as he exited the restaurant.

"His office is on the top floor. You can't get there until..." Zeus cut her off.

"Dawn," Zeus bellowed back. "I know."

The hotel that Zeus was directed to was really just a desk in the center of the station. A concierge, or what amounted to one, stood behind it with absolutely no life in his eyes. *At least this one isn't a puff of smoke,* he said to himself.

The discussion with Kali at the Ether Pit led the King of Storms to a conclusion he wasn't fond of. He knew who *The Lucifer* was, and he would've liked it better had it been the fallen prodigal son of Trinity Inc. At least Lucy was a better host. This Lucifer, the former Dawn Bringer of antiquity, was originally known as Hesperus Phosphorus.

Zeus had to make some tough personnel decisions many moons ago, shortly after the end of the Titanomachy. With the forced retirement of his uncle Helios, who ended up in the Tartarus

Correctional Facility with the rest of his kin, the job of bringing light to the mortals was open. Hesperus Phosphorus, the Dawn Bringer, was a natural fit and did the job with distinction for a number of years. However, in what would become a theme during the early years of the Olympus Administration, nepotism became policy, and Phosphorus was replaced by the favored son of Zeus, Apollo.

It didn't take a genius to recognize the pickle Zeus currently found himself in. He had no power here. The issue with calling the bolt to his aid proved that. And then there was the fact that sometime since Apollo had claimed the position that used to have been his, Phosphorus had adopted a name that was most often identified with an agent of a rival administration. It was clear to Zeus that Phosphorus was trying to appear to be something, or someone, of major importance.

"Greetings, traveler. What kind of accommodation do you need? We have all manner of luxuries for your soul. Can we have your name?" the lifeless attendant said, waking Zeus from his introspection.

"Zeus Jupiter Olympus," the King of the Gods said dryly, only half paying attention. There were so many things on his mind, so many thoughts scrambling to be the focus. *What did disconnected mean? How did a poet get power enough to nearly kill the Lord of Storms? Would he ever get home? What was happening in Olympus with him being dead, or only mostly dead?*

"*Sir!*" the attendant yelled, snapping Zeus out of his daze. "If you please, you are expected, Zeus Jupiter Olympus." The voice seemed to be a script, with his name being a line tacked on at the end. *Even in the AfterWorld, robots do the work,* Zeus thought to himself while trying not to make eye contact with the empty shell of a bellhop.

"Please see yourself to the nearest lift. Your room is on the 29th floor. Mind the gap," the attendant droned on, holding an arm out wide to indicate the direction Zeus needed to walk.

Expected? he thought. What the hells did that mean? Slowly, he headed towards the nearest lift, confused, weary, and defeated. He paused as he came to a platform that hovered just above the ground. It was an elevator without a tube, only the square base to stand on. No sides, no handholds, and exposed to the environment. As Zeus approached, the blue beam of light extending between two pillars on either side faded, opening the way for him. He stepped tentatively onto the raised floor and nearly fell as, a heartbeat after he set his feet in place, the lift took off. It was an incredibly odd sensation, objectively seeing the ground beneath him get farther and farther away, yet feeling no air or gravity against his form. He felt nothing at all. The only reason he knew he was moving was that he saw it with his eyes. Had they been closed, it wouldn't have registered. Zeus took a chance and looked up. The floors above were rapidly coming into focus, but the feeling in the pit of one's stomach, of weightlessness or movement, never happened.

"29th floor. Mind the gap," a disembodied voice chimed.

The moment he could, Zeus exited the lift. The sensation was disconcerting and foreign, and he didn't like it at all. On the interior balcony, he counted down the doors to find his room. He realized that he didn't have a key. It turned out it wasn't an issue when the door opened on its own as he got close.

"This is fucking creepy," Zeus blurted out, entering the room. Inside, he found absolutely nothing that indicated this was a hotel room. There was no bed, no bathroom, no closet. The creepiest bit was the lone office chair sitting in the middle of the room, an envelope perched on the seat. The rest was barren.

"Remind me never to die again," Zeus chided himself for being in this position. He closed the door and moved farther inside, picking

410

up the envelope from the chair. Zeus had an impressive number of epithets and titles. Some were self-given, others earned through various deeds, or more often misdeeds. The one word printed on the heavy paper was common in the mortal tongues of old, but among the many titles that Zeus had, this one was unique. This name was one of the few things he had left of *her*. It was the name his mother called him when he was hidden away on the island of Crete. *Basileus.*

Zeus turned and sat in the chair, examining the envelope. The seal was of an eagle, a majestic animal that he was fond of changing into from time to time. Heavy wax, strong vellum paper, it was an old envelope. It had to be. He hadn't seen his mother for so many years. *How long has it been?* Zeus felt an emotion he had thought lost to him for all time. Guilt. He and his mother had a complicated relationship, and history only told parts of the tale.

Zeus was the youngest of the six Olympians, the only child not to be swallowed by his father, Kronus. She hid Zeus on Crete, guarded by protectors, for nearly twenty years. Perhaps it was twenty, maybe more. The Olympians aged so differently than mortals. Time wasn't such a limited thing to them. The Titanomachy had strained everyone's relationships. Zeus became king, the Basileus, Sovereign of Olympus.

In his hands, he felt the envelope tremble and drop. He couldn't bring himself to read it. *What would it say? Where has she gone?* There were questions that even he, the King of the Gods, had no answers to. She had missed the lives of five of her children while they were trapped by Kronus, and immediately upon their release, a war broke out. Kronus eventually ended up in prison. Rhea had no husband, a tumultuous relationship with her children, if any relationship at all. So, she left. Now, in this place, Zeus realized he missed his mother in a way he could not reconcile alone in this empty room.

He knew he had to read it. There was nothing else but the letter. "This is some bullshit, Mom," he said, as he leaned over to pick the envelope up from the floor. He was scared. That was the tingle in his throat. Fear. Zeus had always been brave. He had fought beasts and monsters, even a rogue Olympian or twelve, but he had never been afraid before. The one thing he wanted in this universe, more than anything, was held back by something he was afraid to experience. Grief.

Zeus took the letter out of its envelope and unfolded it. The words on the page were carefully and expertly written. The language was old, ancient by mortal standards, and in a tongue Zeus hadn't spoken aloud in millennia. But he could still read it:

I know this is not the way it should go, but we never really had a chance to talk, did we? I suppose this is me not grasping the reality of our circumstance. I do not expect you to approve of my departure, but I do want you to understand why I felt it was the right thing to do. Kronus was the love of my life (I know that the stories may say something different, but this is why we replace Scribes from time to time, is it not? They cannot tell the story as it is, only how they think it should be.) I loved him, and for a time, he loved me. To my horror, that was not enough. When Gaia saw in him the same evil that infected his father, Uranus, she wanted to warn him. The prophecy was only for him to take caution of his father's sins, not to repeat them. When we had children, it was not the joyous and miraculous affair they all should be. No, it was a daily nightmare. Child by child, he took them, swallowed them away, and hid them from me. By the time I had the courage to fight back, he had already taken five of you. I have fought with myself, and even with the Fates, to understand why it took me so many years, and children, to take a stand. By the time I realized what I needed to do, I only had you left. I will always feel I failed them, leaving them to be alone with a father who thought they would be his ruin.

I have left word for each of them to find in time. I trust that they will know the truth, as well as I can tell it. For you, my youngest, I know the burden that was thrust upon you. I never wanted to have you grow up to fight against him and our kin. I feel that I am, in no small part, responsible for the war that tore us apart. That is not what a family does. A family should never be the source of pain and sadness. I could not bear that burden. It was all-consuming to be the catalyst for war. A family should be the greatest source of strength anyone has. If only they can see it. Our place in the sky is to be an example for the mortals to see and take into their hearts, yet I fear they only see war, anger, hate, selfishness, and vanity.

Forgive them, Zeus, forgive all of them. Our immortal lives are not worth living if they are only lived to punish and resent those who have wronged us. I see in you the greatest parts of what our kind can be. Use it to build a home for all of them. Your children, your kin, they are not your enemy. I wish I could be there to see you be the man, the king, that I know you are capable of being. It was my choice to leave, difficult as it was.

Be good for them, my little Basileus. They need to know that kindness is the way, not punishment. Be the strength and the power behind the light, not the focal point for the empty and evil.

I will always be your mother. Just look to the stars, and you will see me.

Zeus let the letter fall to the ground. He just sat there, staring blankly at the blank wall in front of him. *What the hells did I think this would be?* he thought, stirring in the chair, discomfort rapidly building in him. He shifted side to side in the seat multiple times. Finally, he jumped up and grabbed the back of the chair, and with all the strength he could muster in this "in-between" realm, he smashed it against the wall.

"I fucking died, Mom!" he screamed, remnants of the chair falling to his feet. "I died! And you're not here!" he cried out. His hands trembled as he ran them through his long, braided hair.

"I don't know what to do, and you're not here to tell me." He slumped onto the floor, bits and pieces of the broken chair bounced a bit when he landed.

"I lost," he began, "I fought, I lost, and I died." The release of anger quickly turned into something else. The rage that the King of Storms was known for evaporated, and now he was struggling to keep his emotions in check. His thoughts stuck in his mind, and his words caught in his throat. The warm sensation of liquid spread down his cheeks and into his beard. Zeus cried openly. He nervously kept running his hands through his hair, searching for something he could hold on to, needing a reason to remain angry.

"Dad was a fucking tyrant, and I beat him! I won!" he yelled loudly to the walls. "You should have stayed! You should have stayed and been with us! We needed you! I needed you!" Anger rose in him; the familiar tension in his shoulders, the racing heartbeat, tears flooding his vision. He launched himself into the air once more and began recklessly pounding against the wall.

"You should have stayed!" he cried out again, striking the wall with each word.

"Why didn't you stay!" His fist landed flush with the wall, and still, it gave no ground.

"I built an empire, and you were gone!" Another strike, the wall continued to hold. Punch after punch, strike after strike, the wall held. Zeus felt each blow land, his anger rising with each attempt, and yet the wall showed no signs of defect.

"I died, and you aren't here!" the King of the Gods screamed at the top of his lungs. He called upon all the strength inside him, using the pain in his words to punish the wall for not bowing to his violent command.

"I don't know what to do!" he cried to all the heavens. His words carried all the weight and power of a man who had lost all direction. With one final blow, one ultimate and vicious strike, he struck the

wall. A sudden and bright explosion of lightning shot from the fist of Zeus. The bolt had returned! The build-up of aggression and grief too much for this *in-between* realm to handle, and the entire room shattered. The walls exploded outward into the void, fragments and shards of the facsimile of a structure faded. A shield of electricity surrounded Zeus, the familiar embrace of the lightning that he was famous for.

He paid no attention. Zeus was on his knees, resting on whatever made up the floor of this now wide-open space.

Zeus wept for the first time in his life. An immortal sovereign, a powerful god, a king of the skies cried, for the first time in forty thousand years.

Years upon years of pent up sadness fell away. The epochs and centuries he had lived with this pent up inside of him, all released in a deluge of tears.

When his eyes could no longer cry, and when his lungs could no longer carry air, Zeus fell onto the floor and drifted into a deep and dark expanse of nothingness. The void carried him, such as it could carry anyone, safely held to its breast, and allowed him an earned level of peace.

The darkness was calm. There were no dreams, and there were no voices. It was a silence and a peace that Zeus had possibly never felt. He stirred, a return to consciousness. His eyes opened, and the colors of the sapphire and azure surroundings reminded him he was still in the Ethereal Realm.

"Oh, come the fuck on," he groaned and blinked his eyes open.

Zeus found himself inside the remains of what was, prior to his passing out, a hotel room. It was now a gaping wound. Blue and black shards, of whatever the Ethereal Realm used for building materials, laid around him in a massive sphere of destruction. A bomb had gone off. Zeus was that bomb. He rolled over onto his knees and lifted himself off the floor, his body slow to respond to commands.

I am so tired, he thought. A massive exhale brought him back to focus. There was someone standing in what was left of the doorway.

"You destroyed the whole floor. Do you have *any* idea how expensive etherstone is?" the man said while eating what looked like an apple. "At least I know you can afford it."

"Phosphorus. It's been a long time," Zeus said, not turning to look him in the eye.

"Shhh, shh. Dude, secret identity," the man said after one big bite of the apple. "Do you know how much work I've had to do to get people to call me Lucifer? You probably don't understand. Everyone trembles at *King of the Gods*." Phosphorus walked closer to Zeus. "I should be angry. I really should. Trouble is, you've got bigger problems at the moment."

Zeus raised an eyebrow, not sure what *Lucifer* was talking about. "Problems? Beyond being dead, what other problems could I possibly have?"

Phosphorus finished chewing and tossed the apple onto the pile of rubble at his feet. Just another piece of garbage on the heap.

"You're not dead, dumbass," Phosphorus said, earning himself a narrow-eyed glare from Zeus. "Whoa, whoa, don't take that face with me, you're not the boss up here. However, I will answer some questions for you. First, you're not dead. Pretty damn close, though. Orpheus? The poet?" he said with no small hint of mockery in his voice. "How the mighty have fallen."

Zeus felt his level of irritation rising and cocked his head to the side, waiting for Phosphorus to get to the point. Phosphorus held his hands up to placate Zeus.

"Second, you've become disconnected from your physical vessel. It happens on a rare occasion. Normally not to guys like you, but whatever Orpheus used to take you down, it's strong. Incredibly strong. Frankly, the only reason you're *not* dead is because you're you. Now you've become an untethered spirit, lost in my station."

Zeus couldn't hide his confusion as Phosphorus continued, "We need to get you reconnected. Find something that your soul can use as an anchor to your body. Sorta like a magnet. Something to pull you back to the Prime Material plane." Phosphorus opened his hands towards the results of the blast. "Part of that you've already done." Phosphorus took a breath, resigned to the damage in front of him. "You found the bolt, and it's part of you again. I would have wished for a less destructive discovery, but I digress. We need to get you in contact with the other side."

Zeus nodded, finally understanding what was necessary. "What are my other problems?"

Phosphorus turned his head and whistled. "Not that you pay attention or care, but time here doesn't really function like it does downstairs. Something like two or three weeks of regular time has passed. I'm sure Hades could tell you. Honestly, I'm surprised he hasn't called me looking for you, but again, I digress." Phosphorus shuffled uncomfortably then turned to look Zeus squarely in the eye.

"The Titans are loose."

The words triggered a visceral and immediate reaction in Zeus. His eyes flashed and sparked, causing Phosphorus to take a step back.

"Get me home, Lucifer," the King of the Gods growled.

Phosphorus bolted out of the blast zone, and Zeus kept pace. They traversed the internal walkways of the Ethereal Transit Station. What was initially a hotel now led down into a massive open space filled with souls waiting for the call to their final destinations. Zeus was passing through so many people, or former people, who just stood still. These unmoving, unemotional, seemingly lost figures of blue energy were the remnants of living, mortal people. Free-floating souls. Zeus had lived for thousands of years, had ruled over millions of mortals, yet not once had he ever seen where they went when they died.

"Is this what it's like all the time?" Zeus asked

Without stopping, paying no mind to the souls they passed by, Phosphorus spoke with the authority of a CEO that would rival Zeus doing business inside the God Complex.

"Business is booming. Numbers are up, and transits are pushing record highs. Not since the second mortal World War have we seen the like." They passed into a corridor beyond the central hub. "For some reason, the mortals keep killing themselves. Heard something about a virus worse than the flu. Hells, it could be climate change. Don't know, don't care. We transport all of them. I'm sure Hades and Thanatos do their fair share, but all of you down in Olympus forget you're not the only administration in the game."

In the shadowy blue corridors and depths of the station, in this transit hub to whatever eternal resting place the souls of the mortal realm went to, Zeus found himself presented with a plain and nondescript door.

"This is it, Zapados. The gateway to the material plane. Doesn't look like much, does it? On this end, we have to disguise it to look like a boring freight door. We can't have wandering souls thinking they can just cheat death." Phosphorus coughs. "You know, like you guys let happen in Tartarus." He moved forward to unlock the door, then turned to Zeus one last time.

"You can expect to have my repair bills sitting on your desk when you get back." The man called *Lucifer* by the transient souls of the Ethereal Realm stared Zeus squarely in the eyes, a deadly serious look on his face. "Word to the wise, if I ever see you here again, I own your soul." Phosphorus paused, letting the tension hang in the air. "Best you avoid guys like Orpheus, unless you want to spend eternity cleaning toilets in the Ether Pit."

Phosphorus slapped Zeus on the shoulder, then made his way down the hall, leaving Zeus standing alone. "Open your mind and phone home, big guy. I'm sure someone's around."

CAN'T GET ENOUGH OF THE GODS?
THEIR STORIES CONTINUE AT:

IN THE PANTHEON

WATCH FOR MORE ANTHOLOGIES
COMING FROM REWRITTEN
REALMS IN THE COMING
MONTHS!

www.ingramcontent.com/pod-product-compliance
Lightning Source LLC
Chambersburg PA
CBHW021124260626
47169CB00005B/1442